WHATEVER MAKES THEM DANCE
By
Lindsay Wesker

Mea Sharmaine!

Thank you for coming to
my reading!
You survived!
Hope you enjoy the rest of it!

xxx

24.01.19

This book is dedicated to the people that make my life so good:

My wife, Claudette
My mum, Dusty
My father-in-law, Darkon
My children: Natasha, Werner, Clarissa, Katie, Jerome, Shadae, Elijah & Josiah
My nieces/nephew: Phoebe, Miriam & Jonatan a.k.a. Yung Lean
My goddaughters: Alicia & Nicole
My siblings: Daniel & Elsa
My family
My friends
The Beautiful People (my gang)
The Music Programming Department at MTV UK
The staff & DJs at www.mi-soul.com
Everyone that listens to my weekly radio show and/or attends my gigs
Everyone that interacts with me via Facebook, Twitter, Instagram, WhatsApp
& text messages!

Many thanks to Marie Harvey-Harris and Tania Cordeiro for their proofreading skills and editorial input.

This book is also dedicated to all the songwriters, musicians, singers and producers that make the music. Without music, what would our lives be like?

And, of course, everything I write is dedicated to those we have loved and lost.

Chapter One (Sunday a.m.)

I slept in an office doorway last night.

Not sure for how long? Might have been a few hours? I must have been tired?

As it was an office block and, as it was Saturday night, I wasn't disturbed by anybody on Sunday morning; the cold of the pavement woke me up. At first I thought I was dreaming, until my eyes began to focus, and then I realised I was fully dressed and warm in my overcoat and scarf.

I began to collect my thoughts. I'd been out with my mates: Tony, Tony, Tony and Melvin. My crew. My gang. My comrades. There was great affection between this group of men and, initially, we were too afraid to say the word but, with the integration of hip hop culture and pirate radio into modern parlance, we expressed 'big love' and 'much love' with almost gay abandon!

We were all single. It was Saturday night and we were all going to do the predictable, male, Saturday night thing: eat spicy food, drink cold beer, laugh at each other's misfortune, attempt to dance and try to impress pretty girls with conversation of varying quality.

We'd taken a train to Dalston Junction. There's all sorts of nice bars and clubs there now. It's so different! When I was growing up, I remember the area being rather forgotten. The main road, Kingsland High Road, was busy but ordinary. There was a vibrant market, Ridley Road, but the area always looked unloved.

But now, with The Square Mile spreading, the city boys needed somewhere to live, so they were straying north beyond Shoreditch and Hoxton. Christ, they'd be in Stamford Hill soon! At that point, the trendy beardies would meet the orthodox Jews: a lot of facial hair!

It was a normal Saturday night. I'd spent a long and vexing day at work (Saturday is always the busiest day for a disco equipment hire shop); gone home for a quick shower and then out I went.

It truly was a very normal Saturday night for us. It's what we always did. We looked forward to it. It's what Saturday nights were made for! Even if the music was crap, even if the girls didn't bite, the people-watching was priceless!

Were we predators? Not really. We weren't notches-on-the-bedpost guys. (Well, maybe Low was?) We just enjoyed a good laugh. Laughing was the most important thing. Laughing at other people, laughing at each other, or just laughing at the sheer awfulness of a bar, a club or some couple trying to look like Fred and Ginger on the dance floor!

I suppose that was the best thing about these guys: the laughter never stopped. Some of our best memories were just of us losing it; uncontrollable, almost-painful laughter. Those memories were forever tremors.

As I continued trying to focus, I remembered walking and laughing, queuing outside a club, drinking bottles of beer, talking to random girls. I remember getting drunk, but I couldn't remember much after that.

I sat up and leaned against the front door of the office. I suddenly needed to piss really badly. The right side of my face felt cold. I gingerly got to my feet and wondered what the time was. Behind the reception desk was a clock; 5.17am; nothing would be open. Calculated I'd been asleep about two hours. An outdoor disco nap!

My legs felt like Bambi and I stuttered out on to the pavement. Even at this early hour, there were cars honking impatiently. Behind a door, I could hear the muffled sounds of an all-nighter; the rigid heartbeat of some processed bass drum, pounding mercilessly into the ecstatic faces of weary kids.

I found a pitiful patch of lawn stranded in the middle of all this commerce: a concrete square, some benches, some bushes. Made sure no one was near and relieved myself into the soil.

I reached into my coat pocket and found my phone; six missed calls. How drunk had I been? Beer never did that to me.

Or had I moved on to something else? Some mind-numbing, over-priced spirit; specifically created to destroy the inhibitions of cautious credit controllers and timid traffic wardens. These garishly-coloured spirits had sinister names that made them sound like sedatives and caused the user to spit luminous vomit. Had I really succumbed to this pantone pus?

I looked at my phone again: the missed calls were from Tony, Tony and Tony. Nothing but fucking Tonys! Why were no women calling me? God knows I'd given my number to enough and yet, on a Saturday night, none of them needed me. None of them were bored or lonely; they were all fully-occupied and fully-satisfied. None of these women were curious to meet me or had even given me a second thought. All I had on my phone was fucking Tonys!

What did this say about me? Was I unmemorable? Unlovable? Or, given the choice of people to have a conversation with, why was I NOT the person you call? Did I really give such bad conversation? No, that wasn't true. I was a salesman. I owned a shop. I dealt with the general public every day. I was polite, my patter was topical, my jokes were of standard. I was charming in a goofy, self-deprecating way.

What was it about me? Boring? Bland? Unlucky? I was careering towards 40 and I'd only had one serious relationship to talk of. Was I really going to die one of those sad, pathetic bachelors who still thinks he's got 'it'?

I started walking and looking for a bus that might take me in the general direction of home. I needed ablutions quick; the inside of my mouth felt like a Christmas mitten and probably smelt like an armpit.

When I finally found a night bus heading north, I realised I was not alone. Some of these Muppets were in a worse state than me; dull-eyed, staring into space, collapsed on their boyfriend's shoulders, coughing, spluttering and spraying tired phlegm all down the window. I looked like a groomed, catwalk model compared to some of these corpses.

Never had my front door looked so welcoming. In the hallway, there was still a faint smell of aftershave, where I'd given myself a last-minute squirt before heading out the door.

I turned the heating on, went upstairs, undressed and threw my clothes on the floor. I stood in the shower without moving; I needed hot water to remove that initial layer of dust, and then I scrubbed myself quite vigorously with a flannel, in case bugs had crawled into my crevices.

I slumped on the sofa in my front room, wearing bath robe and slippers, watched Sky News and ate cereal. It was too early to call anyone; figured I'd let London wake up in its own time. I didn't need another phone call; it was probably going to be someone called Tony anyway!

Almost as soon as I dozed off, my phone rang. It was Tony. Tony T the jeweller. One of my gang of five: three Tonys, Melvin and me. We'd all known each other a long time and we usually travelled *en masse*!

"What happened to you?" he said.

"I don't know, I thought you could tell me!"

"Well, we were talking to two girls, and you said you needed to pop out for some air, and that's the last we saw of you! This girl was still waiting for you at 3.00 in the morning and then she went home."

I remembered that. I remembered talking to her, I remembered thinking I felt a bit hot, a bit clammy, a bit dizzy and that the dry ice was getting in my eyes. I remember feeling a bit overwhelmed. Shouting in someone's ear is hard work and not very sexy. Plus, I was tired from the day; sorting customers' logistics is taxing.

"So, what did happen to you?"

"I had a nap in a doorway," I said. I must have sat down and nodded off?"

"Nodded off? Why?"

"You tell me! What were we drinking?"

Tony thought. "We started on beers and then, when the girls arrived, we moved on to spirits."

"Jesus, what kind of spirits were they? They knocked me out!"

"Anyway, I got her number for you. Her mate left my flat a few minutes ago. What a delightful young lady!"

"Cheers, Tops! And what happened to everyone else?"

"They all seemed to have their hands full, as it were. We should go back there again; it's full of gorgeous women!"

"Yeah, definitely, but stop me from making a prat of myself!"

"That's gonna be hard to do!"

"Ha ha! Send me her number, will ya?"

How did I know Tony T the jeweller? We'd met each other at a party. We must have been about eighteen. It was one of those chaotic Skins parties. Nice house, as it goes, but these kids were hell bent on breaking something or someone. Carnage! Empty bottles on the floor, food up the walls and someone had even cracked the toilet! The girls were so stoned; it wasn't even worth chatting them up! We'd escaped at the same time and gone on to another party; the first of many great nights together.

Tony T was an ordinary Joe, medium height, average body but full of chat. He wasn't anything to look at – I'd even heard girls say that – but he was happy, conversational and very easy to get on with. Girls liked him because he could make them laugh without even trying. He wasn't even much of a dresser but girls could rely on him; they were guaranteed a good gossip and a good laugh! He knew a little bit about everything! Almost like a doctor's bedside manner. Whatever they wanted to talk about, he could offer a view! When women needed someone to talk to, they called him! Not me! Him!

As you would expect, Tony T the jeweller always had interesting rings on his fingers or things hanging around his neck. Interesting stones or crystals, interesting symbols or shapes. Talking points. Ice breakers. Women would finger these decorative items and ask him questions. Conversation, smiling and laughing would follow. The three simple steps to seduction. Tony T was very good at being single. Unlike me.

This gang were a group of guys I was happy to do nothing with. We could go anywhere and have a good time! In fact, we could actually do nothing and say nothing and STILL have a good time. It was nice being a member of a gang. I'd never really been part of one at school. 'Gang' sounded a bit gay disco but we liked it. We didn't have a name for our gang but we were definitely more than a group of friends. We liked going places together.

The five of us. Like the 'Entourage' boys. It didn't seem worth doing anything unless my friends were there.

The only stuff I did on my own was 'relationship stuff'. They whispered it in hushed, reverential tones: 'relationship stuff'. "Ooh, we won't be seeing Wezza on Saturday; he's doing 'relationship stuff'!" But I liked being in a relationship and they accepted that. I'd only ever had one steady girlfriend. Trish. Good thing they liked her or they'd have made her life a misery!

We'd never talked about friendship. When we were kids, the protocol was so much simpler: you just walked up to someone and said, "Would you like to be my friend?" With these guys, a casual remark had become a conversation, had become a good night, had become a friendship, and now what we shared was really quite magical. Almost like the rapport between John Paul-Jones and John Bonham? Almost.

I put the kettle on and, while in the kitchen, I heard my phone 'ping'. This was the girl's number arriving from Tony T.

Then, the decision was: how to approach this situation? What to say to this girl? Could I really tell her the truth? What would she think? Would she wonder if I had a medical problem? Shit, not even I knew if I had a medical problem! I didn't drink that much; why did I pass out?

It was now 8.10 a.m. There was little to do, bar domestic chores, so I had time to work on my story. What was her name? I looked at my phone. Roz. Short for Rosalind? Roslane? Rosa? Roswell? Roz: it was a punchy, business-like, asexual abbreviation.

I knew I'd get an earful but I was ready for that. She was probably used to haphazard men but I didn't immediately want to be categorised as 'flaky'. There was plenty of time for that!

What should I say? Only the truth would excuse me. I could say I was "exhausted and stressed", making myself seem busy and important. Whereas, I was actually just the owner of a disco equipment hire shop and a part-time mobile DJ. By telling the truth, I could effectively convey an image of being a work-hard/play-hard kinda guy; a very masculine look.

I looked in the fridge: leftover Chinese, leftover Indian, uncooked diced beef, uncooked chicken breasts, assorted packets of uncooked vegetables. I wanted to cook, just never found the time.

It was all a matter of confidence. I probably needed some kind of adult education class; a gathering of pathetic men with an intimate knowledge of the take away restaurants in their locale. While there was a campaign behind take aways called 'Just Eat', I needed a campaign called 'Enough With The Eating!'

Besides, cooking was sexy! Like Tony T and his expert knowledge of jewellery, if I could just learn to throw these ingredients together, I would be more of a hunter and gatherer, less a collector of Nectar points!

I pulled some milk out of the fridge and threw it into my coffee. I stared into my cup and tried to recollect the evening.

It had started at around six, with the usual set of phone calls: one to Tony F the wine merchant, another to Tony G the *maitre d'*, one to Tony T the jeweller and, finally the freak of the whole bunch, Melvin. Why couldn't he have a normal name like Tony? Actually, Melvin was a blessing! He had devised a graph called T.I.T., the Tony Identification Tree, in which he had placed the Tonys on an evolutionary scale based on their mistakes.

As Tony G already had one illegitimate child, one failed marriage, one failed business, one case of Chlamydia and one ropey tattoo, he was right at the bottom of the diagram. He was Low Tone. Or Low, for short. He worked as *maitre d'* in a restaurant inside a five-star hotel; the clientele were nice but dim trust fund kids, Russian oligarchs, oil-rich playboys, and good-to-go good-time girls. In short, oceans of arrogance and little thanks but it suited him. Great food every night and pretty girls a-plenty! Plus he rocked a suit!

You could imagine girls thinking Tony G was handsome, in a David Cassidy/Tom Cruise kind of way. His highly-styled hair and well-arranged features actually caused women to walk in his direction. What must that feel like? To actually have women walk towards you!

Next on the T.I.T. (Tony Identification Tree) was Tony F or Mid Range, but we called him Midders or Mids for short: six points for speeding on his driving licence, a conviction for handling stolen goods and one failed marriage. He'd eventually found a niche for himself in wine. He had a warehouse under the train tracks in Camden Town, a staff of four and a loyal clientele. The middle classes don't want one bottle of over-priced wine from their supermarket; they wanted six reasonably-priced cases of small-town vino delivered to their front door. Plus, they loved the neighbours seeing wine being delivered!

Tony F had that jolly, portly thing going on! He had a bit of good restaurant belly out front. His plump cheeks were a happy, smiling rouge and his bulbous nose looked as if it had enjoyed many glasses of the finest. Tony F was the embodiment of good wining and dining. Life was for living and the taut belt around Tony F's waist bore witness to that!

Finally on the T.I.T., Tony T: Top End, Topper or Tops, for short. The eternal romantic but a hundred failed relationships and no wife, three points for speeding and a mono-brow. Tony T designed and made jewellery, and repaired sentimental items for his customers. He had a tiny workshop in

Hatton Garden. In school, he'd been a natural at metalwork, making all sorts of handy items for his mum's kitchen and ornaments for her wall.

Jewellery was the natural progression and Topper was good at it! Making jewellery involved talking to women about rings, necklaces and bracelets; emotional business transactions that led to drinks and dinner! He was slight, almost petite but muscular. You could imagine him circling a woman like Prince dancing around Wendy Melvoin in his video for 'Kiss'.

And Melvin made five. A lovely, sweet-natured man. Very kind, gentle and considerate. Almost like our own holiday rep, making sure everyone was well and abreast of all the arrangements. There was something different about Melvin and we couldn't work out what! We knew he was in touch with his feminine side but we also knew he wasn't gay. Nah, he couldn't be? Not possible! There were women sniffing around him like footie fans around a meat pie stall!

Of all of us, Melvin definitely had the best moves and, more important than anything else, the ability to dance WITH a woman! Women love a man who can hold them right and move in syncopation with them! They figure if he can dance, he can make love!

Melvin had a black dad and a white mum, a huge amount of insanely-curly hair on his head and big, innocent-looking brown eyes. His perfectly-white teeth were slightly crooked but that barely detracted from the dazzling gleam. Melvin loved being single! He was forever disappearing! We knew not where! With his trusty holdalls, he was always ready for an overnight stay!

I'd been born Wesley, shortened to Wes, and then bastardised into Wezza or, if I'd just urinated, Wazza! Those were our nicknames. They ebbed and flowed, depending on how drunk we were!

Who was I? I was actually The Sensible One. Bordering on being The Boring One. With every madcap idea, I was always saying to them, "Are you sure?" And they were always saying to me, "Aah, come on! Don't be soft!"

Did I like my role? Not really. I yearned to be carefree and reckless but that wasn't me. I needed well-thought-out, well-executed plans, I needed times and destinations, I needed sleep.

Was I boring? Of course not! (He said with conviction.) If we'd all been nutters, there would be anarchy. Within our clique, I was designated driver. Within our circle, I was the quivering voice of reason. So, why was I the butt of so many jokes? Probably because it had to be someone? Probably because I didn't mind? Probably because the jokes were funny?

Wes The Wife. Wes The Woman. Wes The Wallflower. They were all jokes about me and my girlfriend, and my intrinsic need for a partner. The jokes were all about me being less of a man, half a man, almost a woman, reliant on my girlfriend like phone charger to plug socket.

Before the end of the day, I was sure I'd hear from all of these clowns. Clowns they were but I loved them all. They were a prosperous but not exactly eligible set of bachelors; far too concerned with wringing the last drops of bravado from their youth. If you can still call late-thirties 'youth'?

The gang were all single but far from 'on the market'; they cherished their singledom. It was the last link to their thirties. Sever that and it would be the steady slide to old age. They definitely were NOT looking for wives. Wives represented routine and responsibility! Wives represented mind-numbing boredom (family functions, shopping trips etc.), although we stuck fairly rigidly to our weekly, single man routines! In fact our weekly schedule was written in stone and we were adrift without it!

I loved these guys because they were a solid set of friends, friends who could be called on to help and friends who would actually help! Subtle distinction: friends offer their help but only true friends actually turn up! These were real mates; guys who'd known me since I was a virgin.

Down the years, we'd actually had a few blokes trying to edge their way in to the gang, but they never felt right. One bloke thought he was a stand-up comedian and made crap jokes all night long: he had to go! Another guy was always looking to muscle in on our action, as if he didn't want to date a girl but would be happy to be involved in any threesomes going! He definitely had to go!

So, it was just us five. The Gang. A motley crew. A patchwork of five different personalities that, for some reason, gelled. We didn't question the strength of the bonds. We knew they were strong.

Three cups of coffee later, I'd built up the courage to call Roz.

"Didn't think I'd hear from you!" she mocked.

"I am so sorry," I said.

"What happened? I waited until 3.00 for you to re-appear."

"Thanks for waiting … to be honest …"

"To be honest? For God's sake, don't start the sentence with 'To be honest'!"

"I dozed off in an office doorway last night."

"What?"

"I went out for some air and that's the last thing I remember! I must have sat on some steps and dozed off?"

Roz paused and digested all this. I knew it sounded highly implausible.

"Honest!" I said, foolishly hoping it would make me sound honest.

"Dozed off? Are you narcoleptic?"

"I don't think so."

"I think I'm just … tired."

"Tired?" she squawked, not buying the story.

"And probably very drunk?" I quickly added.

I could hear her wrinkling her nose. Wherever she was in London, I could hear her nose wrinkle and feel her disapproval. The silence was full of wary trepidation.

"Tired and drunk?" she enquired.

"Very tired and very drunk," I re-affirmed.

And then I began to question my own story! Could I really have been that tired and that drunk? Add to that my advancing years, yes, it was plausible!

"I've heard some stories!" she said.

"I'm sure," I said. "All I can say is sorry? We were getting on well, right?"

"We were," she admitted. "You were asking me questions! You weren't trying to seduce me!"

"Christ, no!" I said. Seduce? Seduction? That was not what I did!

"Anyway," I continued, whimsically, "here I am!"

"Yes, but how long will you be awake?"

"Okay, okay, I deserve that! Listen, imagine how I feel? I'm freaked out! I slept in a doorway last night!"

"So you say!"

"I did!" I bleated, pathetically.

"As you can imagine, I've heard some whoppers in my time. Falling asleep in an office doorway is just weird!"

"I know, I know. Let me buy you brunch?" I quickly added, hoping I would sound generous, urbane, paternal or any combination of the three. "We'll meet at 11.00. I'll come to your neck of the woods. Where is that, by the way?"

"Chiswick. And you should go see a doctor!"

"I will, I will."

I had the normal male dread of doctors. I'd managed to get used to giving blood but I was not ready for probing. And what the hell would I say to a doctor? Falling asleep in a doorway could just be attributed to laziness?

We agreed on a venue and I looked at the clock. I had about 40 minutes to get dressed, 40 minutes to find the perfect 'Fucked-Up-The-First-Impression-Let's-Try-To-Do-Better-With-The-Second' outfit.

My wardrobe was a sorry mess of gifts, jeans and promotional items: free T-shirts, free sweatshirts, free hoodies. The only things that weren't free were birthday and Christmas presents from well-meaning relatives. And all the things that Trish had bought. Why were Trish's purchases the best things in my wardrobe? How did she know me so well? How did she know what looked good on me?

Trish had defined love for me. Before Trish, 'love' had been the traditional view: Hallmark cards and chick flicks. The love I had known before was based on someone else's ideas: roses, candlelit dinners, long country walks. Trish had torn up that script.

"Just stand still, you silly bugger!" I remember her stoically holding on to my shoulders. "Do nothing! You don't have to do anything! Love doesn't have to be about gestures!"

"Don't actions speak louder than words?" I'd asked.

"No, they don't! Any fool can buy a bunch of flowers!"

Trish felt that love was spiritual. "It's like that old soul song," she said, "If you don't know be by now, you will never ever know me. Love is NOT about saying, 'I love you'."

"It's not?"

"Again: any fool can say, 'I love you'. If you can't write original lines, where's the sincerity?"

But Trish was my past. Trish was gone. Trish had disappeared. Literally, disappeared. She was nowhere to be found! Doubtless, her family and friends knew where she was but I wasn't going to ask them!

It had fizzled out like a damp sparkler. I was never sure if she'd got bored of me or just felt I'd never get it. Why had Trish and I ended? Did I stop calling? Did she stop calling? Or had one of us fallen out of love? Were we ever in love? I thought about her constantly. Had she really just lost interest and drifted away? Could that be possible?

I looked at myself in the mirror. Thirty seven, paunchy, pale, poor posture, dank hair and dead behind my eyes: practically irresistible! My life was simple. I went to work, I went out with the boys. There was no gym, no grooming. Such matters were for a girlfriend to worry about and, if there was no girlfriend, these things fell by the wayside.

I thought about Trish constantly. Of course I was still in love with her! It was stupid to suggest I wasn't! I still wanted to call her and tell her about my day (mundane, as ever!) I still wanted to ask her opinion. Still wanted to hear her voice. Our photos were still in my phone. A pair of her worn-out trainers were still on my shoe rack.

Such a lovely face! Trish had a head-turner of a face! Guys would crash into lamp posts catching a few extra moments of that face. And she photographed so well! Effortless. No make-up, no posing. Trish just turned up and looked beautiful.

Slim, elegant, feminine. A self-made woman with her own business designing greetings cards. Together, organised, disciplined; a driven person with a structured life. What did she see in me?

Over time, she had just faded away. She'd got busier. There were less dates, less phone calls, less text messages, and I could do nothing to stop it! Like grains of sand slipping through my fingers, I was powerless to stop her extracting herself from my life.

Why had I not talked to her and asked her why? That kind of 'stuff' is scary! I can talk about most things but ... well ... that kind of emotional stuff is not my forte! The truth is often terrifying anyway! Asking a woman, 'Why?' Only bringing a child into the world and moving house are more stressful experiences!

Where had she gone? I almost didn't want to know. I feared the worst. Someone taller, someone smarter, someone more dynamic than me. Worst of all, Trish's smell had left my nostrils. I could no longer recall what she smelt like. In some ridiculous, juvenile fantasy, I imagined her returning and regretting her decision. When my phone rang, I prayed it was her. When a text arrived, I hoped for a miracle but, as yet, it hadn't occurred. Clear signs of hopeless, puppy love. A new woman was my only hope!

What to wear? I banged the same old hangers against each other and hoped a great outfit would suddenly materialise. It didn't, so I just wore something Trish had bought me.

I stood in front of my only full-length mirror and beheld this bland, neglected. A half-decent pair of trousers and matching shirt. Smartish by my standards. If I really hoped to get over Trish, I needed to face facts: she'd gone, she wasn't coming back, and I needed to attract a new Trish. I needed someone dynamic in my life who would show me how to turn raw ingredients into a meal, someone who would shake my wardrobe out of its stupor, and someone who would help me to grow up. I loved being part of my gang but you can't live like that forever! Can you?

Drove to Chiswick, parked the car and made my way to trendy, brunching bistro. Found a corner seat where I could see people coming in and out, and waited. Roz was one minute late. I was impressed. We pecked each other on both cheeks.

"All cleaned up?"

"Yes," I replied, remorsefully. "I'm so sorry about last night. It was going so well."

Roz was of indeterminate ethnic origin. Were these Brazilian features or was she Sri Lankan? Portuguese or Pakistani? I waited for more clues. There was a riot of black, naturally curly hair that cascaded over her shoulders, mesmeric brown eyes and a full mouth that would not quit. They looked like great kissing lips but, it must be said, people with great lips don't always know what to do with them, particularly if they lunge at you with their tongue!

I'd had little chance to ask questions last night, as she'd talked for most of the evening; an engaging monologue about her parents, her sisters, her school friends, her collection of stuffed animals, the family business (flowers) and her teenage crush on L. L. Cool J.

We ordered coffee and croissants.

"So, I assume you'll be going to see a doctor tomorrow? About your narcolepsy?"

"Yeah," I lied. "It's top of my agenda. I think it was just tiredness and alcohol, though. We'd been at it a while before we met you! I'm not the biggest drinker in the world. Pushed the boat out a little too far?"

She looked at me, sceptically, as if she was fairly certain that most of the facts coming out of my mouth were bullshit. No explanations and excuses would make a jot of difference. There was nothing I could do or say, but I persisted.

"The long and short of it is: I haven't got a clue what happened!" Amateurishly, I re-folded my serviette. "I was really tired, so I sat down on some steps and just fell asleep."

"That must have been one comfortable doorway!"

"It was!" I began. "I was wrapped up snug in my jacket. I was comfortable!"

"Just as a precaution, you should go to the doctors. What is it with men and doctors?"

"I will go to the doctors. I promise." I rested my hand on my heart. "I swear on my record collection!"

She nodded approvingly, "Now I know you're serious!"

The restaurant was starting to buzz and there was a glorious smell of bacon in the air. I was suddenly very hungry and, as she talked, I fantasised about long strips of lean bacon cooking on a grill. It made me feel warm and toasty like tea time at my nan's farm.

From the way she controlled the conversation, I could see she was used to orchestrating things. She finished my sentences, so she could rapidly move on to her point and curtailed subject threads she had no interest in.

That mouth was certainly going like the clappers! She'd finish a chapter, laugh, toss her hair, laugh and start up again, but it was an enjoyable show. She told good stories.

I sat and listened. Trish had told me that sometimes all a man needs to do is listen. Listen and remember. So, I listened. I sat, and smiled, and nodded, and laughed (with sincerity) and tried to remember all the details this girl was imparting. Not just times, dates and places but subtle nuances about her psyche. Was I anxious for her to like me? You bet I was! I didn't like being single. Some people do, I don't!

"If people don't like you, fuck 'em!" Trish's words always banged around in my skull like demented dodgem cars. Long lectures about self-esteem! Maybe Trish had grown tired of giving me pep talks? Thankfully, the more absorbed I became with Roz, the less I thought about Trish. It was working!

Seven days prior, I'd been replaying Trish quotes in my head, but now this talkative tootsie was pushing Trish memories aside. She had one appealing quality that Trish had lacked: a sense of the surreal. How I love a delicately derailed and deranged sense of humour! Every so often she'd lapse into some weird, hybrid dialect, pull a wholly unattractive face or collapse her words in some non-sensical way, and I loved it! I like eccentrics. I don't trust people who are too sober. She was clearly capable of some world-class lunacy and it was very appealing!

I could no longer resist and we ordered cooked breakfast. Roz looked relieved. With all those anecdotes, she'd developed an appetite. She ordered a lot of food that she had no hope of finishing, and she looked positively aroused when it arrived.

She was clearly worldlier than me. We'd both gone to Uni but she'd then spent a year travelling, whereas I'd lurched straight into the allegedly-glamorous world of the DJ; weddings, birthdays, christenings, dodgy pubs, seedy clubs, some hospital radio, a bit of in-store radio, and even some late-night local radio.

She talked lucidly about Vietnam and Singapore, while all I had was tales of me playing The Nolan Sisters at trailer trash weddings, but it seemed to amuse her. I was making Roz laugh and I knew this was a good thing.

Trish's words replayed in my head, "If you can make a woman laugh, you're almost there! Her defences are down and her legs are virtually open!"

Why had she told me these things? Was she preparing me for life after her?

Roz's face was completely transformed by her smile. She had no visible fillings and quite the whitest teeth I'd ever seen. I was relieved to see her smile and laugh at my repertoire of wedding reception nightmares.

"I promise you, wherever I go, there is always someone who thinks he can do my job better than me. You can see him on the dance floor, shaking his head disapprovingly, and then he'll sidle up beside you and say, 'Now, if you really want to get people dancing, you should play … this ... or that ...'

"All of us DJs have got a few standard responses. I say to them, 'Where do you work, mate?' and when they ask 'Why?' I say, 'Cause I'm coming to your work place on Monday to tell you how to do your job!'

"And then people will ask you for the most obscure shit in the world and, when you say you haven't got it, they look at you like, 'How can you call yourself a DJ and NOT have my tune?'

"How can I possibly carry every tune ever made? There's even a Facebook group for DJs called 'Do I Look Like A Fucking Juke Box?'"

Roz was smiling in her eyes and listening intently to my stories. This was a good sign. She buttered another piece of toast and crunched into it. "I'm guilty of that," she said. "I give DJs stick all the time!"

"Thanks! You should try it?" I said. "See how hard it is."

We ordered some more coffee and drifted into lunch. The restaurant was filling up with families ordering Sunday lunch, and the air was suddenly alive with chattering children, screaming babies and cutlery hitting the floor.

I had ascertained that she did something called 'production' at a TV production company. She actually made television programmes! It sounded fascinating to me but she was blasé about it. Bored and a bit battle-weary!

"Working in TV must be fun?" I ventured.

"It has its moments," she began. "At least I'm not stuck behind a desk, looking at a screen, doing the same thing every day. Every day is different. I've travelled the world, we've filmed people in amazing places: music festivals, beaches, deserts, the best hotels in the world, parks, London Zoo, in the middle of a football pitch, a protest march, the McVitie's biscuit factory …"

The words had stopped but the internal monologue continued in her brain. I could see her thinking. These thoughts were private. I wondered if I should pry but I figured, if she wanted to share, she would.

She caught herself, deep in thought. "Sorry," she said. "My brain went off on a tangent."

"About what?"

"About everything else. All the other things outside of my job. Out there is life!" She waved her hand, like someone trying to get Sellotape off a sticky finger. "The rest of your life is out there!"

"Yes ..." I said, with that tone you use when someone has stated the obvious. "Life is out there ... and?"

"Oh, it's okay! I've just got work/life balance issues! I've been working a long time. Guess I'm a little burnt-out? Work's not really giving me what it used to. Maybe I need more from my life?"

"You looked like you were daydreaming? How far is daydreaming from narcolepsy?"

She looked at me competitively. "Well, let's drive a car and find out, smart arse!"

"We don't know if it's narcolepsy!"

"No, we don't," she conceded. "What do you think it is?"

I shrugged my shoulders. "Don't know," I began. "Life's hard, you know! Sometimes ..."

"Sometimes?" she prompted.

"Sometimes ..." I paused, "... sometimes I struggle."

"Struggle with what?"

"With life!"

She thought about that for a second, acknowledged it, nodded her head and filed it in a filing system.

"Interesting!" she smirked. "Struggles with life."

Why the hell had I said that? Not really a great card to play! In a misguided attempt to impress her, I'd played the Honesty and In-Touch-With-My-Emotions cards! Why couldn't I just keep it light and fluffy? There was no need to reveal so much.

I suddenly got a flash of her playing Scrabble or Backgammon, and then a quick mental image of her jubilantly slamming her dominoes down. She had a competitive glint in her eye but then – I suppose - dating is warfare. You need to keep your game face on until a marriage ceremony occurs! Of course her guard was up! She looked like a no-nonsense gal who relished a challenge. Someone who would momentarily take offence at being rejected and then say, "Right, I'll show you!"

She was so chatty, it gave me a chance to study her closely. She really gave her hair a thorough working-over. Her hands were always in it; twisting it, primping it but, more often than not, just luxuriously running her fingers through it. It was a huge and healthy head of hair and worthy of a shampoo ad. I pictured her standing beneath a waterfall, soap bubbles cascading over her shoulders.

And I was still mystified as to why this dazzling woman wanted to brunch with me? Had she really run out of options? I was surely the short straw?

"Married? Separated? Divorced?"

"Completely single," I said. "How come you're only asking that question now?"

"It's not important," she said, sitting back and displaying her perfect teeth in a smug smile. "If you fall in love with me, it won't matter if you're married, will it?"

"No?"

"Because you'll be in love with me! And how you handle THAT is your problem!"

I found her confidence beguiling. Why was I attracted to strong, dominant women? Did that make me a wimp? Did that make me a strong candidate for pussy-whipping?

Amateur analysts would be thinking Oedipus Complex but it really wasn't that. It was more the need for a P.A., a decision-maker, a go-getter; someone ambitious, organised and pro-active. All things I was not.

Like Trish had been, Roz was a cornucopia of knowledge, wisdom and opinion. It was like watching a fascinating, factual TV programme on architecture or a lost civilisation in the Amazonian rain forest. I just sat back and enjoyed the show.

"Ever been in love?" she casually enquired.

I probably looked like a horrified rabbit in some blinding headlights. Again, not a good look!

"Is this a painful subject?" she asked.

I was not doing well. In fact I was doing really badly. I was umming and erring and struggling to form a word, let alone a sentence!

She looked at me pitifully. "Okay, I am assuming you have been in love and it was a painful break-up? Just nod for 'yes'."

I nodded obediently.

"Can you talk about it?" she asked, nervously. She was trying to be sensitive, not knowing what kind of hornet's nest she was about to stir.

In truth it was just me and Trish. No hornet's nest. Just uni friends who'd fallen into a relationship. Fallen into a routine. What was there to say? I couldn't tell her why Trish had left because I didn't know.

"I've had one long-term relationship, with a girl called Trish. We got together when I was 21 and we actually only separated last year."

Again, not a good look. Why was I making every attempt to sabotage my own date? For some reason, this girl was still across the other side of the table. For some strange, impenetrable reason, this delightful damsel was interested in me and my pitiful past.

"That is major!" she said

"It was."

"What happened?"

I had to tell the truth. She already thought I was a lightweight narcoleptic and a habitual liar!

"I really don't know. We just drifted apart. I didn't ask her why we were drifting apart. I think I was too stunned, too depressed, too afraid of the answer. I just accepted it. And now I can't even find her! She's disappeared!"

"Don't her folks know where she is?"

"Probably ... but she doesn't want me to go looking for her!"

"Were you in love with her?"

"I guess I was?" I said. "But love probably feels different to everyone?"

"I think you would know," said Roz. "You would know! And how do you feel now?"

"Still numb." And that was the truth too. I was still numb. I'd 'fallen' into a relationship with Trish. We'd gone to the cinema and I'd walked her home, and the next day we were making plans to see each other again. And so it went on! Fairly soon, we were living together and, fairly soon, we had routines!

She did the ironing, I did the hoovering, she did the cooking, I washed-up the dishes. Was it a relationship or was it a set of routines?

And, at night, she would begin to kiss me and that's all it took! Her kisses excited me. Once she had begun to kiss me, everything fell into place. At that point, there were New Year's Eve fireworks and all the feelings I'd been told you could associate with 'being in love'.

"Not really ready for another relationship, are you?"

"I am," I quickly replied. "MORE than ready to make new friends!"

She looked taken aback and smiled. "You were with her a long time! Am I your rebound?"

"No," I said, confidently, quite impressing myself. "In the immortal words of Dr. Dre, you are the next episode."

"The great philosopher, Dr. Dre!" She laughed again. As long as she was laughing, I was in business!

"And what about you? What do you want? Do you want to get married?"

"Part of me does," she said. "It's a nice gesture but it's not the institution it was. Marriage seems to turn men into even sneakier bastards than they were already! Slip that ring on and a man turns into an MI5 agent; suddenly, he's got complex aliases and alibis. But those convoluted answers are always a give away! I can always tell when a man's lying to me."

I sipped at my coffee. It was stone cold. "Yeah, what's that about? Why get married if you're not ready to settle down?"

"Well, that's the million-dollar question, innit?"

"Have you got a boyfriend?"

"Well," she began, not knowing how I would respond, "On Facebook, you've got Single, Married, Divorced and It's Complicated. Well, with me, it's really fucking complicated!"

"Would you like to tell me how 'complicated'?"

She smiled, nervously picked up a sachet of sugar and began rolling it between her fingers.

"I have numerous men in my life who want to sleep with me. Some of them have even made it into my bed. I have a few who want to date me and I even have a few who want to marry me. I am spoilt for choice and yet I'm not convinced any one of that number is someone I want to spend a prolonged period of time with. I'm a fussy bitch!"

She fixed her eyes on me. "Does that answer your question?"

"No," I said, firmly, shocking myself.

Good God almighty! What kind of answer was that? This woman had just calmly told me that her sex life was full of men! Was it true? Or was it a test? Whatever it was, I had to look cool. I had to look unfazed and confident in my ability to compete.

I opted for a mildly-amused smile but I suspect I looked like a Labrador trying to take a quick dump on a pavement!

"You want to know if I'm seeing anyone regularly? The answer is: no."

And then I asked the question that my male ego demanded but, as it was coming out of my mouth, it sound ridiculous.

"So, I would be part of a harem?"

She laughed. "Silly man! That would just devalue sex!"

I liked her laugh. It was the laugh of child-like wonder and delight, part evil scientist but also quite melodious.

"I'm just a normal girl, Wes. I do not want to die a spinster. That is not how I'm going out!"

She raised her eyebrows and expected me to understand.

I nodded, feebly, and tried to make it seem as if I understood the word 'normal'.

"By that, I mean," she began, "I have this set of clowns who view me as a 'booty call'. Imagine that? Me? A booty call. Amazingly, there are this group of men I have given my phone number to and, whenever they get horny, they call me, assuming that I will drop everything and be a warm, inviting hole for them! Imagine that, Wes? The fucking audacity! And every modern woman has male friends like that: men that will just prod, just in case. Just in case!"

"I don't make booty calls," I quickly added.

"I know you don't."

How could she know? How had she assessed my personality so quickly? I was still processing information about her, how had she read me so quickly?

"I know you don't make booty calls, Wes, because our conversation is not about sex and my sexual past. By now, most men would've tried to find out how many men I've slept with. They will never know. You will never know! We've been talking about our lives, our work, our hopes and dreams. No talk about sex. It's been nice. Refreshing."

Families began paying for their lunch and heading out to the park for some Sunday afternoon fun. Waitresses were swirling around us, collecting debris and mopping up spilt ice cream.

"And what about you?" she teased. "Do you want to join the queue?"

"The queue?"

"The queue of men. The queue of men trying to impress me and failing miserably."

It didn't sound appealing! In truth, I needed her to say something very simple, you know, the stuff we used to say in the playground: 'Would you like to be my boyfriend?'

Who was I? Far from dynamic. How on Earth would I be a better option than these dynamic, professional men? Me and the boys were just plebs. Consumers. Commuters. Lab rats. What the hell was I doing in this restaurant with such a smart, sexy minx? She would see through all my modest ambition. Her clever housemates would look down on me and urge her strongly to "be rid of the troll".

From somewhere, foolhardy courage took hold of my body. "Well … we could go out on a few dates. See how it goes."

"Do you want to date me, lovey?" she mocked.

"Yes," I began, decisively. "I'd like to date you. There: I said it!"

"Well, that makes a very welcome change!" She laughed, unzipped her purse and placed a £20 note on the table.

"My shout!" I said.

"No way, Jose! Money can screw up a friendship. We'll be toasting Amsterdam after every meal!"

We made a very loose arrangement to see each other in the next few days and, even though there was no time or date, it seemed like a plan.

The date had gone well and I stepped out into the weak afternoon sunshine feeling satisfied. I had redeemed myself; pulled myself back from the embarrassing brink of calamity. There was no more talk of me falling asleep in a doorway. Except from my friends.

I got into my car and returned my phone calls.

Tony G the *maitre d'* couldn't make any sense of it. "Just fell asleep? Just like that? Don't make no sense, geez. You seemed fine."

As a *maitre d'*, Tony G's constitution was legendary. He could drink with the best of them. His body could handle anything. His liver was probably beautifully marinated but he still looked fit and sprightly. He still played football on Sunday morning, whatever he'd done on Saturday night.

On the T.I.T. scale, Tony G was Low End but we called him Low or Lower. He was just over six foot with an athletic frame and an olivey complexion. He liked to pretend that he was some kind of Arabian prince but his family actually came from Whetstone. He had a roguish glint in his eye that women loved and he always looked great in his clothes, as if the fabrics were his friends!

His parents had owned a kebab shop in Turnpike Lane and, sticking with the food motif, he now worked in a restaurant inside a very opulent hotel. The perfect place for a smoothie like him! The trouble is: his patrons were ten times wealthier than him!

"Top End got his leg over again!"

"I know!"

"Lucky bastard!"

"Once he tells them he's a jeweller, the drawers are almost off! You know about women and jewellery! They're talking to him and thinking about that ring they've never mended!"

I parked my car in Sainsbury's car park and pulled up the handbrake. "What were we drinking?"

I found a functioning trolley and pushed it into the superstore. Stray two-year-olds swerved in front of me, while bamboozled biddies crashed into me.

Low re-traced his steps. "Two beers at the first place, two beers inside the club, round of cocktails when the girls arrived, Sambuca shots after that …"

I almost crashed into the Walkers Crisps multi-pack display. "I absolutely hate Sambuca! That is some evil shit! That probably did it! I was out on Friday night and up early Saturday morning. I'd only had four hours sleep!"

"Alright, geez, calm down! So you fell asleep in a doorway? I fell asleep on the train once and ended up in Brighton!"

"I've just had brunch with that girl."

"The one from last night?" exclaimed Low.

"Yes."

"Eh?"

"I've still got some moves!" I quickly asserted.

"Course you have, geez! And?"

"We're going to see each other again."

"Well, that's a result! Maybe she can be the new Trish? Minus the buggering-off bit!"

"Yeah, I want one that stays!"

Taking confidence from that brunch, I began using unused bits of my brain: logic, foresight and inspiration. If I was going to start dating a girl, there would be sleepovers, and sleepovers would involve breakfast. Brilliant! I bought milk, tea, coffee, sugar, bread, croissants, jam. This was grown-up behaviour!

I quickly paid my bill before I became the victim of trolley rage and headed home.

That word 'spinster' resonated with me. Spinster evoked very old ladies with grey hair and dusty black clothes. The girl with the big hair and the colourful garbs was decades from that description, and yet she was already using this word: spinster! I'd read articles about the big 4-0. Was it really that climactic? She'd made her decision. She was NOT going to die a spinster! She'd made her decision and I was the beneficiary! But why me?

Chapter Two (Sunday p.m.)

Sunday gave me the opportunity to see my sister, and make sure she hadn't polished her wood floor into an ice skating rink. I mean, there's OCD and there's my sister! True, her house was amazingly clean and the tea towels matched the curtains, but being with her was exhausting!

My one and only sister. Cruel people might have described her as frumpy but she felt like a good cuddle whenever I grabbed her. Middle age and neglect meant that she now looked more Dorothy Perkins than she cared to admit. She was at that stage in her life where she genuinely didn't give a damn whether you liked her or not. Quite a healthy stance I always feel. As a result, she could appear quite abrasive and lacking in basic diplomatic skills, but I knew she had a good heart.

Marie opened the door, wearing yellow rubber gloves and a Souvenir Of Margate apron. "Oh, don't mind me," she said, kissing my cheek and dripping soapy water down my trousers, "I'm just scrubbing some pots. Filthy! Encrusted with rice, I think! Make us a cuppa!"

We wandered into the kitchen and I filled the kettle with water.

"Got a nice fruit cake from the Farmer's Market yesterday; bugger me if it doesn't taste like the countryside!"

My sister Marie and I were the only remaining members of the family. Dad had passed away six years ago, Mum had followed shortly after, and Marie still lived in the family house. Separating her from home might have been one piece of grief too many; OCD might have matured into something more serious?

Was she clinically depressed? No, not really. She'd just fallen into a well of sadness, where she resided, mournfully wailing for help every now and then, just in case anyone was passing by.

"How did these pots get so dirty?" she muttered.

"They don't look dirty to me!"

"What do you know?" she spat. "You're a male of the species!"

There was currently no man in Marie's life, just her memories. There had been men in her past but none of them could really cope with a genuine, authentic, honest person. There was something a bit too real about Marie. Maybe she was too down-to-earth? Maybe she just wasn't sexy and sassy enough? Maybe she didn't giggle enough?

No matter what they say, men love a Barbie who laughs at their jokes. Until they realise that no voluptuous blonde is going to marry them and they settle down with someone like my sister. Sadly, the male population were still out there looking for that vacuous bimbo, so there were no suitors knocking on her door. Didn't help that she was a virtual hermit!

And now she was fortysomething. Too tired to look. Too tired to flirt. Marie busied herself at work and in the family home. Years passed and nothing changed. No one arrived. That word 'spinster' again!

She was a lovely looking girl but searching for a decent partner takes time and effort, and she really wasn't that bothered!

"I slept in an office doorway last night."

"Did you?" she replied, without missing a beat. "You did what?" She stopped scrubbing and looked down at me. A bead of sweat dripped on to her replica Cardiff City top.

"I got so pissed, I just passed out."

"Silly bugger," she said, returning to her pot.

"I went out with the boys."

"Melvin?"

"Yep."

"He's a nice boy! I can never remember the others."

"They're all called Tony!"

"Well, that's why I can't remember their names!"

Marie's logic was faultless and quite unique.

The kettle boiled and I made two cups of tea.

"Don't know how Mum kept these so clean!" Marie complained, twisting her arm, changing her angle and applying more elbow grease.

"I can see my bloody face in the bottom!"

"Well, I can't! Nearly done!" she said.

My older sister had been my golden gateway into adolescence and through into adulthood. She'd always taken me to parties and always allowed me to hang with her curvy and commanding friends, which is how I'd met Trish. Her friends liked me because I knew about music. I was Marie's trendy little brother; always ahead of trends. I made them cassettes and CDs of hot new bands.

But now, many years later, I was the voice of reason, the soothing voice, the organiser, the motivator. Now it was me dragging her to the movies, dragging her to concerts; anything was better than leaving her to potter around her pristine home.

"Oh, I can't go out," she'd say. "The place is a tip!"

"Marie, your flat hasn't looked a tip since the last owner set the chip pan on fire! Give it a rest and put a frock on!"

"Oh, no, I can't!"

Exhausting! It was bloody exhausting trying to get her out but always rewarding; she knew the best restaurants in town. "Can't go there," she would say, "the dessert menu is atrocious! Let's drive down to Notting Hill, there's a terrific Thai I know."

So, we had some tea and some slices of fruit cake from the Farmer's Market and – from what I could see – she seemed okay. I wasn't sure she'd ever get over losing our parents. Fortunately, I'd developed this hard, outer shell, and had found a way of mourning my parents without missing them. In my head, I was still having arguments with my Dad, and enjoying them as much as I ever did.

In fact, the boys – my gang – had helped me get over my parents. They'd been the constant in my life. Same as they'd ever been.

Being with the boys was like being in my past; a comfortable cocoon in which I could be a gawky, geeky (37-year-old) teen. Somehow, they shielded me from the harsh realities of convention. When I was with them, I didn't struggle. We were a gang, each with a role to play.

For some reason, her school and university friends had faded away; Marie no longer had a tight-knit circle, just a few well-meaning cousins, who had long since gone back to their lives. Not even Trish stayed in contact with her! Maybe Marie's sorrow was too visible and off-putting to others?

"And I've met a girl!"

"Have you now?" she said, polishing the table with her sleeve.

"Her name is Rosalind. Roz for short!"

"Rosalind? Sounds like some kind of Gypsy name."

"She looks like a Gypsy!"

Marie paused. "What the hell is a Gypsy? Are they a race?"

I thought for a second. "I think so. Anyway, she looks a gypsy!"

Marie got up, as if sitting down was wasting valuable cleaning time. She stretched and belched politely into her cupped hand. "Pardon me."

I watched her survey the kitchen. I couldn't see anything untoward but I could also see her scowling at some wayward cups. She moved towards a shelf and began re-arranging mugs.

"So tell me about Rosalind?"

I thought about our brunch. I got a quick mental image of Roz talking enthusiastically about her circle of friends, a seemingly mystical coven of people. She talked about them as if they were superheroes, each with a wondrous power.

"She lives in this huge house with two women and three men. Seems strange to me."

Marie stopped and thought. "Nah! It must be fun?"

"When we were students it was okay," I began. "You didn't mind emerging from your bedroom with some random girl. But this house is full of thirty and fortysomethings! None of whom wants to get married!"

"Maybe it suits them? Listen, Wes, don't have a wife, kids and a mortgage just because everyone else does. There are many ways of living this life!"

Marie was right.

Roz had said she was a "normal" girl but she was far from normal. She took tomboy to new levels! She had said it didn't matter if I was married and that, if I fell in love with her, it would be my problem to deal with. Who says that? It was more cold and callous than any man.

She also lived in a house with five, unmarried, middle-aged people who had no intention of marrying and moving out! Not very normal.

Using the word 'normal' was some kind of joke for her. She knew she was unconventional and, for some unfathomable reason, she needed someone like me in her life. Some demonic epiphany had convinced her to embrace normality.

I looked into the eyes of my beautiful sister. What kind of life was she leading? She hid inside the family home and rarely emerged. It was so much simpler to hide. What kind of impoverished, pre-fabricated world lay in wait for her? Pottering around was not much of a life but it suited her. It meant she didn't have to suffer fools or clean up behind them.

She'd introduced us, we'd courted and I'd begun dating Trish. I'd been with Trish and, because she was my clever older sister, I assumed she'd be fine? Contenders a-plenty! I assumed some Darcy would come into her life and click with her? It hadn't happened. And now she was quietly growing old inside the family house.

"Roz said my job was my job but it shouldn't be my life."

"Work-life balance? That makes sense."

"But my work IS my life. My life has been always been about my work. I love my work. I get paid to listen to music."

"Doesn't that make you one-dimensional?"

"Doesn't it make me focused?"

"Doesn't it make you boring?"

"Am I boring, Marie?"

"Not to me you're not, my love, but then I don't have to date you!"

She picked up a slightly chipped mug and seemed almost on the verge of binning it, when she suddenly got a memory from the mug and it escaped its death sentence.

"Dad loved this mug," she reminisced. "Someone at work gave it to him. I remember." She paused and put the mug back on its hook. "Shame about Trish!"

"Yes."

"I thought you two were perfectly suited. Thought you'd be together forever? But she was always a bit of a perfectionist. Always thought it could be better."

"Maybe she needed 'better'?" I offered.

"That's what people always wonder, don't they? They wonder if they can do better. And everything else ALWAYS looks better!"

I spent a wonderful afternoon at my sister's and it gave me a chance to walk about the family home. Fortunately, the walls were full of photos and paintings, and – just like the Rod Stewart song – every picture told a story.

We had a family friend who fancied himself as an artist. Just to support him, Mum and Dad bought a few of his paintings. They looked a bit clumsy to me but then he was an amateur. By day, he worked with my Dad but took night classes and bought himself an easel. I stopped to look at them closely. What were they meant to be? Lots of lovely yellow splashes but I couldn't make out much more. The best thing about them was that Mum and Dad had given him £50 and made him feel like a professional. A nice gesture. That's the kind of people they were. God knows where the artist was now!

I even paused to spend a sentimental moment in my old bedroom. It brought back ghastly memories of my naivety but also spine-tingling recollections of my first kiss. How lucky I'd been? My parents had allowed early girlfriends to stay over and even developed this brilliant, nonchalant facade when the young lady came down for breakfast. No knowing comments or looks. Just polite, matter-of-factness and "Pass the butter, dear."

I opened a wardrobe to see what was inside and found some of my parents' old clothes. I touched them and rubbed the fabric between my fingers. I inhaled my past and struggled with a maverick tear.

I pulled out one of my dad's suits, looked in the mirror and held it against me. "Fuck, this might even fit?"

I opened my old bedroom door and shouted down the stairs. "Can I try on one of Dad's old suits?"

"You can take them all!" she shouted. "Take them before the moths get them!"

I looked inside the wardrobe and found some jackets and pairs of trousers. They weren't stylish but they were well made. Durable too! There were no holes, rips or stray threads of cotton. A few new shirts and I would have some new outfits! Inspired thinking by my standards! Could I really ask Roz to help me? I'd only known her two days! Why not?

I figured Roz could mix a noughties shirt with a pair of eighties trousers. She looked like a shopping and label girl. She looked like someone who would say, 'You're not going out dressed like that, are you?'

I then spent the next hour trying on Dad's old suits. Not the kind of thing I normally did but it was fun. They smelt of him and, of course, from certain angles, I almost looked like him!

It was virtually a comical, Austin Powers moment: me dressed-up in all these vintage clothes. I looked like I'd stepped out of 'Bouquet Of Barbed Wire' or 'Abigail's Party'.

I came downstairs to get some plastic bags. "I'll take a selection of things and return what doesn't work."

Marie looked up from her skirting boards and mopped sweat with her sleeve. "I think you wearing Dad's old clothes is wonderful! Just leave Mum's clothes for me."

The only other thing that could stop Marie from cleaning was vintage, Sunday afternoon films; something starring Tyrone Power, or Deborah Kerr, or James Mason. Her whole taste in films, music, clothing and art was 'they don't make them like they used to', and yet I never heard her utter those words. Her best years were in the past and she knew it. Now all she needed was a future with someone who wanted to live in the past.

"And what about your love life?"

"What love life?" she guffawed, settling herself into an armchair. "Who'd want me?"

"Well you look like me, so you must know you're gorgeous!"

"Good looks skipped a generation!"

I grabbed her and kissed her cheek very loudly.

"Get off me, you silly bugger!" She casually flicked through the TV channels, trying to find today's matinee idol. "Here it is! 'Send Me No Flowers': 1964, Rock Hudson, Doris Day and Tony Randall. Perfect!"

"There is one bloke at work," she began.

Marie worked for a firm of architects: organising, administrating.

"He's just started. Quiet. Looks a bit craggy like Daniel Craig. Just the way I like them! He only drinks herbal tea!"

"Sounds promising!"

"Chance would be a fine thing!" she snorted.

I sat on the sofa in the front room of the family home, as I'd done a thousand times before and, out of corner of my eye, it felt as if my mum was sitting in her customary chair, knitting and chewing her tongue, as she always did. I half-expected my dad to pop-up with what he considered a witty remark but, in fact, it was just me and Marie, half-watching, half-dozing with the TV eventually watching us!

I finally got home just after 9.00 and stretched all of Dad's clothes out on the bed. The trousers were okay around the waist but the legs looked strange on me. With those slight flares flapping, I looked like Dr. Who.

It wasn't vintage designer, just well-made British clobber. I sat and looked at the trousers and jackets laid-out on my bed, and I could hear Dad loudly tapping his fingers in the hallway, muttering under his breath, waiting for the women of the house to add the final touches, so we could leave for a family function.

"You know I don't like being late," he would repeat.

At the time, those words made me nervous. I was scared they were going to escalate into a row, but now those words made me smile: "You know I don't like being late!"

Would Roz enjoy dressing me in my Dad's clothes or would she find it morbid? Maybe she would think I was being cheap? I'd only just put our friendship back on track. It was a truly mad and impulsive idea. This girl was going to think I was a headcase!

But that's how I was. What did I know about clothes? What did I care about clothes? I didn't give a second thought to clothes. I permanently looked as if I'd dressed in the dark! I needed guidance. I needed a stylist. Tony G (The *Maitre D'*) spent a fortune on clothes, particularly flashy suits and shiny, pointy black shoes. Working for a female boss, Melvin was in and out of designer shops all day, which suited him fine. Me? What did I know? Clothes were just bits of material that kept me warm during the English winter.

I looked at the suits laid out on the bed and tried to imagine the right shirt. Should it be lime with pink stripes? Maroon with yellow stripes? It was hopeless. Every combination had me looking like a Flamenco dancer! This is why I needed a woman, dammit! These were the bloody decisions I couldn't make.

I nervously dialled Roz's number.

"Hey, sorry to disturb you so late!"

"It's okay," Roz said.

"I've just been over to my family house, was looking through the wardrobes and found a lot of my Dad's old clothes. Suits! Some of them look really cool! It's the kind of stuff they're selling in retro shops! I was wondering if I could get your opinion?"

I heard her laugh. "Wow! You are different! First, you fall asleep in an office doorway, now you want to wear your Dad's old clothes, and you want me to style you!"

"Erm … yes!"

"You don't like buying new clothes, do you?"

"I don't mind buying new clothes but I'm not very good at it!"

"These are seventies suits?" she asked.

"Late seventies/early eighties."

I could hear her thinking and tapping on her mobile, checking her diary.

"Okay, it's an unusual second date but you've talked me into it! Tomorrow night?"

"That would be great. I know it's a bit premature but ... will you come over to my place."

"As long as we're just looking at clothes?"

"Of course! C'mon, I'm not that much of an idiot!"

"Are you sure?"

"Yes," I replied. "Strictly business!"

I looked at the suits again. White shirts would work but someone with a sense of style would be able to solve the riddle: somewhere out there there was a perfect colour for these suits, but fucked if I knew!

Feeling pleased with myself, I called Tony F (the wine merchant), who was grappling with a piece of IKEA furniture and getting aggravated!

On the T.I.T. Scale, he was Mid-Range, so we called him Mids or Midders.

I told him all about Roz.

"I'm glad you've put that right," he said. "She seemed a nice girl. Lots of hair. Always playing with it. Nice girl, though."

"We had brunch this morning!"

"Well done, Wezzer! And?"

"Gonna see her again!"

"Happy days! You've had a face like a slapped arse since Trish buggered-off!"

"Have I?"

"Well ..." I could hear Midders grasping for a tactful reply. "Without a girlfriend, you're miserable! You like having a girlfriend! You like being attached!"

"That I do! And how did you fare?"

"Well, I don't have the success rate of Topper, but I got a phone number. If I can get her into the warehouse to taste some wine, I'll be laughing! Fantastic girl! She teaches PE at a school. We talked about sport most of the night! Ah, fuck it!"

"What's up, mate?"

"Whoever designed this IKEA stuff is a complete bastard! It's meant to be simple but, by the end of it, you want to take an Uzi and waste the neighbourhood!"

"Easy, son! I'll get off the phone, so you can concentrate."

"Alright … and don't forget about my friend's engagement party on Friday night!"

I froze in horror. Engagement party? I HAD forgotten about it! I quickly made a note on a piece of paper.

I gathered my thoughts and tried to piece together bits of information I'd clearly been given over the past few months. Amazingly, over the last few months, I'd had numerous conversations with Mids about this function, and they had slipped down the back of my mental sofa. Since the disappearance of Trish, I'd been absent-minded, lack-lustre, disinterested in most conversation, virtually like a hesitant zombie, unsure whether to kill or be killed!

"Nah, Mids," I lied, "I've got it in my diary. Looking forward to it! I've spoken to the girl, found out what she wants to hear. The usual: disco, dance, pop, no rock, no techno. It'll be fine."

"She's a client and I recommended you, so you need to deliver!"

"Don't I always?"

I looked back at my e-mail correspondence with the bride-to-be and checked all the details. How had that slipped my mind? What was happening to me? I used to have a rough plan of my month in my head but now I was forgetting dates and falling asleep in doorways.

This was getting ridiculous! I had an A4 diary in the shop, a calendar on the wall and my ever-reliable internal diary and, to be honest, I relied on my brain more than anything else, but now it was failing me!

Maybe I did need a doctor after all? But what would I say? I didn't feel unwell, but then many men say that and die of prostate cancer a year later! It was almost like the forgetfulness of old age?

"Aah, bollocky bollocks! I can't put this thing together."

"Take a break, son! Come back to it in ten."

D.I.Y. was not Midders' forte. Like most men, he wanted to do it himself, but he just didn't have the patience. Fly him to a vineyard, get him to sample wines, and he could tell you what would fly off the shelves, just not shelves built by him!

What would I say to a doctor? "I fell asleep in an office doorway?" It's not really the same as, "I've got a nasty rash on my penis." That you can see, that you can treat, that you can deal with. Falling asleep after a bunch of sambucas was just a regular Saturday night hazard, but totally forgetting functions was NOT something I did! Functions were my business! My income!

I looked again at the e-mails and tried to recall the details of our conversations. It was a fairly standard booking. As it was so ordinary, maybe it just hadn't registered? Normal venue, normal customer, normal music. They all blended into one homogenous groove like a four-hour re-edit of Pharrell Williams' 'Happy', Outkast's 'Hey Ya' and Amy Winehouse's 'Rehab'.

And, suddenly, the correspondence began filtering through, as if my brain had been buffering. I remembered it all. Her specific needs. Her special song at midnight. 'Candy' by Cameo at 11.00pm. It was all coming back to me.

I stuck Post-It notes all over the wall to remind me about the gig. A desperate measure I'd never used before! If my memory was about to go, the business was in trouble!

Chapter Three (Monday a.m.)

Monday was a normal day for me. Monday was the day that people brought back their gear, and Monday was a day of checking that every appliance had its lead, and that all the bulbs in the lights were still working.

I looked in my diary. Yep, the booking for the engagement party was there, and all the details. How had I forgotten that?

Working with me in the hire shop was my trusty assistant Max. Another aspiring DJ and, like all teenagers, tribal about his favourite genre. For hours, I had to endure the latest bassline releases and, even though they were all shit, I enjoyed his passion. As he hopped and bopped around the shop, extolling the virtues of this primitive crap, I felt slightly envious. 90% of new music had stopped sounding good to me ages ago.

At just after midday, the door swung open and a sweaty, father-of-the-bride burst in carrying a speaker cabinet. "Fuck, these are heavy!"

"I prefer the word 'sturdy'."

"Spare me the semantics and give us a hand, will ya?"

We pulled the rest of the stuff out of his car and I began sorting through it. There was the smell of cheap champagne in the amplifier but it still worked, so I gave him back his deposit cheque.

The old man breathed a sigh of relief. "Well, I'm glad that's all over." He took a cotton hanky from his breast pocket and wiped his brow. "Never have a daughter, mate!"

"It's out of my hands, isn't it?"

"Well, if you do have a daughter, don't let her get married!"

I sprayed some cleaning fluid into the amp and wiped the surface grime off. "And that's out of my hands as well."

He paused and sighed heavily. "Well, if you do have a daughter, and if she does decide to get married, a 14-piece salsa band is not necessary!"

"I shall remember that," I said. "Cheers! Everything else okay?"

"Oh, yes! My daughter was very happy. My wife and I will be eating bread and water for months, but at least my baby's happy. Got any kids?"

I shook my head. "Not yet! Well, none that I know of!"

"Kids are bloody expensive! Every time my daughter opens her mouth, it costs me money!"

"Well, now it's her husband's problem, isn't it?"

The father looked up at me and smiled, and his shoulders relaxed and broadened, as if the weight of the world had just been removed.

"You're right, son!" he exclaimed. "It's HIS problem now!"

The father-of-the-bride disappeared, tearing-up his deposit cheque and chuckling as he went.

We piled his gear neatly in its rightful place and Max returned to his customary position, behind the record decks.

"Listen to this one!" he said.

Something that sounded like a rubbish truck colliding with a klaxon blared out of the speakers.

"Sounds like the last one, Max."

"How can you say that, bruv? It's completely different!"

I stopped and listened, but the tinny beats and ringtone melodies did nothing for me. "Whatever makes them dance, eh?"

That was our catchphrase: "Whatever makes them dance!"

As in, the object of the exercise is to keep the dance floor full. As in, ours is not to reason why. As in, you won't understand everything. As in, some things just … are.

Max pulled up his baggy jeans. They were hanging around his knees, so this brought them to just below his nuts. "They loved this one! The girls were screaming!"

"I bet they did!" I got a quick mental image of the drunk, delirious and sweaty teenage girls at his clubs; excitable, impressionable teens, anxious to snare a rapper or at least a pirate radio DJ.

Max pulled at his baggy jeans again but, as they were around his ankles, it didn't make much difference. "Some girl came up to me on Saturday night and was all up in my face, about how I was the best DJ in the club and could she become my personal assistant. She must think I'm rich!"

The phone rang. I picked up the phone. "Wheels Of Steel: how can I help?"

A classic Hyacinth Bucket voice came over the phone. A blue rinse prude full of Orpington outrage!

"Do you provide DJs as well as equipment?"

"Yes, madame, we do."

"How much would that cost?"

"Well, if you hire equipment from us, we can provide you with a DJ from £60 an hour."

I could hear her doing the sums in her head. "Will he be a professional DJ?"

"Not sure what you mean, madame?"

"I mean … will he be polite? Well-mannered? Punctual? Smartly-dressed? Will he know that the customer is always right?"

"Of course, madame. The customer IS always right. You tell him what you want and he'll play it."

"Very good."

She sounded relieved and we finalised the details.

"Blimey!" I put the phone down. "That's our first booking for the new year!"

Max began doing his own sums. "That's six months away, bruv!"

"I know!"

I'd inherited the shop from my dad. We'd always been in the business of hiring out 'disco' gear. In the seventies, business had boomed. In those halcyon days of wide collars and wider trousers, Dad had been one of the first to grasp the concept of adding dancing to a drunken night out. Most people don't dance and most people can't dance but, in his unscientific way, Dad had seen the ability of dance music to make people happy.

We didn't make a fortune but business ticked over. There was always a private party somewhere that needed a DJ. And even though I was sick to the back teeth of The B52s 'Love Shack' and The Killers' 'Mr. Brightside', there was no doubting the durability and enduring popularity of these tunes. Like very few other things, these tracks were built to last.

Having said that, I knew the rent would be going up soon and, at that point, I'd probably have to come off the high street and go to an industrial estate. Who cares about the high streets? Certainly not greedy landlords! No shops equals no community but who cares?

In a quiet moment, I thought about my mental health. Did I really need to see a doctor? Or was my brain, like an aging body, just going into decline?

I went online and looked up Alzheimer's. It said it usually started around 60 but, amongst 5%, it could start as early as 30.

What was happening to me?

I thought about my dad's side of the family. How had he ever wooed someone as sweet-natured as my mum?

Don't get me wrong, my dad's family were salt of the earth but they lived in their own world. My grandfather had been a Teddy Boy and that's where my dad had inherited his passion for music.

Their family home in Streatham was a shrine to Elvis, Jerry Lee Lewis and Johnny Cash. Framed posters on the wall. Memorabilia on the shelves. Music always blaring from the front room hi-fi. God knows how my grandmother put up with that!

And the family never left that house. My grandparents, my dad, his two younger sisters (Auntie Lucille and Auntie Peggy.) Every night, my granddad would regale his children with stories of the greats of rock & roll and, by the time I came into the world, those stories were getting vaguer and vaguer.

Dad managed to snare Mum, but the two sisters never left the family home. For some reason, no man was good enough (or had the same swagger as their heroes), so the girls remained, trapped in time, stranded in Streatham.

I remembered Dad taking me and Marie down to my grandparents, and there'd they be: same clothes, same food, same routines, same stories but, with each visit, my granddad would forget a detail.

"No, Dad!" my auntie Peggy would wail, "It was Memphis NOT Chicago!"

"Don't you tell me!" my granddad would threaten. "I remember it clear as day."

They never seemed to go anywhere. Seemingly, nowhere was as interesting or as glamorous as my granddad's memories. They just sat in front of the TV, slaves to the TV guide, talking about the cost of living and reminiscing about how good things used to be.

Suitors came and went, but my aunties never followed anyone out the door, and I watched the steady decline of them all. The conversation and the scenery never changed, so their brains began to stagnate and fossilise. That word 'spinster' again!

I wondered about my own brain. Did my brain need stimulation or did I just have a selective memory, choosing to remember the things that really mattered? That seemed logical. Maybe DJ-ing at another private function wasn't what mattered to me? If not ... what did?

Maybe I was still in mourning about Trish? Midders was right: I really did enjoy being in a couple. I wasn't a gifted conquest-machine. The other guys absolutely loved the thrill of the chase! They were good at it. I just liked the laughs.

I loved their friendship, I loved being part of the gang but, for me, nothing was quite as sweet as the union, the bond, the companionship. Nothing was quite as satisfying as two hearts beating as one.

If my life lacked love, the necessary chemicals couldn't flow to my brain. Chasing women caused confusion in my head. Their names and faces and stories were all blending into one. I'd even forgotten the names of some of my early conquests! Instant and forgettable gratification!

Chapter Four (Monday p.m.)

On Monday evening, I met up with Roz. She was punctual and arrived at my place with a baking dish full of pasta bake.

She noticed my appreciative smile. "I love cooking!" she said.

"Do you?"

"But don't expect me to cook all the time!"

"Of course not!" I said, assertively.

Something about her was different. There was still lots of hair. Tons of it! But she looked extra colourful, as if she'd selected every single colour in her wardrobe. There were bold splashes of everything and even some ear rings with violet feathers in them!

"You look different. You look ..." I stumbled for the right word, nervous I'd say the wrong word.

"Like a paint box?"

"Christ, if I'd said that, I'd have got castigated!"

"It's cool," she said, "I'm going for the non-dowdy! I'm fed-up of black! Nothing is the new black! Black is the past, present and future black! Black is for funerals and fucking. I've got my little black number - what women hasn't? - but let that be an end to it! There are so many colours on the spectrum, why not celebrate them?"

"You're like a poster girl for the paint industry!"

She smiled. "Don't mind if I wander around, do you? You knew I would!"

I quickly scanned the rooms in my head. I'd had a quick clean-up before she arrived. What had I forgotten? All the dirty clothes were in the wash basket (a present from my sister), all the dishes had been washed, there were no hazards on the floor, no traces of single life on the shelves (condoms, sex toys, DVDs etc.)

I was still nervous. She would be clocking every single fashion faux pas, every blemish, every visible sign that I was still a juvenile jerk. (What's my age again?) Doubtless, she was storing up a list of searching questions, in which my answers would indeed display that I was mentally malnourished and still a teenager trapped in a weedy, adult body.

She sauntered around my tiny, terraced house and ran her finger over every surface. The dust didn't seem to bother her but there were other, unidentified sticky substances that troubled her.

"Like a typical man, you walk around your house with a plate of food, don't you?"

There was no need to answer.

It was an unlovely suburban box, lots of small rooms and low ceilings and, in my case, non-existent decor. Even my walls looked like a kid's bedroom, covered with huge, crass rock concert posters and tasteless, sexist images bought by well-meaning mates.

She stopped at one particular image of Rick James with two topless floosies hanging off his bass guitar.

I shrugged my shoulders. "It's Rick James, innit?"

"Of course!" she replied. "Cultural icon."

I didn't need to ask any questions, I could see her face responding to my humble abode. As she walked around the place, picking up ornaments, she was now able to see why Trish had made a run for the hills.

There were family photos in stylish frames that Marie had given me for my birthday and a striking sunset on a canvas (painted by Trish's friend, Dawn). These were the only things with any taste and Roz knew it but, amazingly, she didn't take back her Pasta Bake and beat a hasty retreat. She stayed. She actually wanted to be with me!

She was anxious to see the clothes and emptied them excitedly out of the big, plastic sack. She fingered everything lovingly, and oohed and aahed with pleasure.

"Lovely old fabrics," she said.

She held a jacket to her nose. "It even smells of the seventies!"

"Dad was quite dapper!" I added.

"Right, we need a fashion show! Get 'em off," she demanded.

"Eh?"

"Your jeans! Not shy, are you?"

A taunt guaranteed to remove the clothing from any posturing male.

I removed my jeans and she threw a pair of Dad's trousers at me. I quickly slipped them on.

"And the grubby t-shirt!"

She threw one of Dad's shirts at me and sat back, assessing her work.

"Turn round."

I followed her instruction.

"Good fit! Weirdest date I've had in ages but it's working for me."

She rifled through the other items spread on the bed and threw another shirt at me. I put it on.

"You know what? You might be right? We CAN use some of these. We need to go shopping, though."

She saw me grimace. "What's your problem?"

"I hate shopping!"

"This is only going to work with a mix-and-match approach. We need to buy some standard, contemporary items to go with all this. Otherwise, you'll always look like you're going to a fancy dress party!"

I didn't want that. Systematically, she had me try on everything. As far as I could tell, not necessary, but she enjoyed using me as mannequin and, having watched me undress and dress for an hour, she finally announced, "Right, it's dinner time!"

We wandered downstairs and she began looking around my minimal, single man's kitchen. She looked inside my impoverished cupboards and pulled open the fridge.

"Oh, you are classic!" she laughed. "Is there a bottle of wine to go with the food?"

I reached into the bottom of my fridge and pulled out a bottle of cheap plonk the local Chinese restaurant had given me for Christmas. They told me I was their "most loyal customer". I was actually the laziest bastard on the street.

She looked at the bottle dismissively. "Oh, this will do." Then, she spooned out portions of pasta bake on to plates and we sat and ate. She looked at me, like she'd never really looked at me. "You remind me of one of my exes."

"Is that good?"

"He had that same 'lost' look."

"Lost look?"

She fiddled with her hair again. "Most men have this cocky look. And most of them haven't even got anything to be cocky about!"

"Ah, now, that's interesting! I actually have many things to be cocky about! Does that make me modest?"

She smiled shyly. It was a look I hadn't seen before. It was a mischievous look.

"I like the way you look. You look innocent. Pliable."

Pliable? Christ, what a word! I'd been called many things but, of course, she was right. I was pliable. The problem was: I liked it. Well, not a problem, really. Not a 'problem' to me. Let experts be experts. Women are better at certain things. Let them crack on with it!

Being with her was like being with Trish. I liked that. She was 'together' and full of killer anecdotes. She also did most of the talking, which was a blessed relief, after making the running for many years. My tales were tawdry; my stories were deathly dull with no structure and no punch line.

Roz filled my kitchen with colour and laughter and personality and I was desperate to find out why she found me interesting, but I knew that would look pathetic. If I were to ask that question, I'd look far from cocky! It just didn't make sense. Trish and I were teens and we'd fallen into a relationship, but here was a woman meeting Wes the adult and she actually found me appealing! Why?

I looked at my bare walls and began to feel ridiculous. How difficult was it to buy and frame a painting?

"What does 'pliable' mean to you?" I asked.

"Nothing sinister!"

And yet the look on her face was very sinister and I got another quick flash of her coven. The usual images: dark cave, pointed black hats, bubbling cauldron, eye of newt etc.

"So, tell me more about your friends?"

She sipped cheap plonk and rocked her head back with laughter, "God, how I love them!"

"So you keep telling me!"

As she laughed, I suddenly caught the glint of metal. Ha, she had a filling! She wasn't perfect!

She spooned more pasta bake on to our plates. "Let me start by saying that: a) I live with three men, and b) I have many platonic, male friends. Is that a problem?"

I had too much food in my mouth and was unable to talk, so I nodded my head back and forth, slowly and nonchalantly, as if I was completely comfortable with her sharing a house with three young, healthy, fit, professional men.

"No, you've already told me about all the men in your life," I finally, replied. "Of course you have lots of men in your life!"

"I live in a house with five other people: two girls and three guys and, I promise you, the guys are just mates. I know where they've been! It would literally be like fucking my brother! Not happening!"

"It's not a problem," I assured her in my special, metrosexual voice reserved for smart women.

"Raymond is a strong, dark, powerhouse. English, Jewish mother, Italian father. Very masculine, very dynamic. He's a do-er. Knows how to create excitement, knows how to make money, runs his own film production company. Came from a TV background like me. He directed his first short film a few years back and has been visiting film festivals ever since!"

I was jealous already. If this was how she described her platonic friends, how did she describe her lovers?

"Heston is tall, athletic, beautiful, charismatic, has a heart of pure gold and a very sensitive, almost vulnerable core. He's a painter. If he's anything, he's an impressionist. Big hit with the ladies! He's got the looks and personality and boy does he work it!"

"And Benjamin ..." she continued, "Christ, how do I describe Benji? He thinks he's above it all. He's a teacher at the local comprehensive, but he thinks he's above living with us, thinks he's above all his work colleagues. A smart guy but so bloody arrogant! He describes us all as 'peasants!'"

Who were these clever bastards? Not like anyone I knew! My mates were drunk and illiterate, like me.

"And the two girls?"

She hesitated and picked up her wine glass and, in a moment of brilliance, uncommon in me, I picked-up on why she was hesitating; she didn't want to paint too good a picture of her female housemates.

Roz gobbled up another mouthful of dinner and thought about her answer. Using the right words was important to her.

"Well," she began, "let me start with Jill. Jill is Mother Hen in our house. She's works in HR at a bank and she's like the general manager. She makes sure all the bills are paid and we never run out of toilet paper. You don't argue with Jill. You won't win. Jill knows best and, even if she doesn't, it's best to let her do it her way!

"Jill's a touch older than us. Maybe that's why she's taken command? And even though she's got no husband and no children, she seems really happy in our house. As if we're her husband and children?

"And Wendy? Well, Wendy is an NHS nurse. Long hours and low pay but she still takes care of us all. Patches us up. Gets rid of our colds, aches and pains. Kind-hearted. Loving, giving, caring. Funny girl! You will love her!"

She paused and thought about her gang. "Good friends!"

While my mates were quite happy feeding Cosmopolitans to the members of a hen party, her friends were probably dissecting an installation at Tate Modern? Christ, the difference between her mates and mine! Guess they served the same purpose, though?

"And what makes a good friend?"

She began playing with the hair again and, as she had a tiny piece of pasta bake on her index finger, I could see a dinner-in-hair catastrophe unfolding before me. I waved my fingers dramatically, as if I was trying to loosen a sticky piece of mucus.

"What?" she asked.

"You've got food in your hair."

"Don't worry. I'll find it later."

I found her casual attitude to hair care very comforting. Fussy women are irritating at the best of times. Waiting for a woman to get ready is like falling asleep on a freezing cold bus stop while waiting for the night bus on a December morning. Maybe worse?

"Some people imagine that good friends need to see each other every day," she began. "I don't subscribe to that. A good friend is someone that makes no demands at all. Not one! You might not see them for a week? A month? A year? But when you see them, you are excited and grateful. When you're not with them, you think about them, worry about them, feel their pain, share their joy."

Was this how it was with me and the boys? Did I feel their pain? I suppose I did. When Low lost his dad, he cried. I remember putting my arms around him and feeling him cry into my shoulder. Brought a lump to my throat.

I liked her definition. That's how I felt about the boys. My glorious gang of beer-swilling, chest-beating charlies were always in my thoughts. Of course, we were never apart for too long! We even did holidays together; the customary and very outrageous package holiday to somewhere hot. It didn't matter where we were. As long as there were cold drinks and girls dressed in not very much, we were happy!

I pictured Roz and her housemates, sat round a big, wooden table, several empty bottles of great red wine, a big pot of goulash on the stove, fiercely debating Descartes and Spinoza!

I pictured quiet, Sunday afternoons reading books or expansive vocabularies analysing the weekend broadsheets. I pictured impassioned debate, hearty laughter and lusty kisses, and I wondered where I fitted into all this.

"And what do you and the crew do for fun?" I asked.

She hesitated. For the first time, the noise stopped. The talking had come to a halt. She was either lost for words or unsure what to say.

"God, what haven't we done?"

She fingered her bra strap nervously. "We're all busy people. Independent. All over the place. Rarely in the same place at the same time."

I looked at her. Again, more fingering of the bra strap. Fierce twisting of the fabulous mane."

"You never hang out together?"

"Of course we do! But we're all single! And free!"

Roz suddenly noticed that the plates were both empty and cleared the table. She squirted some soap over a sponge and began doing the dishes.

"We live together! Of course, we hang out! God, we've all been through a lot."

She was silent again. Her back was to me and I could see her eyeing-up the meagre display of household cleaning products. I always forgot that there was 'bathroom cleaner' and 'kitchen cleaner' and, amazingly, a significant difference between them!

"We've been through a lot," she repeated. "We still are."

She span round and looked at me. She really had gone all out to be as colourful as possible. She was an extremist. This was now dawning on me. This marvellous, mysterious woman was about to light a fire under my life.

We enjoyed our first moment of silence. She looked at me and smiled, and I gazed at this pallet of extravagant shades. And, in that moment, I understood it.

I was low maintenance. Within that company, the pressure to perform was high. She'd have to be firing on all cylinders or get devoured! With me, it was quieter, simpler, easier.

She looked down at her potential simpleton of a boyfriend and smiled again. "Since we've been living together, we've done so much!"

"Like what?"

"All sorts! Christ, we had a Rummy phase and played Rummy every night for three months! We started with day trips, pub crawls, riverboat cruises, paint balling and wine-tasting, moved on to sporty things like archery and golf, then extreme sports like sky diving and snowboarding, we've done every kind of holiday, we went to South Africa for the 2010 World Cup, got totally involved in the London Olympics, and we even dabbled in the occult!"

I sat back, stuffed and sleepy. "Yeah? The occult? Was it fun raising The Evil Dead?"

"It was interesting."

"You can't really take The Evil Dead wine-tasting, though!"

She smiled at me. An unnerving smile. She turned and looked at all my fridge magnets and fingered my map of Corsica. I knew my magnets were tacky but they brought back great memories.

What was the unnerving smile about? Could she hear that I was envious of her exploits? Or could she actually hear that I was intimidated by her circle? The word 'compatible' began rolling around my head and I wondered what it actually meant.

One of the fridge magnets was shaped like a large pan of paella, she pulled it off the fridge and began running her fingers over it. Fidgeting nervously for the first time. Not in control but rather anxious, as if she had something important to say.

"No need to go somewhere and do something, as it were. We live together!" she said, triumphantly. "Which means we spend a lot of time in each other's company. Cook together, shop together, holiday together, watch TV together. We really get on. I'm so lucky!"

She smiled and looked at me. It was that infamous look of discovery where the other person scrutinises you like an MRI scanner. I felt a little uncomfortable as she perused my every pore, but it was something I had to allow her to do. I tried to look nonchalant but probably looked like a homophobic man waiting for a colonoscopy.

"What are you looking at?"

"You're quite cute, aren't you?"

Now, 'cute' is not how you want to be described. In your deluded fantasies, you hope someone will describe you as 'hot' or 'sexy' or, at the very least, 'handsome'.
But ... 'cute'?

"Cute like a puppy? Cute like a detailed Lego model? Cute like an intricate snooker shot?"

"No, no," she smirked, clearly enjoying my discomfort. "You're just boyfriend cute. Good-enough-to-show-off-to-my-friends cute."

I suddenly realised these weird and wonderful 'friends' needed to approve me. I would have to audition for them as well. And what if they didn't like me? Did I still have a future with Roz?

"And what else do you and your friends do?"

She had a fumble around in her memory to gather up stray thoughts.

"Ah yes!" she began, "and then we moved on to sex."

My heart stopped. I tried not to look un-cool but I guess the fine sheen of perspiration on my forehead gave me away. "Sex?"

"Yes."

"What kind of sex? Kinky sex? Group sex?"

"All sorts of things."

Trying to appear un-phased was not an option. My heart was pounding and my leg was now trembling uncontrollably. She watched me suffer and giggled.

"We went to an orgy. We went to a naturist spa. And we went to a pretty full-on S&M party: lots of heavy techno and trance, lots of leather and PVC, and lots of very swollen testicles!"

I nodded with interest, and tried to look as if she'd just told me the cheese in my sandwich was Edam. "Interesting."

"The best thing about it …" she began

"Kinky sex with well-endowed men?"

She looked at me with the disappointed look of a TV contestant who's just let a mortgage-size sum slip through her fingers (and all she'll be going home with are some department store vouchers!)

"You mean that's NOT the best thing? There's something better?"

"The best thing about it," she continued, "is that it's crystallized what kind of people we are. We finally know what we are. We finally know what makes us happy. What makes us comfortable. We finally know how we like to escape. Work hard, play hard. You relax, you escape. If you can't relax and escape, you can't function!"

I looked at her blankly.

"Escape," she repeated. "When we leave work, we like to escape, right? 5.00 p.m. arrives and we all scatter in different directions. Some people switch on their PC or Mac and escape into websites. In websites, they can be someone totally different; somebody cool, sexy and alluring. Others escape inside a dark cinema. The lights go down and, suddenly, their world is full of super-sexy, super-strong people, car chases, talking animals, aliens and zombies. Some folks go down the pub and, a few hours later, the inhibitions are gone, they're telling shaggy dog stories and dancing like Kevin Bacon!"

Made sense. What did me and the boys do? Where did we escape? Our favourite pub, the clubs of London, holiday destinations. Most of the time, though, we just escaped inside our laughter. It was the easy laughter of familiar banter. Taking the piss out of each other never got tired!

I suddenly remembered I had some Ben & Jerry's in the freezer, so I rescued it, brushed off the ice and handed her a spoon.

She looked at it approvingly. "Cherry Garcia: my favourite!"

"And where do I escape?" I asked, peeling the lid off and trying to dig my spoon into it.

"Well, from what I saw the other night, your mates are your escape. You seem like a tight bunch. I assume you get up to your own adventures?"

As it happened, our adventures were restricted to normal stuff: chasing girls, eating curry and getting wasted. Nothing as exciting as raising The Evil Dead!

"So, you've been to these sex parties," I began, partially bending my spoon in the hard ice cream, "and they've helped you work out what you are?"

"Like I said, once we'd been to a few parties, we all realised what we were. Three of us were dominant, two of us were submissive, and one of us was a switch; probably 60% dom, 40% sub. In every kind of relationship or friendship, there are subs and doms. In every marriage, there is one that likes to be in control, and one that likes being controlled. In some cases, it's almost master and servant."

"And what about you?"

"Hmm ..." she hummed, "I think I know what I am but, some days; I'm not so sure. I guess we all have different needs on different days?"

If I'd asked any more questions, I'd have looked like a right div, so I acted as if I knew what she was talking about, and made a mental note to look it up online.

I now had a strong mental picture of both her social and sexual life. A calendar full of art gallery openings, film festivals, lingerie fashion shows, fiercesome dinner debates around a long, dining table, and illicit liaisons with swarthy and devilish deviants. Where did I fit into all of this?

Roz's account of her own brand of domestic bliss brought back a vivid memory of Trish, who multi-tasked like it was her last day on Earth. She was a great list maker. It was almost a game for us. Trish would make a list: we would spend the day checking off the items and reward ourselves when the list had been ticked. Paint spare room: check. Iron shirts: check. Throw out recycling: check.

She was a good organiser and I enjoyed that. It meant I didn't have to do it. There it was: my day planned out before me on a list. And I looked forward to my treat!

What did that make me? A faithful pet. Where on Earth did I fit into Roz's life? What role would I play?

"Six singletons?"

"Yes, six singletons!"

"Forever single?"

She kicked off her shoes, sat on my well-worn sofa and wiggled her toes. I was interested to know why this singleton wanted to spend so much time with me.

"It really is a very special house and we're all really happy."

I could hear a 'but'.

I waited.

And waited.

"But?" I prompted.

"But," she began, "even though I love my housemates ... I think I'd like a boyfriend?"

And there it was!

She was smart and sophisticated, she was cultured and well-travelled but, when it came down to it, she was still a human being, she was still a girl and, thankfully, I was a boy! A very old boy!

In my own primitive way, I observed a pendulum swing. I had what she wanted. I definitely didn't feel lusted after. She was not all handsy! But I definitely had something she wanted! What was it? Companionship? Nah, she had that already! A sex life? Nah, she could get that anywhere! A friend? Nah, she had people she could talk to and rely on!

"You want a boyfriend?" I asked. "And how do your housemates feel about that?"

"They think I'm mad!"

"Mad?"

"Yes," she smiled, "completely out of my tree mad! They think I've crossed over to the dark side and I am now the butt of all their jokes! I am 'the good wife'. I am 'her indoors'. I am 'the other half'."

"Harsh!"

"It's almost like they feel that, if I become someone's girlfriend, my brain will waste away!"

And that made sense too! I knew that being in love could sometimes make a brain turn to mush! I'd seen it happen to my sister. And couples fall into zombie-like routines but – damn it – I loved those routines!

"So your friends think you're mad for wanting a boyfriend and they're taking the piss out of you?"

"Yes."

"That must hurt?"

Roz looked sad and quite angry. "It does. After all we've been through, it really does!"

I'd never been here before. Girl ridiculed by housemates for wanting a boyfriend. It seemed ridiculous.

"So, what now?"

"I need to win them over. WE need to win them over. So, when are we going shopping?" she asked, quickly changing the subject.

The ice cream was starting to soften and we were finally able to share dessert. I was way out of my depth. It was clear. She had the confident demeanour of someone who'd got some answers, while coasters like me and my mates were happy to fumble in the dark. How did I feel about her being smarter than me? I wasn't bothered. When I'd taken the lead in the past, I'd fucked up on every occasion.

"Shopping," I stumbled. "How much is this going to cost?"

"Oh, you are looking at The Queen Of The Bargain! I never buy expensive clothes and I never buy labels! Labels allow clueless people to look good!"

She swallowed mouthfuls of ice cream and moaned with pleasure. What did the woman that described me as 'pliable' want with me? All of Trish's words kept coming back to me. I knew, if I kept listening, she would finally reveal her hand.

How was I possibly going to pass The Friend Audition? She wanted a boyfriend and they were already mercilessly ribbing her! I was on a hiding to nothing. Their feedback to her was going to be "Dump him!" I could feel it.

"The high road is full of hidden gems," she said, licking her spoon. "Must stop eating this!"

"Considering I screwed-up so badly on our first night, you're being very generous with your time. Thank you!"

She smiled and slowly rotated her neck. "You don't have to thank me! You seem a decent guy. You have a strange medical condition but you seem genuine."

"I do not have a strange medical condition!"

She laughed and looked very beautiful.

"At brunch, you said you wanted to take me on some dates. So, are we dating?" She smiled mischievously and had another spoonful of ice cream

She absolutely loved provoking me! Who didn't? I was the butt of everyone's jokes!

As she was so much smarter than me, I hadn't even entertained 'dating'. Why would a whiz-kid like her want a *schlub* like me?

"Dating?"

"C'mon, you know! Dating! If we're going on some dates, we must be dating!"

"Let's see how the dates go, huh?"

My internal computer was whirring furiously. What did I have? What did she want? Normality. Stability. I kept coming back to these words.

"I'm fairly certain you'll like this boyfriend/girlfriend business! It has its perks!"

"Perks?" I enquired, excitedly.

"You get a goodnight kiss!"

I trembled and grinned.

"Listen, if my housemates are gonna take the piss out of me, you might as well agree to be my boyfriend?"

"Well, as you asked so nicely."

She leaned across my kitchen table, grabbed my head with both hands and kissed me on my lips.

I looked shocked, which pleased her immensely.

"That's got THAT out of the way. Right, I'm off. I have to be up early."

I watched her put on her coat and walk towards the door. I may have been walking behind her but it felt as if I was floating. She was a killer mixture of ass and sass! Had I really been lucky enough to find another Trish?

Except she was no Trish! She was Trish with added attitude and pizzazz! The stars had finally aligned. I was finally in the right place at the right time.

"Speak tomorrow, Hot Lips!" She waved and walked down the path to my front gate. "And stop looking at my bum!"

I waved feebly, she shot out another dazzling smile and disappeared into the distance.

The Friend Audition. Could I prepare for it or should I just be myself? She'd called me a "decent guy". What did that mean? Maybe I was better boyfriend material than the beefcakes? Maybe they gave better banter but I was someone she could actually call her own?

And what would my gang say? Nothing. They'd be fine. They wouldn't mind, as long as it didn't mess with too many of our routines!

I stood in front of my hallway mirror. What was 'cute' about that? Who was I to argue?

Chapter Five (Tuesday a.m.)

The next day, I got to the shop and called Tony F the wine merchant to finalise more details about his friend's engagement party. He was taking delivery of some new stock.

"This is lovely stuff! Not even available on the high street! I'm bringing some of this to Helen's party.   Bit too good for them but why not?"

"Is she going to want disco lights?" I asked.

"Yeah, give her the whole works! Cheesy as you like!"

We had three huge, mirror balls, guaranteed to make any party look like 'Saturday Night Fever'. What was it about disco that made everybody happy? The clubs were ostentatious, the huge collars and flares were ridiculous, and the dance moves were as close as white people were ever going to get to looking good on a dance floor! It was almost a black music that didn't sound like it was derived from the blues; it came from idealism, optimism and hope, and sexual liberation!

And, to match the high-camp, Las Vegas showgirl nature of the scene, the music had to be fast and dramatic like Puccini on poppers! The melodramatic sit-com plots of 'I Will Survive', 'Tragedy' and 'It's Raining Men' never failed to make people smile. That was one of the best parts of my job: making people smile. We promised to play whatever made them dance and whatever made them smile.

I could hear Tony F shouting at delivery drivers and boxes of bottles being piled high. In a weird way, I was quite proud of Midders. He'd recovered from his wife running off with one of her employees and he'd turned his life around. His business was growing and, if anyone was gonna be rich, it was him!

"Right! Finished!" he said. "So? What's happening between you and that girl with the hair?"

"She was over here last night!"

"Crikey, you work quick for such a dopey bastard!"

"No, no, not like that!" I quickly assured him.

"Well?"

"Bit of dinner, bottle of wine. I've asked her to sort out my wardrobe."

"What wine were you drinking?"

"Just something I got free from the local Chinese!"

Tony then uttered some profanity that I don't think I'd ever heard before. It sounded very coarse and highly insulting. Could have been Polish or Ukranian? Either way, he was NOT happy with me.

"What are you like, son? Couldn't I sort you out with a decent bottle of wine?"

"I don't drink wine!"

"Well you do now, mate! God knows why but some classy girl wants to go out with you! You need wine in the fridge and wine in the rack, in case she pops over."

"I don't know what wine she drinks!" I said.

"Don't you worry about that, Wezza! Don't you worry your pretty little head with those details! I will sort you a wine for every occasion."

Sometimes my mates treated me like the gormless little brother. As if nothing would get done without their supervision! Little did they know: I'd just been kissed by this woman called Roz and I was about to wake up next to a naked woman, every morning!

"She's going to sort out your wardrobe?" Mids asked. "Is she a chippy?"

"No, sort out my clothes!"

"You haven't got any clothes!"

"I picked up some of my dad's old stuff from the house the other night."

Midders was silent, trying to compute what I'd just said. "Your dad's old stuff? Helen's party is not fancy dress!"

"Yeah, hilarious, mate! Listen, it looks fine and Roz is going to find some newer bits to go with it. It fits me and she says it looks fine. Women do it all the time: mix old with new."

Tony was still trying to get his head around it. "It'll be like raving with your dad!"

It was a mad idea but it had Roz's endorsement! A no-nonsense girl like that would quickly shut down something naff!

"She's classy! She knows what she's doing!" I assured him.

"Classy girls like that won't drink cheap wine forever! I'll bring you a case and charge you cost. Good wine works wonders! Didn't you know that? Like flowers!"

I thanked Midders for his advice and offer, and left him to get on with his day. How nice it would be to offer Roz some decent wine! How dopey was I? Of course! The best ingredients make the best meals.

All of the gang gave to each other. We gave what we could. Subtle distinction: acquaintances talk about giving but real friends actually give!

Max wandered into the shop. "Morning!" he said.

I looked at the clock. 10.15. Our hours were fairly flexible. No one wanted to talk about hiring disco equipment until after 10.00, so we didn't bother opening until then.

Max pulled off one faded, black T-shirt to reveal another faded, black T-shirt underneath. It hung lifelessly over his baggy, blue jeans. He feebly pulled up the jeans but they quickly fell back down.

Couldn't quite get my head around the baggy jeans thing; some fashions made no sense to me at all. The trousers fell and no one bothered to pull them up! These skinny, shapeless boys were attempting the show off their form to members of the opposite sex, like apes exposing their buttocks in order to mate, but it didn't quite have the same allure.

The shop looked particularly grubby today. I dreaded raising the subject of cleaning to Max. Cleaning was definitely part of Max's job description but he didn't fully appreciate the removal of grime. To him, grime was a music genre!

And how was I going to tutor Max in cleaning when I didn't know what I was doing? I'd seen this thing called a feather duster but surely that just moved dust from shelf to floor?

"Wes, you've done radio, haven't you?"

"I have."

I fondly recalled my many years of hospital radio. How exciting it had been back then. I'd had so many dreams of being a radio star (then moving into TV like Noel Edmonds!)

I'd listened to radio so closely when I was younger, captivated by this seemingly endless stream of patter. How could these people talk so clearly and concisely for so long? How did they know what to say and how did they say it so perfectly?

I'd built myself a little radio station in my bedroom, with one record deck, one cassette deck and a microphone with a stand I'd found in a charity shop. For hours, I'd practice talking into songs and talking out of songs. Why did being a radio DJ seem so appealing? The thought of millions of people hanging on my every word was intoxicating.

"What's it like, bruv?"

"Radio?"

"Yeah!" said Max, wide-eyed. "How do you do radio?"

I'd never thought about it.

"All that talking!" he continued. "What do you say?"

"Why you asking?"

"Some dude's asked me if I want to get involved in a pirate radio station!"

I looked at Max and suppressed a smirk. This was a kid with a passion for music and an innate gift to make people dance, but talking was not his forte!

Conversation with Max was an arid desert populated by a few manky vultures! Conversation with Max was always the same few subjects: Chelski, girls, music, his mates and clothes; typical young man stuff but never with any insight.

He would never say, "Girls are very interesting because ..." He would merely say, "She is well fit and I bet she swallows!"

How was he going to become a radio broadcaster?

Maybe it was my fault? Maybe I should have engaged him in conversation? But what did I know about anything? My knowledge was gleaned from free newspapers and the questionable wisdom of my mates!

We were stuck in this shop for eight hours of every week day, why didn't we talk about politics? Or the economy? Or the arts? I had time to educate this boy but I was wasting it online, looking at gadgets and You Tube clips of cats and dogs.

I looked at my assistant and, for the first time, he was starting to look like a man. He was tall, skinny and angular, with cheekbones, floppy hair and a small, black tattoo on his bicep. In truth, he was starting to look model material. If he could make it as a pirate radio hero, the sky was the limit.

In fact, despite his gormless, teenage opinions and his complete lack of perspective, my trusted aide was probably going places! Before long, he'd be strutting the catwalk and spinning for toffs at society soirees!

Max was looking well pleased with himself. His jeans were balanced delicately on his knees but, somehow, he was still dancing, grooving to some juddery piece of dubstep nonsense in his head.

"How do you do radio?" I repeated. "Well, Max, it might sound strange, but you will have to learn how to talk!"

Max looked crestfallen.

"Ah, shit!" he moaned. "I knew it would be complicated!"

"Maybe you could just mix and play jingles?" I suggested.

"Yeah!" said Max, enthusiastically. "I can do that!"

Max was happy. He could now become a celebrity.

Unlike me. A faded star. All I knew was: I needed a girlfriend who was smart and decisive, and could help me remember all this shit I was forgetting! Roz seemed to be up for the job, so things were looking good?

I wandered into our small kitchen and turned the kettle on.

"You don't want a cuppa, do you?"

"Nah, bruv!" Max shouted.

I decided I needed to urinate and opened the door of the toilet. As I washed my hands, I looked at my face in our broken and cracked mirror. Not a pretty sight. My hair fopped in a bored and lank way. It could have looked like Robert Redford in 'Barefoot In The Park', but instead it looked like bedraggled student at the end of Fresher's Week. I couldn't remember the last time I'd had a decent haircut.

There was a barber's literally two doors away from our shop and I'd been visiting there – out of convenience – for the last ten or so years.

This was just a high-street barber, with no pretensions of ever being trendy. The men in the photos on the walls looked crap, why did I ever imagine I would look any better? The shop was run by two hopelessly mis-styled Greek brothers, born and bred North Londoners with a fierce allegiance to Arsenal. They told tall tales of famous footballers that had passed through their shop, and every haircut took forever as the stories ambled on.

Their own hairstyles were throwbacks to the pre-disco era and my hair always looked like a hurried, botched (and ultimately unsuccessful) operation. I looked at myself. Everything about me was weary and unkempt. No wonder Trish had run far away! I was the picture of poor maintenance.

The kettle had boiled, so I opened the fridge, hoping to find some milk. There was the merest splash left in the carton. I made myself some tea and reached for a stale something from inside our metal cookie jar: the last, lonely digestive biscuit.

I heard a female voice inside the shop and Max making primitive grunting noises as a form of communication. I looked at myself in the mirror again. Did I look presentable and ready to face a member of the public? No. I looked pale, malnourished and badly in need of some nasal hair clippers!

Carrying my mug of tea, I came back into the shop and there was Roz, browsing, smiling to herself, making Max very nervous, and asking him questions he couldn't possibly answer.

She pretended to ignore me and I watched her run her fingers over the gear, as if inspecting it for dust. Sadly, she found not only dust but wedding cake and probably vomit, but she didn't flinch. I vowed to learn the difference between kitchen and bathroom cleaner, and buy the shop some rugged and chunky kitchen towel!

She was wearing these figure-hugging jeans that did a great job of showcasing her derriere and, just when she knew she had my full attention, she bent over to inspect a well-travelled speaker cabinet.

Nice move!

She turned round to look at me.

"Good afternoon," she said, brightly. "Are you the proprietor?"

"I am."

She extended her hand. I shook it.

"My name is Roz," she began, "but my loyal subjects call me Queen Rosalinda The Merciful. You may address me as 'your highness'."

Max looked up and wondered what was going on. What had the woman just said?

"Thank you, your highness," I began, "we are honoured by your presence."

"Your name, surf?"

"Wes, your highness. Short for Wesley. Wesley Thorpe."

"Thorpe?" she said. "A Thorpe is a small village. So, Wesley Of Thorpe, which small village do you rule?"

"Erm ..." I stuttered, "Tufnell Park. And the surrounding areas."

"I see," Roz said, looking regal, with all that amazing hair cascading over her shoulders.

"And you, your highness, what is your domain?"

Roz looked around the shop, looked up at the cracks in the ceiling, looked me up and down, and snarled in disapproval. "I am the ruler of all I survey."

Max was now looking totally bemused, and furiously tugged at his baggy jeans, as if trying to make a good impression. He wondered if he was really looking at royalty, or just one of the nutters that wandered the streets shouting at pigeons?

"So, Wesley Of Thorpe? What sort of services do you provide?"

"We rent out equipment on which to play music, your highness. We will install it in your venue, make sure it's working properly, then come and collect it once the function is over."

"And, do you provide disc jockeys?"

"We do, your highness. Both Max and I are highly competent, plus we have others at our disposal."

Roz turned to look at Max. His jeans were hovering nervously around his ankles and there was a small bead of sweat on his upper lip.

"Too young!" she snarled.

Max looked visibly relieved.

She looked back at me. "You'll do!"

I bowed in deference. "Thank you, your highness. And what is the function?"

"Function?" she sneered, derisively. "One does not organise functions! There will be nothing functional about this event! It has to be the best!"

"We always try our best!"

"It's a surprise 40th for one of my housemates. He has reached this monumental age and has begun sobbing uncontrollably into his food. Stupid boy!"

"What music?"

"He thinks he's at the cutting edge of fashion, so just play him whatever trendy crap you can find!"

I looked at Max and he winked back at me!

"My people will be in touch," were her parting words, as she sauntered out of the shop.

I dunked the digestive in my tea and took a bite. I liked this girl more and more. Roz was funnier than Trish. Trish had actually been quite sombre at times. Roz was entertaining, quite comical and very convincing. She'd clearly fooled Max.

He looked at me. "She's not all there, is she, bruv?"

"The customer is always right," I reminded him, "even though they might not be right in the head!"

Max laughed. "Good one, Wes! You're not wrong there! Do you think she'll call?"

"Oh, she's deadly serious! You'll be seeing her again."

A text buzzed into my phone. It read, "Get yer coat. You've pulled!"

I reached for my jacket. "Max, will you look after the shop for a short while? Just have to pop out."

"No worries, Wes."

I walked out of the shop and there was Roz. Leaning up against the shop window, looking at herself in a compact mirror and applying Sheer Plum lipstick.

"Where are we going?" I asked her.

"Shopping."

And that's what we did for the next two hours.

Roz was in her bossy element, leading us in and out of shops, barking out orders, telling me what to discard and what to purchase.

But being with her was enjoyable. She reminded me of Trish in so many ways. Trish loved a project or a crusade! Rolling up her sleeves and marching into battle, Trish was never happier, and Roz had that same determined glint in her eye.

She loved shopping and loved my discomfort. She was gurgling with glee! It gave me pleasure to see Roz laughing, clearly enjoying herself, and gesticulating wildly like the conductor of an orchestra trying to hail a taxi.

I saw more changing rooms that morning than I had in the last three years, and who knew that body odour could vary so much? However, with a clutch of new shirts in some carrier bags, Roz was happy.

"A good morning's work, you scruffy vagabond! These nice, new shirts will bring those suits to life!"

"What you doing on Friday evening?"

She thought. "Nothing."

"Can I interest you in a truly awful engagement party featuring a lot of very tipsy Greek girls in a pub on the Holloway Road. The food may be cold but it will be Greek, and the sparkling rosé will be in plentiful supply!"

"I am SO there!" she squealed with delight. "What kind of music?"

"Well," I began, "you'll probably hear a few decent tunes by the Human League and Heaven 17, but you might also hear some pretty dire eighties disco."

"I look forward to it. And that surprise 40th is next Saturday!"

I made a mental note not to forget this date and hoped to God I'd remember the mental note!

We kissed, parted ways and I trudged back to the shop, laden with trendy new attire.

Max looked at me as if I'd grown horns. "Shirts? Are you trying to impress some girl, bruv?"

I realised I was.

"We need to clean up this shop, Max."

Max looked genuinely horrified. He surveyed the worn-out, bespeckled carpet and the pock-marked walls. "Really? Looks fine to me!"

It looked like a shit heap, so I got out our antique Hoover from under the stairs, poured some pine-flavoured Dettol into a pail of hot water, found some rags, and we spent the rest of the day cleaning. And, when a female customer wandered in around 3.00, she looked well impressed with two sweaty men wiping decades of party off our record decks!

By the end of the day, the shop no longer smelt like Pale Ale, and everything was put away tidily and symmetrically. We almost looked like a prosperous business!

"So you'll teach me how to do radio?" Max asked, hoping that I'd be rewarding him for his endeavours (actually the first sweat we'd broken in years!)

"Course I will!" I assured him, knowing full well that he stood a better chance of reaching my dreams!

Chapter Six (Tuesday p.m.)

That evening, I met up with the boys for a quick, mid-week drink. Traditionally, we met on Tuesday or Wednesday to make plans for the weekend.

We had a variety of pubs we'd frequent but there was one we liked in particular, the innocently-named Dog And Duck, which we'd nicknamed The Fog.

The Fog was brilliant, not only because the landlord had installed several virtual-cinema-sized TV screens, but because he had a several satellite boxes, which meant we could watch any sport from around the world any night of the week. The landlord – one Alfredo Pena – also had the most spectacular array of snacks I had ever seen in a pub. A global array of tasty treats with almost one suited for every single drink in his establishment. Fredo would bring you your drink and say, "Try this!" and you knew it would be the perfect snack accompaniment for that beverage.

Back in the day, The Fog had probably been a very traditional local but, down the years, Fredo had added touches of his home town (Madrid) and The Fog was now a busy mixture of English pub and Spanish bar.

Everywhere, there was Atletico Madrid memorabilia. Faded, framed photos, pendants, autographed football shirts. It would've been a trendy sports bar, if it weren't for the crusty locals still stuck in their favourite spot. These old boys were sporting the same cloth caps that were now back in fashion and, when they talked about the good old days, they were not talking about the swinging sixties!

These trusty residents had seen the pub go through many guises and probably not even noticed! They were still having the same, safe conversations they'd always enjoyed, something along the lines of "They don't make footballers like that anymore!" It was the pub on the corner of the road. Their local. And they would always pop in for a "swift half" which quickly materialised into a night out (out).

I arrived first, got a bottle of cold Peroni and sat down with the Evening Standard. How the fuck had London got so expensive? A tatty, terraced house in Shadwell for half a mill? No wonder there was so much crime! Only the most effective criminals could afford to buy in the capital!

Tony G the *maitre d'* was the next to arrive, tired and sweaty after a 10-6 shift on his feet. "What a fucking day, geez! Every arrogant shit in the world descended on my restaurant today!"

Low went back to the bar, bought two bottles of Peroni and settled down.

"Aaah, feels good to be off my feet! Thought it was going to kick off today! Some old witch was not happy about her soup! First, her soup was cold, then it wasn't what she'd expected! 'This isn't Mulligatawny!' she whined. I said to her, 'Every chef interprets a dish in his own way.'"

"You can be charming when you want!"

"That is a huge part of my job! In fact, I'd say it's the most important part of what I do. Yes, I stand at the door and sort out the table bookings, but I am at the very front of the front line!"

I watched Low getting animated. This was his Good Service Rant! I'd heard it before.

Where had I met Low? On a football pitch. At one point, when I was a teen, we'd actually played in the same Sunday morning team. To think, at one point, I was almost as good as him? Now, I just didn't have the upper body strength to shrug off a tackle, whereas Low was hard and brawny, with a menacing growl and a lethal five o'clock shadow!

I knew I wasn't good enough, so I drifted away from football. Low had all the talent and could have made it but he loved women too much, and they all loved his handsome face and athletic body. Hence, the illegitimate child, the failed marriage and the bout of Chlamydia!

He'd miss training sessions because he was chasing tail and, eventually, managers lost patience and cut him loose. Now, he was just a great, Sunday league player. And he was also a great friend. I loved having him in my circle. He was a tall and chiselled magnet which meant, at the very least, single women gravitated towards the gang.

And this was one of Low's two rants. One was his Good Service Rant, the other was his Safe Sex Rant. Both were very entertaining.

"I know her type," Low continued. "She thinks that England has gone to the dogs and now she complains about everything! She's the kind of broad who begins a sentence with 'In my day' and she probably feels like saying, 'In my day, the coloured people knew their place!' I know her type but – you know what – by the time she left, she was nice as pie! I had bent over backwards to make her feel special and she'll be back. Why? Good service! People love good service. We all love good service! By the time I'd finished massaging her ego, she was nice as pie! Can't beat good service, can you, Wezza? You know that!"

I raised my bottle of Peroni in agreement.

I loved The Good Service Rant! Sometimes Low would employ it when we went to a restaurant! Oh, he was a terror in somebody else's restaurant! Once we'd left those places, the bill had been discounted and we had faithful promises for our next visit. Low stopped at nothing to ensure we got hot, fresh food and attentive service. The rant came in very handy sometimes!

The Safe Sex Rant was reserved for men that aggravated Low. He hated misogynists and men that talked disparagingly about women. He hated men that used the word 'slag' or 'slut' or 'slapper'.

"How would you feel if your mum was described like that?" he'd ask.

Low went through women like a hot knife through butter, and some probably thought he was callous and disrespectful, but he hated the sore losers who threw insults.

"Those are the cruel men that do the emotional damage! They're weak and insecure, so they bully women!" he'd say.

With his sleek, imposing demeanour, Low was good to have in your camp, and we never got into any fights. We didn't want to fight! Sod that! Who wants a boxer's broken nose!

"So what about the girl with the hair?" he asked.

"It's going well. We went shopping for shirts today?"

Low looked at me as if I'd suggested that his Peroni had been brewed by aliens. "Did I miss something? You're already shopping together? Has the deed been done?"

I know that men are supposed to enjoy talking about sex and swapping war stories but I actually didn't feel comfortable doing it. They would all blather away, talking about this girl's tits and that girl's flaps, but I kinda felt it was private.

"I'm not talking to you about any deeds, mate!"

"Aww, c'mon, geez! Did it all go in her hair?"

I looked at him blankly. He was not getting any details. Not that there were any!

To be honest, before Trish, sex had been crap! It just didn't make sense. The girls didn't know what they wanted; I didn't know what I was meant to be doing. It was all short, chaotic and messy. Not loud and pyrotechnical like I'd seen in porn films.

Trish was the first person who'd taught me how to kiss and, with practice, I got quite good! Trish had taught me to be patient. And now that I'd been kissed by Roz, I was looking forward to learning things from her.

Had there been that spark? That crackle? Had there been that necessary electricity between us? You bet! But I was keeping it to myself. It was mine. Low was asking about sex but I just didn't want to get into it.

"She's been too busy," I lied.

"And you're straight on to buying shirts? No shag but you've moved on to shirts?" It wasn't making sense to him. "Why shirts?"

"I went and got some of my dad's clothes from my old house."

Low looked at me as if I'd suggested that his Peroni had been hatched from the egg of an Osprey.

"Your dad's old clothes?"

"They look great!"

Low was always smart and very well-groomed. He had to be for his job but he also needed it for his conquests. Women will always notice bushy eyebrows and dirty nails.

"Buy some new clothes, you tight git!"

"Women mix and match decades! You should know that! And Roz says I look great, so I'm well happy!"

Low was not convinced. He couldn't understand why I'd been rifling through my dad's old clothes. What he didn't know was that, when my parents were alive, things had been better. My life had been simpler and I found these clothes quite comforting. It was almost as if, in these suits, I could be as confident and dynamic as my dad. I needed my own Superman outfit!

In the distance, we could see Melvin walking towards us, carrying one laptop case, one sports bag, and two carrier bags, one containing groceries and the other containing some newspapers he had planned to recycle. We called him Baggers because he was always carrying bags. Think of the polar opposite of 'travelling light' and there you will find Melvin.

"Baggers! How are ya, geez?" Low looked at all the bags and chuckled. "You leaving home?"

"I meant to put these newspapers in the recycle bin at the supermarket!"

Melvin put all his bags under the table and headed towards the bar. He returned with three Peronis. I'd just finished one and now I had two more waiting. See what happens?

"How was your day, son?"

Melvin shook his head with dismay. "Non-stop. Frantic."

Melvin worked as PA to the female CEO of a chain of clothes shops. She worked long hours, so Melvin worked long hours, following two steps behind this busy, demanding woman.

In truth, Melvin loved his job. The pay was good, the perks were good and he got to travel. Every day was different and, every day, he seemed to accumulate bags.

And he was a vital member of our little crew because, as he was an organiser/fixer by day, he was our personal concierge too!

How had I met Baggers? I'd actually met him in a branch of Boots, where I was struggling to buy shampoo. He'd actually convinced me that shampoos and conditioner were a waste of money and that my hair would clean itself. All that was required was hot water. And he was right!

And, as we chit-chatted in that branch of Boots, I got a real sense of what a lovely, generous guy he was. I wouldn't call it a man-crush but there was a definite bromance rapport between us, as if I knew we'd always be friends.

Other than Trish, he was the most helpful person I'd ever met. He just gave unconditionally; advice, tips, recommendations, encouragement. He gave freely. Who was I? A total stranger but he still offered me tips on ironing shirts, growing indoor plants and the right vitamins for me.

"Wes went shopping for shirts with that girl today." Low whispered, in a conspiratorial tone.

Melvin looked at me as if his Peroni had started Moonwalking across the table.

"You're already shopping for shirts? Must be going well?"

Even though Melvin was a bag lady waiting to happen, he was probably the most sensitive amongst us: a genuinely nice bloke. Women didn't just find him attractive they fell in love with him! He wanted to hit and run, and was desperate to be a bastard, but he just didn't have it in him. So, not only did he accumulate bags, he accumulated women. They definitely were not a harem – he didn't have time to sleep with them all – but they were a huge group of women who all wanted time with Mr. Sensitive: The Great Empathiser! Though Melvin was far happier just hanging with us!

Melvin had more hair than was necessary and all it did was pose him problems! He had a seventies, disco afro; millions of tight curls pulsing up and out, and while it was always clean and buoyant, it often got caught in doors and windows. In his attempts to carry as many bags as possible, he would open doors with his foot, get his groin and two bags outside, leaving half his afro and two bags inside! It just made him even more lovable.

"Shirts?" he asked. "I've never been shopping for shirts! I've never reached that stage in a relationship!"

"Yeah," said Low, "but you know about shopping and you know about clothes. Wes doesn't know about either. Trish used to choose his milk for him!"

"Wes, what milk do you drink?"

I looked at Melvin, blankly. "Semi-skimmed ... I think?"

Melvin swigged at his Peroni with fervour and shook his head. "Let's hope this girl is the new Trish. Or your tea will never be the same!"

Melvin then embarked on this long tale about his boss, who seemed half 'The Devil Wears Prada' and half Attila The Hun! She had this annoying habit of relationship-switching, as in, when it suited her, Melvin was her friend and, when it suited her, Melvin was just a lackey. It meant Baggers had to endure wild variations in behaviour; one minute she was praising him to the heavens in public, the next minute she was berating him in private. Nevertheless, as we'd never seen Baggers lose it, we knew he had infinite reserves of patience and vats full of good nature.

Melvin had ridiculously cool parents, who we'd sometimes see out and about. He had this funky, outgoing dad and a former hippie chick mum. I'm sure, in their minds, it was still the sixties? We'd find them smoking spliffs and grooving in the middle of Hyde Park, or wandering around Kew Gardens looking at the trees! Melvin had clearly got his social graces from these two very sociable people.

Tony T The Jeweller sauntered through the door, plonked his bag on a chair and looked at all the debris beneath Baggers' chair. He looked closely at the bags. "One of them is full of newspapers!" he said. "A bag full of used newspapers!"

"I forgot to dump them at the supermarket! Give me a break! You look tired!"

"My eyes hurt," said Topper. "I've been busy. Lots of small, fiddly detail."

He wandered over to the bar and came back with four Peronis. I had finished one but I now had three in front of me. I swigged from the second.

"I'm bringing Roz to that engagement party!" I said.

"Cannot wait!" said Topper. "A room full of happy, inebriated women! What could be better?"

"They went shopping for shirts today!" Low said to Topper.

Topper looked at him and tried to process what he'd just been told. Somewhere inside of him, his on-board computer had crashed and he was speechless while it frantically tried to re-boot.

"The girl with the hair took Wes shopping for shirts?"

Low nodded. "No shag yet but they went shopping for shirts! What's that about?"

"Have I lost a year of my life?" Topper complained. "Have I really been holed-up in that workshop for a whole 12 months? How can you possibly be buying shirts already?"

"They haven't even done the deed!" complained Low.

Topper's world was spinning off its axis. "Let me get this straight," he began, removing an old, black, Ralph Lauren jumper, "there has been no sex but you have already been shopping for shirts? Next you're going to tell me you've popped to Vegas and tied the knot?"

"Look," I began, swigging from my beer and feeling decidedly light-headed. "I went to my sister's place and found all of Dad's old suits. They really don't look bad! Some of those styles have come back into fashion! Roz said all we needed to do was buy some new shirts. I've practically got a whole new wardrobe! A whole new wardrobe! Now, THAT is working for me!"

Top End was still looking at me blankly.

There were a lot of curious facts in there that the boys were struggling to digest. Talk of clothes, talk of girlfriends, talk of shopping, talk of my deceased father. Understandably, the boys were confused, but then Roz was a bit surprising. A pleasant surprise!

"Is she some kind of stylist?" asked Melvin.

"Nope. She works in TV production, but she fancies herself as a bit of a style guru." I swigged on my beer again and wished I'd had more for lunch (a less-than-satisfying Cornish Pasty), as the beer had gone straight to my head! I wondered how much I should tell them about my adventurous new friend. Telling them about her house would have them wondering why I was dating someone from a dangerous and pervasive cult.

I was saved by Tony F, who staggered through the door with a box of wine for me. He plonked it down at my feet. "Don't let me hear that you're serving paint stripper to some nice girl!"

"They're getting on famously, Midders!" said Low, revelling in the novelty of my situation. "Getting on famously! She took him shopping for shirts today!"

Midders just stood there gawping. "Shirts?"

And I had to go through my story all over again. As these were guys whose relationships lasted a fortnight at the most, shopping for shirts was not something they did. Dates happened in bedrooms, not in the men's section of Gap!

Midders was still seething at the cheap plonk I'd fed Roz!

"She's a classy girl! And he served-up some free bottle of wine from his local Chinese! How is he gonna find (and keep) another Trish with that kind of brutish behaviour?"

Find another Trish. Christ! Those were the words that had come out of his mouth. "Find another Trish." Someone to babysit their dopey mate! Did I really need another Trish? Was I totally worthless without a girl on my arm?

I needed to make sense of it. Was I useless? Was I lonely? Or was it just more fun to share a life with someone?

Tony F went to the bar and ordered four more beers. I looked at the bottle wearily. I would need food soon.

We sat around and caught up. Chit-chat about last week's games. Speculation about next week's games. Hammers-mad Tony F was speaking sagely about their new manager and recent good form, and we all listened patiently, as you do with West Ham fans.

Finally, the ever-romantic but miserable love failure, Tony T, piped-up. "The one with all the hair: I want to know more about this girl."

Topper was what you might call 'dapper'. Despite working in a pokey workshop all day, he always emerged from his workplace looking neat and tidy. As a jewellery-maker and mender, he had more accessories than most men: ornate bangles, gothic rings and a complex shamballa. Plus, he always spent his money on good quality, gentleman's clothing. Not trendy, skinny boy clothing but classic items that made him look like the idle rich.

He was Mr. Average in so many ways (height, weight, hair, face) but women found him attractive, and not just because he was conversational. I think they liked his patter about relationships, true love and finding 'The One'; they loved his optimism and idealism. How ironic it was: he talked about love and romance (big female favourites) and yet he'd never had a relationship past one doomed holiday to Gibraltar!

Topper was great at Dates 1 through 10 but, after that, he forgot his lines. Ran out of steam. Topper was an expert at the romantic date but when the ugly subject of 'the future' raised its horned head, suddenly, he was out of ideas.

Nevertheless, Topper was always interested in my dates. As if I held out the greatest hope for long-term happiness? Good God! What a damning indictment of my circle! I was the great white hope! Me? Hopeless, feckless me!

They all leant forward. Anxious to hear my verdict. Comical. Literally, hanging on my every word.

"She can cook!" I replied.

"Nice!" Topper moaned.

"Delicious, moist, cheesy pasta bake!"

A collective moan of pleasure.

"Can she kiss?" asked Tony G, our resident lothario.

"I can confirm," I began, "she can kiss!"

Light applause broke around the table.

"This is good news, geez!" he replied. "And when you get to the sex, I trust ..."

"No, you fucking can't trust," I snarled. "I'm not telling you Muppets anything!"

"What will Wes say?" began Tony F. "Fumbled around a bit, spunked all over her dress, went home."

They all laughed, except me. I glared at him.

"Alright, son! Only joking! If you serve decent wine, at least she'll excuse your premature ejaculation!"

They all laughed at my expense again.

"I don't need another Trish!" I exclaimed, proudly and, in that moment, I realised what had happened. Asleep in that cold doorway, my body had virtually shut down, as if I wasn't needed. No girlfriend: what's the point? With no one on my arm, I ceased to have a purpose, so I fell asleep. This was worse than low self-esteem. This was worse than losing your social skills. This was: I date therefore I am. Though, in my case, it was: he has no girlfriend therefore we might as well unplug this unit (to save on the electricity bill!)

I truly was an ineffective single person. The boys happily etched little notches on their respective bedposts. The conquests were like computer games. Win, lose, re-set. Turn it on the next morning and start all over again. It didn't even matter if the sex was bad. You could always laugh at bad sex. The boys were happy with this lifestyle, but not me!

It was a joy to live in my parents' house. I loved the family jokes, I loved the smells of the kitchen, I loved the living room habits and the holiday traditions. I loved my parents' relationship; support, teamwork, compassion, hugging, teasing, private jokes, laughter. I wanted all that. I wanted that for myself. With someone.

Suddenly Melvin woke up. "What you need," he began, "is a Hollywood!"

I looked at him, blankly, and shrugged my shoulders.

"It's a waxing treatment for men."

"Fuck, no!" shouted Tony G. "What for?"

"A lot of men are having it. It removes all the hair from your arse, from your knob, from your nuts ..."

"Fuck, no!" shouted Tony G again, wincing with pain. "Baggers, what are you going on about?"

"Wes should do it!" insisted Melvin. "Especially if he's about to have sex! His new partner is gonna be well impressed! He wants to make a good impression!"

"Actually, it makes sense!" said Tony F. "She is clearly an educated girl, a stylish girl, and she will appreciate a modern, metrosexual man. Like I say: good wine, good food, nice clothes, and exceptional standards of personal hygiene!"

Tony T was warming to the idea. "It's a nice gesture! Women do that for us, don't they?"

"You want me to get a Hollywood?"

I looked at them all, nodding earnestly. My mates. I trusted them because I loved them and I didn't mind using that word. I think we'd all got used to using that word without feeling embarrassed. We even kissed each other on the cheek or head every now and then. It was comforting to know these buffoons were in my life; traditional, roll-up-your-sleeves mates.

My circle was very similar to Roz's friends but mine all knew that it had to end one day! One day, they knew they would have to 'grow-up', get married and have kids. That's how it works, isn't it?

True, they were all close to 40, with no sign of maturity in sight, but at least they all knew – one day – they would want a wife; someone to grow old with; someone who would listen to their stories for the 900th time; someone who would mop up their piss when they dripped on the toilet floor. The parts of a marriage that everyone forgets about!

Roz's friends seemed to love their dynamic so much; it was never going to end. They were all going to live in that big house together and no love affair or marriage was going to blight their kibbutz-style arrangement.

"Why am I having this wax done now?" I asked. "I don't know when we'll have sex! How do I know when we'll have sex?"

"We'll make the appointment," Melvin began. "Just in case?"

"Appointment?" I asked.

"There are experts in this field," said Melvin. "Specialist therapists for this kind of thing. You have to make an appointment."

"You're serious!"

"Yes, we're serious!" affirmed Tony T.

"Geez, it's up to you. Nice to make the effort, isn't it? I'm sure she makes an effort for you!" Tony G sipped on his beer, belched and looked around him. "We should eat."

So, we made a rough plan to go and eat after the beers, but we never left The Fog. There was some Spanish football game on one of Fredo's over-sized screens. We ordered some chips (with cheese) and just stayed. It was easier to stay.

The pub was full of mid-week regulars, all needlessly getting juiced-up, and the boys and I were quite happy to do nothing. Being with each other was enough.

As they chatted amongst themselves, I thought about sex with Roz. Yes, the wax was a nice touch but what next? What would I do next? I couldn't actually remember the next move! Trish had kissed me! Trish had initiated sex. I couldn't just assume Roz was going to lead me by the groin!

"Oi," said Topper, staring at the pub door, "isn't that your girl?"

I turned around and there was Roz, looking very pleased with herself.

"Good evening, gentlemen!"

The boys were all gawping, half in amazement, half in lust. She really looked dazzling! Not quite sure what it was, but it was a very tight and sheer top that left little to the imagination. She wasn't blessed with ridiculous seaside postcard boobs, but she was definitely showing off what she had!

"How did you know I'd be here?" I asked.

"Which one is Tony Gordon?" she asked. Tony G put his hand up.

"Tony Gordon updated his Facebook status and told us all where he was!"

Low looked a bit sheepish.

"I was in the area," she said. "When you're done, you can walk me home."

I grabbed a chair for her and she sat with us. She took off her jacket, wiggled and made herself comfortable, then kissed me softly on the cheek and winked.

It was unlike our normal evenings! Evenings usually full of crude and inaccurate jibes aimed at me. It was easy to ridicule me. I was the most ridiculous. In a way, I was the most easy-going, the quietest, the simplest, the most accommodating. It was easy to make me the butt of all jokes. I didn't mind. It made the evening flow more smoothly. Everyone laughed at my expense but, on this evening – ha ha, ya bastards! – on this evening, I was the envy of my mates, because I now had a real girlfriend, who liked me, and actually wanted to be with me! And had great tits!

None of the boys said much. They just carried on watching the game, ensuring they kept their language in check, while stealing sly glances at Roz's boobs! Midders bought her a large glass of good wine from the bar and she sat with us, observing my crew, wondering if it would give her insight into me.

The boys were on their best behaviour. Shouting at the TV, but not obscenities, and being very attentive to Roz's well-being, constantly offering to buy her drinks which, if she'd had accepted them all, would've rendered her inebriated. Maybe that was their plan? But she turned them all down.

The boys would ask the odd polite question but Roz knew she only had 50% of their attention. No point embarking on some rambling anecdote, as they were intently watching a meaningless football match.

Roz was more than capable of handling herself anyway. It was a cagey game of cat and mouse, both parties listening to the other, hoping to hear something incriminating.

I actually spent most of my time watching Roz watching my mates. She was scrutinising their every gesture and every word, and she was more than interested in the bags underneath Melvin.

At half-time, Topper, the conversational one, decided to engage in a little banter with Roz. He turned and smiled at her. I could see Roz grinning with evil intent, as if she was ready for whatever ill-informed nonsense he could throw at her, but Topper wasn't like that! He genuinely liked questions and genuinely liked answers.

"So," he began, "does Wezza really look good in these suits?"

"He does!" she confirmed. "He now looks like David Hemmings in 'Blow Up'."

Topper looked at her blankly.

"Classic, stylish, sixties movie about a fashion photographer."

The boys all turned to look at her. The effect was dramatic. Inside me, I could feel my heart swelling with pride. They were looking at a woman who was about to turn their figure of fun into a style icon. Wezza had always been a running joke but now he was going to be moulded into a fully-formed homo sapien. My evolution was about to be accelerated! (Not before time!)

"I've heard about this movie," began Melvin, "but never seen it!"

"The plot's a bit clanky but it's beautifully shot!" she replied.

Wezza had found himself a culture vulture. I could see the boys wondering if I had the chops to play with this girl. It didn't matter. She liked me. For some unfathomable reason, she liked me! Or maybe she just liked the normality and the stability?

She turned to look at Melvin. "You seem to have a lot of bags under your feet?"

We all laughed.

Melvin blushed a little. "I like to be prepared for every eventuality! You never know!" he said, raising his eyebrows in a very suggestive way!

"Ah!" said Roz. "Get you!"

The second-half began but I could see her checking her phone; probably time to leave. Forcing her to sit through a mid-table La Liga game would not score me any lucky stars.

"Okay," I said, half-curious to see The Haunted House On The Hill! "We can go."

So, having got Midders to agree to drop the wine at my house, we said our goodbyes and left.

We walked up Highgate Hill, past Whittington Hospital, and I tried to tell her about my life. It wasn't a great story, so I was embellishing it. In truth, the most interesting person and chapter in my life had been Trish, bringing much needed dynamism to my bland existence.

"When I get to my front door, don't ask to come in! Not sure my mob are ready for that yet! Not sure you're ready for them!"

Wasn't quite sure what that meant!

But it was a straight-up statement! I was loving the honesty! She wasn't sugar-coating anything. I loved it. I always got the feeling that Trish was tap-dancing around me. Not really telling me how she felt. Not really telling me her reservations. As if I was a make-do. A second choice. Someone she had settled for. I got the distinct impression she had reservations but these were locked-away in a discreet, female compartment marked 'The Down Sides'.

Some meals with Trish were like Sunday dinner with your parents. Superficial subjects. Nothing too heavy. It can't have been easy for her. It must have been frustrating! She was gently trying to prise this butterfly out of its cocoon but it just wasn't budging!

Maybe that's why Trish left? The frustration. Maybe there are millions of couples sitting around dinner tables every night, studiously avoiding the white elephant in the room; nervous about discussing the burning issues, for fear it will inject a lethal injection into an already condemned relationship.

With Roz, the one burning issue for me was: why me?

Women will often say, "I just knew!" Ah, that fabled intuitive sense!

Women will often say, "There was just something about him." Which means he was the best of a bad bunch. He was the only one that didn't chew with his mouth open.

"Why me?" I asked.

"I've got a good sense of intuition," she said, smiling. "I know what I like about you."

I smiled, weakly. "Dazzled by my charm?"

"I am," she said, "but my life is full of charming people! I've got charming men coming out of my ..."

"Arse?" I offered, helpfully.

"Well, that wasn't a great image, but you know what I mean! My life is full of men that can charm the birds from the trees, and charm the knickers off a willing wench! But that's not really enough to sustain a friendship!"

We paused in Highgate Village to look at some clothes that had caught her eye. "Hmm ... I'd look good in that!"

This was a very feminine, summer dress in striking shades of topaz.

"Yes, you would," I said.

"But, I'm on a diet," she said. "No more clothes this month. My closet is full anyway."

"A clothes diet?"

"Women are brilliant at justifying why they should spend money. Sometimes it can be something as simple as, 'I deserve it!' That works every time!"

"So your intuitive feelings about me are good? I'm not just charming?"

She ruffled her hair vigorously and tossed that mane again.

"No, Wes, you're more than charming. In a world full of artificial things: processed food, auto-tuned vocals, canned laughter, you are real and down-to-earth. You are bravado-less, thankfully! I don't think I could stand one more piece of narcissistic nonsense!"

It sounded like a compliment. It felt like a compliment. All I knew was: down-to-earthness was making this pretty girl smile and, out of all my virile friends, I was the one with a girlfriend!

We walked a little and said less. She was at the end of her day and getting tired. We were walking up hills too, so our words were fading into the night sky. I thought about the guys. I knew they'd been impressed by her. In their sordid little minds, they were thinking about me and her in a bedroom. They were wondering if my life was suddenly about to improve? Maybe this girl would make me a better man? Better than them?

And then I remembered that the boys really didn't WANT girlfriends! They just wanted good, old-fashioned poontang! No attachments, no commitment, just momentary flashes of exhilarating passion. Quick, hot and steamy encounters: no names, no strings. Women were for thrills. They had geezers for friendship. Friendship with a man was simpler. In the future, they'd need wives but, for right now, women were strictly for pleasure!

She bravely plodded up the hill and talked about her housemates again. They were a group of friends like mine but she really hyped them. It almost sounded like she was selling them to me, or was she hoping these glowing portraits would show her (and them) in a better light? Were they really as loving, supportive and together as she described them? It sounded like hard sell!

She clearly had a lot of affection for the men in the house. They were like an amalgamation of a boyfriend. They each gave her something different; all three combining to give her the ultimate male experience. Three men combined in one perfect but fictional man.

It was almost midnight, I was tired, sweaty and still a bit inebriated. We reached the front of a tall, foreboding house.

"Can't invite you in. I'm tired."

"I understand," I said, trying my best not to seem disappointed.

She grabbed my face and kissed me hard. All of that Italian beer inside me began to gurgle like Vesuvius.

She turned and dived into her front door. I stood there for a moment, still recovering from the kiss. What on earth did this stunning woman see in me? I resolved to find out what!

I stood there looking up at this huge house. What was the rent like? I turned on my heels and trudged back down Highgate West Hill. It was after midnight and I was still full of beer. Under cloak of darkness, I disposed of the Peroni behind hedges. I felt like I was sleepwalking. My head kept replaying moments from the last few days and, suddenly, I was at the bottom of the hill. It was all happening very fast and my thoughts of Trish were in decline. I had found not another Trish, but a really exciting replacement; an improvement, in many ways.

But would I pass The Friend Audition? What would these titans of industry make of a drip like me?

Chapter Seven (Wednesday)

I opened the shop on Wednesday morning and pushed open every window I could. The shop smelt of take away food and Max's Christmas after shave.

The shop still looked like it had when my father had acquired the lease back in the late sixties. Working with such grubby, re-heated merchandise, was there any point in modernising? If we'd been selling shiny, German, digital toys, all well and good, but these were old bits of electrical gear that had passed through a million jaundiced hands.

I looked around the shop. Maybe it could do with some brighter lighting? Then everything would look newer and more powerful? Or maybe it would just show up the cracks and stains?

Max meandered in and presented me with a Tupperware container full of cake.

"What's this?"

"It's from my mum. Carrot Cake! She said we should have it with our tea!"

"You thank her for me."

What a nice gesture! I'd met Max's mum at her 40th birthday party and she'd been complaining she couldn't motivate her lifeless son. She was eternally grateful that I'd offered him employment, not that I was having much luck motivating him!

Max was not only a different generation to me but seemingly a different species. Back in the eighties, we'd talked about 'generation x' and feeling totally alienated from a stuffy, conservative establishment. Back then, we questioned everything, but at least we got an education, went to work and started families.

Max was part of a generation that didn't question anything and didn't care. It would be easy to say Max had no respect for authority but 'authority' meant nothing to him. He couldn't even spell it, didn't know what it was; it played no part in his life.

The one major, redeeming feature he had was that he was a nice kid. A nice kid with a good heart. He didn't know how society worked, or how to spell 'society', but he was a nice kid! He had good friends that passed by the shop. Some of them were employed, some not, but they were all good-natured, pleasant guys. Gentle souls. Products of gentle souls and, when they talked, I sometimes understood what they said, and sometimes I just observed the banter.

I could always rely on Max to be courteous to the customers. He would patiently listen to their inane questions, he would dextrously demonstrate the gear for them, and made it look so easy, people would invariably say, "That looks easy!" It wasn't, particularly when you had a drunk uncle shouting in your ear!

It was a relatively quiet day when, suddenly, a very tall man appeared at the door. He looked inside the shop, as if he wasn't quite sure what we sold. He took a step inside and looked around. He liked what he saw. Despite the foul stench, I actually saw him inhale and exhale with pleasure!

"Do you sell gear or hire it?" he asked.

"We just hire it."

The tall man looked disappointed, but he strode into the shop with long, purposeful and almost comical steps, in order to take a closer look. As he perused our equipment, his face was locked in deep concentration, as if he was the Dr. Dolittle of disco gear and these grubby components were talking to him. He put his hand on a meaty, silver pre-amp, as if hoping to feel vibrations.

"I've always wanted to be a DJ," he softly murmured.

"What do you do?" I asked.

"I drive buses. I've driven buses ever since I got my driving license. Always wanted to be a DJ."

The tall man walked around the shop and smiled. Looking up at the disco lights and looking down at the dry ice machines. Max and I just watched him quizzically. Who was this lanky clown? And what did he want?

"You could still be a DJ?" I said.

Max looked at me nervously. He wasn't sure whether the tall man was a head case or not. He seemed harmless to me, plus he was in his bus driver uniform.

"I've always spent my money on the music, never the gear. I'm thinking I should buy gear?"

"Have you ever DJ'd before?" Max asked.

The tall man looked Max up and down before responding to his question.

"Have you ever heard of Gary Glitter?"

Max looked at him, blankly.

"Never."

"I DJ'd at this function once. A 50th birthday party, it was. Quite posh people. And I start playing a Gary Glitter song. 'Rock And Roll', I think it was. And this woman comes up to me and says I shouldn't be playing Gary Glitter 'cause it's in very poor taste. Now, this is a man with twelve Top 10 UK Pop hits. This is a man who knows about popular music. And she says don't I know he's a convicted paedophile? And I said, yes, I do, but he makes great dance music! And then she calls the host of the party to come and talk to me! I said to him, popular music is full of drug dealers, paedophiles, perverts, drug addicts and wife beaters. Look at Jerry Lee Lewis, Chuck Berry, Sid Vicious, 2Pac, Phil Spector, Rick James, Ike Turner, James Brown! If we stopped playing all those who have stood before a judge, we'd be playing Vera Lynn all night!"

Max looked stunned.

"You've learned your lesson, though?" I asked.

"The customer's always right. I know. I know."

He was tall with a dramatic, bleached-blonde quiff. He looked a cross between Billy Idol and Christopher Lloyd as Dr. Emmett Brown in 'Back To The Future'. He continued to stalk around the shop, inhaling the faint smell of Cava from a thousand evenings of matrimonial bliss.

And, at one point, he seemed to hug this tall stack of speakers, like it was bringing him comfort. Max and I looked at each other; he was weird, even for a DJ!

"You don't have to buy gear if you want to be a DJ. I might be able to find you some work?"

The tall man stopped abruptly. "Find me work?"

"We hire out gear AND we supply DJs."

"Really?" The tall man smiled for the first time and the sun came out. His whole mood and body shape changed. He suddenly looked very upright and quite eccentric. "I've got the tunes. I've got every Top 20 hit since 1974."

"Everything?" I asked.

"Absolutely everything!" he said proudly. "In chronological order."

Max suddenly had a new-found respect for the tall man.

"Vinyl?" asked Max.

"They didn't have CDs back then! Seven-inch vinyl. Neatly-stacked. Away from sunlight."

I could see Max's naive noggin computing the shelf-space. "Wow!"

I held out my hand, "Wes."

The tall man shook it. "Percy."

"I've never met a Percy," said Max, extending his hand.

"After Percy Sledge," he said. "'When A Man Loves A Woman' was my mum's favourite song!"

"And if you DJ for us," I began, "you won't need to buy your own equipment!"

Suddenly, the tall man grew an inch or two, as if his self-esteem had increased or as if he'd grown into his life. Whereas before he was loping like John Cleese at The Ministry Of Silly Walks, now he was strutting like a peacock, like Liberace on heat!

"Hire me to DJ at functions?"

Percy pondered the concept, cocked his head and smiled at the ceiling. Within the space of a few seconds, a stranger had made his dream come true. He smiled, shook his head and mumbled something incomprehensible.

"Our philosophy here is: whatever makes them dance! We don't care what it is, if they like it, we'll play it: whatever makes them dance! People come in all shapes, sizes and colours, we play for people of all ages, so we play ..."

"... whatever makes them dance," said Percy. "Seems fairly straightforward."

What had I just done? Employed a man with no application form, no job interview and no references! Had Roz softened my brain? I looked at this stilty, angular freak and wondered about my sanity but, the more I watched him smile and chatter, the more I liked him.

He was now so happy, he was just chattering about everything: the area, the shop, my neighbours, public transport, the cost of coffee at the local Starbucks. He was right on one! Chattering, smiling, making himself at home.

"You drive a bus?"

"I do and, in truth," said Percy, with gusto, "I love it! My customers know me. I know them. Many of them, I see at the same time every single day. Some even know my name? They're not gonna forget a bloke that looks like me, are they?"

"No!" said Max, shaking his head, vigorously. "What made you get that hair style?"

The tall man smiled and carefully ran his fingers across his hair, to make sure it still looked as loud and ostentatious as ever.

"I modelled myself on Stewart Copeland. Do you know who he is?"

Max looked blank.

"Just like me. Tall, skinny bloke with lots of bleached blonde hair. Used to be the drummer in this amazing band called The Police."

Max just stared at him with this vacant expression. He definitely didn't know who The Police were and I wasn't even sure he knew what a drummer was!

"You should educate him," Percy said to me.

"I will," I assured him.

But Percy didn't wait for me, he began to talk, telling stories, imparting terrifying titbits of trivia not even I knew! He was confidently pacing the floor, spouting this insane tutorial and, fortunately, Max seemed to enjoy the lecture. I wasn't sure if he was absorbing the information or was just transfixed by Percy's barnet, but Max was silent and listening intently to Percy's stories of 'Outlandos D'Amour' and 'Reggatta De Blanc'.

I had to go to this ridiculous waxing appointment, so I picked up my jacket and made to leave.

"Sorry, Percy, I need to pop out. Just leave your number with Max. We'll definitely be in touch!"

"Will do," he said, looking taller and more eccentric than ever!

As I ducked out of the door, I could see him lovingly caress some clapped-out, old cabinets, as he dreamt of playing glam rock at a retirement party!

Who was this character? And why had he come into my life? What a find! He was a DJ and circus act all rolled into one!

Chapter Eight (Thursday)

After much persuasion from the boys, I had agreed to go for this male grooming treatment and our concierge, Melvin, had made me an appointment for the following day.

What was I doing? Roz hadn't mentioned sex. In fact, she'd done a brilliant job of avoiding the subject!

What made the boys think sex was on the horizon? What was I 'grooming' for? Who was I 'grooming' for?

Roz was embarking on the boyfriend route, unchartered territory for her, maybe she was also about to embark on six months of celibacy? Who knew where her head was at?

Anyway, I trusted these alleged experts and followed Melvin's instructions so, while Max took care of the shop, I went off for what the boys had described as a 'Hollywood'.

The room was small, clean and functional. It wasn't silver and shiny like a dental surgery, but it was very clean and smelt of expertise.

"Have you ever been waxed before?" she said.

She was a pretty, willowy Polish girl but not my type.

"No," I said.

"Fill in this form."

I filled-in all the classic registration questions. The form was to see if I had any medical complaints. In truth, I was ailment-free with no history of anything in my family. I didn't think my irregular sleep pattern and frequent napping would be of any interest to her. Was I a candidate for a heart attack? No.

"Strip from the waist below," she said. Not something that had ever been said to me before. Five quite shocking words to say to a stranger, but this Eastern European wasn't going to pretty it up with any politeness; she wanted and needed to make this as impersonal as possible.

"We're going to do your ass crack first!" she bluntly declared. "Get on all fours and go like this!"

She sounded like the director of a porn movie, as she simulated an action that made her look like a twerking, hip hop honey.

I followed her instructions and clambered on to the operating table.

"No, lean on your elbows!" she said. She wanted my rear end higher! She wanted my exposed parts at their most vulnerable!

At this point I experienced Roller Coaster Regret. You know! That bit where you get to the top of the first dip and you think, "Oh, shit! I want to get off!"

So there I was, with my arse and scrotum exposed to the world, and all I could hear was this matter-of-fact woman making preparations to the side of me.

I suddenly felt warm wax being applied to what can only be described as my rim. She was probing parts of me that others had not probed. It was profoundly shocking and I could feel every part of me retreat inwards.

She waited for wax and strip to settle and, with a quick whoosh-whoosh, it was done. I was hairless between my buttocks!

"You can turn over now," she said.

"Is that it?"

"Yes," she laughed. Well used to the question.

"Wow!" I thought. "I can do this!"

As I lay on my back, she pulled my heels together, so that I resembled an inelegant ballet dancer, and began applying more warm wax, pulling my genitals this way and that. To her, I was just meat and, despite this women having my scrotum in her hand, I felt like a corpse. It was not sexy in the least. It was cold and impersonal like a V.A.T. inspection.

"I can do this," I muttered out loud. "I'm a man, I can do this."

She laughed again. "Of course you can!"

Again, I questioned my friends' advice. How were they so certain I was about to get laid? I guess Low had a lot of experience in these matters but Roz was a cut above his bed partners! Roz was NOT fluttering any 'come to bed' eyes at me and would be more likely to signal, "Stay right where you are!"

"Is this popular?" I asked.

"Very! Recommend it to your friends!"

"I can't tell my mates!"

"That's the problem!" she sighed. "No one wants to recommend my business!"

Whoosh! More hair began to disappear. It momentarily hurt like fuck. I was shrinking by the second.

"I can't introduce my mates to pain!"

"Don't tell them about the pain," she smiled. "Tell them how good they will look. Tell them how good they will feel. Tell them how good I am."

I lay back, looked at the ceiling and tried to occupy my mind. How on earth would I broach the subject with Roz? She would think I was a total perv! She would think I was trying to steer the conversation round to sex?

"I can do this," I repeated, more for my benefit than hers. "Look at what women go through for beauty!"

"Yes!" she exclaimed. "Look what we go through: eyebrows, upper lip, legs, and then we make sure our hands and feet feel smooth!"

This I knew. When I was growing up, nails were done at the hairdressers. Now there were dedicated nail shops everywhere and long queues outside. Now, the nails were more elaborate than The Sistine Chapel and marginally less expensive!

I had my arm across my eyes, as if I was watching a zombie horror movie (my least favourite genre.) Not sure why? Maybe I was nervous that watching it would be more painful?

"I need to talk," I said. "It will take my mind off it. Is that okay?"

"Yes, that's okay!" Whoosh-whoosh!

"I'll tell you my life story."

She laughed. "Okay." Whoosh-whoosh!

What was I doing? Why was I going through this surreal charade? And suddenly that light bulb came on in my head and I realised it was a practical joke.

"Oh, those bastards!" I thought to myself. "There's no need for all this! No need for this at all!"

I smiled and muttered and chuckled under my breath. The Polish girl must have thought I was mad but then her job was bizarre in the first place!

I couldn't really be angry with the boys. At some stage, I'd have to do it? At some point, I knew I'd have to smarten up; Roz would demand higher grooming standards. I knew that!

Within minutes, it was over. I was alive. Naked, pink and bald like a plucked chicken. What was it all for? Sex? Roz hadn't even talked about sex!

Would Roz even find it attractive? Who knew? I had trusted my boys: big fucking mistake! Clowns! I'd get them back!

I limped out of the salon like John Wayne and felt decidedly different as I bowled down the road. Roz had sent me a text, inviting me to a very private showcase so, when Max and I had shut the shop down, I headed off to see this new kind of girlfriend.

She was different to Trish in so many ways. For some reason, Trish felt as if I needed mending or correcting, as if I was a problem child that needed extra hugs? For some reason, Trish approached every day as another chapter in her case notes. I was a project and it was her duty to fix me.

I didn't really need 'fixing'. I was just lazy. I'd let Trish do it all because – fessing-up here – I was lazy!

I met up with Roz at a branch of Starbucks. She needed some strong coffee and a Danish, so I set them down before her.

She sighed heavily, as if she'd had a frustrating day.

"You okay?"

"I am now," she said, taking off her jacket and leaning back.

We talked about her day at work and I enjoyed her stories. As ever, she was a pleasing mix of many colours; the skirt, the top, the cardigan, the shoes: all a different but complimentary colour. It was like the transformation from black and white to glorious Technicolour. Suddenly, I was appreciating colours and shades. It was quite emotional!

Not forgetting her signature Sheer Plum lipstick! Other than that, there was no make-up on her face. There was no need for any more colour! She was an unadorned, unfussy beauty and I was quite happy to gaze and moon.

I was looking for my moment to slip in my big news but I needed it to be the right moment. She was talking like the clappers, seemingly without taking a breath, and there was just no room for me to insert my insane front page story. Although this was more a Page 23 (in the women's section!)

There was a momentary pause and I blurted it out. "I went and had my first Hollywood today!"

Roz thought for a second, to analyse the words that had just come out of my mouth. Had she really just heard me say that?

"You did what?" she asked, stirring chocolate powder into her cappuccino.

"Intimate male waxing," I replied, trying to sound as if it were a weekly occurrence.

"I know what it is! What did you do that for?"

"The boys recommended it!"

That didn't go down well.

Christ, what would I say now? I didn't want it to seem as if I expected sex.

"Hygiene reasons," I lied, as we walked out of the coffee shop clutching our coffees. "It's becoming very popular!"

"Hygiene reasons?" She looked sceptical.

"Grooming reasons too! It looks better!" I ventured, optimistically.

"Who do you plan to show it to?"

I must have looked embarrassed. She laughed. Far too heartily for my liking.

"Come on, Wes, who do you plan to show it to? You need to find someone who will appreciate the aesthetic beauty of your hairless privates."

Everyone took the piss out of me. I took it all in good humour. I'd always been led to believe it was 'banter' but, sometimes, some of it seemed rather cruel.

Whenever I took umbrage, someone would invariably say, "It's just banter, mate, just a bit of fun."

I took that on board but some jibes still hurt.

This was the first time Roz had really ridiculed me. It upset me, particularly as I'd waxed for her!

What was I thinking of? The boys had stitched me up. This girl was in no hurry to sleep with me. She lived in a house with three amazing men. Probably former lovers? She was not short of cock!

Bastards! They'd stitched me up!

"I don't need anyone to look at it!" I snapped. "Women don't wax and then immediately drop their drawers so people can mark it for style and content! The boys said I should do it for hygiene and grooming reasons!"

"I'll look at it, if you want?"

I must have looked hurt and sorry for myself. This was Roz quickly trying to make amends.

"Very funny!" I said and quickly changed the subject. "Where are we going?"

"We're going to a very exclusive and very private gig. In a private house. Friends and family only. Everyone will be there."

"Who is everyone?"

"My housemates."

My heart sank. It then dropped a few inches into my digestive system and continued travelling south until it reached the balls of my feet.

This was The Audition. I was being paraded before her friends like a dog at Crufts. My fate was in their hands. A few bad reviews from the chosen few and I'd be back on Single Street.

My palms began to sweat. I was about to meet the Masters Of The Universe, Twelve Angry Men and The Furious Five all rolled into one. She'd painted a perfect picture of these cohorts and I had to confess: I was nervous.

Trish came to mind again. Why? Why was I still quoting this woman?

Trish would always say, "If they don't like you ... fuck 'em!"

So, this mantra rolled around my head. Roz was chattering away, telling me who we were going to see, and I just kept the mantra rolling.

We wandered past Mornington Crescent tube station, managing to manoeuvre our way past tired commuters, frantically trying to get home to their bedsits, and excitable shop assistants, desperate to sip from that first glass of wine and catch-up on a girlfriend's gossip. Suddenly, Roz stopped and looked at her phone.

"This is it!"

I looked up: a large but quite ordinary, Georgian house. Another couple brushed past us and went through the front door.

Roz led the way and I followed. As we went through the door, it sure looked like a house, but it sounded just like a gig!

The house was actually someone's home; tastefully decorated, smelling of lilies, with striking, abstract art up the high walls. The music was meaty and beaty but no one was dancing. The people in all the rooms were talking excitedly and there seemed a real buzz of expectancy.

The first person to embrace Roz was a short, dark guy, about my height, and he held Roz very tightly to him.

"God, I'm so fucking nervous," he mumbled in her ear, and then he suddenly saw me.

"The boyfriend! You must be the boyfriend?"

He shook my hand firmly.

"Yep, that's me!" I said.

"She's been telling us about you!"

Roz glared at him.

"Anyway," he continued, not wanting to embarrass her, "I'm nervous, Genie's nervous, mum's nervous."

"Wes, this is Benjamin," Roz began, "Genie is his sister and that's who we've come to see."

Benji looked manic. His eyes were everywhere. "Lots of journalists here," he jabbered. "A few radio DJs. No record company people, as far I can see. Bricking it!"

Benji's fashionably floppy hair spoke volumes. One of those effortless, non-style styles. It had probably cost a fortune! Here was a modern man that had spent big money on a hand-crafted, designer hair style! He was a living piece of art!

Not like me! I was bog-standard, cheap and cheerful, but the others (particularly Melvin) were quite smart. Smart but not fashionable! Benjamin's barnet had elegant twists and turns, a wisp of grey; it swooped and shimmied, flopped and fawned and ached for attention. I wanted a photograph with it!

Roz's poor friend was fidgeting like a school kid with nits but he still seemed happy to be hosting this event for his sister. Roz held his hand tightly and they exchanged a few private words. He was nodding like a boxer, as if she was giving him the pre-fight pep talk.

Watching them interact, I could see they were close and I could see he was a dynamic guy but, at this point, he needed Roz's calm words and reassurance. Like the typical man, I looked for signs of sexual chemistry but there were none. For this occasion, Roz needed to be big sister because Benji, for all his fabulous hair, was not coping well.

I looked up and coming down the stairs towards us was a very tall and very athletic-looking blonde woman. She hugged Roz quickly and then threw her arms around me. "You must be the boyfriend?"

Her long arms and long hair were wrapped around my face. When she eventually unravelled herself, I was looking into the eyes of this stunning, Nordic beauty.

"And this is Wendy!" said Roz wearily, well-used to men drowning in Wendy's allure.

Wendy looked incredibly happy to see me and scrutinised my every pore and hair follicle rapidly, like some sophisticated police scanner. If Roz's friends disapproved of her having a boyfriend, Wendy did not seem displeased.

We made very quick chit-chat and, with every reply, I could see her analysing my grammar and vocabulary, looking for traces of wit or some shred of intellect.

"We never expected Roz to take up with someone! For years, she said relationships were unnecessary!"

"Yes, thank you, dear!" said Roz, quickly secreting herself between me and Wendy. "Where's everyone else?"

"Upstairs!" said Wendy. "Heston is about to eat some poor little gig-chick! She's got badges on her bag and tattoos up her arm. He says he wants to paint her and she's lapping it up. Raymond has found someone to talk to. He looks like some ancient roadie."

"And here's Jill!"

I turned round and coming through the front door was another gorgeous woman! The Haunted House On The Hill was actually populated with models. No wonder sex parties had risen to the top of the list!

Jill was meticulously dressed, not a hair out of place, shapely and probably muscular underneath those designer threads.

"Wes?" she asked, kissing me on both cheeks. "We've heard a lot about you."

Roz embraced Jill and sort of planted her head in her shoulder, as if Jill was her person to lean on. "We'd better go up: she'll be on soon."

Roz, Benji and Jill disappeared up the stairs and left me in the company of the lithesome Wendy, who towered over me, smiling and waiting to hear what I had to say for myself.

"She talks a lot about you guys," I ventured. "I had pictured Marvel superheroes and that's exactly how you are!"

Wendy laughed. "We are quite formidable."

"I don't want to break-up the party …"

"It's okay," said Wendy. "Roz needs someone. She's been high speed for some time. Too many ups and downs. She needs a bit of normal in her life. No offence!"

"None taken!" I quickly added.

In a matter of minutes, I had met the kind of women that me and the boys never encountered. These were thinking women. Women of prowess and purpose. Not the giggly, flirty types we fraternised with every weekend. Roz's flatmates were a cut above. And yet, for some strange, twisted, universe-bending reason, Roz wanted me. Unkempt, unappealing me. It made no sense.

It's like those couples you see walking along the street and the guy is really ugly, and you're thinking to yourself, "What has he got? A huge bank account? Is he famous?" Never for one moment do you think, "She must be ready to settle down."

Wendy began walking and I knew this was my cue to follow her. There was a make-shift bar in the downstairs front room. We grabbed some plastic cups full of wine and headed upstairs. The upstairs living room housed about 30 people, who were crowded-in, waiting expectantly for the star turn.

I didn't really have much chance to interact with the other two housemates, as the star attraction was soon on. Backed by another guitarist and a percussionist, the audience were shoulder-to-shoulder and the act was three feet from our noses.

Yes, I was a professional, mobile DJ, and had been for almost 20 years, but I hadn't really seen that many gigs. My life was music but it was old music, familiar music. My life was 'Dancing Queen' and 'It's Not Unusual'. This was a young woman singing new songs.

She stood about 5'4" in heels and many people were craning their necks to see her. She had a lot of impassioned vibrato in her voice, sounded like she'd had some operatic training and, like opera, these were dramatic compositions about love, lust and longing, but this trio had a nice little funk to their step and I could feel the assembled cooing with approval, though it was probably people that knew her well.

I tried to concentrate on the singer but I wanted to look around. Where were Roz's housemates? In the main, they'd seemed pleased to see me but also vaguely amused; I was the normal person and yet I was the freak show. I was a 'boyfriend', a weird, little contraption that nobody really used anymore.

The little girl we were all watching was a typical Camden child. Her parents must have been artists or poets in the nineties; her attire was clearly influenced by her mother's wild nights at The Electric Ballroom or Shoom.

Every song was met with rapturous applause and whoops of encouragement by the throng and, as the gig went on, the timid voice began to talk and make the audience laugh.

The songs were Imogen Heap meets Janis Ian, and she clearly had a strong but sweet voice. Was she destined for stardom? It was hard to tell. Her friends and family certainly enjoyed it and, as she finished her last song, there was loud applause and whistles of approval.

I was really a stranger in all of this, but I didn't want to seem like an accessory on Roz's wrist, so I walked about the house, looked at the walls and pretended I understood what I was looking at.

I hadn't been introduced to him but I could clearly identify Roz's flatmate Heston, sprawled across an antique couch. He was a beefy, broad-shouldered man in a rugby shirt, with long, surfer-blonde hair and blue eyes. He was engaged in a deep-ish conversation with a pretty, busty girl with a head full of sisterlocks. As described, he definitely looked as if he was trying to eat her. He was leaning forward and she was trying her best not to be consumed but enjoying his advances.

Heston was clearly a successful lothario. Strong, determined, confident, relentless. There was no way he hadn't put his moves on Roz at some point, but what had she said? What had been the response of my clever new girlfriend?

I pictured her face. She'd probably looked at him with equal parts amusement and contempt but, realistically, there was no way she hadn't spent at least one drunken night with this beefcake. I didn't know this girl well enough to judge.

All I knew was – at some point in the evening – the pretty, busty girl would have her lips locked to Heston's and they would soon fall into a bed, or a cupboard, whichever came first.

Dating Roz was going to involve socialising with three of her exes! Occupational hazard. If you date a pretty girl, she will have exes!

The volume of chatter was still high. The singer we had come to see was covered in lipstick from all the congratulatory kisses and looked elated from all the love she was receiving. Her older brother was hovering close by, absorbing all the comments; he'd clearly appointed himself as her personal manager.

The other housemate I hadn't identified yet was Raymond. As I roamed the vast house, I found him holed-up in a corner, not just sipping from a plastic cup like the rest of us, but swigging from a wine bottle.

He was enjoying an animated discussion with another worse-for-wear guest and, from what I could see, was wearing a dramatic, full-length leather coat. With his five-day growth and tinted specs, he looked ready to step on the set of some teen-appeal werewolf movie.

I felt someone grab my hand.

"There you are!" said Roz.

"Knew you'd be busy with your friends!"

"Let me introduce you," and she dragged me over to Raymond. This tall, imposing man stood up to greet me. He shook my hand firmly and held on to it. It almost felt as if he was going to say, "Young man, take good care of my daughter" but, instead, he said, in a broad, Scottish accent, "You can take her on dates, son, but don't take her away from me!"

"Raymond!" she protested.

"Sorry, son," he said, finally letting go of my hand. "Sorry. I feel quite strongly about this girl."

This was going to be trickier than I thought. Not only was I socialising with three exes, these were people who loved living with Roz and weren't going to let the small matter of a boyfriend get in the way. This was way beyond friendship.

"What does that mean?" I asked.

Raymond stood upright, cocked his ear at me, as if he hadn't quite heard me correctly, and ran his wine-soaked fingers through his stubble.

"We've got a good thing going on. I'd hate to see it end."

I looked over at Roz, who was glaring at Raymond. It was obviously a subject they'd talked about (at length!)

"We've talked about this," she began, "at length! I can't live in a house with five other adults forever! In three years, I'll be 40! You expect me to still be there?"

Raymond was swaying slightly. Drinking on a school night was not wise. He took two, unsteady steps backwards, and sat back down. "Why not?" he asked, plaintively.

Roz was still glaring at him but there was more affection in her eyes. She walked towards him and put her arms around him. His head flopped against her chest. "Ya miserable swine!" she said, fondly.

Roz's two female flatmates Wendy and Jill came into the room. They had their coats on and looked ready to leave. Roz nodded her head, which was her signal to the girls that there was nothing to worry about.

Raymond's eyes were closed and he looked quite comfortable, as if he were planning to nap. This was a housemate whose objections to Roz moving out were beyond affection. Clearly, for him, the house made sense: six adults, living together, forever single. Someone wishing to leave was illogical and clearly in need of therapy.

"I'm hungry," said Wendy.

"That means we're eating," said Roz, so we left the boys and the party, and ventured out, me and these three imposing women. I was definitely poodle on a leash but I went with it. I knew I was about to get interrogated but it was a necessary part of this process.

We found a busy Tapas bar teaming with pretty people and squeezed through the front door. The word 'interrogation' really didn't do the evening justice. I was forced to recount my dating history in painful detail and, as it wasn't a particularly gripping tale, I padded it with sexual escapades from the back catalogue of Tony G the *maitre d*. I knew he wouldn't mind me nicking a few of his notches.

If I'd told the truth, I'd have looked like an idle eunuch, so I threw in Low's almost-legendary, drunken one-nighter with quite a famous, French actress! She was staying at the hotel and was quite taken with Low's mischievous smile. For the first time ever, Low got first-night nerves and, by the time he got up to her room, he was so pissed, he fell asleep with his head in between her legs. He woke up in the bedroom alone. The unnamed actress was not amused and checked out early the next morning!

This story had Jill snorting Sangria out of her nose. It had everything: an illicit rendezvous, celebrity, oral sex and a punch line. I looked like a plonker but the girls seemed to like me which, in turn, made Roz happy!

Chapter Nine (Friday)

It was Friday night. This symbolic, triumphant day in which everyone can break free of the shackles of employment. As if 'employment' is torture!

Friday at 5.00 (or 6.00) is the moment at which you can take your hard-earned money, buy alcohol from pubs and bars and, literally, piss your wages down the toilet.

Friday night worked for me! On Friday night, people wanted to get happy. Friday was when people had parties or private functions. Friday night provided me with work and, on this evening, I had been hired to DJ at an engagement party. Quite an unnecessary party really but who would begrudge a girl that's overjoyed to be getting married. A pre-wedding knees-up!

We were situated in the backroom of an ordinary, very traditional pub. Max and I had set up the equipment at 6.00, as the guests were due to arrive any minute.

As I was going to be playing a lot of old music and it didn't matter if I looked like I was wearing fancy dress, I put together one of Dad's old suits and one of the new shirts Roz had bought.

I was probably breaking a million fashion rules but I felt quite fly! The suits fitted me well and the new shirt had that unworn feel and fresh out the packet smell. I knew I was a walking fashion *faux pas* but I felt great, which is the most important thing. The suit gave me swagger, a quality I was sadly lacking in!

As my sister Marie was doing nothing (as ever), I invited her along. She knew all my mates anyway and, as our new friend Percy needed to observe my 'exacting standards', I told him to pass by as well.

In fact, the first person through the door was Percy, looking as gangly and peculiar as ever, attired in a slightly-crumpled and highly-inappropriate turquoise velvet suit.

"On time!" I said.

"I'm a bus driver," he replied. "Buses have to run on time!"

Faultless logic. I knew I'd never have to worry about Percy's timekeeping.

He wandered around the function room, reading the tatty, homemade signs on the wall, and gazing up at a huge TV showing 'The Fast And The Furious'.

Eventually, he settled in front of the gear and looked it over.

"Seems quite straightforward," he said.

"It is," I replied. "Your biggest problem will be drunk guests slopping their drinks all over it."

"I can handle them," he said, ominously.

"Whilst being incredibly polite!"

Percy nodded, having absorbed this note, and continued to soak-up the non-existent ambience of the anonymous back room.

I began playing some familiar seventies soul hits at low volume and, out of the corner of my eye, I could see Percy convulsing in time to the music.

The sisters of the bride-to-be soon arrived, carrying large and delicious-smelling trays of Greek meatballs and large bowls of salad. One of them was carrying this elaborately-decorated cake with a hand around a penis and the words 'To Have And To Hold' inscribed in icing.

Other guests began to drift in and it was clearly a case of the bride-to-be wanting to make an entrance a little later. The volume of chatter was increasing and, from the numbers arriving, although it was an irrelevant party, it was looking to get busy; these people were looking forward to their Friday night.

Marie edged nervously through the door and I enveloped her in a big hug.

"Get off me, you silly bugger!" she growled. Her traditional response.

I introduced her to Percy, who greeted her with a courteous bow and kissed her hand. Marie blushed slightly, looked up at the curious man with his buoyant quiff, made a few pleasantries and then began talking to him. With their respective lunacies in check, they found common ground and quickly became engrossed in conversation.

Every time I looked up, they were talking. He arched over her, she looking up at him. He was laughing at Marie's stories and, every time he laughed, the quiff bounced. Marie was smiling. First time I'd seen that in a while. Percy seemed to have some good stories of his own, so her cheeks were beaming. They looked ridiculous together but, every time I looked-up, they were talking. I wondered what their common ground was?

Melvin was the first of my crew to arrive. He looked quite dapper, as ever. He already had the afro and, in between the buttons of his unbuttoned shirt, he had this outlandish, flashing pendant. He greeted Marie and introduced himself to Percy. Marie was happy to see Melvin but quickly returned to her conversation with Percy. They seemed to be having big fun!

"Who's he?" asked Baggers.

"Possibly a new DJ for the agency?"

"He certainly stands out in a crowd!"

That he did but he was making my sister smile so, as far as I was concerned, he was alright in my books.

Unsurprisingly, Melvin had a 'man bag', a holdall with some clothes in and also a carrier bag full of vegetables.

"What's with the vegtables?" I asked.

"I plan to get creative with my smoothie-maker!"

Melvin finally looked at me properly. Eying me up and down, he tried to absorb my makeshift ensemble.

"You know what?" he began. "It works!"

"She's got a good eye, your new bird! Mind you, your dad did have some nice suits, so kudos to you for digging them out!"

People complimenting the way I looked never happened. This never happened to me! In a matter of days, Roz had made me something worth looking at! My back straightened and I think I grew an inch with pride! Even my swagger now had swagger!

Roz was having a perceptible impact on my life. Within days, I had become businesslike, witty and stylish. Me falling asleep in an office doorway was my mind and body shutting down. Roz had re-awakened me. As I watched Percy and Marie, and threw down another killer song, I was matchmaker and entertainer too.

Finally, the bride-to-be arrived with her beau. Everyone thronged around them, kissing, hugging, admiring the engagement ring, and this was also my cue to amp-up the volume. It was time for the party to start!

Much screaming from female relatives and friends! Many pats on the back for the groom. The couple were beaming! The cameras were flashing!

An attractive couple, about mid-thirties, no kids. Maybe the bride had worried she'd be left behind? Forever single. Maybe we were all feeling her sense of relief?

Tony T the jeweller strode through the front door, looking particularly pleased with himself. I wasn't sure why? He greeted Marie with a warm hug but he was unable to prize her from Percy's clutches. The conversation was still in full flow, even though they were now shouting in each other's ears.

"Who's that?" he asked me, motioning towards Percy.

"Might be adding him to the agency?"

"Marie seems to like him!"

Percy had bought her a large glass of red wine and her cheeks were flushed with merriment. I really hadn't seen Marie laugh like that in ages. Who knew that bus timetables could be so amusing?

The opening guitar line of The Staples Singers 'I'll Take You There' filled the room and suddenly, as if by magic, Percy and my sister were dancing in the middle of the room. He was six foot five, she was about five foot three. They looked like two stoned puppets but – by God – they were having fun!

Encouraged by this unlikely pairing, the dance floor began to fill and, as soon as they heard the opening piano line of Nina Simone's 'My Baby Just Cares For Me', the floor was full: mothers dancing with daughters, uncles dancing with nieces, groovy, middle-aged couples shucking and jiving!

I loved making people dance. Well, not 'making them' dance, I loved knowing the right songs for the right moment, I loved knowing songs that made them want to dance.

Carrying a box of bottles, Tony F finally arrived. "Give us a hand," he shouted at the others, so Tony T and Melvin went outside to help him bring in boxes.

The boys unpacked the boxes and didn't those 24 bottles of Prosecco look impressive on the food table! This was going to be one long and incoherent toast to the bride and groom!

The party was going well. The disco lights were bouncing beautifully off the drab walls and I could hear the sound of tuneless voices singing along. Many of these people hadn't danced in years, in some cases, decades, but everyone had decided to go for it. The brides pretty young friends were shaking what they had or didn't have!

Once she'd disentangled herself from well-wishers, the bride-to-be came over to see Mids and thanked him for the bottles of Prosecco, then gave me a smacker on the cheek, to thank me for making her friends and relatives dance.

I didn't need thanking but I appreciated it. Now, all I needed was Roz to walk through the door, but the hours were passing by and she was in danger of missing this joyous but tacky occasion.

Tony G eventually staggered in, looking bedraggled. His hair had that just-been-shagged look to it.

He clocked Percy and Marie tearing up the dance floor, and didn't even bother going to greet her! He could see she was otherwise engaged!

"Who's that with Marie?"

"His name's Percy," I replied. "Might add him to the agency?"

"What does he play?" asked Low, looking at his mighty quiff and retro sense of style. "Doo-wop?"

"He's got it all!" I said.

"He looks like he's got your sister too!"

We drifted from old soul and reggae into newer things, which brought the young people out on to the dance floor and this, in turn, encouraged my gang to show off their moves.

Melvin had a respectable repertoire of dance steps. When Baggers hit the floor, the bride's young relatives looked well impressed. Tony G had an athletic buoyancy in his moves, which always attracted attention, while Mids and Topper just tried to establish some eye contact and drag these girls to the bar!

Sadly, no Roz. She'd seemed enthusiastic but maybe something had come up? Maybe I was moving too fast? After all, it had only been one intense week. Or maybe she'd got cold feet? Maybe the witches had gathered round the cauldron and looked deep into her future? Maybe they'd had a high-level conference at the haunted house and decided on an intervention, to stop her wasting time and emotion on an obvious inferior?

Christ, like a woman, I was over-thinking it!

It was quite a standard evening. The usual songs, the usual requests ("Got any Abba?"), the usual accidents (female guest slips on spilt drink on the dance floor), the usual complaints ("Can you play just one more?"), the usual idiot ("Have you got any funky house?")

The evening was standard and ran smoothly. Max arrived at 1.00, to help me dismantle and carry the gear back to the shop. The boys looked happy enough. I think they'd made some new friends and we made vague plans to meet on Saturday night but, when I eventually looked at my phone, there was a text message from Roz apologising profusely and asking me, "Would you like to get naked?"

As it was Roz, I had no idea what that meant! It might have meant sex? Or it might have involved me being a life model for an art class!

I thought about Trish. First time I had in a while. Trish had always enjoyed my gigs. She'd accompany me, have too much to drink, people-watch and then we'd grab some fast food on the way home, invariably falling asleep on the couch.

She'd say to me, "You've got a gift."

I never really viewed what I did as a 'gift'. There were certain records that always made people dance and I had them. That wasn't a gift; it was just a box of custom-made CDs.

"But you know how to play them," she'd say. "You know when to play them. You know the right order."

It all seemed quite intuitive to me.

In the last week, Trish's words of wisdom had not been running through my head. She was fading in the memory. I could no longer smell her; I was even struggling to remember how she tasted.

I was trying hard not to be insulted but Trish had left me for no good reason. I knew my failings better than most but I hadn't betrayed her, or taken her for granted. I hadn't abused or assaulted her. She had no good reason to leave me, other than the fact that she might need 'space', or something like that?

I wasn't going to hound her friends and family in some undignified fashion. They knew where she was. Somewhere, in some room, in some town, she was reflecting. She had her space and she was reflecting. Maybe she was reflecting on me?

Having said that, I had not been reflecting on Trish. In the past week, Roz had consumed my thoughts with her wild hair and kooky mannerisms, and I was more than happy to accompany her, whatever 'getting naked' meant!

Chapter Ten (Saturday p.m.)

"I'm so sorry about last night," Roz said, kissing me. "I would have loved to come, but we really got into it last night!"

We got off the bus and began walking down Kentish Town High Street. "Got into it?"

Roz smiled to herself. This was her inner sanctum. I would have to get used to them.

"Yeah, got into it! Sometimes, the conversations can get a little ... intense!"

Saturday night. My routine had been the same for years and I loved it! Bar first, club later, maybe a party after? It was exhausting but it was Saturday! Like many others, the boys and I planned it, looked forward to it and, yes, I'd sometimes wake up on Sunday morning on someone's couch, or underneath a blanket on someone's floor, but it was our Saturday night routine!

On this particular Saturday evening, all convention was going out of the window. The boys were off somewhere and I was out with my ... what? ... I was out with my girlfriend!

Would wonders never cease? I had a girlfriend!

"Where are we going?"

"Does it matter?" she replied.

It didn't. Blindly, I followed her. I was ready for Roz-style adventures. Calling her a 'free spirit' just didn't seem accurate. Free spirits are people who do things on a whim. They genuinely haven't got a clue where the day or night will end.

Roz was far too much of a control freak to be a free spirit. She knew exactly where she was going and what she was doing. She was testing me, trying to shock me and having a laugh at my expense. I didn't mind. It beat the hell out of pub snacks and European footballers with inflated salaries.

Roz led me to an anonymous doorway on an ordinary high street, and boldly stepped through the door.

"I'm paying for both of us," she said, slapping a twenty-pound note on the counter.

The cashier gave us two, clean white towels and buzzed us through a door and I could immediately smell chlorine. A tall, obese, naked man walked past us, with his towel over his arm.

I looked at Roz and she appeared calm. She'd done this before.

She motioned to her left, "This is the girl's changing room." She motioned to her right, "And that is the boy's. Go in there, take all your clothes off, put them in a locker and I'll meet you back here in five."

She turned on her heels and disappeared into the small room.

My head was spinning. What was about to happen was quite terrifying but I knew I would have to keep calm. Appear as nonchalant as her. This was a test: I knew that. I would have to maintain eye contact at all times.

I entered the changing room and it was full of all sorts, in various states of undress. Short, tall, white, black, thin, fat, many of them bending over, drying their crease, making casual conversation with the next bloke.

"I fancy a big, dirty kebab!" said one.

"And chips!" added his mate.

These were not professional athletes or bodybuilders. These were not even sun-worshippers or naturists. These were ordinary men who liked a sauna and steam after work and, of course, the opportunity to ogle at naked women!

I dutifully stripped off and folded my clothes into a locker. The locker key was attached to a thick rubber band, which I put round my wrist.

I paused and, for some reason, I thought about Trish. We'd had a lot of fun, done a lot of things but it had all been quite conventional. There were no risks. No fear of the unknown. I'd only known Roz a week and already she was plunging me into an experience that was shrinking my penis by the minute!

My time with Trish had been amazing but this ... this was another level! A whole new strata of leisure-time pursuit! I gulped a few deep breaths and took stock of where I was and what I was about to do. My head was spinning! I had finally lost my mind!

I came out of the changing room door and there was Roz, a towel wrapped around her slender waist. As she led the way, I looked around me. There were people on sun loungers, relaxing and watching a huge, wall-mounted TV. Looked like some crap reality TV show! As they lay on towels, they acted like there was bright Spanish sun above them, whereas they were actually in the backroom of a huge shop in North London! Inner city escapism.

We passed a small bar area where there were more people wrapped in towels, drinking fruit juice and conversing, and we finally reached a huge Jacuzzi, full of single people relaxing and a few couples draped around each other.

Roz hung her towel on a hook and walked naked into the Jacuzzi. Not a care in the world! I followed suit, wondering what the hell I was getting into! As I hung up my towel, I could feel eyes on me. Or were there? Maybe it was just my imagination? Who'd want to look at me?

Roz perched herself on a ledge, leaned back and enjoyed the warm fuzzy, water rushing around her body. She closed her eyes and exhaled.

"Aaah, feels good!"

I wasn't quite at the 'Aaah, feels good' stage yet! I was still in a state of shock about being naked in front of Roz and a group of complete strangers, and having a group of complete strangers enjoying my girlfriend's naked bod!

I was still at that stage. Still at the 'Who is this woman and what does she want?" stage. Roz looked perfectly relaxed and at ease, but I was struggling to know where to look and what I should be doing.

"Last night was crazy!" she began, still with her eyes closed. "You would have thought I was hatching a plot to assassinate the president! All I want to do is have a boyfriend!"

"They're trying to talk you out of it?"

"Well ..." she stuttered.

Another naked couple, they looked very German, entered the Jacuzzi and waddled past us. They must have been in their late forties and were so relaxed, they were actually carrying plastic cups of water to set on the side. It certainly was hot and humid in there. Water seemed a good idea.

"No one has a problem with you," Roz continued, "and, of course, everyone wants me to be happy ... but ..."

"But?"

"No one wants the party to end!"

I thought about it. "No one wants the party to end." It was like a happy baby fighting sleep because he doesn't want to stop playing.

What a ridiculous scenario! It was romantic and idealistic but destined to fail! These six people couldn't all live in the same house together forever, could they? Were they really going to keep sharing that house into their forties and fifties? Did none of them want families?

I could hear from Roz's voice that she was unsure and probably a little nervous but I certainly wasn't going to talk her into a relationship!

"So, what do you think?" she asked.

"What do I think? I think you should date me!"

Roz nodded with approval. I guess I'd adopted the right tone? I'd been committed. I'd been assertive. I'd expressed desire. Hopefully, she felt chosen? It's always nice to feel chosen!

"I'd still live there, of course!" she asserted.

"And you'd sleep over occasionally, right?"

"Do you snore?" she asked.

"Like a small woodland animal, I've been told."

Roz laughed but I really didn't want to have this kind of conversation surrounded by naked men, some of whom were lean, muscular and well hung. Who were these men and why were they here? They just seemed to be parading back and forth, pausing momentarily only to flex and moisturise their well-toned flesh with baby oil.

If I was going to have this kind of conversation, I wanted to be the star of the show. I wanted to be the only dick in the room. Sadly, there were dicks everywhere!

Roz seemed totally oblivious. She was fine! Eyes closed. Relaxed. The Jacuzzi was massaging her tired limbs and she had a horny suitor hanging on her every word.

"I'll tell them!" she proclaimed. "I'll just tell them what I want! They're being selfish. Thinking about themselves. What about me? What about what I want?"

I felt reassured. Whatever conversations she was having, she knew what she wanted. She wanted a good, old-fashioned boyfriend. Someone to share popcorn with at the cinema. Someone to tell her problems to. Someone to desire her. That was me! I was ready to fill that vacancy.

It seemed farcical. It was usually an over-protective father trying to protect his baby from a sweet boy in a flash car! It was usually a nouveau riche, suburban mother worrying that her daughter was marrying beneath herself! What was I? A threat? A danger? It wasn't like I was from a lower caste!

"Right, let's go!" she said, getting up from the water. Dutifully, I followed her. She grabbed her towel, wrapped it around her and went into the sauna.

It was only a small room. Three rows of benches with room for about 12 people, at a push. Most of one side was taken up by an old Eastern European couple. I wasn't sure from where. Czechoslovakia, maybe?

He was lying lengthways on the top level, while she was on the lowest level, rubbing some kind of moisturiser into her legs and feet. They looked as if they'd been married a long time, communicating with the occasional word or familiar chirp.

Was this what lay in wait for Roz and I? Saturday nights in a naturist spa? What was the protocol? Should I make conversation or was she here to relax? Maybe comfortable silence was the sign of a good relationship?

She truly was in her element. She'd laid-out her towel and was laying face down, soaking up the intense, dry heat. In fact, as she was saying nothing, we were already like that old married couple! We were already there! The conversation had all but dried-up! Within a few dates, we were an old, naked married couple!

I sat quite still, daring not to move. This exquisite woman was laid-out naked in front of me and I couldn't kiss or touch her. That's not what this was. This was a public place. Yes, we were starkers but we were still in public. I had to respect her space. We had to respect others. I'd been on some bizarre dates but this was right up there!

The old couple in front of us didn't interact with us. Nothing would disrupt their Saturday night routine. They were just there to sweat, and that's what we did: breathe and sweat. And try to look unphased by the whole experience.

"I'll still be living there," she mumbled, picking-up the conversation where she'd left it. "Most weeks spending six or seven nights there! How can they complain?"

I grunted in agreement. Yep, I was already that old, naked, wrinkly husband! Roz sighed with pleasure and turned on her back. Sweat was dripping from every part of her body. She glistened and glowed, and enjoyed my embarrassment and discomfort.

Once Roz had finished in the sauna, she wanted to spend some time in the steam room. Sweat was dripping from my every orifice, I definitely now needed several cold beers but some water would do. The male ego had kicked-in; I wasn't going to comment on the heat or complain. I was going to savour it like a pro and enjoy the ride. This was the test: flexibility, adventurousness and mental strength.

"I need some water!" I said

"Get me one too! I'll be in the steam room!"

I joined her in this foggy hell hole with two plastic cups of cold water. She took one and gratefully sipped from it. I could barely see her with all the steam rising from the floor but this was what she was about, and she wanted to see if I was ready for it.

For some reason, the steam room was even hotter than the sauna, maybe because I couldn't see where the heat was coming from? Couldn't see her and couldn't see where this evil mist was coming from! Within minutes, my towel was drenched. The water had quenched my thirst momentarily but I was soon gasping for liquid again.

As she'd done it before, Roz was quite peacefully soaking-up the therapy. And this is all it was. We were naked but there was nothing sexual about this encounter. Far from it and she knew it!

And so the evening went on: jacuzzi, sauna, steam room, jazuzzi, sauna etc. By the end of the night, I was drained. Shattered. I felt unbelievably clean but exhausted. It was as if all of my pores had been opened by minions, steam-cleaned and closed again.

And, after a while, the naked bodies meant nothing! I became oblivious to them and unbothered by my own unclothed state. There had been no stirring in my nether regions. It had not been a sexual experience.

We got showered and dressed, and staggered out into the night air. She looked invigorated while I looked as though I'd done ten rounds with Tyson.

"We should eat?" she offered.

No argument from me, although I knew sleep would instantly follow food.

We tucked into a family-owned Italian and ordered some Minestrone and some large plates of Spag Bol.

"She did a nice job of waxing you!" Roz began.

"Didn't think you'd noticed!"

Roz smiled. "Women notice everything!"

Chapter Eleven (Sunday p.m.)

On a normal Saturday night, I'd have been out with the boys, carousing in the bars of North or East London, testing my tired chat-up lines on polite but fatigued women but – oh, no - not I! I had been stark bollock naked with my new girlfriend but neither of us had stroked, or pinched, or groped each other, neither of us had touched, save for a long and lingering, pasta-flavoured kiss at the end of the night.

So, to make up for it, me and the boys arranged to meet for Sunday lunch and chew over the events of the previous night.

How did I feel after last night? I felt different, to be honest. I felt clean and actually quite healthy. The effect of all that heat and water had made me feel metrosexual; as if I'd come to terms with pampering, instead of viewing it as a gay pastime!

And I was feeling quite virtuous too. I'd kept my cool. Roz and I had both been naked for a few hours but I'd kept my cool. No compliments. No suggestive remarks. No improper suggestions. If I was being tested, I must have passed!

Of course I was being tested! She was cruel beyond words!

And how on Earth would I convey this to the boys? It really was a "you had to be there" moment. How on Earth would I put this story into context and truly convey the surreal nature of my Saturday night? Even I was having trouble digesting it! Where was I? What had I done? Was that really me? Shopping for shirts had confused them, what would a naturist spa do?

For our Sunday lunch, we'd picked a favourite Lebanese restaurant in Camden where you could get huge plates of mixed shawarma; a meat feast for a group of red-blooded males; delicious spicy food and, hopefully, spicy conversation?

Tony F the wine merchant was the first to arrive and looked worse for wear.

"Rough night, Mids?" I asked.

He could barely speak but managed to order his first beer of the day, which he gratefully gulped, as if it were doing him good.

"It was a top night!" he said. "A bit much after Friday, though. Friday was fun! The client was over the moon! She loved her case of Prosecco, loved the music. Well happy!"

A satisfied customer! Nothing beats positive feedback! I was just your bog-standard, high street DJ, but even I liked having my ego massaged!

"Do you think she'll write a testimonial?"

"I'm sure she will," said Tony wearily. He looked in pain. "And what about you? What did you do?"

Before I could begin my story, the manager Hakim arrived at our table. He greeted us both with strong, sincere handshakes and made pleasantries. We'd been to his restaurant before. Not often, but he remembered us! Not surprising as, last time, we'd stayed for about five hours!

We told him we were expecting three more and anticipating another long-afternoon of analysis. He smiled.

This was an unpretentious, local restaurant full of large families all talking in languages I couldn't identify. For me, a good sign! These were huge families, full of podgy, headstrong boys and sweet, giggling girls.

I've never been to Lebanon but I had to assume these primitive paintings and faded photos were 'home'. I particularly loved the insane collection of camels scattered liberally around the restaurant; stuffed, woolly camels, ornate, glass camels. Wherever you looked, there was some languid-looking camel smiling at you.

"My Saturday night?" I began. "It's quite a story! Let me wait for the others. I'm only telling this story once!"

Mids didn't look that bothered. He didn't look able to listen, let alone talk. He looked tired but seemed to be saying that he was more exhausted than hungover.

"This bloody girl wouldn't let me leave the dance floor! I must have danced for about two hours and I can't even dance!"

Tony F and I had seen some dark times. He'd been married to quite a dynamic woman and she'd left him for one of her employees. In the aftermath, I don't even think Mids was hurt as much as inconvenienced.

He'd clearly been wrong for her but they'd married anyway. They were both busy, young professionals, both working long hours and, like many men, he'd fallen into a relationship. One minute he was dating and – bang, before he knew it – it was a relationship!

I'm not sure why he was wrong for her, he just was! No spark, I guess? She didn't talk to him about it, she just upped and left. One day her clothes were in the flat, the next day they weren't!

It can't even have been some kind of deep, all-consuming love, as Mids wasn't upset, he was just, "Eh? What happened?"

The annulment took 30 seconds and, suddenly, Mids was a single man again.
The trouble was, it had made him very cynical and he now viewed all relationships with mild amusement.

"What's the point?" he'd say to any attached person listening. "Women are as clueless as men!"

He'd not been hurt by the experience but he had been slightly dazed by it. Almost as if he was in shock? He was different for a while. Slightly withdrawn. I'm not sure he dwelled too long on this other man who might (or might not) have been 'better' than him. Tony was forever shrugging his shoulders and blithely waving play on. In business, you can't take things personally, but Mids took nothing personally, not even his own love life!

"Whatever" was one of his default settings. In his eyes, few things were worth stressing about, and your wife running off with another man definitely wasn't one of them!

Tony was too busy and loving his life too much to worry about such matters. He loved his business, he loved his mates, and being single gave him back his Saturdays so he could go and see his beloved Hammers at The London Stadium.

It took him a few months to recover but, eventually, he returned to his former self: full of verve and panache. But today Mids was sorely lacking in both.

"My calves ache!" he moaned, finishing off his first bottle of Lebanese beer and signalling for another.

Melvin wandered in, carrying a laptop case, an overnight bag and some Sunday morning groceries. Even he, usually impeccable, looked dishevelled. He sat down quietly, ordered a beer and fiddled in his bags.

Melvin never did The Walk Of Shame because he was never far from an 'overnight' bag. The same clothes two days in a row? Never! This was something Baggers never did! There was always a clean shirt somewhere in one of those bags!

As Melvin was the best dancer amongst us, he was having the most fun with Tony F's aching calf muscles.

"The passion and the intensity in those moves, mate!"

Midders could barely speak, so he just made abusive hand signals in Melvin's direction.

I wasn't that hungry but the sizzling meats on the grill were playing havoc with my digestive juices. I was gurgling and ready to consume!

Topper and Low arrived together, looking pleased as Punch. I wondered if Punch was the same wife-beating swine I'd seen at the puppet show? And why my parents hadn't said, "Hold on! The hero of this puppet show is beating his wife with a stick! We're not endorsing domestic violence!"

"What are you two grinning about?" I asked.

Low was smirking all over his face. "Hasn't Mids told you?"

"Told me what?"

"He won Strictly Come Dancing last night!" said Topper.

Mids didn't have the words or even the inclination to respond. He just looked up at them wearily.

"She loved my dancing AND I've got her phone number, so fuck off!"

I made sure everyone was settled and had a beer before I began my Saturday night tale and, as I talked, I could see I had their complete attention. After all, my story did contain a party full of completely naked people, including my new girlfriend.

I'd not had this much attention since a member of Spandau Ballet walked into the shop! Now, THAT was a good night and an even better story the day after!

I told them everything about my Saturday night: the naked bodies, the jacuzzi, the sauna, the steam room, and the wholly non-arousing nature of the experience. The only thing I didn't do was describe the finer contours of Roz's hot body! Such details were for me alone!

They were literally hanging on my every word. Not just gawping in amazement but almost a bit sad that we hadn't all shared the experience together. As a gang, we'd shared most new things together.

As I unveiled every detail, I could see them looking more and more incredulous. I was the butt of most jokes; how come I'd experienced this before them? How come the weedy nerd had got there first? How come Mr. Average was existing on this higher spiritual plain?

"No touching at all?" asked Low, scouring the menu.

"None!" I replied.

"Wasn't she waiting for you to make the first move?" he asked.

"It wasn't about that," I said to him, almost sounding as if I knew what I was talking about. "It was just a ... health thing! It was all about well-being."

"Well-being?" squawked Topper. "What's that?"

"Well-being!" I replied. "Like the Blur song! It's all about making your being ... well!"

The boys were silent. Waiting for more. Half gob-smacked, half morbidly curious. They wanted to hear more. More lurid details! Anything that involved naked women!

"I went to the dentist the other day and I was reading about it in some woman's magazine. Being at that naturist spa was like tantric sex: touching without touching, energies passing between us."

The boys were still silent, looking at me, waiting for me to finish. They all sat on the edge of their seats, beers in hand, waiting for some punch line or for me to tell them it was some kind of early April Fool!

"Where is my friend Wes?" Topper asked. "And what have you done with him?"

"Tantric sex?" asked Baggers. "Are you sure? Are you're sure she wasn't just ... you know ... 'holding out'?"

"I know it was a test," I said, confidently. "She's like that!"

And, suddenly, I realised I had knowledge of Roz. I knew how she thought! I was able to say, "She's like that" ... but what was 'that'?

Well, as far as I could see, Roz was playful with a mischievous sense of humour, but she was also a thinker. She was at that stage of life where she was questioning everything and that was definitely working in my favour. She'd been happily living in her high-performance hippie commune on the hill but, for whatever reason, it wasn't enough. Somewhere inside her, there was a very normal girl jostling for position. Part of her psyche needed normality.

I was able to say, "She's like that!" because I now had some idea of what 'that' was!

"Let me get this straight," began Mids, still clearly suffering from aching calves, "this place is on the high road?"

"Just an ordinary door on an ordinary high road," I began. "Full of ordinary people!"

"And didn't you feel a bit of prat?" Mids continued, "you know, with your ugly, deformed Hobbit body?"

"After a while," I began, "it didn't matter. We could have been dressed in pyjamas? We could've been invisible? We managed to transcend it."

All of the boys leaned forward. Had I really just used the word 'transcend' in a sentence? They all looked at me as if I'd told a joke in some obscure Russian dialect.

"You were naked!" squealed Topper, trying not to let the upper reaches of his voice leave him sounding like a hyena. "How can you forget you're naked?"

I shrugged my shoulders. "We just did. We talked, got wrapped-up in the conversation and forgot."

"You've changed," said Baggers. "You've only known her a week!"

Had I really changed? Maybe I had? Roz was like Trish in so many ways but there was something much more accepting about Roz. Trish had this slight tone to her voice as if she were tolerating my inadequacies.

Roz accepted my flaws. She ridiculed my flaws. Roz was able to dismiss my opinions and dissect my theories like a clumsy, drunk butcher! My dignity was in bloody clumps on the floor, but I liked it. It was out in the open. She thought I was an idiot and she actually didn't mind.

Had I really changed? No, not really. I was different to my mates. I always had been. I was the runt! They loved being single! I didn't! I really didn't. I couldn't bear telling women my simple life story over and over again. Chatting-up women was hard work! I wasn't hung up on the conquest. That wasn't me.

Hakim approached us again. "Ready to order?"

In such situations, being a *maitre d'*, Low took over. He always knew what to order, wherever we were! Hakim nodded with approval and went away to supervise our lunch. We were all ready to eat!

Tony T, the romantic, was trying desperately to understand my relationship with Roz. This was a guy who dealt in jewellery and talked to a lot of women. He was meant to know about women!

Ironically, although he had no interest in commitment, Topper was a good guy, someone who liked women and someone that women liked.

"So, she's been to your house and you've stripped off, you've been shopping for shirts with her, you've both been naked and sweaty in a spa together, and you're trying to tell us you STILL haven't had sex?"

I shook my head. What else could I say? I'd been having so much fun talking to Roz; I hadn't really worried about sex. I knew it would happen eventually. And a really perverse part of me delighted in walking this new path. The butt of their jokes was embarking on a new journey. One they might never experience?

It may have been childish but I loved leading the way. Roz was taking me to new places, making me think in different ways; Roz was polishing this unlovely gem and, suddenly, Ordinary Joe didn't look so plain.

"Can we go to this place?" asked Low.

"Don't see why not?" I replied. "Best to go with a woman, though!"

Low looked at me quizzically. "What? Like a date?"

I nodded.

"What a great idea!" he said. "We'd already be naked! Halfway there!"

Boom! The Runt was now the supplier of great leisure ideas to a Premier League playa! I was loving the new me, loving my new status and the boys were looking at me as if I were an alien replicant.

A bevy of waiters arrived with some huge trays of assorted delicacies. Low looked very pleased with himself.

"Are we feeding the whole restaurant?" asked Mids.

"Sharing these platters works out cheaper!" Low clarified.

There was then a lull in conversation while everyone filled their plates, save for the odd orgasmic moan as someone enjoyed something tasty. There was the contented hum of food being shovelled into mouths but I knew they weren't finished with me. I knew there were more questions coming.

They knew I needed a girlfriend and they only wanted the best for me, so my friends weren't nervous about 'losing' me from the gang, they were just worried that I might've hooked-up with a serial killer, or an axe murderer, or a member of The God Squad, or a traffic warden or, worse, a lawyer!

Their questions were partly out of concern and partly voyeuristic; they loved any story that contained partially-clothed women!

"The interesting bit of this story ..."

"There are bits that are MORE interesting?" shrieked Topper.

"The interesting bit," I continued, "is that Roz's housemates are trying to talk her out of dating me! They think it will kill their vibe. They think they'll see less of her and the 24-hour house party will be over."

Melvin looked up from his food. There was a small smidge of taramasalata on his chin. "They're a weird bunch, aren't they?"

"You'd never say I'm 'killing your vibe', would you?"

"Nah!" said Topper. "You like having a girlfriend! You need a girlfriend to do everything for you!"

"Even if you had a girlfriend," began Mids, "she'd still let you see your mates! And, if she didn't, you'd dump her, right?"

"Of course!" There was never any doubt in my mind. Dating Roz could never affect my friendship with these guys. Nothing was breaking-up this gang! No matter how beguiling she was, Roz would NOT be dictating! I didn't know her THAT well and I could see her looking to direct everything but she was not controlling.

Her mob were different! They were almost possessive! It seemed laughable that these clever people actually thought they could keep Roz locked up forever! Or maybe they thought it was in her best interests? Maybe they thought I was a nice guy who would bring her happiness for a few years but ultimately break her heart?

The platters began to empty, the bellies began to fill and, where before we'd been ravenously stuffing food into our faces, now we were groaning and picking and almost at a standstill. We had eaten a lot of food. My belly was almost the size of Beirut. Conversation had almost stopped because we were having trouble breathing!

"So, what's Roz saying?" asked Melvin.

"Oh, she's an independent woman!" I said. "She does her own thing!"

"She certainly does!" said Low, pointing at the door. I turned round and there was Roz, looking dazzling and colourful as ever. Fabulous swooshes of turquoise and orange and purple!

As she headed towards us, every man in the restaurant tried to act nonchalant, while catching a sneaky glance at this vision, and all of them were envious as she arrived at our table.

All the boys stood (quite a polite gesture, I thought) and, for their troubles, they all got a peck on the cheek and a face full of hair!

She picked up my beer and took a swig of it.

"Good evening, gentlemen!"

The boys were too full and sleepy to say too much.

She began making short work of our leftovers. "Very tasty!" she said, finishing off my bottle of beer.

"How did you know we'd be here?" asked Melvin, clearly impressed.

"You boys are never hard to find," she replied, waving her empty beer bottle at a passing waiter. "In fact, the way Low uses Facebook, I think he wants to be found!"

"We heard about last night!" said Low. "Sounds like fun!"

"'Fun' is not the word I would use!" she said, feeding more kebab and salad into her mouth. "That sauna is hot as hell! You'd be sweating from pores you didn't know you had!"

This sounded like an extreme sport to the boys and they all immediately looked interested.

"I've been in saunas!" said Low, his fertile imagination already working overtime.

"Do it!" said Roz, provocatively. "Enjoy it! It's a real one for the senses!"

Cupping her hand over her mouth, Roz belched, but it was louder than she'd anticipated.

"Oops, 'scuse me!" she said, giggling.

It certainly was amusing watching Roz interact with the boys. These lunches, dinners and visits to the pub were boys-only zones. No girls were ever invited. Not even Trish had attended. Trish had allowed me my 'guy-time' but Roz truly didn't give a toss! It was always Roz-time!

Here she was, plonked down in the middle, eating our food, brazenly daring us to treat her like the opposite sex. In our space, she was more than happy to be one of the boys!

"And were you impressed with Wezza's wax job?" asked Tony F.

I watched Mids discussing my dick with my girlfriend and it felt like an out-of-body experience.

"It is a thing of beauty!" she stated. Straight-faced. "And whose bright idea was that?"

No one wanted to take the blame, so they all played with their cutlery.

She knew full well that Mids was trying to make her blush but she would never be fazed by body-part banter. Women are more than happy to talk about dicks but it will always end in tears!

Having emptied a few of the plates, I could see that Roz was done, and I was ready to move on to the next phase of my Sunday.

"Need to go and see my sister!" I said to her. "Sunday tradition."

"Can I tag along?" Roz asked.

"Course you can! She's a bit barmy!"

"Not as barmy as me, is she?"

To be honest, it was a fairly even contest. Roz and my sister each had their own unique brand of barminess.

I reached into my wallet and pulled out some notes.

"I'll see you boys in the week."

"Remember you're all invited to my warehouse on Wednesday?" said Mids.

I had completely forgotten.

"Maybe Roz's friends would like to come and sample some of my new bottles?" Not one to pass up an opportunity, Mids knew Roz's cocky mates would fancy themselves as wine connoisseurs.

These words stopped Roz dead in her tracks.

"We like wine tasting," she said.

"Got a lovely Cotes-du-Rhone Blanc just come in!"

"I will ask them," she said, sweetly, but I could see her wondering if the two sets of friends were ready for one another.

So was I! This would make 'War Of The Worlds' look like afternoon tea at the vicarage! This would almost be like a debating society: the two sides of the house debating ME! Pro-Wes and anti-Wes: each side defending, protecting and promoting their friend. What would my mates say about me? Doubtless, they'd be over-the-top; profuse in their praise! Not meaning a bloody word but backing their boy anyway!

Maybe this would be the pivotal moment when Roz suddenly realised that she moved in higher circles than me? Side-by-side with her friends, maybe mine would look like lovable buffoons? Charming and endearing but ultimately an inferior gene pool?

Roz and I jumped on a bus up to Marie's and talked about Wednesday. Part of her was nervous, part of her was curious. Like an anthropologist, she wondered how these two indigenous civilisations would integrate?

There was definitely a class divide between her friends and mine. Our parents had been shop owners, policemen and waiters, whereas her friends' parents had been poets, set designers and mountain-climbers! In truth, we were 'a bit of rough' but, if Roz could find me attractive, our two sets of friends could mix? Initially, it would be a bit tense and possibly a bit explosive, but it could work?

"I think the boys can come off looking quite arrogant and pretentious?"

"They'll be fine!" I assured her.

I was counting on Mids' wines to undo the buttons and loosen the belts. All that wine would cause one of two things: either lots of hugging and kissing, or a punch-up!

"I think I should warn you," I began, "Marie has OCD like you wouldn't believe!"

"It's fine."

"No, seriously! She fusses and fidgets. Nothing can be out of place. It all has to be symmetrical. The house is spotless! Cleaner and tidier than when my parents lived there! Some people find it overbearing?"

"It's fine," said Roz, calmly. "Really, it's fine!"

"My sister was the one that introduced me to Trish and even Trish found it hard to deal with sometimes!"

"Trish," said Roz. "You don't talk about her anymore."

No, Trish had definitely faded into the background. This dynamic figure who'd once been such a central part in my life was now just a fridge magnet in my kitchen and a small statue of the Eiffel Tower on my key ring.

Roz was definitely an improvement on Trish. It felt uncouth to be judging them like two prize heifers but there had been something aggravating about the dismissive look in Trish's eyes. It was almost a look of pity? As if I were some gigantic project she would never finish?

In Roz's favour, she accepted me. She didn't want to change me. She knew, just by leading me astray, that I would change! She didn't need to speak or instruct or lecture, all she had to do was guide and redirect my life and, in turn, I would evolve and, hopefully, grow up? Well, we all live in hope!

The only thing against Roz was that she wasn't sure. She was still 50:50. Despite her calm exterior, she was chewing over the evidence, trying to decide whether her friends or I were right. I just couldn't believe this clever girl was worried about losing her friends? As Melvin had suggested, they were a weird bunch. They literally planned to stay in that house, frozen in time, forever! They didn't want anything to change. The chemistry was perfect and they didn't want a gormless twerp like me adjusting the temperature!

Why were her friends making it so complicated? Did it really have to be this much of an issue? Why was a man and a woman dating a matter of such global importance? Would it really affect everyone's lives and provoke new conflicts in the Middle East?

We got off the bus and began walking towards Marie's. To be honest, today I was dreading my Sunday visit to my sister. Marie could really be quite cutting at times. How would she respond to Roz? If she didn't take to her, it would not be pretty: personal questions, loud silences and dismissive retorts. Marie's feelings always flashed across her face like a Belisha Beacon! My sister would NOT be getting a job in the diplomatic corps any time soon!

And she did that thing where she put a coaster under your mug and slammed it down in a very judgemental way! Not-so-subtle suburban torture!

When we got to her front door, all the lights were on and there was some cheesy disco pumping out in the front room. The neighbours must have been able to hear it! I tried to knock on the front door but the front door was already open!

I gingerly pushed it open. Roz and I looked at each other. She looked confused but I was concerned! The living room door was marginally ajar and we could both see through the gap.

Dressed only in a pair of baggy, old-fashioned Y-fronts, Percy was literally dancing like no one was watching him. He had no real moves and, for the most part, was gyrating like a seventies hippie tripping at a free rock concert, but he surely was digging the music! He didn't seem like a disco kind of guy but the subtle, punchy rhythms of The Bee Gees had him jerking and twerking like an excitable eel! He looked blissfully happy!

Roz and I looked at each other again. She still looked confused but I knew what lay behind the kitchen door. I pushed the door open and there was my sister, standing at the kitchen table, her hair standing on end and full of flour, her arms up to her elbows in a huge mixing bowl, and a row of freshly-made cakes next to the oven.

The kitchen smelt like your favourite bakery. Vanilla, almond, cinnamon, coffee and nutmeg were all floating in the air. Roz stopped looking confused and her eyes lit up!

Marie looked up from her frantic mixing and smiled. "Didn't hear you come in?"

"The door was open!"

"Oops!" she said, playfully.

Not only was every cup, plate and glass NOT in its rightful place, the whole kitchen looked like it had been ransacked by a horde of hairy Celts! The place looked like a tip and Marie didn't seem to give a damn!

"You alright, love?" I asked.

"Never better," she replied. "Never ... better! Never!"

Blimey! I thought to myself. She and Percy have had some serious, mind-bending sex! I looked at Roz. We were now on the same page and she was thinking the same!

"Marie," I began, trying to catch her attention, "this is that Roz I've been telling you about!"

Marie looked up from her mixing bowl and smiled at Roz.

"I would shake your hand," she began, waving two hands covered in chocolate cake mix, "but ...."

"It's okay," said Roz. "Are these cakes for any special occasion?"

"No, darling! Help yourself and, while you're at it, make us a cuppa! I'm gasping!"

Roz and I moved over to the sink, which was full of dirty plates, half-full cups and sticky knives and forks. The sink was so full, I struggled to get the kettle under the faucet.

Amazingly, having filled the kettle, I had trouble finding a clean mug! In my sister's kitchen, where the mugs are always lined-up neatly and, where possible, in alphabetical order!

So, I began washing up. Without saying anything, Roz started loading the dishwasher. I looked at her and smiled. I liked her. It was easy with her. She knew what to do.

"What are all the cakes for?"

"Cakes?" said Marie, lifting her head and looking at this long row of assorted sponges, loafs, fruit cakes and cupcakes on her sideboard. She looked at them all. Maybe for the first time? The look on her face was priceless! She'd had her head in a mixing bowl so long, she'd lost track of this insane production line she'd created.

Then, with the delighted smile of a child that's just peed in its first potty, she looked up and simply said, "Percy loves cake!"

"You made these for Percy?"

"Percy loves cake!" she repeated and carried on mixing.

Roz looked at me and winked. I handed her a plastic sachet of dishwasher soap and set the machine in motion. We now finally had three clean mugs. The kettle had boiled, so we made tea. The milk wasn't even in the fridge!

Not only had the sex stood Marie's hair on end but she was in some kind of Percy-induced trance. As if he'd commanded her to start making cakes but hadn't told her to stop!

"So, you're getting on well with Percy?" I asked.

Marie stopped stirring her cake mix for a moment and looked at me. She thought for a second and brushed hair out of her eyes, which merely put chocolate cake mix in her hair! Roz and I tried not to laugh!

Marie was glistening with perspiration and panting from all her vigorous cake-mixing! "Percy?" she asked.

Unable to help herself, Roz grabbed some kitchen towel and moved towards Marie. "Sorry, babe, you've got cake mix in your hair!"

Marie watched as this total stranger began wiping cake mix out of her hair. She looked at Roz and there seemed to be an instant connection. "You're a pretty thing, aren't you?"

Roz blushed.

"Where are your parents from?"

"My mum's from Venezuela. My dad's half Irish/half Swedish."

Marie couldn't really help as her hands were covered in cake mix, so she just stood there and let Roz de-gunk her hair. "That's an exotic mixture, isn't it?"

"I've got family all round the world!"

Finally, Marie's hair was mix-free and re-tied back behind her head. I looked at my sister, still waiting for an answer to my question. "She's a pretty thing, isn't she?" she said.

"Yes, she is! So ... you and Percy? I could see you getting on well on Friday night!"

"He's been here since Friday night!" said Marie, triumphantly. "I can't get enough of him!"

That was a little too much information but I was very happy for my sister.

"Can't get enough of him," she repeated. "What an amazing man!"

And suddenly she was lost in a flurry of vivid memories. Roz and I watched as my sister reminisced in her daydream, quite lost in thoughts of whatever Percy had done over the last 48 hours!

The kitchen door opened and a red-faced Percy stood there grinning from ear-to-ear. Suddenly realising he was just in his undies, he turned quickly with a loud "Oops!" and disappeared up the stairs.

"Percy loves cake!" Marie repeated. "And what Percy wants, Percy gets!"

"Just like that?" I enquired.

"Just like that!" she said. "You know when something's right, don't you?"

Roz and I looked at one another and, in that look, we had a major conversation. If Roz wasn't sure about dating me, it was because she wasn't sure it was right and, as Marie had said, even though she was in a Percy-induced trance, you know when something's right.

I handed Marie her tea and she sipped at it. "Have some cake, why don't ya?"

Roz and I surveyed all the different items and Roz finally picked up a knife and sliced herself a piece of – what looked and smelled like – coffee and walnut cake. Biting into it and savouring the flavour, Roz moaned in this exaggerated fashion and giggled with pleasure. I cut myself a slice and, indeed, it tasted good!

Percy re-emerged, fully-dressed. "Evening!" he said, chirpily. "Nothing before its' time!"

I looked at him quizzically.

Striding into the kitchen, he switched the kettle back on and looked for a mug. "Nothing before its' time!" he repeated.

He span round skilfully and clamped his long arms around Marie. "I've waited my whole life to find a woman like this!"

This mad, gangly fool was actually Rhett Butler in disguise! Roz and I looked at each other and, within a few seconds of eye contact, we communicated. I liked that. I liked being on the same page as her. In that look, I knew we were both enjoying Percy's loud and profound declaration of love.

Could it really be love after 48 hours? My sister and this lanky nutter already seemed like a couple. I'd never seen a man behave like that around her. I was happy for her. Truly I was! It totally changed the dynamic of our Sunday.

No longer would I have to beg her to leave her house. From now on, Percy was going to keep her occupied! A terrifying thought but strangely comforting at the same time!

Unlocking my sister from his grasp, Percy span round like a synchronised soul singer and surveyed all the cakes. "Ooh, what have we here?"

We watched him scan the cakes like a quality control machine, back and forth, licking his huge pink lips as he went. Finally, he stopped at this chunky carrot cake and sliced off a huge doorstopper of a wedge. We watched him stuff a huge piece into his mouth and savour every morsel. It took him ages to masticate and swallow this unholy slab.

"My goodness, Miss Marie! What magic have you dispensed here?"

My sister turned round and beamed with a mixture of coyness and undiluted glee. In 48 short hours, this manic geek had taken 30 years off my sister and turned her into a giggling school girl. Equal measures terrifying and powerful.

What was this? Lust? Love? Hunger? Longing? Whatever it was, this new couple were unpicking the nonsense of intellectual considerations and just getting on with the serious business of appreciating one another!

Roz and I finally left Marie's after 10.00. We were both quiet and thoughtful, digesting what we'd both witnessed and processing the data.

I felt relief. I'd been worried about Marie. Worried about how I would deal with her sadness and loneliness. The future had looked gloomy! I'd readied myself for years of hand-holding, years of putting my arm around Marie's shoulder. And now look at her! She was so happy and so orgasmic, her hair was standing on end!

Roz's thoughts were probably different. She was probably analysing the passion she'd just witnessed. And such passion! Percy literally dancing with joy, while Marie made treats for her man like a woman possessed!

It was so simple! Trish had made it complicated and now Roz's friends were trying to make it complicated whereas, in truth, it was very simple.

"Are you okay?" I asked her.

"That was quite intense, wasn't it?"

It was. Even she'd been touched by love at first sight? I was surprised. I didn't peg her for being slushy. Maybe her hesitancy about us was just fear of the unknown? Maybe she'd never felt that ridiculous heady feeling? I tried not to take it personally.

We got to her front door, she opened it, walked in and left it open. She hadn't said goodbye, so I followed her in. My first time inside The Haunted House!

It was a beautiful old house. Hard to put a date on it. No wonder she didn't want to leave! I closed the front door behind me and followed her into the kitchen. A huge room with a huge kitchen table, just like I'd pictured it. Guess I'd watched too many film adaptations of Jane Austen novels with Marie?

Roz headed for the fridge and pulled out a bottle of wine. It was a bit late on a Sunday night for a drink but I wasn't going to say anything. She poured wine into two glasses for us.

Her house mate Benjamin shuffled into the room, dressed in pyjamas, dressing gown and slippers.

"Alright?" he nodded at me, in an informal, blokey way.

"I can't sleep!" he moaned, falling into Roz's arms. Over his shoulder, she gave me a tired roll of her eyes, as if this diva always needed a reassuring hug.

Roz gave him her glass of wine and poured herself another. They both sat at the table, so I perched myself at the end. Not wishing to interrupt, spoil the moment, disturb the dynamic: take your pick!

"Where have you been?" Benji asked, haughtily, half expecting her answer to be somewhere dull and something mundane.

"Well, first, I met this one at a restaurant in Camden Town. One of his mates loves to update his Facebook status wherever they go, so they're always quite easy to find!"

Benji said nothing. This item of her evening was of no interest to him. He sipped at his wine and continued listening to her, daring her to say something that might capture his imagination.

"And then we went to see Wes's sister, which was quite an extraordinary experience!"

Benji's curiosity was aroused and he sat up straight but, before Roz could continue, Wendy came into the kitchen, also dressed in pyjamas, dressing gown and slippers.

"I can't sleep," she wailed, walking over to Roz, sitting on her lap and cuddling her. Roz was clearly the go-to cuddler. She took a sip from Roz's wine glass and shivered with disgust.

"I can't be drinking wine," Wendy said, "I have to be up in six hours!"

"So, what happened?" said Benji, cynically. "Why extraordinary?"

Wendy pulled some milk out of the fridge, threw it into a saucepan, reached into the cupboard for some hot chocolate and suddenly noticed me.

"Wes!" she said. "Didn't notice you!"

She clearly needed a cuddle from me too, so I stood up and we embraced. "What's extraordinary?" she asked.

"Wes goes to see his sister every Sunday, so we've just been to see her. She's been single ages. Become quite a hermit. Bored out of her mind. Become a bit OCD!"

Wendy stirred drinking chocolate into her warm milk and sat down at the table for the rest of the story.

"She's early forties, an attractive woman but no takers. And then, out of the blue, she meets the man of her dreams on Friday night! Where was she on Friday night, Wes?"

All eyes turned to me. I felt a huge, bright spotlight shining in my eyes and my mouth felt dry. The clever people were waiting for me to talk.

"I was DJ-ing at an engagement party on Friday night. They met there."

My heart was pounding. I couldn't remember what I'd just said. Had I made sense?

The eyes were still on me. I was expected to talk more. The clever people wanted to hear more of my story.

"It was the first time they'd ever met. I'd invited her because she doesn't get out much, and I'd invited him because he'll be working for me soon."

The clever people were silent and still looking at me, so I continued.

"They'd never met each other before, so I introduced them, and they spent the whole evening together. They were inseparable! They talked, laughed and danced all night. When I'd finished and was packing-up, they disappeared together and we've just found out that he is STILL at her house! Their first date continued all through Saturday and all through Sunday!"

Wendy looked thrilled by the romance of this story, while Benjamin looked sceptical.

"They both sound unhinged!" he snarled. "Too much, too soon!"

"Benji, you miserable shit!" Roz actually looked quite angry. I'd never seen that before. It was a bit scary.

"Passion is a powerful, fiercesome, raging and spitting fire," he began. "Nothing gets done without passion! We love passion! We write songs about it! But let's not get carried away!"

"Who knows?" said Roz.

"Yes, who knows?" echoed Wendy, cupping her hands around her hot drink. "Who knows? Open your mind to the possibility! Don't you always sneer at narrow-minded people!"

Boldly, I continued. "When we arrived at her house, this guy was dancing around the front room in his Y-fronts! Dancing on his own! Dancing for joy! Not a care in the world!"

"Where was she?" asked Wendy.

"She was in the kitchen baking. Baking as if her life depended on it! He had expressed a liking for cake and that was it! She began baking like she was on a mission! Bloody cakes everywhere! 'Percy loves cake!' she kept saying, like some Stepford Wife!"

Wendy's eyes and mouth were open in amazement. "So, he was in the front room dancing and she was in the kitchen baking?"

She turned to me for confirmation. I nodded.

"They definitely sound unhinged!" said Benji.

"Don't say another fucking word!" Roz snarled at him.

And now I had a much clearer picture of what 'getting into it' meant. When Roz had talked about Friday night, now I knew what she meant. It meant consumption of alcohol, it meant late nights, it meant heated debates, it meant a lot of cruel words said in the heat of the moment and regretted the next day!

Benji dare not speak.

Heston wandered into the room, wearing ragged jeans, flip-flops and a paint-stained sweat-shirt. He surveyed everyone inside the kitchen and clapped his eyes on me. "The boyfriend, right?"

I nodded, meekly.

"Wes? Is that right?"

I nodded again.

Heston looked around the kitchen again and quickly sensed the tension. "What is all this noise about?"

No one spoke. It was a recurring theme.

"Well?" Heston insisted.

"It's just Benjamin's gloomy outlook on life," began Roz. "So depressing! Is anything real? Does anything really exist? In Benjamin's world, what is there?"

"What are we talking about?" asked Heston.

And now there were five of us at the table! It was filling up quickly! Heston found a mouthful of wine in the bottle, necked that and opened another bottle. It was after midnight on a Sunday night and we were ... getting into it!

I re-told my story to Heston, this time with more detail, this time with more confidence. Heston – the romantic artist – seemed to enjoy my story.

"Can I speak?" Benji whispered sarcastically.

"Yes," Roz regally responded.

"I think," began Benji, carefully choosing his words, and pouring from the second bottle, "it sounds wonderful! You think I'm such a heartless bastard?"

Roz glared at him, knowing there was a 'but', knowing Benji didn't really believe it was 'wonderful'.

"But?" said Roz. "We know there's a but!"

Benji didn't need his 'but'. Everyone in the house knew his views.

"They're happy!" said Heston, grasping the muscles on his naked arms. "Moments of happiness! Let them enjoy their moments!"

"Moments of happiness, followed by moments of what?" said Benji.

Roz was too angry to talk.

"Let them enjoy their moments," said Heston, calmly.

"Maybe you could do with a few 'moments', darling? Might alter your outlook?" Wendy winked at Benji mischievously.

"We are not discussing my 'moments'!"

His housemates were all smirking and enjoying Benji's discomfort. It was clear he was the dissenter; the main person putting doubt in Roz's heart. While everyone would be sad to see less of Roz, Benji was the one person who thought he knew best and planned to shackle Roz. For her own good! I really was in a Jane Austen novel!

Chapter Twelve (Monday)

Sunday had been a long day! Monday was proving tricky.

Work was painful. I was moving slowly and my brain felt like it was buffering.

My mind was still replaying selected moments from yesterday: my lunch with the boys, Percy dancing in his Y-fronts, Marie's kitchen in a mess, the Spanish Inquisition around Roz's kitchen table. It had been a lot to take in. Enjoyable but a lot for my feeble brain to digest.

It was a typical, busy Monday but my mind was away with the fairies and I could feel Max staring at me. I didn't make conversation with him at the best of times but today I couldn't even nod! I had the energy of a corpse and the people skills of a frustrated warthog!

As ever, we had people returning gear to the shop but, on this day, Max was running the show. I was a bit of a dead loss.

The first couple through the door were quite a picture! She was a tall, buxom woman with long, auburn hair, while he was average height, stocky, with a face full of hair.

While the man brought the gear in from their car, she just sat at the counter applying make-up. Not a word was uttered.

The man was returning a fairly basic set-up (CDs, mixer, amp, speakers) and Max was scrupulously checking through the accompanying bag to make sure all the wires had been returned.

When everything was inside the shop, Max checked it all over to make sure there were no dents or damage, no buttons or knobs missing and, once he was satisfied, he gave me the thumbs-up.

Then it was my turn to return their deposit cheque but, as I was moving like a dead snail, this was going to take a while!

For some reason, this couple were in no hurry. He sat on the other stool at the counter and they both drank from cups of takeaway coffee. She seemed to be getting ready for work, meticulously applying a lot of make-up. He couldn't take his eyes off her. I could hear them mumbling discreetly. Her voice was almost as low as his!

The area behind the counter was organised – desk files, plastic folders, lever-arch files – but I just couldn't find the one bit of paperwork I needed! Sod's Law!

My customers didn't seem fussed at all. He could not take his eyes off her! Their bodies seemed entwined in a motionless tango, their words lost in a private language; he seemed beyond besotted, almost hypnotised by her. She had this cool, aloof look and didn't seem that bothered by his attention, but it was probably some elaborate role play game and he was loving it!

I should have been looking for their deposit cheque but I couldn't take my eyes off this passion play. That's what I wanted. I wanted to be like the words of a soul song. I wanted that natural high or that supernatural thing. I wanted that electricity between two people. I'd seen it in the movies, so I knew it existed!

Eventually, I lifted up an old copy of Metro and there was the paperwork! Not that the couple were going anywhere! Sitting on the stools at my counter, he was getting closer and closer, as if he wanted to climb inside her, and she was playfully pushing him away, so she could finish getting ready for work.

That's what I wanted. I wanted that love. I wanted that light-headed, dream-like state. Even my chronically-miserable sister had found it! Was it too much to ask for?

At one point, Tony G the *maitre d'* had virtually suggested that love was unnatural.

"Unnatural?" I'd asked.

"Unnatural like a mysterious infection! Unnatural like a mental illness that suddenly turns your friend from a normal bloke into a rambling, stumbling mess! Loving your kid or loving your dog is alright but ... falling in love? It's a madness! An unexplained phenomena! People lose their minds, geez! Do weird things! Love changes you, changes your life, makes you soft, makes you insecure, makes you jealous. Count me out!"

"You've never been in love, Low?"

"I stay on my guard!" he said to me. "I move on quickly before it can happen! It upsets your routine!"

That was Low. He was your archetypal, cartoon character Don Juan! Body, looks, patter. He played football and had even dabbled in sprinting when he was at school! He had those strong, muscular thighs and that hard torso that makes women drool.

We'd all experienced our fair share of hurt and wounded women, but Low didn't even let it get that far!

"It's simple, geez! You spell it out! You say to them, 'I am NOT looking for a relationship.' You have to let them know from the get-go. It is what it is."

At one point, Low had even suggested that he should write his autobiography. He was so proud of the furrow he had ploughed; he wanted some ghost writer to document all the gory details.

That was not me! That's not what I wanted.

As I watched this couple enviously, I enjoyed the perversity of their dynamic. She was taller (and broader) than him but she clearly loved his intensity. He wasn't going to be able to throw her around the bed but he clearly had all the masculinity she needed.

"Found it!" I triumphantly proclaimed.

The man took his receipt, took his cheque and smiled at me. "Nice doing business with you," he said, in a broad North London accent (somewhere between Finchley and Whetstone.)

"Everything okay?" I asked.

"Yes," he said. "We had a little party."

I wasn't quite sure what that meant. I dared not ask!

As they left the shop, I decided to follow them out and get some fresh air. He had her pressed up against a wall and they were kissing like it was their last moments on Earth.

I shouldn't have stared but I did. They didn't care. They were totally oblivious to all around them. This was a goodbye kiss of epic proportions! No one was escaping from that clinch without a stirring in their pants!

I wanted those impetuous gestures. I wanted to feel that way and I wanted someone to feel that way about me. Obviously, I hadn't aroused those passions in Trish but, maybe, with due care and attention to my persona, maybe I could reach that level of machismo?

It felt ridiculous even contemplating it!

I'm not even sure how I got through the day! Roz called me around lunchtime to say she was knackered too and was probably going to have a very early night. I was looking forward to a low-key evening. The entire weekend had been an assault on my senses!

For the life of me, I just couldn't stop replaying the weekend. I'd tried as best as possible to convey Saturday night to the boys but I'd failed miserably. Even I was still coming to terms with Saturday night! It's not often you spend Saturday night naked with a hot girl and absolutely nothing sexual occurs. It's like going into a high-class restaurant, pulling out a book and just reading. It's like going to the Tate Modern and just sending text messages to someone!

Max and I closed the shop before 6.00, I thanked him for being so helpful, and I trudged my weary way home. It was just a short bus ride home but I was nervous of dozing off and ending up in Highgate Village!

I managed to get off at the right stop and dawdled my way the remaining 200 yards. In the distance, I could see someone sitting on the wall outside my small, terraced house.

"Cheeky bleeder!" I thought to myself.

As I approached, I suddenly realised it was Trish, not looking like herself, not smiling, looking quite subdued. I stood in front of her. She looked up at me. Did I look the same? She studied me closely.

Here she was: the woman I had doted on. The woman I had given my all to, but a woman who had analysed 'my all' and decided it was not enough.

No, I was not quite good enough for her. I was a work in progress. Someone she had tried to mould but failed. Someone she had tried to 'educate' and 'civilise' but someone who had not responded to treatment.

In her eyes, I would never quite make the grade. It had been unsatisfying for her and, as a result, she'd drifted away.

What had she been looking for? Perfection? Close to perfection? I was NOT going to deliver anything close to that!

"You look the same," she began, "but ... you look different!"

She lifted herself to her feet and threw her arms around me. She almost looked pleased to see me! I could feel her relaxing into the embrace, as if it was a reassuring and comforting hug.

I'm no expert here but it almost felt as if she'd missed me. I wasn't holding my breath waiting for those words, though.

We went through a familiar front door, hung our jackets on familiar hooks in the hall and went into the front room. I sat on my sofa and she sat in her favourite armchair.

She looked around her. "Nothing's changed."

"Why should it?" I replied.

She looked startled.

Had those words really come out of my mouth? That response was very unlike me! Yes, I did look the same but THAT response was the difference. If I'd changed in the last six months, THAT was the change. I'd finally learnt to love myself. There wasn't much to love but I was no longer going to apologise for my personality, my tastes and my needs.

"No reason," she replied. "There's no reason why anything should change."

She stiffened her back, as if she knew she'd have to come correct. This was a conversation she wasn't going to have to lead. For the first time, we were talking as equals. I no longer needed her and she knew it!

"Where did you go?" I asked.

"Nowhere," she replied. "I just needed a little time on my own."

"Was it enjoyable?" I asked.

She raised her eyebrows. She wasn't used to this Wes. Again, she looked startled. She'd been so used to making the running with me, she wasn't used to barbed, slightly condescending questions.

"You're upset with me," she stated, confidently.

Was I upset? Not really. Maybe, if I hadn't found Roz, I'd be lonely, but now that my head was full of new experiences, new people (and alarming new feelings), I wasn't upset with Trish. She had surprisingly faded very quickly. Roz really made her look quite high street essentials, whereas I was now moving in chic, backstreet circles!

"No," I replied. "I'm fine."

She looked at me. She wanted more. She wanted to know what 'fine' meant. She wanted to hear that I'd missed her. She wanted to hear that I was ready to buckle down and complete our mission; Mission Wes; the seemingly impossible journey from boyhood to manhood. She wanted to hear every detail of everything I missed about her but, in truth, I didn't feel I owed her any answers.

She had disappeared and virtually ensured she'd be impossible to find. Not a goodbye note. Not an explanation. Not an existential theory. Nothing.

A month had passed; I'd waited. A second month had passed; I'd started to worry. A third month had passed; I'd become depressed. A fourth month passed; I started to become angry. And, after six months, my mind and body began to shut down and I was dozing in shop doorways.

Six months of no communication and a chocolate assortment box of pain.

I didn't feel I owed her any kind of response at all.

I got up and made us some tea, and brought out some chocolate brownie I'd nicked from Marie's house.

Trish savoured her first mouthful. "It's good!"

"Marie made it. I saw her last night. I think she's in love!"

Again, Trish looked startled. It was an evening of surprises for her! "In love?"

"Seems so! A weird bloke! She's a bit strange, he's a bit strange, but they get on like a house on fire! In fact, 'house on fire' is understating it! They began dancing on Friday night and he was still dancing, in his underpants, in her living room, on Sunday evening! No dating site would ever have matched them! You never can tell, eh?"

"No," said Trish, sipping from her tea. "You never can tell."

The conversation between us was very strained. Both of us wanting to bitch and whine in a very accusatory fashion but managing to maintain our dignity.

She probably wanted to tell me what a drip I was and how we could have had something special, and I definitely wanted to tell her that she was shallow and, if she'd looked hard enough, she would've seen I wasn't such a bad bloke.

I wasn't Clooney, Downey and Hardy rolled into one, but I did have my own business, I did have all my own teeth, and I had been quite happy being her boyfriend!

Trish had made it complicated; she'd made our relationship scientific. She'd over-analysed it and certainly mis-read her data. No, I wasn't a hunk. Not by any stretch of the imagination. Not tall, not muscular, not handsome, not striking. I was fairly ordinary, a bit non-descript and a tad indecisive, but I wasn't ignorant, abusive or violent! I wasn't a glue-sniffing psycho! I wasn't manipulative, or lazy, or cruel. There was a whole lexicon of faults I could have had and I still got dumped!

That was the bitching and whining I wanted to do, but it wasn't a good look. It wouldn't have got me anywhere. It was probably better to keep my cool and keep cutting her slices of chocolate brownie.

She talked about her parents, her siblings and her wider family. These people had almost become my in-laws! As she talked, I looked at the woman whose every word I used to treat as gospel. I looked at this woman who had kept my diary for more than a decade. I looked at her and listened to her and, as she spoke about the ordinary people in her ordinary life, I realised I was going places and she wasn't and, like the U2 song, she still hadn't found what she was looking for. Hence her appearance on my front wall.

When she'd left, I was in love with her. Well, as 'in love' as I can do. Now, she was meeting a different Wes. Not only had my love for her dissipated but she no longer looked that dynamic. I had witnessed dynamic. Miss Dynamite and her cast of friends.

I listened and listened, and all I heard were tales of a very ordinary life, featuring this bright, peppy girl who used to be the poster girl for her circle of friends. They say you shouldn't compare but you just can't help yourself! I hadn't even had sexual relations with Roz but, despite her dour housemates, she promised much. There were no guarantees of anything but Roz really promised a lot!

I knew I shouldn't but I did! I compared Trish to Roz, and Trish really looked and sounded like yesterday. Roz was the new world order!

There was suddenly frantic banging at my front door.

Trish and I looked at each other and jumped up. I rushed to the front door and there was a sweaty and tearful Marie, holding on to my door, trying to catch her breath. She'd been running and could barely speak.

"Don't you ever answer your phone?" she choked.

I was feeling so lethargic, my phone was probably dead and sitting in the bottom of my bag.

"Come in," I said. "Sit down."

"Where's Percy?" she spluttered.

"How would I know, babe?"

"He just disappeared!"

The veins were pulsing in Marie's forehead and there was a sickening look of terror in her eyes.

"I don't know where he is," I said. "Don't you have his number?"

Marie thought for a second. In all of the breathless whirlwind of the last 48 hours, they hadn't even thought to exchange numbers. They'd been so busy talking, laughing, dancing and God knows what else, they hadn't even done the basics!

"Fuck!" she shouted very loudly to no one in particular.

Trish suddenly appeared behind me.

Marie looked up. "Trish?"

"Long time," said Trish, remorsefully.

But Marie didn't have time for small talk or to question why Trish was in my house.

"I might have his number written in the diary at work."

"Really?" said Marie, waiting for me to offer to go back to the shop.

I was shattered, I really didn't want to go anywhere. The shoes had come off and I was enjoying a post-brownie haze. I was ready for bed! Marie just stood there, waiting for the words she knew had to come out of her loving, compassionate brother.

"Okay, okay, we'll go!" I said, going back into the house to get my keys.

This was going to be one fun road trip: a bemused and broken ex-girlfriend, a tearful sister suffering Percy-withdrawal symptoms, and an exhausted, unloved mobile DJ. In our own way, we were all suffering. We clambered into my car and headed back to the shop.

Even though Marie had introduced me to Trish, and even though these two had been friends since forever, not a word was uttered in the car. Marie was still panting, while her brain was in overdrive, trying to understand why Percy had left and where he might have gone.

Trish could see that Marie was madder than normal and just let her percolate. Her old friend was clearly distressed and catch-up chit-chat was not required.

The shutters went up, the front door got opened, and these two punch drunk women fell into my shop. Marie leaned over the counter, willing me to find the number quicker.

I flicked through the pages of my thick, A4, page-a-day diary and found a mobile number for Percy.

"Here it is!" I said.

Marie snatched the diary from me and quickly punched in the number to her mobile. It rang and rang and rang, and then went to voicemail. What remaining life there'd been in Marie's eyes had quickly been extinguished. She looked distraught.

"Now what?" she asked.

"Maybe he had a family emergency?" I offered.

"Then why didn't he leave a note?"

"Maybe he needs some time to think?" said Trish.

Marie looked at Trish and finally registered who this woman was. "Trish? Where have you been?"

"I needed some time alone."

"You disappeared!" Marie continued.

"Yes," was all Trish could say.

Marie processed the response and ran her sweaty fingers through her thick, ungroomed, slightly wayward hair.

"Of course. Time to think? People need time to think?"

I could see her slowly rationalising the situation.

"Thanks, Wes. I'm gonna go home now. Percy probably needs time to think?"

"I'll drop you home?"

"No!" she said, defiantly. "I'll walk."

Her house was about four miles away. It was getting dark and getting chilly, but I wasn't going to argue with her. In the space of a day, I'd seen my sister happier than I'd seen her in decades; higher than a kite and, here she was, 24 hours later, lower than a slug's nut sack.

Where the hell was that long streak of piss? I had my own plans to wring his freakishly-long neck! What the hell was Percy playing at? I'd only introduced them so Marie would have someone to talk to.

Trish stood on the periphery, watching this scene unfold. The last time she'd seen Marie and I, we were both leading quite uneventful lives, but now she'd stumbled into some car crash reality TV show masquerading as real life. Or was it the other way round?

"She seems a bit ..."

"Disturbed?" I offered.

"Yes," said Trish, "she seems quite affected by this Percy!"

"This time last night," I began, "my sister was in the throes of a passionate affair. Today ... well ... I'm not sure what's gone on!"

Trish and I shut up the shop (for the second time) and stumbled back into the car. I was beyond exhausted.

The streets were dark and virtually empty. We were both low on energy. As I drove her home to her flat, she talked about everything and nothing, avoiding the one question she wanted to ask.

I'm not very bright but even I knew the question she wanted to ask.

I wasn't an accomplished sadist by any stretch of the imagination, but making her suffer was really giving me great pleasure. An ugly quality, I know but, if she wanted to know about my private life, she was going to have to ask. She talked and talked about her work, her work colleagues, her holiday plans, everything but the one question she wanted to ask, but I wasn't going to offer any information. I wanted her to ask. But she didn't.

I dropped her back to her flat and we made a vague plan to speak soon.

What did she want? Friendship?

I switched on my phone and there were 11 missed calls from Marie. Each one more frantic than the last. My poor sister!

Somewhere out there was a tall and very strange bus driver, who was in severe danger of being clobbered by my very partisan group of friends, who all loved my sister to bits!

I turned the corner of my road and – lo and behold – there was another person sitting on the wall outside my house.

"Cheeky bleeder!" I thought to myself but, as I parked the car, I realised it was Roz.

Nothing with this girl surprised me. I didn't even have to ask.

I opened the door for her and in she came. I was more than happy to see her but too tired to hear some long explanation why.

"I'm very tired," I said, kicking my shoes off.

"Can I stay?" she asked.

"Of course," I said.

"Sometimes," she began, "it just gets a bit too intense in there!"

"Do you need to talk?" I said wearily.

She smiled. "No! I don't need any more words."

Today's colours were this striking combination of blues. Pretty much every colour worked on her but this bouillabaisse of shades looked spectacular in the dim of my front room.

"Just one question," I asked.

She sighed. "Okay. One question."

"Why me?"

She thought and formulated. "Two reasons. I don't want to get to 40 and be single. After 40 … it becomes that much more difficult. Secondly, you will love me. You are ready to love me and you will love only me. I trust in your ability to love me."

That made sense to me. After a day of drama, I was at peace. There's nothing quite like the sound of truth to calm your soul.

"Three things!" she added, smiling. "You waxed for me! I know that must have been painful. That touched me! A very touching gesture!"

Within minutes, we were both cuddling in bed and, the next thing I knew, I was being awoken by my 8.00 a.m. alarm call.

I turned over. Roz was gone. I laughed to myself. Never had such a great relationship contained so little sex!

Chapter Thirteen (Tuesday)

Tuesday was a very normal day at work. Quite satisfying. A few bookings: one for equipment hire, two for equipment hire plus DJ. One of them would have been perfect for Percy, if I could just find him and/or resist the temptation to throttle him!

When I woke up, there'd been no missed calls from Marie. She'd clearly now retreated back into her shell. Percy had been a nice distraction but, for some reason or other, he'd retreated to the hills.

Could I still employ him after he'd treated my sister in such a cowardly fashion? Probably not!

I knew I'd have to pop in to see Marie. It wouldn't be pretty.

Max and I had just enjoyed a very tasty chicken wrap from the Turkish kebab shop when Roz's housemate Benjamin wandered through the door of the shop.

My hands were full of chicken grease so, when he extended his hand, I waved them in that 'you don't want to shake this hand' way. He nodded in agreement.

"There's still a lot of lunch on these fingers!"

Benjamin smiled. First time I'd seen him smile.

"Do you work near?" I asked.

"Not far."

What was he doing here? He was unexpected! It narked me a bit. I knew he wasn't a customer. The audacity! Just showing up unannounced! If you're a gorgeous girl and you've brought your milk shake to the yard, you can turn up unannounced, but not if you're a grumpy, scowling school teacher with no goodies and no discernible reason!

He wasn't much for pleasantries and didn't even attempt to talk. He looked the shop all over, scrinching his nose at our unlovely selection of equipment, and smiled in a confused, unable-to-process-data kind of way.

"Equipment hire?" he asked.

"Yes," I replied. He'd not even bothered to ask Roz what I did. Not important. Me and my business were not important.

"Private parties?" he enquired.

"Yes," I replied. "Roz has hired me and some gear to play at a party. Happening at your place very soon?"

"Ah!" he acknowledged. "It's making sense."

"Are you here to warn me off?" I asked.

I guess he'd been waiting for a few trailers before I launched into the main feature. He looked stunned, like a wild animal that's just been hit with a tranquilizer dart.

He composed himself. He hadn't really thought this through. Yes, he wanted to observe me in my natural habitat but, now we were here, he had to impress and/or impose himself on me, whichever came easiest!

"I have no power over Roz," he said, suddenly looking quite vulnerable.

So, why was he standing in my shop? To do some kind of background check on me? Or maybe just to get to know me better? All would become apparent soon enough.

For a while, Benji just mooched around the shop, making small talk. He was in his lunch hour, so I knew he wouldn't be mooching for long. He seemed fascinated with the assorted light boxes, each one sending a stream of coloured light in a different direction. I could see him tracing the patterns across our ceiling.

He seemed chirpy enough but I could see there were some burning questions bubbling beneath that brooding exterior.

"How long have you known Roz?"

"A couple of weeks," I replied. "I barely know the girl."

This response perplexed him.

"Strange," he said. "And yet she really seems to like you!"

"Why wouldn't she?" I asked.

"She doesn't do boyfriends!" he exclaimed, in measured frustration. "It doesn't make sense."

I tried not to take it personally but the subtext was, as expected, he didn't think I was good enough.

No, Roz didn't 'do boyfriends' but this one was looking to stake his claim. He was going to introduce her to Boyfriend 2.0, a newer, sleeker, more sensitive brand of boyfriend.

I hadn't dated many girls and this was my most unnerving experience. I'd never been chased by angry fathers or irate brothers. My dating years had been relatively drama-free; simple, uneventful, bordering on bland.

What was Benjamin? A former lover? A current lover? Or somebody who still held a torch for Roz? Couldn't blame him: she was a cracker; a cocky, cheeky, almost-insolent woman. Just the way I like them!

He wore classic, scruffy teacher garb: cords, shirt, jacket, comfortable shoes. He looked like he should wear glasses, but he didn't. In a strange way, he almost looked like me. We had similar, floppy, mongrel hair; a fusion of colours, lengths and styles. There was a few days' growth on his face, which he kept touching nervously, as if he knew he should shave, but couldn't quite be bothered because shaving was unimportant.

He was truly mooching for England, not really doing anything, not really saying anything, but dying to say a million things! I wasn't going to make it any easier for the bugger! Like (I'm sure) he told all his students, if he was going to quiz me, he'd have to speak clearly and with confidence. He hadn't really thought through this strategy. His lack of rehearsed script was causing him discomfort. It amused me. I was enjoying this new devil in me, ironically donated to me by the lady herself.

The more I thought about me, the more I liked her. She made me a better Wes, she gave me swagger, she gave me the confidence to keep this interfering bastard at arm's length and make him squirm at the same time.

He turned to me, as if he'd finally found the words.

Not sure where this came from but I managed to summon the sweetest yet most insincere smile possible. "Is everything okay, Benjamin?"

Direct hit! He was bubbling! I flashed my crooked teeth at him again.

At this point, the brooding one became a bit agitated, and graduated from simmering to boiling. "Not really, mate!" he said, rubbing his five o'clock shadow like it was a six o'clock plague of soldier ants. "What I'm trying to work out is: why is she so captivated with you? What have you got? Some huge, fucking cock?"

It took all my strength not to laugh my head off. In fact, in an act of supreme self-control, I managed to suppress any kind of snort or guffaw. This fool was actually teaching future generations. This humourless clod was actually given a monthly salary cheque by the education system!

It would be so easy to allay his fears and say that Roz and I hadn't even had sex but, at this point, I wanted the brooding one to suffer a bit, so I said nothing and left him with the horrific mental image of me harpooning his friend.

Expertly hovering on the outskirts of this scene was the ever-reliable Max. He could barely take his eyes off Benjamin. It was as if Max had fallen into the lion's den and was watching the hungry beast circling him. Every so often, Benjamin would catch his eye and give him a cold, lifeless glare. Nevertheless, Max was fascinated with Benji, particularly as he clearly hated me. Max wasn't that bright but that much he had gleaned.

"What have you got?" he repeated. "What have you got? You haven't got money. No disrespect but you're not some bulging-bicep gym-bunny or runway model! You're not some dazzling intellect, unless you keep that side of yourself very private?"

This was too much fun! He had accelerated beyond agitated and was fast approaching aggravated. I didn't have to say anything. Saying something might've tipped him over the edge, so I just carried on pointlessly shuffling paper, while he blathered on about what I'd got or had not got.

I wasn't totally sure what I had but, whatever it was, the beguiling, colourful girl wanted it! The way this guy was behaving, he was clearly still madly in love with Roz and, watching him stalk around the shop, I could see why she was giving him a wide berth. He was FAR too intense! She needed whimsical distractions and mindless fun and, as I wasn't that bright, I could deliver!

The tension was so great, I could even see Max starting to get twitchy! His natural instinct was to help a browsing customer but this one was making him nervous. Prowling, sneering. I could see Benji was about to blow and I was loving every minute.

I'd dreaded going to the house! Initially, I'd been intimidated by these bright young minds but, upon closer inspection, they were as in control as the next person. As in, not in control at all! For all his knowledge and ability to instruct and inspire, this glowing beacon was a spluttering mess.

And then, in an afternoon of surprises, Max leaned forward and began talking to Benjamin. "Would you like a cup of tea?"

Benjamin looked at me, as if I'd let one of my prize lemurs shit on his front lawn.

"Well?" I asked. "Would you?"

Benjamin turned back to look at Max. "No, I'm fine. Thanks, though." And, in that moment, Benjamin suddenly realised I was a nice person who employed nice people. In that instant, he suddenly understood the simple, primordial chemistry between Roz and I. I was nice. I was a nice bloke and she liked me. Nice. A wholly ineffective and much-derided word but it was working for me!

"Oh, Jesus!" Benjamin exclaimed in a theatrical way, though he actually sounded like a fake, donations-accepted preacher! "Won't you say something? Won't you help me understand?"

I was under no obligation to help this plank! It definitely wasn't part of my job description! I had half a mind to tell Roz to keep her mates in line, but I was having too much fun watching Benjamin writhe in his own torture chamber!

"What do you want me to say?" I said, calmly. I knew the timbre of my disinterested voice would drive him nuts. "Do you actually want me to list the reasons why Roz might like me?"

He laughed. He would not be stifling his laughter! "Yeah, mate! That's a peachy idea!" And, with those words, he took a menacing step towards me! Stretching his chicken neck in an aggressive way, he repeated himself, "Yeah, mate! Why don't you entertain us with a list of your redeeming features?"

"Steady!" said Max, taking two steps towards me, and placing himself between me and Benjamin.

This was priceless! Max, with his calamitous jeans dangling comically off his thighs, had got between me and Benjamin in an attempt to break-up a fight. A fight between me and the brooding one? Nah! It wasn't going to happen! Handbags at dawn, maybe?

Benjamin laughed again. "What? Are you getting your girlfriend to fight your battles?"

The wrong thing to say! Max turned towards Benjamin and squared up to him, virtually nose-to-nose. "What did you say?" he asked.

Now, this was a tone of voice I'd not heard before. It was surreal hearing this forceful, guttural noise come out of Max's mouth but there it was! He sounded like a huge and menacing bouncer, which was funny because he was probably ten stone sopping wet!

Amazingly, Benjamin took a step back and, suddenly, his concern was Max and not me. "Sorry!" he backtracked quickly. "That came out wrong!"

Max turned to me to see if Benji's apology had been accepted. Part of me wanted to say, "Smack him, Max!" but I actually said, "It's okay."

Max returned to his customary post but took every opportunity to glare at Benji. This was turning into a fun day for both of us.

"I'm just trying to understand," wailed Benjamin but, before he could finish his sentence, a drunk and bedraggled Percy staggered through the door and collapsed to his knees.

"Help me!" Percy cried. He clearly didn't need any help. He was just pissed. It was 1.45 in the afternoon and I had two lovelorn Muppets in my shop. This was not good for business but very entertaining nevertheless.

Max's jaw was on the floor. He could not believe what was happening.

Benjamin turned to look at the broken fop who had now stolen his limelight. "What kind of shop is this?"

A valid question.

"Percy!"

Percy looked up at me. His bloodshot eyes were full of tears and, by the sound of it, lager!

"What is going on?"

Benjamin looked down on this pathetic scene and was probably thinking one of two things. Either, "Who is this basket case?" or "What kind of madness is this man bringing into Roz's life?" Neither thought was particularly perceptive.

Max hadn't seen such melodrama in the shop since the great headphone scandal of 2012! (Long story.) He hopped around in his little corner, watching intently, wondering who next was coming through the front door. We'd already had one grumpy bastard and one snivelling wimp, what was next?

"Get up!" I said to Percy, who was still silently sobbing on his knees.

Percy managed to get himself upright and propped himself up on one of the stools.

"Hold on," said Benjamin, "this is the guy from your sister's house?"

"Yes," I said. "Percy meet Benjamin. This is one of my girlfriend's house mates."

The two men shook hands.

"Sorry," said Percy, "am I interrupting something?"

"No, Percy," I sneered, finally expressing an emotion (disgust, by the way!) "You weren't interrupting anything important! Just Benjamin trying to understand why Roz likes me."

Benji said nothing but stood his ground, hands in pockets, not making much eye contact with anyone. Plus, I think he wanted to stay for the show.

"Right," I said firmly, turning to Percy, "what the hell is going on?"

Percy really looked a mess. There were clearly trails of snot down his well-worn uniform and he kept sniffling gunk back up his nose like a ravenous junkie. It was early afternoon and Percy had clearly knocked back a few bottles of strong beer on an empty stomach.

"Have I messed it up?" he asked.

"What are you going on about?"

Max and Benjamin watched this soap opera intently. Watching this huge caricature of a man in a crumpled heap on my counter was better than

Emmerdale and Holby combined. It was like watching the final moments of 'Godzilla' before it meets its tragic end.

"Your sister!" Percy cried. "Messed it up!"

"What have you messed up? How have you messed up?"

Watching Percy reminded me how we tie ourselves in knots. You start out with a fairly innocent and rational thought and, before you know it, you've pondered yourself into a trough. Within minutes, you can easily depress yourself! A pathetic and unnecessary waste of time and emotional energy! And then, moments later, with a few choice words, someone can make you feel stupid for even wandering down that path!

"Percy, I'm going to ask you a simple question. Think before you answer."

Percy looked up at me plaintively, his eyes full of white and nerdy tears.

Benjamin was probably late back to work but he was anxious to see how this scene played out, plus he was still grappling for his own answers: why had the love of his life turned her back on all his curmudgeonly charm?

"Do you like my sister?" I said slowly and deliberately.

Percy looked and listened and shook his head. "She is ..." he began.

The pause was almost unbearable. Max was on the edge of the seat of his pants, Benjamin was holding his breath, waiting to hear the answer to a question that has troubled scholars down the decades.

"She is ..." Percy continued, "the most beautiful, the kindest, warmest, funniest, most generous woman I have ever met."

He paused again. Catching a memory in his brain and reliving some cake-filled moment on Sunday evening.

We all waited. Nothing.

"Percy?" I urged. "What's the problem?"

We all watched Percy, still shaking his head, still caught up in his (probably sordid) memories.

"I'm scared."

"Scared of what?" asked Benjamin, now totally caught up this engaging tragedy.

Percy looked up at Benjamin. He didn't really know him but there was a look in Benjamin's eyes that comforted him. In Benji, he could almost see a fellow sufferer; a kindred spirit. Another poor man put through the wringer by those dastardly, cruel and devilish creatures: women!

"I'm scared of this love," he replied. "What if she stops loving me?"

Benjamin looked at me. Having spent some time in my company, in my place of work, amongst my employees and friends, he now had a better idea of what kind of being had captured his loved one's heart.

Was Benji capable of providing comfort to Percy? Did he have any wisdom or guidance that he could pull out of his locker? Could he help Percy with his dilemma or was he as nervous and clueless as the weeping one?

Benji seemed like a sensitive guy and, probably, in moments of high excitement, a passionate man too but, at this moment, he had nothing for Percy. It was down to me. Good God, it was down to me! At that moment, in that shop, unbelievably, I was the most emotionally mature. It had never happened before. (It will probably never happen again!)

"You can't be scared, Percy."

He looked up at me and his eyes began to clear.

"You shouldn't be scared of anything. It's no way to live your life."

I could feel Benjamin shuffling on his feet, as if he was now anxious to go.

"I should probably get back to work."

Often in life, you hark back to a moment and think, 'I wish I'd said that.' Saying the right thing at the right moment. Choosing the perfect epithet is a fine art and, as Benjamin began to make his way out the door, I said, "I won't tell Roz you were here."

Gotcha! Benjamin's face was a sloppy collage of emotions. Resting a sympathetic hand on Percy's huge shoulder, he muttered a weak, "Thank you" as he left, daring not to look back at my new security firm, Max!

Telling Roz about his impromptu appearance would have embarrassed him in a glorious variety of ways and my magnanimous gesture put us – dare I say it? – almost on an equal footing.

Yes, he was pissed off that his girl wanted to spend time with me but at least he knew that, should he choose, we could converse. On a scale of one to ten, what's worse? Losing the love of your life or staying friends with the love of your life knowing she's chosen someone else (and having to be cordial to that bastard!) Either way, Benji was about to endure a world of pain. Pain I wouldn't wish on any man but – sod it – it was nice to finally be chosen!

Percy was beginning to compose himself, become more upright. He had taken a large tissue out of his pocket and was starting to expunge some of the hurt from his nostrils.

He was gratefully taking huge breaths, clearing his throat, clearing his mind, mentally preparing himself for that ridiculous tail-between-your-legs moment.

"I suppose I should go and see her?" said Percy.

"Yes, you should," I said, frantically trying to remove the mental image of Percy mercilessly shagging my sister.

"And say I'm sorry?"

"I think," I began, clutching hopefully for some unchartered wisdom, "you need to say more than just, 'I'm sorry'. You need to tell her what you've told us. Tell her that your love for her is so strong ... it scares you! She'll like that!"

Percy nodded. "I will," he said. "I'll tell her. I have to be honest with her."

He found another clump of tissues in another pocket and honked loudly, clearing snot and confusion from his head. He had regained some colour in his face and a little of the eccentricity had returned to his eyes.

"She won't break my heart, will she?" he asked.

This really wasn't my field of expertise but my sister had been alone for decades and, having reached a certain age, the dating game was not next on her agenda. For Marie, to have a loving man walk into her life was literally like winning the lottery two Saturdays in a row! I didn't know much but I knew they'd be happy. There would be music, laughter and cake. Percy would take care of her and that made me happy.

"No, mate, I'm fairly certain she won't. She seems to really like you and, if you're happy to stay, she'll be happy to have you."

Percy gave us a weary, remorseful smile and nodded in acknowledgement.

Knowing my sister, she'd have the right cup of tea and the right piece of cake to make it all better.

Chapter Fourteen (Wednesday p.m.)

When I arrived at Mids' warehouse, he was wearing a pinny and waving a feather duster.

"What kind of kinky sex game is this?" I asked.

"Just trying to make the place tidy for your mates! Make a good impression?"

Bless him! Was it him being a good friend or him wanting to sell wine? Probably a bit of both?

Mids had invited Roz and her friends to this wine-tasting session at his warehouse, she and her friends had all accepted, so I had to assume they were curious to meet my circle? To socialise? It can't all have been about free drinks?

Or were they just doing it to pacify her? Were they all coming over to the warehouse so that Roz could have enough rope? I was tying my brain in negative knots. Young love was not supposed to be this way!

The guests were soon to arrive. I felt I had the measure of Benji, and Jill and Wendy seemed quite open-minded, so it was just Raymond and Heston that needed some work. It's not that I felt I needed a charm offensive, it just seemed strange that me and this house full of top minds couldn't make it work.

There had to be a way Roz could be my girlfriend and still be a member of that household! What really was the problem?

Roz's female housemates seemed seduced by the romance of unlikeliness. As Benji had said, Roz didn't do boyfriends. Added to that, I wasn't someone who had swept her off her feet. So, for those two reasons, I was a dark horse. A rank outsider. For some reason, Wendy and Jill seemed to like the fact that we were an unlikely pairing. Different backgrounds, different interests, different worlds. To them, it just seemed quirky and serendipitous, and they liked the fact that I was (almost) from the wrong side of the tracks.

From their stories, they seemed to be intimating that Roz's previous boyfriends had ticked almost all the boxes but had still turned out to be worthless shits, so they held out hope for someone who maybe didn't tick as many boxes (no offence taken!)

Yes, I was out of her league, but the girls liked that fact, and they liked the fact that I knew it too! What they didn't know was that I was loving my out-of-her-league-ness because, whatever league I was in, Roz liked it! And was willing to upset the status quo to get it!

Mids had really done a nice job with the warehouse! Every box was stacked neatly. There was a long table with a dazzling white tablecloth on it, there was an impressive selection of uncorked bottles to taste, lots of pristine glasses to drink from, a few ice buckets (for civilised spitting) and even the sinks had been given an extra splash of Mr. Muscle!

The first person to arrive was Roz. I was glad to see her! Not just because I was glad to see her, but because it felt right that we should greet our guests, like two parents thanking people for attending their son's bar mitzvah.

I hugged her tightly and it felt good. I didn't want to let go.

"Are you okay?" she asked.

"I missed you!" I said, in an uncharacteristic display of affection.

"Missed you too!"

"You still worried about this evening?"

"A little," she replied.

"Why?"

"My friends can be unpredictable. You never know what day it is!"

And right there was another of the differences between her mob and my mob. You could rely on my mates to be exactly the same, all day, all night. Yes, maybe they had too many die-hard habits? Maybe some of their chat-up lines were past their sell-by-date? But there were no mood swings or drunken tirades that might be regretted the morning after!

That's right: we had no idea what mood her housemates would be in. It could be laughter, banter and flirtation, or it could be accusations and recriminations. Fuelled by wine, anything could happen!

Wendy was the next to arrive. No surprise! I had a lot of time for nurses. I saw how they took care of my grandparents. If anyone deserved a lot of wine, it was Wendy. She embraced Roz, embraced me and I introduced her to Tony. He was very gracious and charming, and there was an instant connection between. I knew they'd get on fine.

Now, don't me wrong, I am not blonde-ist. I wouldn't lump them all in the same bag. Some do! I love them! There's nothing quite as upbeat as a blonde on form! Wendy was a classic blonde. Her mannerisms, the sound of her voice. It was almost like the hair shaped her personality, but there was nothing classically dumb about her. She was literally like a surgeon's scalpel, cutting deep through layers of pretence. She seemed to love the truth! She fed off it! No matter how painful.

Nurses need to be matter-of-fact to do their job and Wendy liked to strip the conversation back to the bare bones: the facts and the motive. At that first meeting, she'd not only asked questions but she'd pondered the reasons behind those decisions. It was like dining with your shrink!

As she'd done when we first met, she clung very tightly to me and acted like we were the couple and Roz was the outsider. Roz was well used to her antics.

I made chit-chat with Wendy, while her eyes followed Tony wherever he went. She seemed fascinated with the process and he, flirtatious as ever, kept winking at her.

"I think your friend likes me!" she said.

"He's very friendly!" I replied.

Tony F fondled a wine bottle very provocatively, while Wendy sucked her index finger deliberately. That friendship was off to a flying start!

Roz dragged me away to a quiet corner and whispered in my ear, "What happened with Percy?"

"He was in the shop today!"

"No!" she said.

"Turns out he's madly in love!"

"No!"

"I'll tell you the story later."

"I can't stop thinking about them!" said Roz.

That couple had definitely been on my mind too. Percy's performance in the shop was one that Max and I would never forget. He was clearly a sensitive man, maybe a touch too sensitive, but he adored my sister and, in a weird way, it was a huge weight off my mind. As long as those two were dancing and baking cakes, I could rest easy.

There was something pure and almost spiritual about their bond. Not sure I'd ever experienced something like that. I couldn't remember any of my relationships being that intense, not even Trish!

From the outside, their new relationship seemed quite simple. I envied that. Sex, dancing and cake. That's how it should be! Some folks like to over-think it. As if life is meant to be problematic! I didn't want my life to be a Rubik's Cube. I wanted it simple. It didn't look as if I was getting sex anytime soon, but the dancing and cake would be nice?

Mischievously, Wendy began sipping wine and soon began harassing Tony F, who was more than happy to be harassed!

Tony G the *maitre d'* bowled through the door, headed straight for Roz and made sure he got some sugar off her before saying anything to me. Roz virtually had to fight him off but she was laughing all over her face. "Your friends are affectionate, aren't they?"

"Aren't they just!" I replied.

Wendy was instantly at Low's side, assessing and sniffing.

Low looked to his right and there she was. He was used to female attention but this one seemed very enthusiastic.

"Wendy, this is Tony!"

"Two Tonys?" she asked.

"Yes, with one more to come!"

"Three Tonys?" she asked. "How do you tell them apart?"

"Oh, they're very different!" chimed Roz.

"Are we?" said Low.

"Very!" affirmed Roz, with a grin.

"They have nicknames! Tony T is yet to arrive. We call him Topper. Tony F is your host for the evening. We call him Midders or Mids for short. And this one to your left is Low," I said, motioning towards Tony G, who was now a bit perturbed by the willowy blonde wrapped around his torso.

"Funny nicknames!" said Wendy.

"Melvin will tell you the full story."

"Melvin?" asked Wendy.

"We call him Baggers because he's always carrying loads of bags!"

And, right on cue, Melvin arrived, carrying an Asda bag of groceries, a rucksack with gym gear, and an old record bag full of day-to-day stuff.

Suddenly, Wendy had a new toy to play with, so she left Low and went to greet Melvin. "Will you tell me about the nicknames?"

Melvin looked bemused. He hadn't even taken his jacket off or greeted anyone, and Wendy was up in his face asking questions and demanding answers. Polite as ever, Melvin began telling her about the T.I.T.

Raymond was the next to arrive. I hadn't really spent much time with him; not at the showcase, nor at their kitchen table, but I'd remembered his words from the showcase. "Don't take her away from me!" A clear view on our relationship and a virtual warning.

He embraced Roz, shook my hand and then shook Low's hand without saying a word. "Raymond," he eventually said, in that deep, Scottish brogue. Low nodded in typical, non-committal, male acknowledgement. Raymond couldn't even get to Wendy because she and Baggers were screaming with laughter.

"Three more to come," I shouted at Mids.

"Whenever you're ready!" he said, without looking up.

Raymond looked around him. We watched him smile. I knew from the showcase that he enjoyed his drink, so he was clearly looking forward to the evening. I could see him eyeing up the display of wine bottles!

Low decided to break the ice. "We haven't met. My name's Tony but they call me Low. What do you do?"

Raymond looked at Roz. Not sure why? Maybe he imagined that Roz had told us all about him.

"I'm a film maker," he said. "I made a short film about an Irish poet three years ago and, ever since then, I've been promoting it. In the last three years, I've attended about 40 different film festivals around the world, and that might sound like fun but it's not!"

This was way out of the realms of Low's experience. He knew little about the film world and less about poetry, but he did spend his day mixing with very wealthy people, so he knew how to conduct a conversation and gave exactly the right response; feeding the ego.

"Where can I see the film?"

"Ah," said Raymond, "that's the problem! Getting it shown in public is hard work!"

I squeezed Roz's hand and pulled her gently towards a quiet corner, leaving Low and Raymond to talk.

I didn't really have much to say, I just wanted to touch her and rub myself against her. I wrapped my arm around her waist and pulled her towards me.

"Careful!" she chided. "Don't get yourself excited!"

"I saw this article online today about waiting. You know … new couples waiting before doing it for the first time!"

Roz smiled. "Aww, are those balls getting blue?"

"Alright for you to say!"

"You shouldn't be reading those online articles! There's not much wisdom online, just opinions!"

It had only been a few weeks, I rationalised. Subconsciously, she was definitely allowing a time period to elapse, just to make sure I wasn't a hit-and-run. Yes, I'd finally hit the jackpot, and I was more than happy to undergo this rigorous interview process!

"What do you want from me?" I asked. Half expecting an answer but also attempting some rhetorical humour.

"Just be you, Wes."

Amazingly, the colourful girl just wanted me to be me. Trish had never been that impressed with me but this girl was!

"Am I late?" shouted Topper, as he walked briskly through the door.

"No!" shouted Mids from behind a pile of boxes.

Topper embraced Roz, then shook Raymond's hand.

"My name's Tony," he said to the one person that didn't know. "One of Wezza's oldest friends! And you are?"

"Raymond."

"One of the housemates?"

"Yes."

"Pleased to finally meet you!"

Raymond was a bit taken aback by Topper's bonhomie. In truth, Tops had been locked away in his workshop all day and was probably quite happy to talk to anyone. "We've been hearing all about you from Roz," he continued. "We're a fairly tight group but I couldn't imagine living with these guys!"

Again, Raymond looked at Roz. Did he need her to respond? He thought for a second, although thinking was quite difficult due to the high-volume hilarity occurring between Wendy and Melvin!

"We got on really well," Raymond finally replied. "I suppose it is quite unusual but we've all been living in that house for so long ... we've just got used to it. You know who the morning people are, you know not to engage them in conversation too early ..."

He smiled at Roz.

"You're not talking about me!" she protested.

Raymond rolled his head around his neck like a prize fighter, cocked his head to one side and suddenly looked quite melancholy. "You get used to people. You grow to like people."

Roz was smiling but she began to look a bit tearful.

"You grow to love people!" Raymond added, emphatically. "You grow to love people!"

There was clearly a lot of affection between Roz and Raymond. He was a big, strong man, but she'd probably seen his dark days and his weak days, and days when he wasn't so imposing and forceful.

Out of the corner of my eye, I could see Benjamin skulking through the front door, and he joined our group. He embraced Roz and Raymond and shook our hands.

"Benjamin, these are two of my friends, Topper and Low. That one behind me is Melvin, who we can't seem to tear away from Wendy."

Benjamin was still looking embarrassed and a bit sorry for himself. He'd obviously had time to reflect on his pitiful performance at the shop. I figured I'd have to get used to that hangdog face. Wherever Roz and I went, he would be there wishing it was him.

Desperate to keep the ice broken, Low continued talking, making small talk as we waited for Heston and Jill.

"I can vouch for this warehouse!" he began. "I work in the restaurant inside The Connaught Hotel, and our sommelier is a frequent customer, and not just coz Mids is my mate!"

"He fancies me!" shouted Mids from the other side of the warehouse. "That always helps!"

"So, we've brought you here not just to taste some new wines but also to meet you. Figure we'll be seeing you on a regular basis?"

There was a stony silence from Benjamin and Raymond which, in my books, was pretty damn rude!

Roz was anxious to keep it bright and breezy, so she began to contribute to the conversation.

"I don't think the guys are quite sure how this will work."

I could feel Benjamin and Raymond hanging on her words, anxious to see how she chose to resolve this delicate *coup d'etat*.

"Of course you'll all see each other. Two sets of great conversationalists. The debates will be epic! I can see us all chewing over current affairs until the early morn."

Low and Topper liked the sound of that. Raymond and Benjamin did not look convinced.

But some people don't like change? Just like the British aristocracy, why would they want to change anything? Living in that beautiful house with that unique alchemy, why would Raymond and Benjamin want to change anything? It wasn't me. There was no point taking it personally. It could be anyone that Roz brought home? They would resist them all.

Finally, Heston and Jill arrived at the same time and the evening could begin. We managed to drag Wendy and Melvin away from their conversation and Mids herded us into place. There wasn't much need for his lecture on etiquette, we'd all been here before.

Mids was truly a masterful master of ceremonies. He'd done this many times and, having been lectured by Low on customer service, he made the evening a real pleasure.

Naturally, Roz's friends had no desire to waste any wine at all, and I don't think I saw them spit out any but this didn't seem to impair their judgement. Mids immediately identified that Heston knew what he was doing, so they were getting on fine, Wendy and Melvin seemed to find everything funny, which just left Topper and Low dealing with the other three.

Benjamin was sinking slowly into depression, Raymond was quickly getting very drunk, while Jill stood on the outside, ensuring that everyone was well. Mids had laid on some delicious, designer crisps, but Jill had also brought some nibbles, to ensure that no one was drinking on an empty stomach.

"Oh, this is superb!" boomed Heston. "Very dry but very fruity. My taste buds are singing!"

"That's my favourite Merlot," said Mids. "I eat red meat just so I can drink it!"

"What do you think, Jilly?"

The wine was still in Jill's mouth and she was swilling it around thoughtfully. "I like it," she said.

Jill was the one with the purse strings. Jill was the one that handled the combined incomes and the collective shopping basket.

"Definitely a case of this!" Heston said.

"Yes, my love," replied Jill, patiently.

"Maybe two?"

Jill raised her eyebrows.

"Definitely two!" said Raymond.

Jill made a note on her phone and the tasting continued.

As I observed my friends attempting to mix with these strangers and engage them in wine-tasting small talk, I suddenly realised I had made a terrible mistake. It had been a bad idea. Yes, it had been Mids' idea but, if I'd had any brain cells at all, I would've vetoed the idea.

The atmosphere was tense and artificial, and I could see Low and Topper frantically pissing in the wind, trying to interact with these difficult people. No matter how her friends felt about me, or us, or my mates, common decency should have come into play. They fancied themselves as artists, academics and professionals, but where was the common decency?

"And what do you think, Wes?" said Raymond. "What do you think about this Merlot?"

I knew the confrontational moment was coming. I just didn't know where it would come from. This was Raymond putting me on the spot, seeing how much I knew. Roz could say nothing. She knew I had to fend myself.

I smiled at Raymond. I was holding all the aces. The previous night, I'd had Roz in my bed. True, I'd fallen asleep and fluffed my lines, but the colourful girl had escaped their clutches and come to me last night, so I was holding the winning hand.

"Something I learnt a while ago," I began, "there are some things I know a lot about, and some things I know nothing about. If I don't know about it, I listen to the experts. Now, my mate Mids is an expert, so I leave wine up to him.

"Some people," I continued, probably unnecessarily, "some people insist on having an opinion about everything, whether they know what they're talking about or not!"

Raymond looked deep into my eyes, probably trying to convey something profound like, "Who do you think you are, you jumped-up, little shit!" But all I could see was pain and wine. I didn't want to take his Roz away from him. I just wanted a girlfriend.

At this point, the mother hen Jill intervened. She definitely didn't want anything as undignified as bad blood. She couldn't bring chit chat to the table but she needed her boys to retain their dignity.

"Right, two cases of that Merlot, what else are we taking?"

Heston looked up and down the line and licked his lips.

"Two cases of this!" he said, tapping a bottle of Muscadet. "That will go lovely with my fish and chips!"

We wrapped-up the evening and said our goodbyes. All a bit sullen. All a bit stilted.

Wendy wrapped her arms around me. She was about four sheets to the wind. Her face red with all that laughter. "Thanks for organising this, Wes. I never would have met your beautiful friend. I always seem to get on well with gay men."

I'd heard what she'd said but it hadn't quite registered yet. I questioned myself. Had I heard right? Had she really said "gay"? I brushed it off. She must be mistaken?

The boys went their separate ways, the housemates went back to their house, and me and Roz went in search of a guilt-free takeaway. We were going back to mine for some TV and cuddles.

"Wendy thinks Melvin is gay!" I said.

"She's probably right. Loads of her mates are gay men. She's got a hospital full of male nurses."

I'd known Melvin for about 15 years. We'd been on holiday together, shared a bed together, we'd stayed up all night playing drinking games and strip poker with girls. We'd spent so much time together and I'd never known. How stupid was I? And how painful must that have been for him? He chased girls like a professional athlete! I'd seen him kiss women and grope women. He had me fooled!

Gay! Christ! How had we all missed that? Melvin was a very convincing actor. What should I do? Maybe he liked pretending to be straight?

"What?" said Roz. "None of you knew?"

Pathetic. No. None of us had picked up on it.

"What do I do? If I tell him I know, it might affect our friendship?"

"So what's he going to say to Wendy? 'Don't tell my mates that I'm gay.'"

I felt wretched. I felt insensitive. I felt ignorant. I was now reliving my whole friendship with Baggers. All the things I'd said, all the things I'd done, and all the gay jokes I'd told!

In a weird kind of way, I could feel my own group of friends unravelling. I didn't give a monkey's who Melvin slept with but a group of straight guys behave like a group of straight guys. It was a straight guy lifestyle with a straight guy dynamic. How long would Melvin want to live like that?

Roz was too busy to worry about that. She had a mouthful of burger and there was chilli sauce dripping down her face!

"Come on," she said. "We can watch 'Empire' and then, if you're very good, I'll let you massage my feet!"

Chapter Fifteen (Thursday)

I remembered to get provisions and stopped in at the local supermarket. My mad, little shop seemed to be getting busier. Not necessarily with custom but definitely with drama! Who knew what would happen today?

It was only when I put the new biscuits in the biscuit tin that I realised we needed a new biscuit tin. Everything needed upgrading and updating.

Finally! A full carton of fresh milk in the fridge! We had biscuits, we had beverages! We were ready for any eventuality! Would it be my ex? Would it be my future? Would it be Roz's interfering friends? Or would another bus driver stride through the door and declare his love for my sister?

While I waited for something to happen, I browsed DJ equipment web sites. Enviously looking at beautiful devices I could never afford! Those new gizmos sure looked bright and shiny! More buttons, more lights.

Part of my brain was thinking about new developments in DJ gear, while the other part was thinking about my mate Melvin. I'd never been here before and truly didn't know what to do! Of course I knew gay people! You can't work in dance music and not know gay people, but how come I didn't know one of my oldest friends was gay? Not that it mattered! I just wasn't sure what to do!

Who to turn to? I'd asked Roz for enough advice; I wasn't going to call her again, Max was of no use, Marie's brain was still in Percyville and, as for the rest of my crew, I hadn't even told them Baggers was gay! THAT was going to be an interesting conversation!

At that moment, Trish came through the front door. Perfect timing! I would ask Trish for advice. I didn't want to backtrack but – damn it – this was an emergency!

Max was pleased to see her! She'd been like an older sister to him. They embraced.

"Where have you been?"

"Long story, Maxi. I'll tell you one day!" She looked him up and down. "You don't look like a scrawny kid anymore!"

"What do I look like?" he asked.

"It's only been six months, but you look grown up!"

Max blushed. "I'm gonna be a pirate radio DJ!" he said, proudly.

"Perfect!" said Trish.

"They've taken my photo and everything!"

I watched them interact. She'd known Max from his first day on the job. She'd known him from when he couldn't even talk to customers! Now, he was a bona fide cheeky chappy, giving the female customers shy smiles and single-handedly stopping the shop from looking like a place where old DJs go to die!

Trish turned to me. "I was thinking," she began. "This shop could do with a kick up the arse! More gear! New gear! New services!"

I smiled. "I was thinking the same thing!"

And I suddenly remembered why I'd liked Trish so much! When she wasn't with me, she still thought about me, and she'd demonstrated it time and time again. I'd have a problem, she'd go away and come back with a solution. We'd have a conversation, she'd go away and come back with a new perspective. I was always in her thoughts. Not out of sight, out of mind. Almost as if she carried me in her pocket wherever she went?

"As it happens, I'm glad you're here."

"Oh?" she asked.

Where to begin? After all those years of friendship, I was still in shock. I didn't even know how to formulate the words.

"What is it?" she prodded.

I hadn't even told her about Roz, or Roz's friends, or last night! So, to save myself all that back story (and all the questions that would follow), I just spat it out.

"Melvin's gay!"

Trish looked unphased. "Not surprised!"

"Really?"

"Always smart, loves shopping, able to multi-task, loves bags: makes sense!"

Christ, why hadn't I noticed that? Trish had noticed, of course! For so many years, this is the woman I had virtually idolised. She noticed everything!

"So, what should I do?"

I was asking Trish that question again. Those same five words. How could she possibly love a man who kept turning to her for advice? No wonder she'd drifted away and wandered off! Unless I could find the decisiveness and *chutzpah* to solve my own problems, Roz would follow her!

Trish looked at me and waited for me to answer my own question. The rusty cogs in my brain began to turn.

"I need to speak to him, right?"

Trish just kept looking at me. Of course this was the right answer! I'd seen that look before. For years, Trish had been waiting for me to think. Not just react; to actually think and respond in the right way. Count to ten and let the magic happen!

I quickly got on the phone to Baggers and made an arrangement to see him that evening. He was curious to know why but I fobbed him off with "a delicate relationship issue." This intrigued him greatly. He fancied himself as an agony aunt.

"Well done!" said Trish, trying not to sound patronising, but a grown man making his first major decision at the age of 37 was pretty pathetic. "And what will you say?"

I looked at her blankly. Again, I could hear those rusty cogs turning in my brain. The solution was in there. Somewhere.

"I'll ask him what he wants to do. He may want to keep it to himself?"

Trish nodded. "You've changed!"

"I have?"

"Yes," she said. "You used to lean on me for every decision, every answer."

"You're smarter than me!"

"Don't do that, Wes! That self-deprecating stuff! That is your least attractive quality!"

Wow! Not quite a dagger to my heart but naked, unadorned truth. That's what a good dose of the truth will do for you: it will blow through your system like a course of laxatives!

My least attractive quality! That's really what I wanted to hear: my least attractive quality!

I looked at her with one raised eyebrow. "Not my second least? My rock bottom least attractive quality? Really, Trish?"

"While I've been away, I've been thinking."

I was very happy for her. If she'd been fishing, I'd have been mightily disappointed!

"And?"

"You've got some good qualities. And you're not stupid!"

That was high praise from a woman I'd idolised, a woman I'd invested in, and a woman who'd buggered off without warning, leaving me wondering if there was something drastically wrong with me!

This was high praise from a woman who had been very short on praise. In fact, it had been a praise-less relationship! She'd been so busy tutting, raising her eyebrows and shaking her head in dismay, she'd forgotten how to acknowledge my good points.

True, I was not a gushing faucet of goodness and great ideas every day, but those few words from her were the best I'd had in ages!

Why had she returned? Why had she come back into my life? It had been six months of silence with no explanation. Surely she didn't want to reconcile? That would just be too tragic and too funny, especially as I'd just found this very hot and very colourful girl who had taken me to a naturist spa!

Her response was so shocking and patronising, all I could say was, "Would you like a cuppa?"

"That would be nice?" she replied.

And so, with my fresh milk, I was able to make us all tea, and I even brought out our battered old biscuit tin so everyone could have a dunk!

As we sat around drinking tea and making small talk, I was reminded of Roz's friend Benjamin a few days ago, shuffling around our shop, unable to really express himself; unable to say all the stuff that was on his mind. I'd had to shock him into speaking and it looked as if I would have to do the same to Trish, even though she'd already spent the whole of Monday night beating around the bush!

"I hope you don't mind me asking," I finally said, "but why are you here? Why have you come back? I'd just got used to you being gone!"

And now it was her turn to be speechless, almost flustered. As she sipped nervously on her tea, it was her turn to tax her brain.

She was fidgeting in her seat and twisting her hair (but not in a suggestive way) and I could see her heart rate increase as she attempted to justify her actions. It gave me no pleasure to watch her stutter and stumble. Alright ... maybe just a little?

"Perspective," I suppose. "I needed perspective."

"Don't let me break up the party!" boomed Mids, as he strolled through the door.

It's was always nice to see him but – damn it - I was just about to get some answers from Trish! Mids grabbed hold of her and almost dragged her off her seat! "Fuck me, Trish! Where have you been? You're looking good!"

"Thank you!" she blushed. "I just needed some time away."

"Six months?" he exclaimed. "Blimey! That's a jail sentence! Get the kettle on, Wezza!"

I made Mids some tea while he and Trish caught up on old times. I would have to wait until he'd gone. I was curious to hear Trish's tall tale. I wanted to know why she left, where she'd been and why she'd come back. This tall story would have to be bloody entertaining!

I didn't need volatile behaviour. I liked things smooth. No, actually, I liked them smoooth! Need that extra 'O' for extra smooothness! I didn't want up and down. I wanted consistency. Did that make me OCD like my sister?

From inside the kitchen, I could hear the two of them laughing. I stood there and paused. Today would be a day of truth and getting people to face their future. I was a long way from boozy backrooms playing 80s cheese to blushing brides. This was proper, grown-up stuff!

I brought Mids his tea and he was looking sheepish. Trish was smiling all over her face.

"Sorry, Wezza, I didn't know Trish didn't know about Roz!"

"She sounds interesting!" said Trish, although she had no idea how 'interesting' she was!

"No worries, matey. I'll fill Trish in when you leave. So, to what do we owe the pleasure?"

Mids triumphantly placed a vintage-looking bottle of wine on my counter. There was still dust on it! "Save this for a special occasion!" he said. "Serve it with steak; it will bring out the flavour of each!"

"What's this for?"

"Just a thank you," he replied. "Roz's mates came through with a sizeable order! Sizeable! They're having a party this Saturday, right?"

"They are!" I said. "And they love to drink! I'm playing the music but I'm dreading it! They're hostile as it is!"

Trish's face was trying to process all this information. "Hostile?"

I looked at Mids; he shrugged his shoulders. There was a lot Trish didn't know, but did she really need to know everything. She'd disappeared for six months. Did I really owe her anything?

"This Roz," he began, "lives in a big house with five other people. Cool people. Professional people. And they've known each other since university. And they all decided to live together!"

Trish wasn't quite understanding. "How old are they?

Tony looked at me. "Late thirties?"

I nodded.

"Late thirties," Tony continued, "and they're all still living together. Six single, middle-aged people, all living together in this old house up Highgate Hill. Weird, huh?"

"Very!" said Trish, looking at me, as if I'd chosen to date the most deranged inmate in the institution.

"And this Roz girl has decided she wants to date old stroppy bollocks here!"

Trish looked at me again. Waiting for me to add some detail. Very little of this was adding-up and she needed to know how I felt.

"The rest of the house are NOT happy!" Mids concluded. "She's breaking up the band!"

Finally, Trish was up to speed. She smiled to herself and gobbled the rest of her biscuit. "Well," she said, "breaking up is hard to do."

Mids finished his tea and went back to work. Trish sat on a stool in my shop, looking at me (that look again!) while Max sat behind the counter, answering enquiries, totally disinterested in the relationship nonsense Trish and I were discussing.

"So, Wes? Tell me about Roz?"

Did I really owe her an explanation? Did I really owe her anything! The more I thought about it, the more irritated I became. Six months. No contact. No word. Nothing! I knew the relationship wasn't going well. I knew we were drifting apart but, I suppose, I was shocked and offended when she upped and disappeared! Where had she gone?

Because I was the easy-going Wes, because I was Mr. Soft, Mr. Simple, Mr. No-Frills-No-Fuss, I just got on with my life, as if a butterfly had flown out of my window, but it still hurt. Yes, it hurt! There I said it! It hurt! I knew ours wasn't some kind of rocket-fuelled, sex-injected, full-on passionate romance, but it was my romance and it suited me and, when she left, I had missed her. There I said it! I had missed her. Bed's too big without you and all that!

So, did I really owe this woman an explanation? Not really, but I was going to give her every pertinent detail, to let her know that somebody appreciated me!

So, I began my story. I'd only known Roz two weeks. Christ, it had only been two weeks and already my entire life had been turned on its head! This relationship came with a lot of baggage, a lot of drama and a healthy dose of conflicting emotions!

I told her about me falling asleep in a doorway, the brunch with Roz the next day. I told her about the waxing, the showcase, the engagement party, the naturist spa, the house on the hill and the wine-tasting. It had only been two weeks but it was a good story!

Roz and I hadn't had sex yet. That was the crucial and unbelievable detail Trish probably wanted, but I wasn't going to ask her about her last six months, so she would have to be left wondering. Roz and I took some believing! No, the first sexual encounter still hadn't occurred! And it didn't matter. It almost added to the mystique?

Trish sat and listened. In fact, the story went on so long, she got up to make us both another cup of tea! She sat, and listened, and smiled and nodded. I wondered what she was thinking?

I couldn't really calculate what she was thinking because I didn't know why the crazy girl had come back! If Trish was totally, 100% over me, she would be thinking, "Ah, that's nice! Wes has found himself a new girlfriend!"

What if she was looking to reconcile? Christ, if she was looking to get back with me, that would be comedy! Two gorgeous women fighting over a nerdy twerp like me? No, it wouldn't be comedy, it would be tragedy!

I was growing impatient. She began asking questions about Roz and I. She wanted to know how I felt. She wanted to know how Roz felt. She wasn't wishing me good luck for my future. She was trying to gauge my status.

Was I fully involved or was I just dipping my toe?

And, right there, I had my answer. Unbelievably, this woman, who had disappeared from my life, from my area, without an explanation or even a goodbye, was now sitting before me wanting to pick up where we had left off. She wanted to press the pause button on her old cassette player and hear me sing the next line of the same song.

This was all doing my head in. Dealing with Roz on a daily basis was eventful enough, but now Trish was back! Trish with all her new coyness! This is why I didn't want to be single; I liked my life to be smoooth!

Trish was doing this evasive tap dance in the middle of my shop, asking me questions about my friendship with Roz and trying to calculate if the friendship was built on strong foundations or soon to crumble. In truth, I could shed no light on the matter, as Roz was still trying to placate the different personalities in her house.

It felt cruel trying to get an answer out of Trish. She was bravely holding on to her dignity and it seemed unnecessary to force the words out of her mouth. I now had my answer. I knew why she was here on my doorstep. After a six-month sabbatical, this woman wanted to re-start our engine. A car engine left dormant for six months will sometimes start? Sometimes not.

It actually looked as if Trish was trying to secrete herself back into my life without anyone noticing. Insane as it sounds, she seemed to be hoping that, without uttering a word, without offering any kind of excuse, she could just plonk herself back in the middle of my life!

After a few hours of going around the houses, Trish made her excuses and left. I'm not sure if she'd heard the answers she was hoping for but, as she left, she still seemed affectionate. We made a very vague plan to speak soon but what else was there to say? She'd left without a word and, six months later, I'd moved on. Simple.

Max and I shut up shop and I headed off to see Baggers. I loved this geezer. I really did. So kind, so supportive, so generous. He always made sure I got home safely, no matter how pissed I was! He always made sure there wasn't a huge dollop of tomato sauce on my shirt. He always made sure my glass was full and that I never went without.

I couldn't imagine my life without him. All I wanted to do was make sure everything stayed the same. I didn't want a damn thing to change!

I needed Melvin's input. I needed to know what he wanted to do. Would it matter that I knew? Would it matter if we all knew?

This grown-up shit was hard work! What would I say to him?

Baggers and I met in one of our favourite bars. A noisy, woody, cowboy-themed establishment screening old rodeos and banging out classic, twangy rock. Why was it special? Probably because they made some pretty authentic burritos? I think there must have been a Mexican in the kitchen?

We hugged each other, as we normally did, and we got ourselves two bottles of Dos Equis to get things started.

Melvin had his normal selection of bags: a rucksack, a record bag (containing no records), one Alexander McQueen bag containing a pair of shoes in a box and a small bag of household cleaning products.

"So?" said Melvin, excitedly. "What's up? Everything okay with Roz? Wow, she's got some wicked friends! That Wendy is absolutely outrageous! Properly outrageous! She's a nurse, right, and you know they don't give a damn!"

"I had dinner with her!" I said. "When she began going into detail about vasectomies, I had to hide under the table!"

"We're going for drinks tomorrow night! She's got some leaving do! More nurses!"

I sipped at my bottle of beer and tried to compose myself. I was taking exaggerated deep breaths, which made it seem as if I was distressed and having major relationship issues with Roz.

"So, talk to me, Wes? What's going on? Is it all going well?"

I felt deceitful. He was such a warm, genuine guy and I'd led him there on false pretences. He looked concerned for me and I didn't need him to be. I had two gorgeous women both wanting to date me. Yeah, go figure!

"On Wednesday, you met Wendy for the first time ..."

I paused. I could see Melvin looking puzzled, wondering where I was going with this.

"Yes?"

"And, when she was saying her goodbyes, she came over and told me how much she'd enjoyed meeting you and what a lovely guy you were ..."

Melvin was still not really seeing how this related to my relationship woes.

"Yes? And?"

"And Wendy said, 'I always get on really well with gay men!'"

Melvin froze in horror and bowed his head. He couldn't even look at me. We paused for what seemed like an eternity, while Melvin just stared at the floor. I'd had the words to come this far but I didn't have any more. I didn't know how to comfort, how to pacify, how to rectify this situation.

I wasn't sure I knew what I could or couldn't say. There was just silence, as Melvin stared at his feet, too afraid or too ashamed or too embarrassed to look at me.

I had to break the silence. This was getting silly. This was my mate. We'd always been able to talk about anything.

"Baggers, it doesn't matter to me!" I blurted out.

He looked up at me. His eyes were a bit red where he'd tried but failed to cry.

"Seriously, mate" I continued, "it doesn't matter to me. Why would it?"

Melvin just looked at me, sadly, as if the party had come to a screeching halt and everyone had to go home.

"It doesn't matter to me," I said. "Nothing will change between you and me. Why should it? We'll still do what we do and go where we go. You'll still carry a million bags and we'll still take the piss out of you. You'll still organise everything, like you do, and we'll all still have a right good laugh! All I want to know is what you want to tell the boys?"

Melvin still hadn't spoken. This charismatic, effusive boy was still silent.

"We'll do whatever you want to do," I added.

Pain and regret were etched all over his face as, like me, he thought about all the amazing experiences we'd shared together; many, many years of beer swilling, belching and farting, testosterone-drenched, typical, macho nonsense and, for some weird reason, Melvin thought it was about to change.

"I can't tell them," he finally said. "Not yet."

"That's fine," I said.

"That's it?" he said.

"That's it. Just wanted to know what you wanted to do!"

Baggers was shaking his head and trying to start a sentence, and not really forming any words, just mumbling. I grabbed his hand and squeezed it. He looked at our hands locked together and looked up at me. I squeezed his hand tighter to let him know I meant business. "Baggers, it's going to be fine. Nothing, nothing, nothing will change. I promise you. I faithfully promise we will still tell terrible jokes about gay people. I faithfully promise nothing will change."

He smiled at me and I could see he was going to be okay. The panic had left his eyes. He had started to breathe and function again.

"You're a top bloke, Wezza! A really top bloke!"

"So your mum keeps telling me!"

He smiled and squeezed my hand.

"I'm sorry," he said. "I should have told you."

"I don't want anything to change!" I added. "I love what we have!"

"I guess that's how they feel in Roz's house?"

He was right, but we'd all have to find a way to adapt and refine. That's what real friends do: adapt and refine.

Chapter Sixteen (Friday)

I'd barely known the man a few days but already I knew far too much about Percy.

I'd seen him dressed in his uniform, I'd seen him in his Y-fronts, I'd seen him dance, I'd seen him strut around like a peacock in my sister's kitchen, I'd seen him fall to his knees and weep, and I'd listened to him declare his undying love for a woman. The only thing I hadn't witnessed was childbirth but, with Percy, anything was possible!

He'd expressed a desire to DJ, I knew I could get him work, I'd promised to get him work and, in a world of so little honour, I felt duty-bound to pass on this job I'd been given.

Within 48 hours, this lanky fool had turned my already fragile sister into a jibbering wreck but, hopefully, by now, they'd patched things up and returned to their happy co-existence of bonking and baking. (Jesus, those mental images of Percy and Marie had taken up residence in my brain and just wouldn't move out!)

I'd invited him to the shop to talk about the gig and, punctual as ever, he parked up his bus at the garage and took his 11.00 coffee break with me.

Percy and Max gave each other a nod and a fist bump, and he presented me with a large cup of Costa coffee. This plastic cup of frothy something was huge and threatened to strain my wrist, so I put it on the counter. Percy settled himself on a stool to listen to the brief.

"This is a very nice couple I've worked with before."

Percy nodded.

"Very easy-going people. Love to drink and, once they've had a few, they like to dance. This is their friend's 50th. Stick to the brief and you can't fail!"

Percy nodded.

"The secret," I began, "is knowing how old they were in their clubbing years. They're 50, they were clubbing 30 years ago, so we're talking the mid-eighties. They'll be happy with 'Relax' and 'Don't You Want Me Baby' but don't play 'I'm In The Mood For Dancing' or Kelly Marie's 'Feels Like I'm In Love'."

Percy nodded.

"They're rock people more than soul people, so you can also give it some 'Living On A Prayer', 'Town Called Malice' and 'Heart Of Glass'. And even some recent, retro-sounding stuff like Kings Of Leon?"

Percy nodded.

"You sure you're getting this?" I asked.

Percy nodded again. "Seems straightforward."

"Try to play requests. It's a good look. If somebody wants something, look for it, even if you don't have it! Let them know you take their request seriously. If the request seems off-piste, then run it by the birthday girl first."

Percy nodded vigorously, as if he agreed with my point wholeheartedly.

"And, if possible, sing along and dance to the tunes you're playing!"

Percy looked at me quizzically. "Really?"

"If you're not enjoying them, why should they?"

Percy nodded again. "Makes sense."

It was a simple brief. Easy to follow. Percy couldn't screw it up! I knew he'd be there on time; all he had to do was keep in his lane.

"Oh and finally ..."

Percy took a long and luxurious slurp from his plastic bucket and licked the froth from his lips.

"If you can mix, all well and good but, if you can't, don't try! Nothing worse than beats crashing!"

"I can't mix!" said Percy, nervously.

"That's fine," I said. "Just be good at what you're good at."

Percy was smiling and there was a vague smirk of confidence on his lips. "I can do this!"

"I know you can, mate!"

There was little more to say. He knew our motto. His mission was to make people dance. If a DJ can't do that, then he might as well hang up his headphones!

Right, that was the first part of the conversation over. Managed to navigate that tricky slope! Now, we had to deal with the murky stuff: feelings, relationships, etiquette, behaviour, timing, trust, support. This was NOT my specialist field and yet I felt the need to have a quiet word in Percy's shell-like, just to keep him from coming off the rails again.

"My sister," I began, "and she hasn't asked me to say anything ..."

"Yes?" said Percy, wearily, as if he'd had his ear chewed-off and spat in his face by my sister.

"I don't want to come off like the over-protective brother ..."

"Wes, I promise you, you don't need to say anything. I'm not a young man. I grew up in the sixties, so I'm far from being young! I've known a lot of girls and women. Not saying I've slept around! That's not really me. But I've known a lot of women. They talk to me! They like talking to me!"

He paused. Trying to find the right words. Somehow, no words were right. No words could truly illuminate the shining beacon that was my sister.

"Your sister ..."

He shook his head and waved his finger like some doddery old rabbi trying to make sense of a passage in his holy book.

"Your sister ..."

He was struggling.

Finally, triumphantly, he found the words! He found the few words that would accurately reflect his circumstances.

"After all this time and after all those women," he shrugged his shoulders like a market trader feigning offense at your bartering skills, "you know when it's right! You KNOW when it's right!"

Percy now looked very pleased with himself, as if he'd summarised the meaning of life into a handy catchphrase! He took another lengthy and potentially dangerous slurp of his coffee, and sat back looking very pleased with himself. "You know when it's right ... and it is."

"So, what was the breakdown about?"

Percy looked a bit shame-faced and I could see his body retreat within itself. Not only was his tail between his legs but much of his dignity too!

"I was scared! It was a scary feeling. To feel that vulnerable!"

Max could only look on and speculate about Percy's feelings. Max had experienced lust and crushes, he'd probably done his fair share of fumbling and fingering by now, but this stuff that Percy was talking about? Even I was having trouble grasping it! This was real and true love. My sister and this very tall bloke were about to become an item. He would be at my Christmas table forever!

Percy returned to an old theme, "Nothing before its time! My God!" He slapped his thigh like a country singer about to launch into his signature song. "I never thought I would find someone like your sister. It's nothing to do with her. It's not like she's anything ... no offence ... it's not like she's anything special! But, when we get together ..."

Again, that grotesque mental image of Percy and my sister!

"When we get together," he continued, "we make the perfect couple! She plus me is something really magical!"

He sounded like Julie Andrews telling us about a spoonful of sugar! Max and I were dumbfounded. Every time Percy came into our shop, it was some kind of dramatic performance. It was almost as if he were incapable of sitting still and being normal.

"I'm just worried about my sister," I said.

"I understand, Wes, truly I do! It caught me unawares. I wasn't expecting it."

I was hearing Percy and I understood what he meant but he was talking about some kind of chemical reaction beyond the realms of my experience. Trish had provided me with a real, live, supportive bosom; love, warmth, security. Good, wholesome stuff but not the destructive kind of whirlwind Percy was describing. This was a coughing and spluttering, lethal injection kind of love. This was bringing bilious fear to the back of his throat!

"You can't bugger off and go walkabout, Percy!"

Percy raised his hand like an evangelist about to spin some fresh falsehood, "I'm good. I'm ready. It's scary but I'm ready!"

Not much more I could say. He seemed full of conviction. He seemed to be speaking with such sincerity. It was a curious sound (rarely heard in these parts) but, if he planned to keep that smile on my sister's face, he could stay!

Max looked at me mystified. Like me, he could hear what Percy was saying but it just made no sense. Nevertheless, even Max, with his unevolved heart and his patchy knowledge of the female psyche could appreciate the soul in Percy's croaky voice. "You must really love her!" he said.

"I do," said Percy, "I do."

How had my humble DJ equipment shop turned into a hairdressing salon full of troubled people and their emotional issues?

Once we'd shut-up shop, I headed home. There was nothing in my calendar, so I was looking forward to catching-up with some TV but, more importantly, I needed a little time just to stop and think. There was a huge amount of information in my head. Well, much more than usual. Even though I was mentally exhausted and prone to doze off at any moment, I'd gone from being a pussy-whipped wimp to being The Dalai Lama. Suddenly, people were consulting me and I was counselling others with my home-baked remedies.

As I approached my front door, I could see not one but two people sitting on the little wall outside my terraced house. "Cheeky bleeders!" I thought to myself but, as I approached, I realised it was not only Roz but Trish as well.

A million conflicting emotions. Blind panic. Should I run? No, not a good look! Whatever happened, this evening would not end well. I knew that.

I looked down at the two of them. They looked up at me.

"This has become quite a popular park bench!"

"Thought I'd surprise you!" said Roz.

"Sorry," said Trish. "I needed to talk."

"It's alright," said Roz, chirpily. "I was here, so she's talked to me!"

My heart sank. Roz now knew that Trish was home and sniffing around.

"Have you now?" I replied, desperately trying to put on a brave face, and quickly formulating answers in my head.

I shuffled clumsily on two uncertain feet. I wasn't sure whether to invite them in or give Trish a rain check!

Roz was smiling, as ever. Not bothered by my discomfort. Not bothered by Trish. Compared to the high emotions and high decibels in her house, Trish was a peaceful walk in the park.

"Should we?" I motioned, ushering them towards my front door.

God, how ironic was this? I'd gone from boring homebod to polygamist in six months. I'd gone from being Trish's other half to being the sharp end of a love triangle! Not that I could imagine Roz fighting over me; I was cute but not that cute!

We all went into the kitchen to make ourselves snacks and drinks. It wasn't a big kitchen, so we were all side-stepping and bumping into one another; a quite ridiculous piece of modern ballet, gracefully trying not to spill our drinks.

"So," I began, "what have you girls been talking about?"

No response from either of them. Great! More tap dancing!

"Trish has been telling me about the last six months. It must have been difficult?"

Oh, really? I thought to myself. What was so difficult? Thinking? Shopping? Spending time with other men? I hadn't asked her questions about the last six months. All I'd heard was her standard response: she'd needed some time to think.

"I've had pregnancy scares too!" said Roz.

I froze. "What?" I said in my head. "Stay calm, Wezza!" I needed to compose myself very quickly.

It reminded me of a stupid teenage Wes, who'd decided to take half a tab of acid one evening. In the middle of giggling and hallucinations, my mother had called with some family emergency involving my cousin! Jeez, I had to put the brakes on hard! Like trying to stop piss in mid-flow!

I went from a pleasant post-work buzz to quite the most traumatic words I'd heard since the death of my parents. I had to come down from that high very quickly!

'Pregnancy scare': what did it mean? She was pregnant or not? She'd almost lost the baby or not?

I turned round very slowly and, as calmly as I could, looked into Trish's eyes. "Pregnancy?" I asked.

"Oops!" said Roz, looking crestfallen. "I am so sorry. You didn't know."

"No, I didn't know."

Trish was having trouble looking at me. She fiddled nervously with her hot cup of tea and slice of cake, and eventually put them on the side.

"Should I go?" Roz asked.

I looked into her eyes and, trying to convey the severity of the situation and how much I needed her calming influence, I said, "No, please stay!"

Roz looked unsure, then said, "Why don't I take my laptop upstairs and do some work? Give you kids some space?"

"Thanks," said Trish, exhaling and heading into the front room.

Collecting up my bowl of hot soup and slices of crusty bread, I joined Trish in the front room and sat looking at her. Again, she was struggling with her words but, now that her cover had been blown, she had little reason to be hesitant, other than sheer embarrassment.

"I'm sorry, Wes!"

"What for?"

"For running away!"

"Were you pregnant?"

"No," she said, sadly. "I thought I was, but I wasn't."

"You needed time to think? About what?"

Trish sipped at her tea and broke off a tiny piece of cake to fortify herself. She spoke slowly and very softly. I ate quietly to make sure I caught every word! This would be a story worth hearing!

"When I thought I might be pregnant ... I wasn't happy! And I thought to myself, that can't be good! If I was happy in my relationship, I'd be happy to be pregnant!"

I listened patiently. Making sure I followed her logic accurately. I knew our relationship hadn't been good but we'd always muddled through. I knew that Trish found me useful but unspectacular, I knew I wasn't as dynamic as she'd like but we always managed to share a good evening, and making love always made us smile, so I thought everything was okay? Obviously not!

"When I couldn't be happy about being pregnant, I thought, this is all wrong! I should be thrilled!"

"So you ran?"

"So ... I ran!"

Fortunately, my Country Vegetable soup tasted delicious. I particularly loved the peas! Reminded me of the fat, juicy peas my Nan used to serve for Sunday dinner, fresh from my grandfather's garden.

I was trying hard to approach this new twist from a mature point of view, taking Trish's feelings into account, trying hard to feel sorry for her and her predicament, but I was struggling with that because she'd just told me I wouldn't have made a good father!

She'd run away and had her six months of soul-searching and now, here she was, in my front room, with my girlfriend up in my bedroom, sniffing around to see if there was any hope of reconciliation. Never in my wildest dreams had I imagined this. Some of those nights during that six months had been pretty cold and lonely. Not knowing where she was. Not knowing how she felt. And here she was! Innocently enquiring if I could kindly forget about the last six months and just pick up where we left off!

"So, what changed?"

"I think I missed you," she said, matter-of-factly.

I'd never heard anyone say that before. I'd heard them say they'd missed the bus, or breakfast, or their childhood pet but never me.

"You missed me?" I asked, hoping for some kind of clarification.

"I just missed our rhythm. I missed our routine. I missed ... us!"

Trish pulled off another piece of cake and sipped at her tea again. She looked around her conspiratorially and lowered her voice even further. She didn't want Roz to hear. "But it looks as if your situation has changed?"

I plunged another piece of crusty loaf into my delicious soup and pulled the soggy mess into my mouth. Yes, my situation had changed but it was far from secure. Dealing with Roz's friends was like dealing with a rogue terrorist group. We might meet their demands but they might move the goalposts?

Who knew if I was dating Roz? It was dating after a fashion but the twelve angry men were still deliberating! I wasn't going to let Trish know the minute details of my insane dating dilemma. I was going to let her twist in the wind a little while longer. The last six months had not been pleasant. I had been so depressed, I couldn't even be bothered to stay awake!

"Yes, my situation has changed!" I said, with as much confidence as I could muster. I wanted her to think that I was madly in love and enjoying raucous sex on an hourly basis. Though this was far, far from the truth. All I really had was the vague promise of much ... but little else.

"I see," said Trish, bravely.

Even though I was not seething but simmering with anger at Trish for buggering-off, and even though I was still reeling from her assumption she could just waltz back into my life six months later, and even though I was still smarting from being told I'd make a poor father, I felt sorry for her. I genuinely did.

She finished off her cake and drank the last of her tea.

"Poor timing," she concluded. "Maybe I should have left you a note?"

"A note would have been nice!"

She got up to leave and brushed cake crumbs off her top on to my floor. "Sorry!" she said.

"I'll Hoover at the weekend," I replied.

She paused and looked around her, as if it was the last time she'd ever see my little house. "Still friends?"

I shook my head. "Stupid question!"

She smiled. "You've changed! Maybe I was wrong?"

"Maybe I <u>will</u> make a good father?"

Trish now felt really foolish. She'd left town with so much conviction.

"Why wouldn't I make a good father?"

"The boys!" she began. "Your lifestyle. You didn't seem to be growing up. I couldn't picture you as a father. When I thought I was pregnant and thought of us bringing up a child, I couldn't see you being around! However, I could see you in a nightclub, several sheets to the wind, laughing at Low's crap jokes."

"I'm a good friend," I began. "I'm a good man, I'm a good friend, and I will make a good father. Me and my kids will be good friends. I appreciate love and I appreciate friendship!"

What were these words coming out of my mouth? I was unrecognisable. Trish looked at me wondering where the timid and transient Wes had gone.

"You've changed!" she repeated.

She gathered up her coat and bag.

"You'd better get upstairs. Roz came to see you."

A brief peck on my cheek and she disappeared down the road.

She'd left suddenly. She'd left no note. She hadn't given me a second thought, really, until she began to miss me! She'd treated me like an absent father. I shouldn't have felt sorry for her but I did.

When I got upstairs, Roz was asleep on my bed, her laptop still on and open beside her. I gently placed it on top of my chest of drawers, covered us both with my bed cover and turned off the light. Passionate sex would have to wait.

Chapter Seventeen (Saturday)

"Smashed it! Absolutely smashed it!" said Max, swaggering into the shop.

From somewhere, he'd grown an inch taller and even his shoulders looked broader.

"Smashed what?"

I immediately pictured one of our new CDJs crushed under the huge wheels of a Jeep.

"Did my first radio show!"

I breathed a sigh of relief. "It went well?"

"People were calling me, texting me, they were on Twitter, Facebook, Instagram. People listened!"

Even Max's speech patterns were different. There was less stuttering, shorter pauses. He sounded more confident.

"A pirate radio station?"

"101.1. Cool, huh? And online!"

"Ah, the worldwide web!"

"Worldwide?" he asked.

There was a look of terror all over his face. That geographical detail hadn't quite sunk in.

"Online means anyone in any country of the world can hear you, just by logging into your website."

I could see it still sinking in. "I had all those people listening to me?" he asked.

"No," I replied, wondering how it was possible for someone so simple to get from their house to my shop. "All of those people COULD listen to you if they wanted, but there are thousands of online radio stations, thousands of TV stations, and thousands of websites, so people are spread out doing all sorts of things!"

"Oh!" he replied, despondently. "So how many do you think were listening?"

It could have been as few as 20 but I didn't want to burst his bubble! Neither of us knew where this journey was taking Max but I planned on being nothing but encouraging. "Being on FM is huge!" I span. "Who knows how many people were listening?"

Max's phone was pinging more often than usual. As he was sending a text message, I heard a different kind of ping! From the inside pocket of his jacket, Max produced another phone!

"Two phones, Max?"

"One for business, one for mates."

I nodded like I understood but I wasn't sure Max was THAT busy! Nevertheless, these two phones were chirping like the dawn chorus! Max was networking his arse off; answering this one, answering that one; expertly juggling trains of thought, short-term plans and long-term schemes, which was a pain because I needed to talk to him.

As I'd committed to providing the music for this party at Roz's house, and as her vague brief had been 'trendy shit', I needed to find out from Max what 'trendy shit' actually represented these days. The last time I was up-to-date with fashionable music was back in the dark days of rave!

Finally, Max's phones stopped ringing and pinging, and he stood in the middle of the shop gawping at me. He was in such shock, he could barely talk. "They want me to do my show every week! Every week!"

"Quite a commitment!"

"Every week!"

"This is it, Maxi! You're on the road!"

Max hadn't even started and already he looked overwhelmed, but I was happy for him. He was young and enthusiastic, and he still had that passion for music I'd lost long ago! We managed to get his phones switched off, so I could get a quick crash course in the new music genres.

When my Dad used to say to me, "Turn that racket down!" I used to say, "Dad, stop listening to it and try to feel it!" So, while Max played me lots of painful noise and tried to explain the subtle nuances, I thought back to my dear old Dad and the advice I'd given him.

Within an hour, I knew the difference between two-step, half-step, dub-step, doorstep and quick-step, and I had a few choice tunes that I could play; some very 'now' floorfillers to show how cutting edge I really was (or wasn't!)

The way it is with trendy parties, you play them these unfinished symphonies until somebody realises they're The Emperor's New Clothes, then you stick on some disco, the floor fills up and everyone goes home happy!

Max and I had agreed to set up the gear at the house at 7.00; so everything was up and running when the first guests trickled in. I thought the cool kids would appreciate some psychedelic lighting, so I made sure I brought with us a cacophony of gimmicky boxes, though I stopped short of a dry ice machine because they can sometimes go horribly wrong! Much choking and spluttering!

Good thing our Saturday at the shop was quite normal. Orders came in, equipment went out. It was a Saturday night. If you didn't catch a fever on this night of the week, your body was probably in need of an M.O.T. Saturday night is the night you dance, even if you can't dance, and the Wheels Of Steel motto was to play whatever made them dance!

We shut up shop and headed to Roz's house. Amazingly, Max's phones were still pinging like Tommy playing his pinball machine! By end of the day, his Twitter following had increased by 100, he had one girl wanting to do his PR, another girl wanting to cut his hair and he had a new club night at a local venue.

"What did you play, Max?"

"Just all the new stuff I've been sent!"

"New records?"

Max reached into a small pocket in the arm of his jacket. "New files!" he said, holding up a memory stick.

This was the new world: songs that sounded like ring tones sent via phone. Trendy kids love new stuff, whatever it sounds like! Being 'in the know' is so crucial to a cool kid, until you realise it's just reams and reams of derivative 'product', which sounds dated within six months.

We arrived and Max looked up at the imposing building. The house was older than his gran; he looked like he'd stumbled across The Addams Family.

"Cor!" he said, in comical, Beano fashion. "Your girlfriend lives here?"

No wonder Roz didn't want to move out; it was a house with a wow factor. Why leave this classic abode to live at my place?

"It's huge!" said Max.

"She shares it with five others."

"Bet they have wicked parties in here!"

It truly was one of those storybook houses where you could imagine, centuries ago, the master of the house had cavorted with the maid in her chambers, and the mistress of the house had seduced the gardener in his potting shed. The house lent itself to evenings of extravagance and excess and, tonight, I was going to be part of it.

Roz opened the door to us and showed us into the main living room. Much of the furniture had been removed, so it was pretty much all dance floor. It would be interesting to see how the uncoordinated Caucasians coped?

We began carrying gear into the house but Max was clearly distracted. "I want a house like this," he said.

"Work hard and anything is possible!" I replied, probably out of habit but more because logic seemed to have disappeared from my life. Everybody's life! Max becoming a superstar DJ would be no big surprise to me. He had the looks, the tunes, the drive and, by the sound of his tuneless phones, business was looking up!

"I'm going to have a house like this!" he said, more assertively.

"I don't doubt it!"

"It's all thanks to you, Wes!"

"Nah!" I replied, flapping my hand, as if to dismiss such a suggestion.

Once we were all wired-up and knew everything was working, Max went off to his Saturday night gig and I settled-in for a long shift. It was going to be five hours at least! Fortunately, the toilet was in close proximity. For such biological needs, it was wise to carry the 15-minute version of 'Rapper's Delight'!

Roz quickly scurried into the living room and secreted herself behind the DJ console, so we could have a quick smooch before it was time to put her lippy on.

"You can invite the boys, if you want?"

She smelt of sweat, onions and garlic, where she'd been preparing food for the evening. She smelt good enough to lick but I resisted the temptation.

"Are you sure?" I asked.

"Why not? Wendy and Melvin get on well. Heston and Mids can talk about wine. Low and Topper can show off their dance moves and chat-up girls, which is what they would normally be doing on a Saturday."

It was true. She had my crew down to a tee.

"As long as your friends won't mind sharing their canapés with the hoi polloi?"

She wrapped an arm around my waist and squeezed my bum. "You never know," she said playfully, "they might enjoy it?"

So, while Roz went off to get dressed, I played some classic ambient/Cafe Del Mar tunes; Hoxton massive old skool jamz: Air, Portishead, Moby etc.

I sent a text to the boys and waited for their response. I wasn't even sure they'd want to sacrifice their Saturday night with the sweet and pretty girls of Central London but, as it happens, they seemed quite enthusiastic to come up to the house. They were probably curious to see the place and pit their wits against Roz's clever and caustic friends.

On a normal Saturday night, the pretty girls of London Town would be up-for-it. Not necessarily promiscuous but ready to party, whereas Roz's friends would be much more circumspect. Plus, they'd require a higher level of conversation; asking them their star sign was NOT going to cut it!

Nevertheless, the crew seemed up for the challenge. Jovial texts back from all of them! They were confident boys; they knew they could handle themselves. I wasn't worried about them 'fitting in' or causing trouble. As Roz had said, they would do what they normally did on a Saturday night. My only worry was The Brothers Grim; would my merry band be too happy for them? Roz's male housemates did not strike me as happy-go-lucky disco dancers!

First one into the room was Wendy, wearing a mesmerising low-cut dress that was giving cleavage a thoroughly bad ... or good name! She looked happy to see me and immediately asked about Melvin. She'd already had her first cocktail, smelt of something coconutty and was clearly very excited about what lay ahead. When I told her the boys were on their way, she shrieked with glee and began twirling around on my dance floor like a wayward wooden top!

The front door knocked and Wendy went to answer it. Much screaming in the hallway. Friends began arriving and the general volume of chatter increased rapidly; the enchanting sound of excitable women squealing with joy. Nothing quite like it! It felt as if the mood was about to change. We were now ready to party!

Raymond wandered into the room and came to shake my hand.

"Love this song," he said. "It's one of those things I always hear but I've never known who it's by?"

"It's called 'Destiny' by Zero 7."

"I know I'll forget that."

"I'll send a file to Roz."

And there was our bond. A little act of kindness and we were friends.

"Thanks," he said. "Just so you know: this whole event is for Benjamin. He's turning 40 and he's in a fairly deep depression."

This 40 number seemed to be causing problems for someone else, but I sensed an opportunity to turn Benjamin's sneer into a smile. If I could get him dancing and merry, he might even find himself an attractive companion to take his mind off losing Roz?

As my room began to fill, I altered the tempo and graduated from chill to groove. Some quality, sing-along, foot tapping music: 'Fast Love', 'Frankie', 'Red Red Wine', 'Somebody Else's Guy', 'Ain't Nobody', 'I Found Lovin'', holding back the new and trendy stuff for later in the evening.

This was quintessential female music. I could see the girls singing the words perfectly. If we could get the birthday boy in here, we could get him caught up in some kind of funky routine? Maybe he'd even smile? If I could get the grimace off this bugger's face, we might even forge some kind of bond?

I was caught in Roz politics. I needed to campaign and get these people onside, or I'd forever be known as the marriage-wrecker!

Finally, Roz appeared looking absolutely stunning! The girl of many colours was dressed in just one colour this evening. Her dress was this glorious shade of cherry red that sat beautifully against her skin colour. It was a simple dress but devastatingly effective. I stood, transfixed, looking at her. She came over to stand beside me. I almost lost track of my timings and missed my cue!

"You like?" she asked.

"I love!"

She looked very pleased with herself and I suddenly realised I was dating a very glamorous woman. Elegant. Stylish. It truly was an out-of-body experience. Within a fortnight, I'd gone from slumbering depression to being one lucky bar steward! Here I was: shoulder-to-shoulder with a real, live beauty!

I felt myself leering and she quickly noticed it. "Play your cards right ..."

This was premier league flirting. I was finally in the big leagues! A gorgeous, glamorous girl was making eyes at me and promising me sex! Did it get much better?

Trish was a beautiful woman but Roz had that star quality. That pin-up-ness! She could easily have been a soap star or TV personality? And it wasn't too late? She stood out! Nothing about her appearance or personality was normal. I loved that maverick part of her make-up.

The birthday boy appeared at the door of the room and Roz beckoned him. Benjamin skulked over to my corner of the room, looking as sullen as a local politician who's been caught with his fingers in the till (again!)

"Thanks for playing!" said Benji, begrudgingly! "The music sounds great!"

"I've been hired!" I replied. "I can't work for free on a Saturday night!"

Benjamin looked confused.

"My birthday present to you, babe!" Roz said to him.

Benji's expression changed from dour and distracted to something verging on surprise and delight. I wouldn't say his face lit up but there was definitely some mild illumination. "For me?" he asked.

"Yes," Roz assured him, "it's all for you."

But nothing could quite move that perpetual look of anxiety from his eyes. The thought of Roz having a boyfriend and possibly moving out of the house (combined with him turning 40) was a little too much.

Hoping to shock him into action and steer him in the direction of gyrating, nubile bodies, I pointed in the direction of the dance floor. "They've all come to celebrate your birthday!" I said.

Benjamin nodded, gravely, forced a weak smile and headed out of the room, probably to fill his blood stream with alcohol? Roz pecked me on the cheek and went off to be hostess. The floor was now filling and there were whoops of delight at favoured tunes! I knew I'd be playing 'Uptown Funk' more than once!

The boys appeared at the door, quickly surveyed the talent and waved at me. They were off to the kitchen to put down their drinks and say hello to the housemates; a little preliminary mischief before they hit the dance floor! They looked in good spirits! Baggers was wearing an ostentatious hat, quite the campest thing I'd ever seen him wear!

Heston ambled into the room and was heading in my direction but he never quite made it! He was immediately accosted by two writhing women, who turned him into a sandwich on the dance floor, and began rubbing themselves against him. He had one hot chick behind him and another wiggling her bum into his crotch, but he barely seemed aroused, as if this was a daily occurrence. He waved feebly and I waved back; getting to me might prove tricky for him. Heston had that tall, square thing going on and, even if he wasn't their target, it was fun for the girls to tease him! He seemed fairly used to this game.

Finally, Jill came over to say hello and I got a very matter-of-fact welcome. She was different to the first time I'd met her. On that night, she was quite open and chatty but, on this night, I wasn't Roz's bofriend, I was 'the help'. What had happened between now and then? Had her view of me crystallized into cold indifference? She asked me if I needed a drink or something to eat, which was thoughtful of her, but I didn't feel as if I was about to become part of her family. Maybe she was happy for Roz to have a boyfriend but I would have to know my place?

Jill seemed friendly enough but maybe she was letting Roz know the conduct that was expected of her; no casual male friends allowed inside, unless they were offering-up an engagement ring! Jill was a young woman but rehearsing diligently for middle-age and severe frumpiness. There was no need for her to be so formal with me. She didn't know it yet but I was a nice guy. Nicer than many of the men that would enter her life. Yes, she had her trio of housemates, sure to be lifelong friends, but none of these boys wanted her in their bed. She behaved like someone who hadn't been kissed properly in a while.

In the distance, I could see the boys returning from the kitchen, they all loitered around the door, making it difficult for girls to come in and out of the room.

"Well, if you need anything, just let me know!" said Jill, the person in charge of dealing with the window cleaners, meter readers and other menial staff.

Over the other side of the room, I could see the boys interacting with the female guests. These girls knew they were strangers and wondered why they were there. I saw them pointing at me, as they explained that I was Roz's new boyfriend.

It was time for the music to increase in tempo, so I began spinning some anthems from the new romantic era: Spandau Ballet's 'Chant No. 1', Heaven 17's 'Temptation' and Human League's 'Love Action'. Some of the crowd were probably a bit young for this era but they still seemed to know the words. Kids listen to whatever their parents play.

Melvin, as ever, was the first on the dance floor, and I could see the regulars eying him suspiciously. Who was this person using his body in this unusual fashion? This was a house big on drink and debate, dancing was something girls and gay men did!

Tony G the *maitre d'* eventually dragged a young woman into the centre, and she was positively cooing at his tactile approach to dancing. Low had a hand on her waist, a hand on her shoulder, and he was twirling, pulling and pushing her like a window dresser working over a mannequin.

I could see the regular visitors to the house surveying the scene. Who were these interlopers expertly gyrating with their girls? Mids and Topper were less sure on their feet, but the centre of the melee was where business transactions would be completed this evening, so they both grabbed a girl and began communicating with their bodies. It wasn't complicated and, at times, it wasn't pretty, but the boys were doing their Saturday night thing and, one way or another, it would result in some high-class Highgate hi-jinks!

There was so much whooping and hollering occurring in my room that Roz and Benjamin wandered in to see what the commotion was. Roz seemed delighted that everyone was enjoying themselves but nothing could lift Benji's pallor. She dragged him out on to the dance floor and the two of them attempted to synchronise. Roz was moving smoothly to the beat but Benji's off-key motions made him look epileptic and one feared for the toes of passing revellers.

In a spirit of brotherhood, I could see the boys smiling with Roz and Benjamin, but Benji just wasn't getting it! This enjoyment thing seemed beyond him. For us, dancing and smiling went hand-in-hand but Benjamin seemed to be dragging his body like he was wounded and Roz eventually gave up. I could see them returning to the kitchen. Obviously, enough alcohol had not been consumed. A smile was still a few hours away.

It was time to nudge the tempo up, so I went through some classic early house: A Guy Called Gerald's 'Voodoo Ray', Paul Simpson's 'Musical Freedom', Adeva's 'Respect' and Alison Limerick's 'Where Love Lives'.

This brought new people into the living room and it began to get hot and decidedly sweaty. The boys took this opportunity to get some drinks, but not before they'd all come over to harass me.

"What a house!" said Low, shouting in my ear and dripping sweat on my arm.

"The girls are mint!" said Topper, shouting in my other ear.

"Why is Baggers wearing that hat?" I asked him.

"Says it will attract women! Says it's a conversation piece!"

Topper and I looked at each other. It made sense but it didn't quite seem right! Wouldn't a monocle or a time piece have had the same effect?

"What are you drinking?" said Mids. "The bar is well-stocked!"

"Get me a vodka and cranberry!"

Baggers looked completely distracted. I looked in the general direction of where he was looking and spied an upright hunk making eyes at him.

"You okay, Baggers?" I asked him.

I managed to capture his attention for a few brief seconds. "It's going to be a good night, Wezza!"

"I bloody hope so! Just keep those girls dancing!"

The boys all trooped off to God knows where and left me to entertain Roz's regular guests, all of whom seemed to be loving my early nineties selection. The wooden dance floor in the living room was clacking like some castanets.

Wendy and Melvin had clearly decided it was their time to shine and made a grand entrance on to the dance floor. Even though these genitals would never meet, what a handsome couple they made! As we moved into the prime time disco set, Baggers and she of the cleavage drew admiring glances with their primal bumping and grinding.

Mids brought me my long drink and I sucked at it through a straw. I almost emptied the glass, so Mids went off to get me another one.

After a while, Benjamin returned to the main room, this time accompanied by Raymond. Raymond had clearly told him to enjoy himself and was virtually pushing him on to the dance floor. Benjamin was already the wrong side of a bottle of wine and was getting animated, aggravated by his friend, who I could see lecturing him at length. Not the buzzkill you wanted on a Saturday night! It almost looked as if these two were squaring-up, but I knew it was just an expression of their intense friendship.

Mother Hen Jill wandered by just to make sure everything was okay. I could see her whispering something in Benjamin's ear. I could only speculate what she was saying.

The smart thing would be to say, "It's your birthday, babe. Do what you want!"

But she was probably saying, "Enjoy yourself, you miserable bastard! We've organised a big party for you: now enjoy it"

He was still scowling, so I guessed she'd employed the latter strategy. Raymond and Benjamin still looked like they wanted to fight, but it was just animated conversation.

Out on the dance floor, Roz was giving Low a run for his money, while Baggers and Wendy were twinkling their toes like Fred and Ginger. Even though Benji was a disgruntled onlooker, his guests were having a great time! Roz kept winking at me, so I knew I was doing okay.

The sight of Roz and Low laughing and interacting seemed to agitate Benji. Having an outsider boyfriend was one thing but now she was almost sleeping with the enemy. In a clumsy fit of teenage pique, he barged his way into the middle of the room, and suggested to Low that it was his turn to dance with Roz. Low was used to this ritual and graciously backed away, leaving Benji to maul poor Roz with his sweaty palms and inelegant limbs.

As a Sunday league player, Low was a competitive athlete so, for some reason, he decided it would be sport to bait the birthday boy. He allowed Benji a few songs with Roz but then strode on to the dance floor to reclaim his dance partner.

The protocol would be to allow the incoming man his chance but Benji was having none of it, and I could see him motioning Low away! Low was not impressed but he was making a melodramatic meal of it and gesticulating wildly. Topper stepped in to pull Low away but he was having too much fun aggravating Benji. I could see this would not end well.

Baggers cleverly positioned himself so that he could dance with Wendy and still make eyes at the hunk across the room. The rest of my crew were blissfully unaware of all this.

As I was new to Melvin's world and modus operandi, it was intriguing to watch him at work. He was full of winks and smiles, to complement his swirls and twirls, and the intended hunk was grinning from ear to ear.

As predicted, in the distance, I could see Heston and Mids deep in conversation, it might have been about wine but at least they were away from the fray, although I could see Heston casting a bouncer-ish eye over everything, as if he was the in-house security person.

Even the normally-sombre Raymond was enjoying himself? He'd found someone who found his film festival stories fascinating, and she was smiling with approval, as if she was about to award him her own prize. The alcohol had clearly loosened Raymond's limbs and he was leaning in towards her neck like a vampire yoga instructor!

Having given Benjamin a few more songs with Roz, Low went back out on to the dance floor to demand what was rightfully his. Again, Benjamin tried to rebuff him. Roz did not look impressed at being treated like mere chattel and disappeared out of the room, leaving Benji and Low arguing about nothing.

Once they realised she was gone, they began blaming one another for that, and I could see Benji getting very hot under the collar. I began getting angry with Low myself because I could see he was provoking him.

As the temperature increased at the centre of the room, it was time to kick-in those nineties club anthems: 'Free' by Ultra Nate, 'U Sure Do' by Strike, 'I Love You Baby' by The Original and, inevitably, Real To Reel's 'I Like To Move It'.

These joyous, sing-a-long dance records usually made people smile (even though nobody knew what the hell he was singing in The Nightcrawlers' 'Push The Feeling On') but they merely seemed to inflame our two stubborn rams, who were about to lock horns in a very comical fashion.

It never got to punches but, within minutes, they were in each other's faces and pushing each other quite violently. The dancers edged away skilfully, as if someone had just puked-up their Margarita and, as soon as Heston saw this sea change, he quickly stepped in and placed his body between the two of them.

Neither of them wanted to fight, so neither of them tried to edge Heston out of the way. Out of nowhere, Jill swooped in to rescue her wounded chick, while Topper pulled Low to one side and tried to lecture him on the error of his ways, but the two of them were laughing too hard.

One way or another, I knew I'd be getting it in the neck from one of the housemates but, ultimately, it didn't seem to matter. The floor soon filled up again and the party continued apace. There was no broken nose, broken glass or spilt drink; everyone was still on course to get laid and wake up with a painful hangover!

Carrying a plate of delicious savoury goodies (made with her fair hand), Roz sidled up to me and began apologising for Benji's behaviour. Thankful that I wasn't getting the hairdryer treatment, I began apologising for Low's behaviour. I was mightily grateful that Roz wasn't upset with my friends, but then I hadn't heard from Jill! Jill was the reprimander. Judge and jury in this parish!

The party was going well. Smiling faces, hugs, kisses and high-fives from guests. I was covering all musical bases; there was something for everyone! I was playing whatever made them dance. It was fair to say, I had achieved a sense of satisfaction akin to a high. I was feeling good! A full floor fuzzy feeling! And then Jill marched over looking like someone had stolen her favourite surgical stockings!

"Our parties are never normally like this!"

"Full of happy, smiling faces?" I ventured.

"No need for sarcasm!" she spat, in a less-than-impressed tone. "I mean there is never any unpleasantness! Our friends drink and get boisterous but there's never any unpleasantness!"

Jill was now severely killing my buzz. I was trying to concentrate on the job at hand (which she'd paid me to do), I was trying to look happy, I was trying to read the crowd and I was trying to select the right song, none of which I could do with Jill lecturing me!

"There's no need for sarcasm when you're in the wrong!" she clarified. She was clearly a last-word person. Even if you disagreed with her point, she would have the last word!

I found the right song, making sure it was long-ish, so I could respond to Jill's thinly-veiled accusations that my friends had, somehow, lowered the tone!

"When me and my mates go out on a Saturday night, there is never any – as you call it – unpleasantness! Why? Because we're polite, well-mannered people, and we know how to hold our drink! If we're guilty of anything, it may be that we showed up your friends for being stiff and lifeless, and injected some good old-fashioned party spirit into this alleged celebration! If you're suggesting my friends instigated that incident, you are mistaken and merely adjusting your rose-tinted glasses!"

Jill looked shocked at my words and my tone and, if I wasn't very much mistaken, looked as if she was warming to me! There was a faint tinge of rouge in her cheeks, as if she was aroused. Perverse! What's the point of being Mr. Nice Guy? Some women clearly need you to prevent them from asserting themselves. In old fashioned-terms, Jill appreciated masculinity!

She said nothing, but tossed her hair loudly and stormed off. By standing up for myself (and my friends), I'd earned her respect, but I still didn't have her approval. Benji was the least of my problems; it was Jill who was whispering in Roz's ear!

Jill definitely didn't want to get left behind, so she was planting classist seeds in Roz's head and, doubtless, suggesting that me and the boys were beneath her. Surely Roz would never be swayed by such propaganda?

Jill didn't want Roz to go off and be happy, possibly get married? It was Jill who wanted everyone to stay in place, it was she who wanted everything to stay just as it was, and she had Benjamin as a strong ally!

The rest of the evening passed off without incident and I introduced something to the house: slow dancing. Instant foreplay! The seductive power of the love song. As I drew to the end of my five-hour set, I began playing slow songs. Heatwave's 'Always And Forever', Luther Vandross's 'So Amazing' and Extreme's 'More Than Words'. The results were astounding!

All of a sudden, these complete strangers were pressed-up close to members of the opposite sex. These were scholars, academics and artists. They were used to red wine, lively debate and plates of cheese, they were NOT used to having a girl's breasts pressed against their chest! Some of these stiffs looked like kids on Christmas Day! Their cherubic faces now smiling like benign leaders. My mob were moving in for the kill! All of them were locked in a tight clinch with a woman. These were the songs where you made your move and whispered inappropriate things in a woman's ear.

Even Heston and Raymond had found themselves dance partners. There would be happy endings a-plenty!

Exhausted, Melvin and Wendy were not so much dancing as propping each other up. This would be Melvin's last dance with Wendy but he would not be leaving the house with her. Baggers had already slipped the young man some kind of 'business card' and, doubtless, they would rendezvous much later, somewhere else!

In the far corner of the room, I could see Benjamin scowling. He wasn't angry anymore, just drunk and powerless. He surveyed the couples scattered around and yearned for intimacy. The party had been a success. People would congratulate him later. Did he realise what a good party he'd hosted.

Roz edged past Benji and steered a course towards me, carefully dodging the writhing couples in the middle. She kissed me, held me around my waist and began swaying in time to the music.

"My clever boyfriend!" I heard her say.

This had been a good day. I was now both clever and, officially, Roz's boyfriend.

Chapter Eighteen (Sunday)

It wasn't difficult to round-up the boys for Sunday lunch; they were all quite giddy and anxious to compare notes about the previous night.

I eventually woke-up after midday and set a time. I could get ready in an instant but Baggers took forever! Matching shirt, matching shoes and all that bollocks!

We arranged to meet at 1.00 but Baggers pushed it to 2.00, then 2.30! This meal was drifting into tea time and, I knew, by the time we'd finished, it would be dinner!

I quite liked our long, rambling, food festivals. We weren't necessarily foodies, but we were big fans of eating out. Even though Low worked as a *maitre d'*, restaurants were home to him. He felt comfortable talking over that hubbub.

Restaurants meant no cooking and no washing-up. No one was up for expensive or experimental cooking; all we required was good quality food that wouldn't cause the runs or give us gout!

We settled on one of our favourite Rodizios because we knew there'd be something for everyone, and plenty of it! Plus, these family restaurants were always full of Brazilian beer and wholesome women!

Having sampled several new experiences last night, everyone was in good spirits! Everyone wanted to talk about the house, everyone wanted to laugh at Benjamin, and everyone wanted to find out precisely what was going on with Baggers and Wendy!

Melvin couldn't even muster a blush because he wasn't embarrassed. There was nothing to tell and nothing to hide!

"She's not really my type!" he said.

"You danced with her all night long!" said Low.

"You were all over each other!" said Topper. "She clearly likes you!"

"Just friends," said Melvin, calmly. "We both like dancing and that's it!"

"Oh, I get it!" said Mids. "Discretion? Protecting Roz's friend?"

Melvin shook his head wearily and accepted another slab of steak from a square and muscular waiter. "You're not getting it, are you?"

"I get it," I said, trying to move the conversation along. "Just friends."

"Those boobs!" said Low. "Wouldn't you like a taste?"

"No!" said Melvin, emphatically. "What I'd like is a new job and a higher salary!"

"I could make you something nice for her? Some earrings, maybe?" said Topper.

"Appreciate the offer," said Melvin, "but I don't need to impress her because I don't want to date her."

Everyone was silent for a second, trying to fathom why their mate was not going to apply his considerable charms to this willing participant.

"Seems a waste," said Low.

"Then, be my guest!" said Baggers, almost with a touch of impatience, which shocked everyone.

"One would think you're a gaylord?" said Mids.

"I am. So what?" said Melvin, casually.

No one said a word. I watched the other three. Not a flicker. They just carried on eating. This wasn't shock or embarrassment, it was just Melvin making a joke. Of course he wasn't gay! How could he possibly be?

"Did anyone speak to Jill?" I asked, wondering if anyone could confirm my suspicions about her.

"I had a quick exchange with her in the kitchen," said Mids. "She was scrutinising the case of wine I'd bought. We got on quite well! I quite fancy her! I can see her in stockings and suspenders, wielding a riding crop!"

"She thinks we're plebs!" I said. "She says that fracas with Benjamin was our fault!"

The boys looked at me as if I was speaking another language. To suggest that we were aggressive or confrontational was just too ridiculous. We were a bunch of peace-loving beatniks compared to some of the cavemen we met on a weekend. We spent more time breaking up than causing fights! It gets to that chaotic segment of the morning when most people are looking for either a shag or a fight and, nine times out of ten, we were pulling people apart and calming a situation.

"Us?" exclaimed Low. "Our fault?"

"Ridiculous!" said Topper, snootily. He even sounded like a toff, full of arrogance and entitlement! "That Benji is a miserable bastard. Plain and simple. No wonder Roz chose you over him!"

And then the boys began talking about Roz. A curious experience. Normally, in a conversation about me and women, there was laughter, ridicule, cruel jokes and farmyard noises but, when they talked about Roz, they spoke of her looks, her elegance, her dress, they spoke about her dance moves, her organisational skills, her sense of humour. Were they really talking about my girlfriend?

"I really like her!" said Low, a bit too enthusiastically. "She's fit and healthy."

I wasn't sure how relevant this was and looked at him blankly. A little more detail was required.

"She'll always be up for going out and having a good time. She's a laugh! And she doesn't roll her eyes the way women do! I hate that!"

This was true. Roz was not one for judgement and lecture. Roz genuinely didn't give a damn how I dressed, how I talked, how I ate. She liked me the way I was. I wasn't some kind of tragic or psychotic narcissist. On the evolutionary scale, I was actually quite advanced; she trusted my judgement. I liked that!

"She'd be good for you," said Mids. "She's got class! Knows a decent wine. Knows how to dress. Knows how to conduct herself. She's got boundaries. Standards."

I nodded. It was true. She was firm but fair. You knew where you stood with Roz. There was no game-playing. You were not required to read her mind. Her thoughts and feelings were projected high and wide across a huge screen.

"She'll definitely be good for you!" Topper re-iterated. "Stiffen your back. Get you functioning at a higher level."

My God! Who was this wonder woman who was finally going to transform me from pedestrian to potent? Were they talking about the same person and was I really dating her?

Now, all I had to do was get her housemates used to the idea. Easier said than done!

"I think Jill is the real problem in there, not the boys! She doesn't think we're good enough!"

The boys all laughed. It wasn't even worthy of comment.

All around us, there were delicious, long skewers of beef and chicken and sausage meat being shovelled on to our plates. We were enjoying our lunch too much to care about the opinions of others. We were stuffed to the gills with meat and beer, and our faces ached from laughing so much. At that point, we cared little for the approval of stuffy, middle-aged women.

"Good enough?" said Topper, haughtily. "When those Kensington and Chelsea girls waltz into my workshop and slap thousand pound diamonds on to my work bench, I am definitely good enough!"

I was just digesting another mouthful of lamb kebab, when I looked up and there was Trish, standing at the side of our table, taking off her coat and looking for a chair to pull up. All of the boys gawped in silence. Trish looked particularly alluring. Even I was taken by surprise! She had this biker-chick meets Boho-chic look going on. The jeans were figure hugging!

Mids was the first to regain his composure. "Hello, sweetheart!" he said, rising to embrace her. "I'll go and get you a drink."

One-by-one, the boys rose to hug and kiss her, leaving me to organise her impromptu place. I quickly grabbed crockery and cutlery from the next table.

"How did you find us?" I asked.

"Lovely to see you too, Wes!"

"Didn't mean it like that!"

"Isn't this one of your regular Sunday haunts?"

It was. Oft-visited. We were never that hard to find.

Mids returned with a large glass of red wine. Trish slurped at it, appreciatively. "Lovely! Let me just go and grab some salad," she said, picking up her plate from the table.

The boys all looked at me. I shrugged my shoulders. "I didn't invite her!"

"What's she doing here?" asked Melvin. He'd never been a big fan. There was just something about Trish that bothered him. He'd always found Trish manipulative, as if we were all toys in her doll house. "I'm confused," he added.

"I guess," I began, not knowing where my theory was headed, "I guess ... now that she and I are in The Friend Zone, she's just hanging out with friends?"

"But now we can't talk about football! Or birds!" whined Low.

"We never really talk about women anyway!" said Topper, slugging down the last of his beer and waving his bottle at a waitress.

Trish returned with a plateful of sensible salad ingredients and began looking around for some meat-bearing waiters.

She was now the centre of attention and, try as we might, we could not stop looking at her. She really looked good!

"What's wrong with you boys?" she began, gratefully receiving a large slice of roast beef. "Cat got your tongue?"

No one could speak.

"Yes, I know!" she continued. "Boy Time! Don't I know about your lunches and dinners? Didn't I date Wes? I know you like your Boy Time!" She made it sound sordid! She was smiling all over her face and chewing a chicken wing enthusiastically, licking her fingers as she went.

Yes, she knew about our lunches and dinners, and all the boys knew her! She was the genius who had brought me from adolescence into manhood. She was the rock-solid, ever-reliable who had given me the strength and *chutzpah* to take over my Dad's insane little shop and make it a viable business! But she was also the person who had disappeared from my life without a word. Vanished!

Having spent the afternoon extolling the virtues of Roz, Trish was yesterday's news! The boys didn't want to talk about Trish, their heads were in Roz-Space! They wanted to talk about Roz's house, the characters she lived with, and how we were all about to step into a new world of smarter, brighter girls with quaint, olde English names and free-flowing, fast-rising skirts!

With Trish's arrival, the mood changed. We were all on a downer, looking at my old life and yet, here she was, looking exceptionally cheerful, fairly motoring through the whole menu, and expecting us to treat her like she was still Top Dog!

Trish looked around her. Everyone was still gingerly sipping on their beer and saying little. "What's wrong with you lot?"

Thankfully, Melvin, well-used to dealing with his boss's emotional issues (not to mention his own) found his voice and began trying to make order in this new world.

"Obviously," he began, trying to open with a compliment, "it's lovely to see you, and you're always welcome at our table but, today, we're basking in the afterglow of a wicked party last night, hosted by Wes's new girlfriend, Roz. And it feels a bit ... funny ... talking about Wes's new girlfriend in front of you!"

We all nodded in agreement and hurrumphed our approval at Melvin's articulate response.

"Oh, I've met her!" said Trish, dismissively. "Seems a nice girl?" Never had anyone sounded so ingenuous! And now I realised why Trish was sitting at our table! Was she really looking to stake her claim? Was she really looking to discredit Roz and win me back?

Roz would NOT fight over me! Oh, no! She was pert and efficient and going places! She would NOT get into an undignified toe-to-toe with Trish! Not over me! Thus, I needed to keep Trish away from Roz! Trish was yesterday! Trish was the old Wes! I didn't want Roz seeing the old Wes! The old Wes was limp and gormless and wholly lacking in direction.

"Hold on," said Trish, suddenly sounded offended, "Am I an outsider? An intruder? Am I piggy in the middle?"

I nodded feebly. Trish had reduced me down to the old Wes. I was back to being the fumbling, bumbling also-ran she'd left. I didn't want to be that Wes.

"Party?" said Trish, quickly changing the subject, clearly oblivious to her unwelcomeness! "Do tell!"

We all breathed a sigh of discomfort. This girl would not be leaving any time soon.

"A beautiful house!" began Topper. "In the backstreets of Highgate Village. By and large, really nice, friendly people."

Trish's ears pricked-up. She could hear a little chink in the armour. "By and large?" she asked.

I realised I'd have to wade in. Trish was manoeuvring. Talking and thinking on her feet. Looking for ways to pull the rug out.

"What Topper means," I began, "I don't think one of Roz's housemates is that impressed with us."

I could hear the boys muttering unkind epithets about Jill.

"Really?" said Trish, absolutely loving this nugget. "Is Highgate Village not that taken with Tufnell Park?" She laughed to herself. "I've met those kind of people before. They put you in boxes and you are forever in that box. You might even climb out of your box ... but they still feel you should climb back in! I foresee problems."

There was tangible discomfort and discontent round the table, and the other boys were slowly realising the not-very-transparent nature of Trish's visit. I could feel them chewing over her words.

Feeling particularly bold, Topper spoke up. "Her housemate might be a bit huffy but Wes's new girlfriend is a quality act!"

Trish looked up and smiled at him. Not a smile of pleasure but a smile of pity, as if he'd made an awful faux pas.

I'd never seen this smile before. Trish had always delivered kind and caring smiles, amused smiles and smiles of pure pleasure, but this was a new one from her repertoire; a cunning, quite determined smile. Amazingly, she was about to dig her heels in and fight for me!

She'd been off the scene for more than six months and experienced some kind of awakening, some series of important epiphanies, and now she'd decided that 'old stand-by' was the best option, which was slightly blowing my mind.

Topper then continued with his thought process and truly showed his colours. "This woman that Roz lives with: I've seen her type! When you make jewellery, you deal with material girls. In their world, there are two types: the haves and the have-nots."

"I quite liked Jill," said Mids, not very helpfully. "I recognise her. She's a bit like my mum: Home Counties, a bit prudey, not very worldly. She'd probably go up to the one black person at a party and imagine she was 'the help'!"

Trish was shaking her head and smiling. Finally, she began waving waiters away. She was full. We were all full but there was still some more drinking and talking to be done. Everyone was starting to think about my housemate predicament. Was I really socially ready to make that symbolic climb up Highgate Hill?

"I foresee problems," Trish repeated. "How can it work? Roz is very close to this Jill woman. To an extent, they must be cut from the same cloth. If there are any problems, this Jill is always going to be in her ear with, 'Told you so!'"

The boys listened intently. There was something about Trish's logic that appealed to them. After all, we were very proud of our group. We'd known each other ages, lived in each other's pockets, cared about each other. It felt ridiculous to hear someone question our integrity. We weren't the finest specimens but we were good, decent, honest men, like a traditional Sunday roast at your Nan's house.

I thought back to the way Jill had talked to me. It was like being back at school and you were being told off for something your mate had done! Dating Roz would mean continued exposure to Jill. Christ Almighty, now Trish had me doubting my relationship!

"Jill will grow to like Wes," said Mids, still fantasising about Jill in racy underwear. "Who couldn't love that little face?" he said, grabbing my chin.

"That's true!" said Baggers. "Jill will change. She will mellow. Now, Trish, why don't you tell us why you're really here?"

Trish calmly turned and smiled at Melvin although, beneath that winning smile, there was a steely glare of epic proportions.

All eyes turned back on Trish. It's not that she was necessarily an attention-seeker but, on this evening, she seemed to want to control the conversation. She had details to prise and propaganda to paste.

"You want truth, Melvin?"

"Tell us why you're here," he insisted, smirking. "Shall I guess?"

At this point, I could see he was being quite playful with her but she did not appreciate her hand being forced.

"Not sure everyone in this group is ready for the truth," Trish said, clumsily, not fully realising how much hurt she was about to cause.

"What do you mean?" asked Low, used to confrontation and always ready for a scrap. "I can handle the truth, so I know you're not talking about me!"

"Trish, leave it!" I pleaded, knowing where she was headed. It was like watching a motorway pile-up in slow motion.

Topper's curiosity had now piqued. He turned to me. "What's going on, Wezza? What does Trish mean?"

"It's just old shit between me and Trish," I lied.

"Is it?" asked Melvin, mischievously. "You sure it's not new shit, Trish. New Roz shit?"

"You really want some truth?" said Trish, her shackles rising.

"Yeah, why not?" said Baggers.

Topper turned to me again. "Wezza, what is going on? This seems to be between you three! I don't know what's going on?"

"Why don't you tell us some truth, Melvin?" said Trish, finally diving headlong into that point of no return.

Melvin and she glared at one another. He had tried to embarrass her, and now she was going to embarrass him!

"Does the truth make you nervous, Melvin?" she asked.

"No," he replied, finally realising that this had become Russian roulette.

"You first!" she replied.

Melvin shook his head and smiled at her.

"Don't the boys know?" she asked.

"Know what?" asked Topper, his irritation growing.

"I'm gay!" said Melvin. "There, Trish, are you happy?"

Topper, Mids and Low began digesting that statement, while Melvin and Trish continued their impasse.

"Now, you, Trish! Tell us what brings you to this table! Are you on the campaign trail? Were you trying to win our support?"

Trish looked a bit rattled and paused. The silence was deafening. I knew what was going on but the other three boys were caught in the crossfire. They were all still digesting Melvin's confession, but also wondering what my cryptic ex was trying to achieve.

"Tell us, Trish!" Melvin insisted. "Tell us the reason you're here! Have you made a mistake? Do you want your ex back? Sex with your ex is very hot, I hear!"

Trish said nothing. I waved at the waiter and signalled that we needed the bill.

"And why don't you tell us why you left, Trish?" Melvin knew! Somebody at the party had told him! Word was travelling fast!

The other boys were growing impatient. We were a tight group. No one was ever on the outside. Everyone's dirty laundry was washed in public. The boys did not like being outsiders.

"Can somebody please tell me what the fuck is going on?" asked Low.

"Shall I, Trish? Or will you?"

"Okay," she said, wiping a napkin deliberately over her greasy lips. "I'll tell you. I thought I was pregnant. I was really late and I thought I was pregnant. And it scared me! It didn't make me happy at all. It should have but it didn't. It scared me. And I was confused! I needed time to think."

We all sat and listened. I'd heard this story but this was all news to the boys. Their heads were now reeling from both Melvin's confession and Trish's bombshell.

"So, you're back?" said Mids, draining his bottle of beer and placing it squarely on the table. There would be no more drinking. "You've had your time away, you've made your decisions and you're back! I've got just one question: why weren't you happy? Why weren't you happy to be pregnant? Wes is a top bloke and would make a great dad!"

I looked at her to see her response. Whatever she was feeling, she had it in check. No flicker of emotion on her face.

"So, why weren't you happy, Trish?" I asked. "Tell the boys!"

Trish wriggled nervously and needlessly wiped her mouth again.

"To be honest with you all, I didn't see Wes as dad material."

This was the biggest revelation of all! It made Melvin's confession seem like a lame joke.

Topper was truly offended. "Not dad material? Not dad material? It's almost like you don't know my friend! This is a good man!" he said, pointing at me. "How long have we known each other? This man has been a constant in my life for more than 20 years. Constant. Solid. Reliable. What are you women looking for, if not men like Wes?"

Trish looked as if she'd been scolded. Her cheeks were redder. "You're right!" she said, softly. "That's why I'm here. It took me a while but that's the conclusion I came to!"

"You've missed the boat, sister!" Mids was not always at one with tact and diplomacy. "Your ship has sailed!" he continued, hurtfully.

Trish noted his words with sadness. "So it seems?"

Chapter Nineteen (Monday)

I was still in a daze when I got to the shop on Monday morning. I'm not even sure how I got showered and dressed. I was on auto-pilot from the moment I woke.

I pulled up the shutters on the shop windows, opened the front door and let the sunshine and fresh air stream in.

I was expecting gear to come back in from the weekend, so I needed my employee to help with the humping. He was late, as usual, so I made myself a cuppa.

It was a lovely day, so I stood outside the shop with my brew. Mothers were just returning home from their school run.

Leaning up against the bus stop was this cocky-looking kid, who behaved like a typical school-leaver. Having left school, he thought he was an adult, but he was probably still living at home with his mum. He had on the classic James Dean outfit: jeans, white T-shirt, black leather jacket, and he was pulling heavily on a cigarette. He was only young but he had one of those grim, gaunt, being-poisoned faces. A crackhead in the making!

At that moment, a buoyant, young girl on a bike rode down the pavement. She was pulling a small trailer carrying a large basket of sandwiches and muffins.

I flapped my arms at her in a non-threatening way, and she seemed to understand that I wanted her to stop.

"Are they for someone specific?" I asked.

"Nope. I stop at local offices. Some buy, some don't."

She looked late-twenties. Very pretty face! She could've been Spanish? Or Brazilian? I was struggling not to look at her prominent nose, which fairly dominated her face.

"Haven't seen you before?"

"It's my second week!"

"Hand-made?"

"Everything!" she said proudly. "Not my ideal choice of career. Finished my degree! Got fed up of working in shit jobs. And here I am!"

"Can I have a look?" I asked, eying up the contents of her basket.

"Be my guest!"

It all looked delicious. Fresh from her kitchen!

"I'll have one for now and one for later!"

I gave her a fiver and she smiled.

"Will you put us on your route?"

"No problem!" she said and cycled off into the distance.

I went back into the shop and unwrapped one of my purchases. It was only a ham salad sandwich but the bread was wholesome and the ham and salad were tasty. There was even a little seasoning in there! I heard myself moan with pleasure. All over a ham salad sandwich! I guess: where there's good, there's always better?

Max finally wandered in and I had to look twice. I barely recognised him! New haircut, new jeans, new top!

I stood back to get the full impact! "Maxi: look at you!"

Max looked like he'd just stepped off the set of his first promo video. He looked better than the artists he played! Max was no longer a cliché, he was fashion.

"Who put this together?"

"This stylist contacted me after my first radio show."

"And then there were photos?"

"Oh, yes!" said Max, clicking his phone through to the radio station's website, and there was Max's DJ profile page with lots of professional-looking images of him in expensive-looking clothes.

"Did you get to keep the clothes?"

"Some of them," he said, almost looking disappointed.

I stood back to look at him again.

"You look the biz, Max! You look like a star!"

Max laughed. "Naaah!" he said, blushing slightly.

The morning passed without incident. All the gear from the weekend came back. Everyone looked worse for wear. The gear had been hired for weddings, birthdays, anniversary parties, stag and hen nights, and some company had even staged a 'Success Party', to thank their staff for a great year!

"Look at this," I said, holding up my second sandwich. "There was this girl riding by on a bike. Do you want half!"

"Nah, Mum made me a fry-up for breakfast!"

"She must be so proud!"

And, duly, Max beamed with pride. "She was so excited to hear me on the radio!"

"Good morning, campers!" said a voice at the door. I turned and there was Midders, holding a carrier bag containing wine. "Two bottles for your cupboard; for when that nice young lady comes to visit."

I took the carrier bag and set it behind the counter.

"Just passing!" said Mids.

"Would you like a cuppa?" asked Max.

"What a good lad you are!" Mids took a seat at my counter and span round with a serious look. "So?" he asked. "What are we going to do?"

"Do?"

"About Melvin?"

I looked at him. He looked genuinely worried. Not outraged or offended, just concerned for Melvin and concerned for us as a group.

And this is why I loved that crazy Roz girl: she had elevated my status within my peer group! For so many years, I'd been an after-thought, I'd been back of the queue for suggestions and solutions. For so many years, because I was attached, I was brain dead, they never consulted me, but here was Mids, claiming to be "just passing" whereas, in fact, he'd come to ask my opinion. MY opinion. Little old me! The weirdo who kept falling asleep!

"What are we going to do about Melvin?" I asked. "Absolutely fucking nothing!"

Mids still looked perplexed. "No, I mean, should we do some stuff he wants to do?"

"Like go to gay clubs?"

I laughed to myself. It was a touching gesture but not necessary. "You don't want to go to gay clubs, mate! Baggers is fine just as he is! If he wasn't, he would've gone his own way!"

Mids nodded in agreement. "S'pose so."

"Why do you think he always carries an overnight bag? He never goes home!"

Mids smiled. "I guess he's having fun?"

Max returned with three cups of tea.

"He's looking a bit snazzy," said Mids, eyeing Max up and down.

"He's got his own bloody stylist!"

Mids looked confused. "Have I missed something?"

"I've got my own weekly radio show!" announced Max, polishing his phone screen.

Mids looked at me nervously, "Playing HIS kind of music, right?"

"Yes, mate! You wouldn't understand it!" I replied.

Max stood there grinning. He loved being young and bang-on-it!

"So, did you know?" asked Mids.

In truth, my gaydar was rubbish, but I think that had more to do with my own trivial, internal struggles. Melvin was right, I was just like Roz's housemates. I loved my lifestyle and I didn't want a single thing to change. Not one single thing! It took Stella a while to get her groove back, I had no intention of losing mine!

Mids stayed with us for an hour, told us some cracking stories, then went back to work. The stories that Midders told were usually about his travels abroad. In fact, he hopped on trains and planes so often, it didn't even feel like travel; it was his commute.

He spoke hilarious pigeon-French, which was actually an amalgamation of four different tongues, but he managed to communicate and barter with the locals, which was the most important thing. He'd even been known to seduce in a second language, but we only had his imaginative word for it.

After lunch, the phone began to ring again: enquiries about gear and DJs. Enquiries about dates far into the future! I made a mental note to find some new DJs for the business.

It was Percy's first gig that night, so I was curious to see if we had a new DJ for our books or not? Would he be able to deliver? I half expected to see his long legs stride through the door! There was no point worrying about the lanky Muppet, I'd explained our philosophy to him in very clear terms, either he'd get it or he wouldn't?

Around tea time, Trish wandered into the shop, looking menacing. I wasn't sure how I felt. I didn't mind her dropping in but 'dropping in' was what girlfriends did.

She was dressed in a very un-Trish-like way. She was normally a smart, casual girl, nothing flashy, but this dress was hugging her curves very tightly, like Clingfilm wrapped around melons.

She caught me looking at her. "Stop looking at me!" she said, which was Trish-talk for "Look as much as you want!"

First the Sunday outfit, now this! She was definitely putting herself in a shop window. Did I detect a little make-up? This situation was beyond belief. In a few weeks, I'd gone from having none to having two women!

As far as I was concerned, I was more than happy with the new, re-energised Wes and, despite the drama, I really liked Roz and her circle of friends. Trish was a distraction. Virtually, an irritant. An unnecessary complication. To imagine she could bugger off for six months and just waltz back in like nothing had happened was an insult to me.

But she did look good! And she knew it! Eventually, she clapped eyes on Max.

"Ooh, look at you!"

Max smiled, shyly.

Trish walked all the way round Max. "What has happened to you?"

"I've got my own radio show now!"

"And his own stylist!" I added.

"I can see!"

Finally, Trish plonked herself on one of my counter stools and looked at me. Max quickly picked-up that this was going to be some kind of conversation about feelings, so he busied himself with his phone.

"Firstly ..."

My heart sank. If there was a 'firstly', there was definitely a 'secondly' and, probably, a 'thirdly'!

"Firstly, I want to apologise for last night."

"No need."

The dynamic in our relationship had changed. For so many years, I'd been like an obedient dog; wagging my tail, waiting for my reward. For so many years, I'd waited for her decision, her assessment, her judgement and, here she was, trying to sell herself to me.

She knew that discrediting Roz and her friends was pointless, so she began detailing the highlights of her personal CV.

"Do you remember Venice?" she asked.

I did. She'd organised a brilliant holiday for us in this mad, fairytale city. I'd done a week in Magaluf in Spring with the boys and then a week in Venice in Autumn. One of my regular DJs had watched over the shop for me.

What a contrast! In Magaluf, me and the boys had enjoyed seven, sleepless nights, while Trish had scheduled Gondolas, opera, art galleries, sight-seeing and food in some of the best restaurants. These pasta sauces made London's offerings seem like tinned Heinz! I was loving the pasta so much, I was in danger of turning into a real porker, a detail Trish would not have been slow to mention!

"That food! Jeez, I couldn't fit into my trousers!" I complained, with a smile. "All your fault!"

Trish smiled with pride. Being blamed for a great holiday was something she could handle!

"And what about your 30th?"

My God, she was pulling out all the stops! Indeed, she had arranged a brilliant surprise 30th for me. I had to pull my shirt over my head to stop people laughing at my tears. She'd pulled-in friends and relatives from far and wide, and even created an embarrassing slide show of old photos. I had not been a pretty baby and she took great delight in comparing me to The Ugly Duckling.

"Secondly," she began, "I fully appreciate that the last six months have been difficult."

The mistress of understatement! Someone you've been dating forever disappears from your life, with nary a word nor a note, and you think that won't have some kind of effect on them?

It's not like I was some kind of brooding romantic who had fallen into a tragic malaise but I did miss her. She'd been part of my life for so long and then, literally, she'd vanished in a puff of smoke.

"In my defence," she continued, "I was confused. It was a rough time for me. I thought I was pregnant and I wasn't happy. I wasn't happy to be pregnant but, at the same time, I was excited. And I was also distressed that I wasn't more happy. Confused, excited, distressed. Get me?"

I did. The new-model Wes was hearing her loud and clear! But the poignant fact was about me not her! Her first response had been to discount me as a father. Discount me as loyal, supportive partner. In short, she was NOT a fan!

"I should have been thrilled! But I wasn't. I was anxious for us. I wasn't sure we were ready to be parents and, in turn, it made me think about you. It made me wonder if you were father material. Being a father is big!"

Yes, she had already told me this. I'd had a few days to digest this multi-faceted stain on my character.

"I'd make a great dad!" I said, boldly. Not really knowing whether I would or wouldn't.

She looked at me with a slight rouge of embarrassment. "I was confused," she repeated.

"And, thirdly," she continued, "I like Roz very much. She seems very together. You make a good couple."

These words surprised me. If she was campaigning on her own behalf, this was reverse psychology on a different level. How was she going to compliment us as a couple and character-assassinate Roz at the same time? This would be worth hearing!

There was a large and luminous "but" waiting in the distance. I could feel it. I could hear it thundering towards me. All I had to do was wait for it.

"But," Trish continued, "she's not forever. She's skittish. She's curious. She likes to try new things. And you will become surplus to requirements."

Another kick in the teeth. It's almost like she didn't rate me at all? Which made her pursuit of me even more curious? So, in her estimation, I wouldn't make a good dad and, ultimately, I was simple. According to Trish, Roz would eventually get bored of me and seek pastures new. An interesting theory but one which I refused to entertain! Roz was Trish with enhancements. Roz was Trish-Plus! Roz was Trish plus postage and packing!

"You're wrong," I stated, firmly. "Roz doesn't talk about me the way you do. I'm not her project. She doesn't feel pride (or lack of it.) She doesn't feel disappointment. She doesn't analyse my attributes!"

Trish was unused to me sticking-up for myself. Whatever Roz had done to me, however she'd changed me, giving me a backbone was causing Trish problems! She wasn't sure she liked it or not.

"Oh, you've changed!" She smiled. This was a slightly worrying smile. This was a regrouping and change of strategy smile. She had a whole repertoire of smiles. I knew them all.

"Actually," she continued, "I think you would make a good father."

Ah, she was moving on to flattery! Slick!

"I've seen the way you interact with your little cousins. You're a natural!"

"Well, you're not pregnant, I'm not going to be a father, and I've got a new girlfriend, so it doesn't really matter."

A brief and fairly brutal summary. The smile disappeared from Trish's face. In fact, for a moment, she looked quite demonic! And, to make matters worse, Roz suddenly appeared.

She looked at both of us and could see that some kind of fracas had occurred. "Am I disturbing?"

"No," I quickly said, "Trish and I are just catching up."

"Busting to use the loo," she said, marching through the shop and into the toilet.

Trish looked at me. "I should go, right?"

"I don't know what to say to you," I replied.

I was now the wisest and most experienced person within my circle but not even I had the know-how for this scenario. Should I have waited for Trish and, if so, how long should I have waited?

Six months. No word. Not even a text message. None of her friends or family knew where she was or, if they knew, they weren't telling me. That made me feel like The Ex. My heart was depressed and my body was depressed too! So depressed that I was falling asleep in shop doorways! I was mentally and physically shutting-down, as if I felt worthless. And that had been an act of cruelty.

Yes, she was confused and needed time to think, but she hadn't conveyed any of that to me. I was fairly resilient but her disappearance had been a blow to my ego. The boys had always told me I was a wimp and, when Trish disappeared, I began to agree with them.

"How long should I have waited, Trish?"

She looked at me blankly. "I really don't know."

Roz emerged from the bathroom, shaking her hands frantically. I gave her some paper napkins to dry her hands.

"I really feel as though I'm intruding," she said.

"Not at all," said Trish, now looking morose and almost in pain.

"Are we eating or what?" said Roz, chirpily. "I am Hank Marvin!"

Trish looked at me.

"It's Percy's first night. I want to pop in and see him. Show him some support."

"Dinner first," said Roz, "then Percy!"

Trish looked at me again, wondering if she should stay or go?

"You will join us, won't you?" Roz said to Trish. "I need to be on good terms with Wes's ex, don't I?"

Trish was clearly touched by Roz's gesture but she did not like being described as "the ex", even if that's what she was. In her mind, she was treading water. She was in a no woman's land between adrift and re-attached.

"That would be lovely," Trish said, so we all buggered-off to a bistro in Camden. Max kindly agreed to shut the shop down and I strolled down the street with two beautiful women. I wanted everyone I'd ever known to see me!

During dinner, I barely got a word in edgeways. For two women who didn't really know each other, like each other or have any intention of being friends, they were really getting on well! It's not like they were both trying to out-do each other or impress me, they both seemed to be going out of their way to show how unconcerned they were! The subtext of their every gesture was, "Threatened? Not me!"

Percy's first gig was a 60th at a smart bar in Belsize Park. It was the perfect debut appearance. He knew the target demographic well. These folks weren't looking to pop pills and rave all night, they just wanted some tasty food, some humorous after-dinner speeches, a drink and a dance.

We arrived at the bar just as they had finished eating and Percy was playing them sixties Motown, Atlantic and Stax. We secreted ourselves into a corner booth and ordered some ridiculous-looking cocktails.

One by one, these smartly-attired North Londoners began tapping their feet, before graduating to some slow shoe shuffling. I stopped worrying. Percy had the situation under control. And, once he'd unleashed the classic disco, people were up and dancing. Spinning and smiling.

I made another mental note to update the website with photos of my DJs and testimonials from satisfied customers.

Meanwhile, the two women in my life were sampling other items from the ridiculous cocktail menu, and had both taken a shine to the American cocktail waiter, who they'd decided reminded them of Pete Sampras.

As I listened to them talk about books they'd read, holiday destinations they'd sampled, the declining quality of Oxford Street's shops and the cost of parking in the West End, I looked at these two potent *prima donnas*, both charismatic in their own way, both pretty dogged in their pursuit of the things they wanted.

How did I feel? As I sat there, sipping on Long Island Tea, trying to prevent a long straw from poking up my nose, I tried to transcendentally climb inside my emotions and take my own temperature. How did I actually feel about Roz? What were these flutters?

Well, I liked her. She was smart and witty and informed. She was fashionable and at the cliff face of everything. And I lusted after that hot, shapely bod. Would I ever love her? Was she even lovable? Could I really imagine myself falling in love with her?

And what the hell was Trish's game? What was she playing at? How would getting on with Roz help her case? Was she searching for an Achilles Heel? I wanted to observe Percy but there was an intense game of chess going on beside me.

Suddenly, Percy was playing some iconic sixties British pop by The Beatles, The Rolling Stones and The Kinks, and the dance floor was empty! These were great songs but not songs to dance to.

Maybe these sixty-year-olds were taking a breather? Having a quick drink? Or relieving their poor, fragile bladders?

As Roz and Trish continued to chatter and sample cocktails, I watched as this birthday event unfolded. After about 20 minutes, Percy was back to more familiar dance music and, slowly, the dance floor filled-up again. It was nice to see couples dancing together. They came from that generation. The couples were holding a hand, holding a waistline, and stylishly spinning their partner. People seemed happy. Again, Percy seemed in control.

Then, I observed the hostess approach Percy. There was a slightly fraught exchange of views and, within minutes, we were back to classic British pop by The Who, The Hollies and The Small Faces. Great songs but not great dance records. Again, the same effect: empty dance floor.

I suddenly realised what was going on. The hostess was trying to please her husband, but Percy's only intent was to follow our shop motto: play whatever makes them dance. Playing requests is often a slippery slope. Let experts be experts. If a DJ were to play every request and follow everybody's vision of the evening, it would be a garbled, disjointed mess. Everyone thinks they know best. Everybody thinks they have the solution. Trish felt she knew best. Roz did too.

I could see the evening was not going well. Not through anybody's fault, though. It was just one of those situations. The birthday boy clearly liked what he liked but it wasn't soul and disco, and he wasn't that fussed whether the dance floor was full or not. Percy would not be allowed to make people dance. It was like giving a kid a great toy and not allowing him to take it out of the box.

I knew I'd have to give Percy some kind of father-and-son facts-of-life conversation. The customer is always right. The customer pays our bills.

And it was the same in my chaotic love life.

I could go back to Trish? My old stand-by; the one who knew me; the relationship I understood. Or I could go with the wild-haired sexy one? The one who accepted me. The one who enjoyed stretching me.

All I could think about was my pathetic, depressed body slumped in a doorway, sleeping because there was nothing better to do! I wasn't going back there again. Miss Reliable had proven to be Miss Highly-Unreliable. Trish's disappearing acts were not good for my self-esteem.

This situation was as confusing as poor Percy's instructions. He looked deflated. I could see him going through the motions and wondering whether being a disc jockey was all it was cracked up to be?

By the end of the evening, I had one miserable DJ and two drunk women to manage. Fortunately, the customer was happy and the birthday boy thanked Percy for playing some great music. Percy momentarily looked relieved.

As Roz and Trish got merrier, so the volume increased. Pete Sampras behind the bar was having to contend with some pretty corny innuendoes, predictably including the Sloe Comfortable Screw!

"Don't be upset!" I said, reaching up and putting a paternal hand on Percy's shoulder. "The customer was happy!"

"I wanted to make people dance!"

"Sometimes, all they want is background music? Sometimes, all you can be is the soundtrack to a great evening?"

Percy liked that and it seemed to comfort him. He managed to produce a half-eaten smile and loped off with his CD wallet. He was definitely a name I could add to the roster.

My delivery boy arrived and dismantled the gear. With a nod and a wink, the set-up/break-down crew were in and out. Another successful evening!

Now all I needed to do was get these two boozy vixens home! I threw both of them into the back of a taxi. We dropped Trish back to her Mum's. Roz was winking and gurning furiously, and seemed to be suggesting that passionate sex was on the cards but, by the time I got her home, she was softly snoring on my shoulder, so I just put her to bed.

Chapter Twenty (Tuesday)

On Tuesday morning, Max came into the shop with a look of rock-hard determination on his face. He wanted to talk and it wasn't about a pay rise!

"I need to learn how to be a proper radio DJ, Wes!"

This made no sense to me. He'd achieved more in a few weeks than I'd achieved in a lifetime of feeble radio broadcasts. He had his own profile page, a stylist, new clothes, he was totally up-to-date with new genres and tunes and already had a loyal and passionate audience. My greatest achievement had been playing tunes for the customers at the Virgin Megastore on Oxford Street!

"What do you mean 'proper radio DJ'?"

"I need to learn how to talk, when to talk, what to say."

I wondered how I could help. I didn't really have contacts in modern radio stations. My radio days were behind me. The only thing I could think of was my old hospital radio studio. Really primitive and probably now quite antiquated! I'd worked there on and off for a few years when I was younger, cutting my teeth, making my mistakes, probably playing chart hits to no more than a dozen, drowsy patients.

I made a quick phone call to my old friend Reg a.k.a. The Midnight Rambler, and asked if I could bring Max down. It was a fairly old-fashioned set-up but I figured Max might learn something from visiting a professional set-up?

Plus, everyone would be his dad's age, so it would be an eye-opener to see how old people played music.

As it happens, when we got there, Max was immediately impressed.

"It's so tidy!"

Max shook Reg's hand and thanked him for allowing us in.

"No problem!" Reg said, cheerily.

I hadn't seen him in about 10 years but Reg hadn't changed at all. A few of his hairs were grey but he still had the cherubic face of a pimply teen. Radio still excited him and, even though his audience was small and, in some cases, very unwell, he loved the thrill of opening the microphone fader and addressing a captive audience.

As Max looked around the basic two-room set-up, Reg and I caught-up. It was just a studio and an office, but Max couldn't believe the systems and the order. All of the vinyl was neatly-stacked and filed, as were the CDs, and the central desk didn't have a paper clip out of place. Max almost looked scared to touch anything.

The room still had that smell! Not a bad smell, just a familiar and, actually, quite comforting odour. The carpet was still the same but, down the years, so much beer and so much tea had been trodden into it! Of course, vinyl and old record sleeves have their own smell plus, as a seventies baby, Reg loved to burn the odd incense stick, so all that combined to give the room a very lived-in smell, thankfully drowning out the aroma of hospital food.

"How's business?" Reg asked.

"Ticking over nicely! We're expanding the DJ roster. We're doing different types of parties."

"Good to hear! And do you still enjoy music?"

I winced with displeasure. "One or two things."

Reg nodded, solemnly. "Music's changed."

"You should hear the stuff he plays!" I said, gesturing towards Max, who was transfixed by the guy currently on air. The man inside the studio waved and smiled at Max, and Max gave him a nonchalant nod. "The stuff he plays barely passes for music."

Reg listened and nodded. I'd always found his side-parting worrying. It was hard to talk pop music with someone who looked like your mother's favourite bank manager. Ten years later, Reg was still wearing the same clothes: some clean and neatly-ironed jeans, a brightly-coloured shirt and a V-neck jumper, rounded-off nicely with some very comfortable-looking Clarks.

"I know," said Reg, stroking his beard and rubbing his finger, as if there used to be a ring there. "We play everything that appears in the Top 40 and some of it ... well ... some of it sounds like it was made by accident by monkeys!"

I thought about the kind of music monkeys might make but got distracted by Max, who was hopping around and seemed to want to ask Reg questions.

"He seems so calm and organised!" Max said, motioning to the guy on air. "He doesn't seem nervous at all!"

"Well, the cliché is: failure to prepare is preparation for failure."

Max looked confused.

Reg smiled. "In other words, if you don't get everything sorted beforehand, mistakes will occur!"

"It's so tidy!" repeated Max.

"He knows exactly what's going to happen next; he knows his running order, he knows his features, he's made notes about what he wants to talk about. When he starts talking, it's NOT off the top of his head. He knows what's coming next. Structure gives you freedom!"

Max seemed to understand. Every nod was followed with a "Seen!"

"So, what have you learnt?" I asked.

Max thought for a second. "I guess I should probably get my shit together?"

And, as we drove away from the hospital, Max was deep in thought. In truth, even though his pirate station was probably gallons of testosterone shouting into a microphone, him and his boys were bringing much needed excitement to the airwaves. Real, live, raw passion. True, most of the tunes they were playing were the musical equivalent of sticky, E-number sweets; sugary shit, but they knew how to sell it! For their generation, it was an irresistible offer.

Reg's little operation was a tightly-run ship but, if his listeners weren't already in a coma, his radio station was surely putting them to sleep. It was the polite, inoffensive radio of the Home Counties; as English as small, tight communities in rural villages full of Telegraph readers and wife-swappers.

I wouldn't be able to teach Max to be a 'proper DJ', he was already doing what young DJs are meant to do, talk fast and play disposable music. In time, he would refine his act. He didn't need my help.

"Wanna come down to our studio? See how the other half live?"

I had no other plans. "Yeah, why not?" I said.

I looked at my phone and there was a missed call from Roz. I quickly buzzed her back. "Where are you?" she asked. She almost sounded worried.

"Out with Max," I said. "I've shown him my old radio studio and he's about to show me his!"

"Ah, you're a good man, Wezza!"

And maybe that was my appeal? Maybe that's what made me different from the other men pursuing her? Maybe that's why she'd chosen me?

"You'll never guess what I've just seen!" she said, full of tremor and mischief.

"Tell me!"

"I've just seen your mate with the wine warehouse sneaking out of Jill's bedroom!" Her voice was rising in volume and outrage.

"Eh?"

"She didn't know I was home," she said excitedly. "She thought she had the house to herself! She thought she could sneak him in and sneak him out without anyone knowing!"

Roz was beside herself with glee. "You know what this means?"

I wasn't quite appreciating the significance.

"Jill has been bending my ear. Saying that you and your friends are not like us, not right for us, not good for us."

I'd never encountered this upstairs/downstairs mentality before. I'd never really met people who thought they were 'better' than me. Jill's words were from a bygone age and her view would always be a problem. She was an old-fashioned girl from an old-fashioned family. Times had changed. Opposites were attracting. People were finding themselves magnetically drawn to someone different! Different colour, different religion, different culture, different lifestyle. Just like that Blue Mink song, we were now one big melting pot! There were no rules to dating anymore. People were falling in love with the most improbable people. And even though Jill was sampling "a bit of rough", she would never change her view. In her mind, whatever names you gave them, there was strata. Certain guys were for sex and certain guys were for marriage.

"So, what does this mean?" I asked her.

"It means she'll stop bending my ear and let me get on!"

This sounded good. This sounded like relationship. This anecdote sounded like future and Roz was interested in having that future with me and, as if by magic, the other obstacle in my road – Trish – sent me a text message.

I knew I'd have to finish my conversation with Roz before I read Trish's new tactic.

"What are you doing this evening?" I asked Roz.

"I'm already in my PJs, mate!"

I bid her a good night and looked at Trish's text. It read, "What time will you be home?"

Oh God! What fresh hell was this? What was Trish going to say or do now? At some stage I would have to tell her that I'd moved on. She could hardly blame me for moving on? At some stage, I would have to declare a winner in this local election.

I looked at my watch. I was outside a council estate in Hackney. I sent Trish a text message: "11.00. Why?"

"We're here!" said Max, and he led me up some stairs to this anonymous, second-story, split-level council flat. Max gave the doorbell three short rings and the door opened. He was greeted warmly by a boy about his age, who then looked at me suspiciously. "This is my boss!" said Max. The boy opened the door and I was allowed in.

Nobody lived in the flat but somebody close to the organisation owned it. In every room, there seemed to be little clusters of people, talking, drinking and laughing. It was almost like backstage at a rock gig. These were the super-fans who were just happy to hang out; happy to be part of this movement!

Max led me into a room where the broadcast was happening. The room contained two people: the DJ and his mate. The mate was frantically oscillating between two mobile phones and several different pages on his laptop. His job was to talk to the listeners, while the DJ entertained the hordes with a break-neck blend of funky house, broken beat, jungle and drum & bass, which seemed to be attacking the speakers like an angry percussionist.

The DJ eventually took his headphones off and greeted Max.

"This is my boss," said Max, gesturing to me. "I wanted to show him my radio station."

The DJ nodded, slipped his headphones back on, moved up the microphone fader and began talking to his listeners. I tried to make sense of what he was saying but it was merely a mongrel language, part slang, part London streets, part Jamaican patois and, because he had Greek or Cypriot parents, the odd affectionate but abusive reference to The Wood Green Crew.

By his side, his cohort looked like an orgasmic octopus, arms flailing, fingers pumping, as he attempted to hype the online crowd.

Suddenly I heard a familiar guitar part: 'Shack Up' by Banbarra. This beautiful, funky lick had been woven into this primitive, high-speed car crash of a track. The beats were juddering like a faulty, pneumatic drill and the bass line was so low, only slugs or cockroaches could hear it!

"I know the original," I said to Max.

"Oi, bruv!" Max said to the DJ, "my boss knows the original!"

The DJ looked confused. "'Shack Up' by Banbarra!" I said.

The DJ quickly went online to find the original and I watched him monitor it in his headphones. A big, revelatory grin appeared on his face, as the missing pieces of the jigsaw fell into place. Amazingly, he had the PC on a channel and he managed to mix the original into the new track.

The DJ looked very pleased with himself and gave me a thumbs-up. Max smiled with pride. He was piecing together his own future and it definitely involved linking old music with new music.

As we drove away from Max's radio station, Max's brain was in over-drive. "See, Wes, you can help me become a proper DJ! You've got those old tunes! If I can get my shit together and you can hook me up with the old tunes, I will have a sound of my own!"

Max was shaking his head at the sheer enormity of the task. He had fifty years of dance music to catch up on! "Man, I've got so much to learn!"

Indeed he had. I took my knowledge for granted. I had a million songs in my head and I knew the right occasion for each and every one of them.

"I've got it!" he said, triumphantly. "You should play your music in the shop! Bring your tunes to work and play me what I need to hear!"

It sounded like a lot of hard work. "DJ for eight hours? I'd be dead!"

"Just once a week! We can call it Wesday Wednesday!"

Boy, his brain really was working! This crazy kid, who I'd woken from slumber, was now a top pirate radio DJ, style icon and marketing genius!

Wesday Wednesday, I thought to myself. Christ, it's even got a ring to it! The more I thought about it, the more I liked it.

"We can stick a speaker near the door," Max continued, "so everyone can hear your tunes? Might even attract some customers?"

It gave me great pleasure to see how this boy was developing. I didn't have kids but I knew I'd played a big part in Max's life. He'd told me so himself. Of course I'd make a good father! Trish thought she knew me but she didn't, and that was the irritating thing! She was comfortable running my life, but she didn't really know me! Of course I'd make a good father!

The more I thought about Wesday Wednesday, the more I liked it. It would give me an opportunity to re-visit old tunes I hadn't heard in ages, and Max would get his musical education.

I dropped him off at his Mum's house and made my way home. I needed sleep. Max and I had had a long day together!

The lights were on in my house and there was definitely somebody inside. The house smelt of cooking. I wandered into the kitchen. There was a large pot of homemade soup on the stove. I lifted the lid and inhaled. Potato and leek. My favourite. This meant that Trish had been here or (sharp intake of breath) maybe she was still here?

I hung up my jacket, kicked off my shoes and walked up the stairs. My bedroom door was slightly ajar and the lights were on. I pushed the door open and there, sprawled across the bed, lay Trish, dressed only in a very expensive and unbelievably sexy negligee! She looked amazing! As good as ever! Her curves were on full display and I stood in my doorway, just looking at her.

"Don't just stand there!" she said.

So, this was her new tactic! Quite a traditional and time-honoured tactic. Naked flesh! The ploy that rarely fails.

My feet would not move, probably because my eyes and brain were commandeering all my faculties! This woman! This woman who had once been the centre of my world. This woman who had taken my hand and guided me. Here she was: trying to seduce me! Something she'd never actually done before! Who could resist? Me. It was quite easy, really. It was a huge can of big juicy worms.

"I can't!" I said.

Trish glared at me. She could hardly believe the humiliation she was about to endure. She suddenly realised she was clutching at straws and it was etched all over her face.

"I know what kind of girl she is, Wes! She's cerebral. I talked to her the other night. She over-thinks. She'll try to make love to you with her brain, based on the data she has collected about you.

"She won't be able to feel it, roll with it, go with the flow. She won't do what's necessary. She won't be able to read you and respond. It will be cold and impersonal!"

"How do you know?"

Trish smiled, as if it was ridiculous that I should be questioning her female intuition. "I just know, Wes! I know women."

I was tired, so I closed my bedroom door and laid down on my bed. So, this was her new tactic: a potent combination of naked flesh and discrediting the opposition. I lay on my back and looked at the ceiling.

"I can't," I repeated.

"You're making a mistake."

My eyes were closing. I could feel myself falling asleep. "Let me make my mistake," I said.

The last thing I remembered was Trish telling me about this girl she used to know, just like Roz; robotic, lacking in emotion, lacking in soul, and the next thing I knew it was morning and I was alone in the bed.

I had passed-up sex for no sex. Even no sex with Roz was better than sex with Trish! New-Model Wes was strong and principled and made good decisions. Roz had to take the credit for this. She had enabled me to become a straight-up guy: a good brother, a good friend, a mentor and, potentially, a good father.

Chapter Twenty One (Wednesday)

I definitely needed to speak to the boys.

Not because they'd be full of insightful wisdom, I just needed to talk to someone!

There was only one thing for it: only Paolo's insane Italian establishment would do. The food was wicked but the decor was shocking, the staff were always polite but it was always kicking off in the kitchen! Shouting, banging of pots, slamming of fists. I was always half expecting someone to stagger out with a meat cleaver in their head!

We loved Paolo's. It wasn't cheap and cheerful, it was cheap and chaotic! Paolo was forever firing waitresses. For what, none of us knew! They all seemed like nice girls. Maybe they just couldn't work with Paolo? They'd rush out the door in floods of tears and Paolo would have to serve the food!

After work, we all headed up there and I was the first to arrive.

Paolo waved an arm at me, which meant I could sit anywhere. Deep inside the kitchen, there was some kind of mad barney going on! What were they arguing about? Food? Football? Women?

Paolo didn't even ask me, he just brought me a cold beer and stormed back into the kitchen. A poor, young waitress looked bemused.

The food was good, so the restaurant was quite busy, but orders were taking forever to come out! It was going to be a long evening.

I'd told Roz where I was and she was cool to leave me to it. She had some work obligation to attend, so she was busy.

This was also our first evening together following Melvin's revelation. How would it be? This was 21st Century London. Surely none of them would give a damn?

I sat back with my beer and thought about Trish's body. A wholly unhealthy thought! I tried to banish it from my memory banks but it wouldn't go! Her hotness was not in doubt! Had a man ever turned down such an offer? I didn't feel that virtuous, as I'd felt knackered and might've been too tired to perform?

That had been one devious tactic! What would Trish try next? Or had she finally got the message? "I can't!" sends a clear message, doesn't it?

Low came through the door of the restaurant, eyed-up the new waitress and sat across the table.

"We haven't been here for ages!" he said.

"I need Paolo's!"

Low looked at me. He understood. "Blimey, it must be serious? Is it about Melvin?"

"No! It's not about Melvin! Melvin's not a problem, is it, Low?"

Low looked appalled that I should suggest such a thing! "Nah! My place is full of gay waiters! I'm surrounded by them! One of them knows more about football than me!"

Melvin staggered in, carrying three bags. Just the three. One overnight satchel, one Banana Republic bag stuffed full of new clothes, plus his laptop case.

"We're at Paolo's!" said Baggers. "It must be something serious!"

Paolo's was very traditional Italian fare but Paolo had been in London for about 40 years, so there were all sorts of English things on the menu, like chips! You could have lasagne and chips, which I often did! Paolo also did old-fashioned English desserts like Spotted Dick and custard, which I had trouble resisting!

"It's not serious," I said. "I want a second opinion, that's all. Obviously I can't go back out with Trish! I just need to go through the pro's and con's with you guys."

Low was a big fan of Roz. "There are downsides to Roz? Gimme a break! She's the best thing to ever happen to you!"

She was. She really was. Why was I even entertaining the past? Was Trish really that special? When I was a kid, she'd seemed like a goddess, but Roz was a sharper, snazzier Trish! Roz was a pricier post code!

Topper wandered in and looked around him. He cocked an ear to the kitchen. Loud voices. He smiled. "Nothing changes!"

Paolo marched out of the kitchen, waved a hand of greeting in our general direction and told the waitress to keep the beers flowing.

"Wezza, why are we in Paolo's?" asked Topper. "You having problems with Roz already?"

"Wes has more than one woman in his life!" said Melvin.

Topper looked at Melvin and suddenly realised we – as a group - hadn't really talked about HIS situation. "So, Baggers?" he began. "Last time we were together, you seemed to be suggesting that ..."

Topper paused, unsure of the terminology.

"Well," Melvin began, "let me graduate it from a suggestion to a statement of fact. I am gay. Always have been. Just thought you should know! Trish was about to tell you all anyway, which is fucking out of order! My sexuality should NOT have been dragged into a conversation about the numerous women in Wes's life!"

"Numerous?" I asked.

"So, now it's out in the open!" said Melvin, looking around him for dissenters.

Low and Topper said nothing.

"I suggest," Melvin continued, "that you get all the jokes and comments out of your system. Say what you want! Say it as often as you like! Eventually, you'll get bored! Cool?"

Low and Topper nodded obediently.

Mids arrived, grinning like a stoner with the munchies. "THAT was a good day!" he announced. "And we're all here together at Paolo's, so it will be a good evening too! I love this place!"

Paolo came out of the kitchen and embraced Midders. They got on famously because Mids spoke a few words of Italian, gleaned from his numerous trips to Italian vineyards. Mids managed to ascertain that Paolo was having a few problems with a cocky new chef, who served-up superb food but had an ego the size of St. Peter's Basilica!

The waitress come to take our order and, as we settled in for the evening, I tried to engage the boys in conversation about me, but the conversation was NEVER about me, so it was hard to get them to focus.

Also, it seemed faintly ridiculous to all of them that I should be choosing between two women. They'd got used to the idea that I needed to be in a relationship. They'd got used to the fact that I had a girlfriend and she would always be a group consideration, but me having to choose between two women just caused hilarity.

"Trish says that Roz is 'cerebral'," I began. "She thinks she's some kind of soulless robot who will make love to me based on the data she has collected! Like I'm a science project!"

The boys all looked at me blankly.

"Cerebral?" asked Melvin. "She's a bright girl, that's for sure! Why is that a problem?"

"I suppose, without being too coarse, Trish is trying to suggest that Roz is too posh to shag properly!"

Low began to laugh! "Well, we know that's not true, don't we, Topper?"

Topper buried his head in his hands and shuddered at the memory. "Sloane Square!" he said.

"Yes, Topper, Sloane Square!" Low swigged on his beer. "One of those girls was very enthusiastic, wasn't she, Topper? Squirted so hard it went up the curtains!"

Everyone laughed. Mecifully, the food arrived, and the new waitress made sure we all had beer. We all thanked her and quickly ushered her away from the conversation, in case Low had any more Sloane Square stories.

"How does Trish know anything about Roz?" asked Mids.

"Oh, they had a big night on Monday! I popped in to see Percy do his first gig and those two hit the cocktails hard!"

"Ah, I see!" said Mids. "And what do you think?"

"I know you lot don't believe me, but I still haven't slept with Roz!"

"Maybe you're the gay one?" said Low, loudly.

Everyone stopped eating and looked at him. Low looked up gingerly. "Can I still say stuff like that?"

"Fuck off, Low! Say what you want!"

"I see we've had the Melvin conversation!" said Mids.

"Yes, we have," said Melvin, bristling. "Or do we need to talk about Melvin some more?"

Topper took hold of the situation. "Oi, you! Don't throw your toys out the pram! We all love you and we want to do the right thing!"

Melvin looked a bit shame-faced! "I know. What I'd really like is for nothing to change. Not one single thing. Low: say what you want!"

And that seemed to be it. We were good. Our Melvin moment was over. Things would carry on. As normal. No gay clubs! No gay conversation! Just us.

Which was all very lovely but I was still in my quandary! I still had Trish's bizarre words of caution ringing in my ears.

"I'm just going to sleep with her!" I announced.

Low began to applaud sarcastically, and everyone joined in!

"Very funny!" I said.

"I know where you're coming from!" said Melvin. "My boss is the same. She's 46 and she's still not married. She goes on dates, she gets very excited, but they never call her back. There's something about her they don't like. Personally, I don't think she's feminine enough!"

None of this was really helping. The moment of truth had arrived. I would have to make the first move, and then I thought to myself, 'Why hasn't she made the first move?'

"What does 'asexual' mean?" I said.

Everyone looked at me blankly, so Topper got out his smart phone and looked it up. "Without sexual feelings," he said. "That's what 'asexual' means."

"Maybe that's what Roz is? Maybe Trish is right? Roz hasn't made any kind of move!"

"That's because you look like Gollum!" said Low. "Who'd wanna touch you!"

Everyone snorted! Nothing had changed. I had two women who wanted to date me and I was still the butt of everyone's jokes.

And then I suddenly remembered Mids' midnight visit to Jill's room!

"Maybe you can shed some light on the situation?" I said to him.

Mids looked up from his food and feigned innocence. "Eh?"

"You've now made the acquaintance of one of the women in that house, haven't you, mate?"

Mids shook his head with disappointment. "How the hell did you find out?"

"Someone saw you sneaking out of Jill's room!"

Everyone stopped eating and looked at him. He continued eating and tried to ignore four people staring at him.

"Can I finish eating?" he asked.

"Can you finish eating? Slick lines, mate! No wonder she likes you!" said Low.

"So, Mids? Are those women cerebral? Are they too posh to get down and dirty?"

Mids looked up wearily and mopped sauce from his lips on a linen serviette. "I am NOT discussing my sex life with you pervs! Get your kicks somewhere else!"

I was getting nowhere. I couldn't even get taken seriously. They were all too busy eating and taking the piss out of Mids. I was no closer to a decision. I would have to move forward and take the next step. If she was asexual, I would have to cross that bridge.

As I dipped chips into the new chef's delicious lasagne, I thought how cruel it would be if this amazing woman had no sexual feelings. She was ticking so many boxes! What if there was a piece missing? What if we could never actually make love?

Paolo wandered over to see how we liked the food. We told him that we hoped he settled his differences with the cocky, new chef because his food was killing it!

And we told him not to sack our waitress! He laughed and finally saw the funny side of his mad empire.

Once everyone had finished eating, it was time for Mids to fess-up about Jill. He was wriggling like an eel and desperately trying to retain his dignity but everyone (particularly King Perv Low) wanted the details.

"We had wine in common," Mids began. "We had something to talk about! After the party, she wanted some more of one particular Merlot, so I made a delivery!"

Everyone laughed at his choice of words!

"The house was empty!" he continued. "Or at least I thought it was!"

"The thing is," I began, "everyone is single in there but Jill doesn't like lots of strange men and women coming in and out of the bedrooms!"

Everyone looked at me blankly.

"She doesn't want the house looking like a brothel!"

"She's a strange one!" Topper snorted.

"When we were talking in the kitchen," Mids continued, "there was lots of eye contact, lots of smiling, lots of twirling of hair and, when I moved closer to her, she didn't move! She wanted me to move closer to her!"

That sounded like normal behaviour to me. That sounded like normal flirtation between normal people. Even though Roz and I had slept in my bed, I was not getting those normal signals from her. I was not getting, "Move closer!" from her. All I was getting was: 'Aren't we a cool couple?' An analytical assessment of our status.

Yes, we were a cool couple but now I needed some emotion. I needed some "Move closer!" and preferably some "Take me now!"

Low needed more details from Mids. "It works very nicely. She'll require more wine and you can deliver it personally!"

Mids suddenly noticed his beer bottle was empty and caught the eye of the waitress. "We haven't talked since." Our friend looked troubled. "Nice girl!" he continued. "I hope she calls."

Topper looked concerned, "You alright, mate?"

Mids smiled to himself. "Yes, she's very snobby! She can't help herself! And, yes, she does look down her nose at most people but ..."

"But?" I asked.

"But I really like her!"

Mids hadn't really liked any woman since his wife left him. He had completely buried himself in the business. Long work hours, numerous work trips, punctuated by evenings with us. So, this was quite a significant moment. Mids liking any woman was big news!

"Back to me!" I said. "Back to me!" I had been given little insight and less encouragement.

"What do you need, Wezza?" asked Melvin. "You know nothing about Roz because you haven't slept with her. All the secrets of the universe will unfold once you sleep with her! You will know whether she's passionate or not. Whether she's generous or not. And, most important of all, whether she's sincere or not!"

The boys looked at me pitifully. I'd seen that look so many times. Yes, Melvin stating the obvious had been necessary.

In my defence, I'd been trying to act like a gentleman.

Chapter Twenty Two (Thursday)

So, here we were: more than three weeks later.

Most couples would've had sex and split up by now, but not me and Roz! Oh no, not us! We were too 'cool' to have sex. Too busy having mind-expanding experiences.

Her distinct lack of primal, carnal urges was beginning to unnerve me. She was too laid-back to rip my clothes off and I was too polite to lunge at her! Either way, we were usually both fully dressed and deep in conversation, almost as if sex wasn't important!

Maybe it wasn't important to her? Maybe she had better experiences for us? Maybe she was going to milk my prostate while we listened to Stockhausen in a public gallery? Maybe she was going to feed me a brand new cuisine whilst a naked Icelandic poetess screeched out her new haiku?

I looked forward to all my adventures with Roz. Honestly, I did. We were going places, my wild-haired friend and I, but I still needed to be grabbed and squeezed and lusted-after. I needed a woman who would give me 'the eye' or 'the nod'. I needed a green light, a come-on or just a straightforward command.

I loved the conversation, I loved the wit, I loved her smile and her laugh, I loved her look and her smell, but I still needed to know that I stirred her loins. I needed her to express desire of me. I needed her to fancy me! I needed her to fancy me because, if she didn't, she would one day meet someone who would really turn her on and, by comparison, I would just look like a male companion.

Tonight was the night I was going to be proactive. I was going to make it happen, one way or another, and find out precisely what kind of animal I was working with. Was she a lioness or a cold fish? I didn't really have much of a script in my head, so I was going to have to wing it. It was a poor plan; seduction was not my major.

After work, Roz came over and we tried to work out what we were going to eat. She had her shoes and socks off, and was wiggling her toes on my threadbare couch, so it didn't look as though we were going anywhere.

I went into the kitchen to get one of the nice bottles Mids had given me and she followed me in. Trish's pot of potato and leek soup was still on the stove. Roz's took off the lid and sniffed it.

"Smells good! Did you make it?"

"Trish made it and dropped it in."

"Nice of her!" said Roz, without a hint of sarcasm. She didn't know (and would never know) what that vixen had attempted to do to me! "We can eat this!" she continued. "This'll do!"

So, courtesy of Trish, we enjoyed a hearty supper. I even found some Ritz crackers in the cupboard which were fun to dip in! Add to that the delicious wine Mids had supplied and, within an hour, we were plump and drowsy, dozily watching some terrible C-List, American sit-com with canned laughter and clichéd characters.

Roz was stretched out on the sofa, with her feet in my lap, and I took the opportunity to massage her feet. I didn't really know what I was doing, so I tried to remember the last time some Thai girl had pummelled me in the name of good health. Whatever I was doing, it seemed to be working. Roz was moaning with pleasure and not in a comical, porn movie way. Maybe I was inadvertently doing reflexology? She seemed to be writhing, as if I'd reached other parts of her anatomy!

My massaging of her feet was having a quite dramatic effect. She stopped watching TV, turned over and began to arch her back. I didn't know much about animalistic behaviour but, from the little I'd gleaned from David Attenborough, Roz raising her pubic bone in the air was definitely a good sign.

I needed to get her upstairs to my bedroom but I needed a slick move. I needed a killer line, or a cute phrase or a suggestive roll of my eyebrow.

As I continued to work on her feet, I could feel her mood changing. I could feel her warming to me. There was slight colour in her cheeks and she was smiling. Finally, our eyes met. Not sure where this line came from but I found myself saying, "Early night?"

"Early night?" she replied. "What a good idea!"

And, with that, she was up and walking towards my stairs.

'Christ!' I thought. 'I'm finally going to have sex with this woman!'

There was no time for brushing of teeth or spraying of armpits. This was a rare moment that would have to be seized! I followed her up the stairs and watched her enter my bedroom. Was this really about to happen? She was tipsy and drowsy as well as horny, so there was no theatrical striptease. She undressed quickly and jumped under the duvet. I closed the door and turned off the light, and followed her in.

How I'd longed to kiss her lips and then move down her body. I'd dreamt of doing it and now I finally was. It was amazing to feel her body responding. Down across her breasts, down across her belly.

While making love to Roz, I tried not to think about Trish, but I kept getting flashbacks. Try as I might, I could not stop comparing them. Trish was passionate in a very Hollywood way, as if we were Mickey Rourke and Kim Basinger in '9 ½ Weeks'. Having sex with Trish always satisfied me but it always felt like just another part of our relationship, like cooking dinner or washing clothes or mowing the lawn.

With Roz, it was different. Roz was actually here with me. Sharing something. We were actually joined physically and spiritually. Both of us, right there, in that moment, committed to pleasing one another.

It felt so good. It felt so right. In fact, I was shocked at the fit. Our two bodies literally felt made for each other. When she began to kiss and touch me, I almost felt like I was floating. She seemed in no hurry, took her time, and tenderly made me feel so good! I felt as if someone was actually making love to me.

From the way she breathed, the sounds she made and the way her body convulsed, I knew I was pleasing her. Real men don't ask, "Have you cum?" So, I didn't.

And this was no quickie! We enjoyed each other for at least an hour, crashing back on the pillows, panting, sweating and laughing with joy.

"Wow!" she kept saying. "Wow! Wow! Wow!"

Real men don't ask, so I didn't.

"Intense! Wow! I could get used to that!"

I took that as a good review. I was thrilled. And relieved. A girl like Roz could have anyone and I knew, if the sex was lacking, I'd be the subject of discussion and analysis, and probably shunted to a back burner?

For my part, I was blown away. I couldn't get over the fit. I'd never felt that kind of physical compatibility. It really felt like hand in glove. And, as I lay there drifting off, I felt a huge weight lift from my shoulders. Until Roz completely freaked me out by jumping out of bed.

"Ooh, I'm hungry! Are you hungry? What's to eat? I fancy some hot chocolate."

And, without waiting for my answer, she'd slipped on my dressing gown and slippers and was gone. Mama said knock you out and I'd failed!

I pulled on some pyjama bottoms and followed her downstairs. She was happily pulling packets out of the cupboards and deciding what to snack on.

Like any normal man who's just ejaculated, I was ready for bed. I was spent and ready to sleep but, out of nowhere, she'd got a second wind and developed the munchies.

"I'm hungry! Are you hungry?" she babbled.

"No," I said wearily.

I sat down at my kitchen table and watched her scurry around. She'd assembled a large plate of cheese biscuits, and she'd found a lump of cheddar and some Branston Pickle in the fridge. And she was going to wash it down with hot chocolate! I sat back and marvelled.

"That was wicked!" she said, munching away.

I really didn't need to talk about it. I didn't need a play-by-play critique. What I needed was sleep and I was a tad disappointed that she hadn't immediately dozed-off.

Real men don't ... but I had to! I just had to! I had to know what had happened!

"So ..." I stuttered, "So ... did you?"

"Oh, yeah!" she said, confidently. "Quite a few times!"

"Are you sure?" I asked.

She might've been insulted by this? But she wasn't.

"Quite sure!" she said, blissfully chowing down comfort food.

But I wasn't convinced. I knew about the knock-out blow. I'd delivered it a few times before. This girl was smiling and happy but she was NOT satisfied, and this was unsatisfactory to me. You've got to keep the customer satisfied. Play whatever makes them dance!

Ice Cube "put her butt to sleep" in his classic track 'It Was A Good Day' and I knew that was the only real measure of success. It wasn't 2.00 in the afternoon. It was midnight. If Roz was still awake and buzzing, I had failed miserably.

She'd claimed to be happy. She'd expressed surprise and shock and pleasure. Surely I could be satisfied with that? But I wasn't. I knew I'd fallen short. Now I needed to find out if it was her or me. A delicate conversation. Could it happen tonight?

She seemed to be deriving sensual pleasure from her midnight snack. With every mouthful, she moaned with pleasure.

"Sex always gives me an appetite!" she chirped.

I smiled weakly.

She didn't say much. She just munched and replayed it all in her head.

Finally, she looked up and smiled at me. "You'll do just fine!" she said.

Snack consumed, we retired to the bedroom. Hot chocolate and snacks sent her straight to sleep within minutes. Leaving me to listen to her breathing and collect my own thoughts.

Despite my own fears and insecurities, the following morning, Roz made it very clear that she was coming back for more THAT night! It was not, "Let's do it again sometime?" It was, "I'll see you later." A very definite and deliberate statement.

Maybe I was wrong? Maybe I had delivered? Real men don't ask, so I didn't pursue the matter.

Chapter Twenty Three (Friday)

"Come out with us?" asked Low.

"Yes, come out with us." I replied.

Still elated from her Thursday night, Roz had decided to join us for our Friday night on the town. We weren't going anywhere special but, seemingly, she just wanted to go wherever I was going.

According to Low, girlfriends needed to appreciate the protocol. If it was 'date night', she could go out with me but, if it was a boys' night out, she needed to make other plans.

"Roz isn't that kind of girl!" I explained. "You won't be able to dictate to her! If she wants to come out with us, she will!"

"I don't need her there tutting at me! Tut tut! I am going to drink too much and I am probably going to kiss more than one girl. I don't need her there seeing all that and tutting at me!"

"You won't even know she's there!" I assured him.

Low didn't sound convinced.

Topper was a bit more philosophical. "It will make us look more like a group of friends, as opposed to a pack of wolves. Having a woman in our group will attract more women!" Topper was going through rather a dry spell and needed Friday to go well!

I was making my customary round-up of phone calls to arrange where and when we were meeting and Topper sounded a bit flat. All that tippy-tappy politeness and conversation was getting him nowhere. He needed a more direct approach.

Amazingly, I think Topper had always been a little envious of me. He loved the single man's life but he also really liked the idea of going home to someone. He'd seen me with Trish for many years and, now I'd graduated to the infinitely-classier Roz, I could hear Topper's brain turning over. He was almost ready to settle down. Almost. Men reach this point at different times; Topper was almost there. All that chasing of trim was exhausting. He loved his mates and loved his social life, but a warm body in his bed was starting to appeal.

I'd left Mids to contact Jill, to see if she wanted to join us. When he finally got back to me, he did not sound happy. "Christ!" he complained, "I think I was just there to scratch an itch! Jill sounds like she doesn't even want to talk to me!"

Jill was turning out to be an interesting one! The sensible and reliable one in the house: the organiser, the planner, the person who paid attention to detail. It was her 9-5 job and Jill brought those HR skills home with her. But she was also a control freak and she didn't want random sexual partners coming in and out of bedrooms, so she ran a tight ship! Everyone agreed. Rules was rules.

So, Mids had delivered some wine, brightened her afternoon with some nookie, and that was it! The player got played and Mids was not happy! Most men would be ... but Mids was not!

"Guess I wasn't good enough?" he rambled. "Really? Really?" he repeated with extra ferocity and lashings of sarcasm.

I could hear Mids about to go into one! I was in the shop, on the phone, and there was a customer waiting to see me, so I didn't have time for one of Tony's rants about women. He'd been burned badly once and he was now very sceptical!

"Listen, Mids, gotta go! Speak later?"

Mids was not happy and I had a terrible feeling he was about to do something rash, like pay Jill another visit! Mids was confrontational at the best of times. He loved nothing more than to thrash it through. As a business man that bartered all day, he needed all agendas in full view. He had plenty of time for diplomacy but NO time for games!

I put the phone down and greeted my new customer.

"How can I help?" I asked.

The man standing in front of me was clearly a grandfather. Not sure how I knew. He looked like he'd successfully raised good kids. That quiet sense of achievement and exhaustion. He had grey hair and a grey moustache but he was one of those sporty and sprightly grandfathers! He looked upright and still quite supple, and was attired in some very snazzy garb: professionally-ironed trousers, casual top, shiny shoes.

"I came to my friend's 60th party the other night; the one in that bar in Belsize Park?"

"I was there too," I said. "Seemed to go well?"

"It's inspired me!" he said.

The man held out his hand. "Andrew."

I shook his hand. "Wesley."

He reminded me of my mad Uncle Alfie. Always had an eye for the ladies! Never married. Then, one day, he fell in love, she rejected him, and he drank himself to death. Thankfully, this silver fox was still alive and scheming.

"I'm inspired!" he repeated. "It's my 70th next June. I want a party too! But on a grander scale! More space, more attractions, more people, and I don't just want loads of old buggers like me!"

He'd been thinking about it. He began to describe this opulent feast, which was going to cost him a few bob, but maybe he had a few bob?

He wanted a bouncy castle for the little ones, computer games for the kids; he wanted to make sure whole families came and stayed and enjoyed themselves.

"Do you have a DJ in mind? If not, we have versatile DJs who can cater for a mixed crowd."

"I want two rooms!" said Andrew, his eyes full of excitement and innovation. "How about that?"

I smiled. "We can do that!"

"Two very different rooms! So all my younger nieces and nephews can attend and have fun!"

"Great idea!" I said, and we began piecing together the details: venue, times, cost etc. I put it in our diary and we shook hands again.

I wanted to grow old like that. A 70th birthday with two rooms? Like some kind of cool club night!

'Ping' went my phone! A text message from Roz. No words just a photo of her boobs! My mouth fell open and I gawped. Max looked concerned.

"You okay, Wezza?"

I was speechless. Sharing such an intimate photo with me spoke more than any words she could've sent. Most important of all, it meant she trusted me. Secondly, it meant she was thinking about sex. Thirdly, it meant she considered herself my girlfriend. And, finally, it meant that, despite my niggles about not being some kind of dragon-slaying destroyer, she was more than happy AND she was coming back for more that night!

"Yeah, I'm fine!" I reassured Max. "Just some fucked-up You Tube clip!"

"Don't forget about Wesday Wednesday? I've told my mates about it. You've got the original breaks. You are the holder of the key!"

I smiled. He made me sound like Gandalf!

There was no point sending back a snap shot of my genitals. It would not have the same effect. I just sent her back a message giving her time and place of tonight's rendezvous. I got back a smiley face. She was happy. Despite Jill's hypocritical reservations and Benjamin's emotional blackmail, Roz was going her own way!

This was going to be an interesting evening. The boys and me ... and Roz. Low was already in a bad mood because Roz was upsetting the dynamic. Mids was upset because Jill had used him. Topper was nervous because he was wondering if he'd ever find a wife. While Melvin was just breezing through life, more than happy to observe the low-rent drama around him. And, in the middle of all that, I had to keep Roz happy, while discreetly letting the boys know what had happened last night.

It was a pop-up party in a courtyard in Camden, Melvin was the first to arrive, and I felt certain he wouldn't be interested in my sex life, but it was the first question he asked. Like a woman, his memory was faultless.

"So, how was it?"

I paused. Baggers noticed this. "Is there a problem?" he asked.

"Not really a problem." I paused again.

"What?" asked Baggers.

"Women orgasm in different ways!"

Melvin laughed and held his hands up! "Can't help you mate! If it was an emotional issue, I could give you advice!"

He laughed again and headed for the bar. He was a lovely bloke and usually very helpful but, with this particular matter, I would have to speak to men that had had sex with women.

Roz was the next to arrive and I got a very sensual kiss on my lips. I closed my eyes. I was virtually seeing stars! I immediately felt a twinge in my nethers. She looked deep into my eyes. "More of that later!" she purred in my ear.

Why the hell was I over-thinking this? Why the hell was I fretting about this minor issue? Roz was happy, she wanted more sex and I was more than happy to oblige.

Having a crisis pow-wow with the boys seemed over-kill. I was probably fretting over nothing ... and yet ... it bothered me.

Melvin came back with two beers and Roz embraced him.

"Nice shirt!" she said.

"Jasper Conran."

She nodded approvingly.

Baggers went back to the bar to get Roz a drink, and he left me in the middle of the club with this gorgeous girl, who kept smiling at me.

I was being foolish. Over-analytical. No matter what brand of orgasm she had achieved, she wanted more. More of me! Whatever I had done, she wanted more of it. Why couldn't I be happy with that?

The DJ was playing some dirty R&B and Roz began to do this comical lap-dancing move in front of me. I could feel people staring at us, more for my obvious discomfort than Roz's erotic overtures. It was fun, though. Trish would never have done such a thing. There was no hint of madness in Trish at all. With hindsight, she had been far too sensible!

Low arrived and Roz embraced him warmly. She had a real fondness for Low because he'd been her dance partner all night at Benji's birthday party.

"How are you, young man?"

Low exhaled deeply. "Glad it's the weekend!" His mood seemed to have lightened.

"Let me go and help Melvin at the bar," she said and disappeared.

Once she was out of earshot, Low was instantly at me. "So? What happened?"

I shook my head in awe. "It was amazing! Mind-blowing! It was nothing kinky, but the fit was incredible. The two of us together feels really fucking good!"

Low looked at me quizzically and squinted. "Christ!" he said. "There's a problem!"

"How did you know?"

"I just knew!" he said. "I've been with enough women!"

I was a bit embarrassed to go into detail, but I needed a second opinion. Low really DID know a lot about women! He didn't treat women very well but he knew a lot about them!

"She said I made her cum quite a few times but, once she got her breath back, she jumped out of bed; up, out, downstairs, making snacks; almost midnight, up and making snacks!"

Low listened and nodded and thought.

"No chill, no snooze, just up and out of bed, as if it was nothing!"

"Okay," Low said, processing the information I'd given him. "Okay," he repeated, trawling through his vast female orgasm archives.

"No knock-out orgasm?"

"Precisely!" I said. I knew he'd understand.

"The thing is: it doesn't ALWAYS happen."

We could both feel Roz and Melvin coming back from the bar, so the conversation had to stop, but Low's voice of experience definitely brought some comfort to me ... but ... I was still worried.

Once Topper arrived, we found a little corner and settled in. Roz was quite happy drinking and dancing. Everyone got dragged out on to the dance floor at some point! Still no Mids! Where was he? He never missed a Friday night!

Roz's phone was buzzing frantically but she was in no mood to talk. She wouldn't have heard anyone anyway. The DJ was digging in the crates for some classic boogie and disco, the music was loud and the crowd were whooping and hollering like a compliant congregation.

Whilst Melvin was occupying Roz on the dance floor, I was able to seek further guidance from our resident expert on female arousal.

"Christ, Wezza, women do all sorts of weird things during sex! Some can't cum at all, you know that, right?"

I grimaced.

"Imagine having one of those?"

It was a horrific thought.

"And that can occur for all sorts of reasons!" he said, sagely. "At least she's getting there!"

Topper was listening intently and looked aghast at my concern.

"What do you expect, Wezza? It was the first night!"

They were both correct: I was being ridiculous and probably over-thinking? (Classic female trait!) I'd just been unnerved by her happy-go-lucky leap out of bed, as if we'd just finished a game of scrabble, or just concluded the new season of 'Orange Is The New Black'. I'd done that once and Trish had berated me. "What? No cuddle?" she'd said. So I knew, from past experience, that there had to be some resonance; one had to let the moment complete before moving on to something else. Roz had jumped out of bed like she was on a tight schedule, as if her orgasms had just been hiccups or belches; the earth had not moved, it had merely turned!

"You're lucky the first night was good!" added Topper.

It had been good. In so many ways. She knew how to touch me. Some women don't! And, worst of all, I kept comparing her to the only person I could compare her with.

With Trish, I was aware of what I was doing. It was: this goes here and that goes there. It was good but it was functional, like a formula movie, or a song that's got the same chord progression as a big hit. It was good but it wasn't great. Like a tasteless meal that fills your belly but leaves your taste buds feeling short-changed.

With Roz, it was a trip! I was lost in music! It felt like floating, or falling, or flying. With Roz it felt scarily right, as if nothing else would feel as right.

Within a few hours, Roz's pretty outfit had sweat patches on it, her eyes were glowing and she was laughing all over her face.

"Wezza, take control of your woman: she's wearing me out!" said Baggers, putting his look back into place.

"Christ, four missed calls from Jill!" she said, grabbing her jacket and heading out of the courtyard. "Back in a minute!"

"Give it time," said Low, when he could see Roz was out of ear shot. "She's come back for more! Isn't that a good sign?"

"Are we talking about Wezza's sex life?" said Baggers, slugging from his beer and mopping his brow with a monogrammed white hankie. "She's coming back the next day for more? You MUST have done good?"

Topper was still chuckling to himself. "Wezza thinks he's some kind of porn star and, because she didn't squirt like a blue whale, he has performance anxiety!"

"Be patient!" said Low. "She'll be staining the sheets in no time!"

We could all feel Roz approaching, so the conversation ceased. Roz's smile had not left her face, so it wasn't bad news! Only, now, she was shaking her head in disbelief. "We have to go!"

"Where?" I asked, wondering if her libido had suddenly kicked in.

"Back to my house!" she said.

"It's Friday night, hun!"

"No, you can all come! Jill needs rescuing from your friend Mids! Or maybe he needs rescuing from her? Anyway, he's there, causing a scene! And Jill HATES scenes! HATES them!"

The boys all laughed out loud and rushed to grab their coats. Whatever Mids was up to, this would be proper West End drama! And, even though the boys were excited, I couldn't be happy about an unhappy friend; Mids had been through enough!

We all jumped in Topper's 4x4 car/wagon/sheep-carrier and headed back to Roz's house. Roz gave everyone a quick pen portrait of Jill and we gave her some choice details about Mids. His wife running off had really shaped the rest of his life. From that point on, it was every man for himself! No woman was going to hurt him. He would never be collateral damage again!

I was dreading what I would find there. It would be Mids digging his heels in, Jill trying to maintain her dignity, and the rest of the house wondering what kind of plebs Roz had brought into their life.

Either way, the boys were all looking forward to this grudge match. Jill was clearly working through a lot of issues of her own. She looked to me like home counties, church choir, girls school and tennis club. Who knew what mottos had been handed down by her mother?

When we arrived, the kitchen was a noisy freak show. Jill was red in the face and looked equal parts tired and embarrassed. Wendy looked chipper as ever and was making snacks to feed her rampant appetite. Benji sat at the kitchen table looking morose and aggravated beyond words. Raymond was frantically trying to get in the middle and make peace. While Heston wanted nothing to spoil his spiritual aura, so he stayed on the outskirts of the room and said little.

We all arrived and greeted one another cordially. Bottles of wine and beer were opened and, for one brief moment, we almost looked like a large group of friends. There was a harmony and an understanding between us; the easy rhythm of cool, civilised professionals.

The only thing disturbing this tranquil and peaceful gathering was the impasse in the middle. We had a real problem: a hot, sweaty and argumentative Mids, standing in the middle of the room looking for answers.

"What is it about me?" he boomed.

"Stop asking me that question!" said Jill, wearily.

"You said you wouldn't ask that question again!" Raymond was beginning to lose patience.

"I have to!" said Mids, "because no one has answered it! Why do women feel that it's cool to treat me like shit?"

"We're not getting anywhere!" wailed Jill.

I looked around the kitchen. Every room in the house had a high ceiling, so the kitchen walls had these tall cupboards full of plates and cups that nobody had used in ages. Those top shelves were only accessible via a ladder. The crockery up there looked forgotten.

The kitchen had one of those cooked-in smells, as if all the sauce and gravy had seeped into the oak. People cooked actual raw ingredients and sat down to eat in there. The huge kitchen table and the chairs looked used and appreciated. Despite there being an ugly scrum in the middle of the room, I loved this kitchen.

Wendy had made this large bowl of fish mixture (tasted like tuna, sardines, pilchards, grated onion, Mayonnaise) and was happily dishing out cheese biscuits, so we could spoon some mixture on. Whatever her friend was going through, this sweet girl seemed unbothered, as if she was used to such scenes, or as if she had little sympathy for the house dictator, who had strictly forbidden everybody else from bringing their sex lives into the house!

Benjamin, still wearing the unbuttoned shirt and loosened tie of his workday uniform, sat with his arms tightly folded, listening closely to the tense silence between Mids and Jill. Not even Roz's appearance excited him!

I decided to intervene. "Mids: what do you hope to achieve here?"

"I just want an answer to my question," he said, slumping into a chair. Wendy helpfully handed him a glass of wine, which he drank like water. "That's all I want: an answer to my question."

Heston finally decided to speak-up. "We actually can't answer your question, my friend. We've only known you a short while. We know nothing of your past."

"Ask Jill!" spat Mids. "Jill will know the answer. Why am I good enough to fuck but not good enough to date?"

Jill hid her face in embarrassment. Hearing her private life on display, particularly in front of five strangers, was too much to bear.

"And we all do that, don't we?" said Mids. "Everyone gets put into one of two categories: either good enough to fuck or good enough to marry."

Everyone was silent, as they trawled back though their sexual history: lovers, flings, mistakes. We all thought back to our early conversations and first, tentative fumblings. Was I a friend or just a warm body?

"Why won't you date me, Jill?" asked Mids, innocently.

Jill could barely speak. This was escalating downhill fast!

Raymond the peacemaker turned to Mids. "If you get answers, can we put an end to this?"

Wendy laughed. "Spoilsport! This is fun!"

Jill glared at her. "Not fun for me!"

Wendy popped another snack into her mouth and giggled. "Most fun we've had in here in ages! As I can't bring anyone home, I have to get my kicks elsewhere. This house has almost become a launderette! We used to have fun, but now it's turned a bit sour!"

Heston finally spoke up. "That's not fair, darling. We have a lovely home!"

"Yes!" said Wendy, "but I have to keep leaving it if I want to shag! But Jill doesn't! What? Jill makes the rules, so Jill can break the rules?"

We all sat and watched the inmates bicker. This was not the cool veneer they wanted to project. And that irritated Jill even more! She hated outsiders seeing them squabble. After all, we were just uncouth, uneducated local lads!

"Yes," said Mids. "If I can get some answers, I will be happy."

What on Earth was going to happen here? Was Jill really going to list the qualities that made Mids undatable?

Raymond turned to Jill. "So, darling, can our friend get some answers? This ugly spectacle has to end!"

Jill looked horrified. There was a toxic spillage in her kitchen and, not only that, it involved her sex life! And now some virtual stranger wanted an itemised breakdown of why he was unattractive to the opposite sex. It was too appalling for words! The embarrassment had caused an angry rash to appear on the nape of her neck.

"I can't do this!" Jill said to Mids. "I barely know you! How can I tell you how women view you?"

Wendy continued to dish out snacks and wine, like some trolley dolly, and one could see she was loving every moment of this. Somewhere in the past, there'd definitely been some history between she and Jill!

Benjamin was incredibly quiet. He didn't want wine or snacks, he didn't even look as though he wanted to be there, but he felt compelled to watch the final, pitiful decline of civilisation, as if life was changing forever, and he might as well inhale the last moments of his worthy, former life.

Finally, he got up, walked over to the kettle and turned it on. We all watched him. Low and Baggers were literally on their edge of their seats. This was the best reality TV show they'd ever seen!

"I'm making some tea and I'm going to bed," Benji began. "This is not me. This is not ... us."

"I agree!" said Jill. "We don't do this!"

Roz sat next to me, discreetly holding my hand under the table. Every so often, I'd get a smile from her. And then a cheeky wink! It actually seemed as if she was one of us, observing these deluded, archaic characters.

Heston lumbered over to the cooker and put a gas flame under a large pot. God knows what it was but, after a short while, the aroma was making us all hungry.

"We still have stalemale!" Heston observed, rubbing a taut muscle in his arm. "What kind of bloody Friday is this? We should be out dancing!"

"We were!" said Roz, "but then I was summoned home! I don't need to be here! What can I do? What can we do? Jill can sort this out!"

Wendy snorted, "Can she?"

Now the tension between the two women began to show. The cracks were starting to appear. They were all bright, professional people, but they had the same flaws we all share. They were better actors, though; better at making it seem as if they were in control.

Jill, the systems woman, the rules and regulations woman, the ethical woman was far from in control. If you exchange bodily fluids with someone, everything changes! People then feel they are owed an explanation. Finding a 200% no-strings-attached scenario is hard to do. Jill probably thought Mids would be happy to walk away from some afternoon delight. But then she didn't know Mids very well.

This was a man who'd had his heart broken, his confidence shattered and his business pulled out from under his feet. He was like Michael Douglas in 'Falling Down'. Jill had tipped him over the edge and now he wanted his revenge on a cruel sex.

"So this man won't be able to get any answers?" said Raymond, still trying to mediate.

Heston spooned some of this delicious-looking beef and vegetable stew out of the big pot and held it up. I could see Topper craning his neck, trying to see how much there was in the pot.

"Anybody want a bowl?" he asked.

"Could I?" asked Topper. After a hard day underground in his workshop, Topper rarely saw sunlight, let alone lunch, so he was happy for the bowl of stew.

Heston fixed himself another bowl and the two men began eating stew. Baggers and Low were quite happy sharing snacks and wine with the tireless Wendy.

Despite saying he was going to bed, Benji took his tea and slumped back at the table, looking as feckless and charmless as ever.

Jill was probably desperate to go to bed but, with her last-word OCD-ness, she knew she had to draw a thick black line under this matter, so it would be over. She was running out of answers.

There was a whole variety of things she DIDN'T want to say. She didn't want to say, "It's not you, it's me," because that would just be a laughable cliché. She didn't want to say, "Thought you wouldn't mind a no-strings quickie?" because that would make her look slutty.

"Okay, answer me this," said Mids, "why can't you date me? Let's go out on some dates? Get to know one another? You might get to like me?"

"I can't!" said Jill.

"Why?" he asked.

"I just can't."

"Why?"

Jill sighed deliberately. "I don't want to."

I think I even stopped breathing at one point. I just couldn't take my eyes off this conflict. Their horns were locked and Jill was struggling to maintain her dignity. She was about to blurt out words that would ultimately hurt Mids and she didn't want to do that. Like a child with a few items of vocabulary, Mids kept saying, "Why?" and, for fear of hurting him, Jill kept repeating herself too. Something had to crack.

None of us dared talk. Roz and her housemates could get in the middle but not us. We were still on probation! I could see that Low was desperate to put his oar in, and Baggers was equally anxious to be his normal pragmatic but blunt self, but we had to leave them to it! Raymond, in particular, using the measured tones and amenable body language of a diplomat, was anxious to make peace. After all, we were the new in-laws, and they didn't want to offend Roz's new family.

"Darling," Raymond began, prodding Jill gently, "we understand you don't want to date Mids, but you need to give us a reason why."

"I don't, Raymond, I don't. And I'll tell you why: I don't need to talk anymore. It happened. It's over. That's it! I don't need to explain my every action."

There was little logic at work here. Not even any emotion! It was just random, matter-of-factness. Like much of life, I guess? Characterised by the phrase, "Shit happens!" Mids understood that, and yet it wasn't good enough; he had reached that breaking point: his life was going to change and he needed answers.

"Why won't you date me?" he repeated.

"I don't want to."

"Why not?"

"I don't want to."

"Why don't you want to?" Mids probed.

Jill looked on the verge of a headache or worse! She looked bored, tired and, finally, a little sad. This is not what she and her mother had hoped for.

"I can't!" she said. "I just can't!"

"But why?" he asked again. "Why?"

"Because I'm married!" she said.

There was silence. Everyone looked at her. Digesting Jill's words.

Heston stopped in mid-mouthful, a spoon full of stew on its way to his mouth. Wendy looked wild-eyed and about to combust. Raymond looked around at everyone, to make sure he'd heard the same thing. Benji just sat very still, quietly shaking his head in disgust.

"To who?" asked Roz.

"Him!" said Jill.

"Him?" asked Wendy. "Why?"

"I thought it might help?"

Everyone forgot about Mids. He'd got his answer and actually looked pacified. He sipped gently at his wine and let the chaos unfold.

Wendy stood up to make her point. This was all too unbelievable.

"Let me get this straight," Wendy began.

"Don't lecture me!" said Jill. "I've been through enough!"

"Let me get this straight," Wendy repeated, "this is the man who was living with a woman, had two children with her, shared a mortgage with her, and someone you knew would NEVER leave his happy home?"

Jill looked down at her shoes. "I thought it would help?"

Wendy's words made it all seem so foolish. Jill wriggled in discomfort. She wanted the ground to open up, swallow her and then close up tight behind her. Jill thought back to a similar Friday night just 12 months ago. The day after was going to be her wedding day. It was going to be the beginning of a new chapter. It was going to be the start of a new life with her amour.

"I know he loves me," said Jill and, as soon those words left her mouth, she regretted saying them. She could feel each of us looking at her with a different degree of pity. Some of this pity was mixed with sympathy, while some was just the pity of an audience member, absorbed in the drama.

Roz looked at me and gripped my hand. She looked a bit tearful; she felt for her friend and knew she'd need to spend some time with her.

Jill straightened her clothes, stiffened her back and composed herself. "I thought if we got married, it would help. I know he loves me. He was happy to marry me. We enjoyed a lovely day together. I thought it would change things but ... he couldn't abandon his family. Couldn't do it. And I respect that."

Mids got up from his chair and turned to us. Me and the boys looked up at him. He didn't really know Jill that well but he felt for her. He looked a bit red-eyed himself. She was a massive pain in the arse but he didn't like to see Jill hurting. "This is a private matter. I think we should leave them to it."

We all nodded in agreement and quietly retreated. The inmates of the house had some catching up to do.

We came out of the front door and heard it close behind us.

We stood out on the pavement and looked at one another.

"You alright, son?" said Topper to a flushed and dishevelled Mids.

Mids nodded and put on brave face. Part of him really liked Jill. Part of him had wondered if she might be a full-time thing. She was hard-working, no nonsense and ethical like him. Yes, she was also a terrible, transparent snob with a head full of half-baked prejudices, but he liked her. She was a cut above his usual short-term shag-fest.

"It's Friday night," said Melvin. "The night is but young!"

"Yes," said Low. He put his arm around Mids and squeezed him affectionately. "We need to get this boy absolutely shit-faced!"

"Well, let's go!" I said, and we all piled back into Topper's tank of a vehicle.

"Where to?" Topper asked.

"Back to where we were!" said Melvin. "There was fun for everyone there!"

We knew what he meant. Even Mids managed to squeeze out a smirk. "I'm a bit over this 'fun' lark," he said. "I'll leave all the talent to you boys!"

Topper laughed out loud. "They will be unable to resist me!"

Melvin was riding shotgun, so he was able to fiddle with the radio. Fairly soon, we were all listening to classic house music at pumping high volume and aggravating other drivers. Another night of sex with Roz would have to wait.

Chapter Twenty-Four (Saturday)

The morning after, I lay in my bed alone. I decided to take a moment for myself. Just to acclimatise. Just to adjust to the time and the day. Adjust to my new reality.

I stared up at the cracks in the ceiling and wondered if they needed dealing with. My house had been built in the fifties. It was compact and sturdy. Small, simple rooms. A functional cottage. It needed a lick of paint but not much more.

My head felt very fuzzy. After leaving Roz's house, we'd headed back to that same event in Camden Town and drunk the night away. It had finished at 3.00 and we were there at the end. Melvin had found a friend; athletic-build, well-groomed, Eastern European or Mediterranean, tanned with Hollywood white teeth. He blew us all a kiss and disappeared out the front entrance.

Low had been dirty dancing with this very tall and lean girl all night. She seemed thrilled to meet a man who could multi-task; dance and smile at the same time! At 3.05, we saw them leave the event together.

Even Topper had scored! He and this plump brunette had been talking and there was much laughter and tossing of auburn-flecked mane. It was hard to tell what she was. She may have been Irish, or Italian, or Romanian? Who knew and who cared? He was great with conversation, so she was fully engaged: laughing, drinking, dancing, twisting her hair.

As Mids and I sat slumped at the bar, we watched Topper exit the event and we waved. Topper looked relieved but Mids was in no mood for any female company. His confidence was shot to bits. It all seemed a waste of time. It was hard to feel aroused when he didn't feel desired. It's hard to be exhilarated by the chase when you suspect it will quickly fizzle out like a damp firework.

And, as I lay on my back, looking at my ceiling, I thought about my mate. Mids would now need a dynamic woman to pull him out of his slump; someone who would restore his faith. Not ideal. Women usually require a strong, pro-active man. Mids was now the one that need rescuing! But, at least he had us; his trusty clan of peppy cohorts. That's what friends are for, I thought. That's actually what friends are for. As his friends, we'd just do what we always did, in our own haphazard fashion.

It was Saturday. The shop could open later, but I would need to get up. I needed orange juice, coffee and probably some toast, though I couldn't remember if I had bought bread. There was no need to worry about that! As I emerged from my bedroom, I could smell toast being made in my kitchen.

Roz didn't have a key but Trish still did! Today was the day I was taking back that key!

I descended my stairs gingerly and entered the kitchen with unsteady steps. Trish was stood at my stove and turned her head slightly to observe this pathetic figure.

"Friday night!" said Trish. She knew. I didn't have to say anything.

I sat at my kitchen table and wondered what to say. She put a pot of tea on the table and two plates of bagels and crumpets. The table already had butter, jam, marmalade, Nutella etc. So Trish sat down and began eating breakfast.

I looked at her with hangdog eyes. My head felt too heavy for my neck. Trish could see that I was having trouble focusing, so she poured my tea and buttered a crumpet for me.

"I need my key back," I said to her.

She nodded slowly. "I see," she said. "So you're going to try it with her?"

"I am."

She nodded again and continued to eat her bagel, sipping loudly from her cup of tea.

"I made a mistake," she said. "I shouldn't have run out on you. It was a mistake."

She hadn't said this yet. She may have been thinking it a while, but she hadn't admitted her mistake. Did it make me feel any better? Not really. I thought back to waking up in a shop doorway. God, how depressed must I have been? I didn't even care. I was drinking too much, sleeping too little, eating nothing but rich restaurant food, forgetting bookings, and not even thinking about where I was falling asleep or waking up. I'd never felt that low. Maybe it was a mental breakdown? I hadn't taken the time to visit a doctor. Men never do, so these illnesses pass through without a name.

"I stand by my view," she continued. "I think she's skittish. I think she'll need some new stimulus. Flutter on to another bloom. No reflection on you. That's just how she is!"

I nodded. It was the best I could do.

I disagreed with Trish. Well, I had the last time I could think! Now, all I could do was think about how right it felt with Roz. As Maya Angelou once said, "People will never forget how you made them feel." It was true. Roz made me feel quite masculine and potent and, after a lifetime of ridicule and tagging along behind, that felt good. Why shouldn't I feel like that? I deserved to feel like that. Through my hungover haze, I remembered that feeling.

Christ, why had I drunk so much? Countless (and very delicious) mojitos! They tasted so sweet and innocent! Plus, I had been consoling Mids. He needed alcohol and conversation, though he did most of the talking.

I nodded, as if to acknowledge what she was saying. I spread some Nutella on my crumpet and bit into it. I sensed melted butter dripping down my face. I didn't care. I sipped at my tea. Too hot! I could feel it scorching my throat.

"You can't even talk, Wes!" she said, trying hard to suppress a smirk.

"Mids needed consoling," I mumbled.

"What happened?" she asked.

I shook my head, which hurt the upper half of my skull. "Long story!" I said. "Really, really long story."

Trish nodded and continued eating breakfast. "I'll be here if you need me. I'll be busy anyway. Probably need to concentrate on my little business? You know you can always call."

I nodded. It was the best I could do. "My key?" I asked.

She reached into her handbag and pulled out my front door key, which she'd attached to a small Eiffel Tower key-ring, a memento of a nice weekend.

It was quite a poignant moment. Something I'd never experienced before. But I didn't feel as if I was leaving or 'dumping' her. She'd disappeared out of my life for six months and someone new had stepped in. That wasn't dumping, that was adjusting! I was merely adjusting to my new circumstances.

Thankfully, I'd met someone incredible who made Trish seem like a tasteless bowl of gruel. Roz was a sumptuous feast by comparison. When you discover something or someone better, it's quite a revelation, isn't it? You look back and think, "Christ, how could I have thought that was good?"

Not sure how I washed and dressed but, by the time I got downstairs, Trish was gone. There were fresh flowers in a vase on my kitchen table. Somehow, I knew she would ALWAYS be there, nestling in the background, just waiting for Roz to slip-up.

When I eventually got to work, there was a small film crew interviewing Max inside the shop: a camera man, a sound man, and a cute girl with a clipboard and two mobile phones, who put her finger over her lips to ensure I'd be quiet.

The interior of the shop was now illuminated by these two huge lights on stands, which made everything in the shop look extra dusty, or extra grimy!

Max was talking about music, and radio, and fashion, and social media. He seemed charming and confident. Who were these people and what had they done with my shop assistant? This handsome-looking young man couldn't really be the same Max, could it?

Suddenly, I heard Max say, "And here is the guy that gave me my first break!" He waved at me, motioning that I should join him beneath the bright lights. I waved him away. I wasn't sure my pounding head could take all that brightness! So, Max began walking towards me, and the camera man and sound guy shuffled around to follow Max.

"This," Max began, putting his arm around me, "is Wes, the owner of Wheels Of Steel. He gave me my first job in music, encouraged me to become a DJ, and has always played me the original breaks behind the big tunes. Most important of all, he taught me our motto, 'Whatever makes them dance', which is how I play my tunes. My job is to make people dance. I play whatever makes them dance."

He sounded like a politician and, in his swish but borrowed clothes, he looked like a media personality. The smile on his face was brighter than the lights! He was looking at me. In fact, everyone was looking at me, waiting for me to speak. I cleared my throat, which made no real difference.

"Max is destined for the top," I croaked. "I've always known that. He takes his work seriously. Serious people want to deal with serious people."

There was a pause.

"Wicked!" said the cameraman/director. "We've got some great stuff here!"

"Thanks, Wes!" said Max, his arm still squeezing my shoulder. I shook everyone's hands, signed the cute girl's clipboard and tried to look enthusiastic.

Max was buzzing. I left him to say his goodbyes and usher these people out of my shop. When they turned off those big lights, I breathed a sigh of relief. I needed more fluids, so I went to make a cup of tea. When I came out of our kitchen, the shop was quiet again.

"They work for some music website!" said Max. "Wanted to interview me! It's all happening so fast!"

"That's good," I said.

"The radio station want me to do two shows a week!"

"You're on your way, Maxi! Just make sure you play good music."

Max looked at me. These final words had completely blown his young mind. He stared at me, unable to speak. Thinking. Digesting. Of course! This was the secret: good music. Seemed fairly obvious to me.

"And keep it down in here today, will ya? Head's a bit sore."

Max nodded. "What time are we leaving here?" he asked.

I had no answer for him. Whatever he was referring to, I'd forgotten about! I flicked through the diary frantically and suddenly realised I was meant to be DJ-ing at a wedding. I looked at the clock, we still had time. I breathed another sigh of relief. I needed some more tea and a little quiet time behind the counter.

"If we leave here at 3.00, we'll be fine. They won't be back from the church until 6.00."

Max nodded again and continued answering text messages on two different phones.

I looked at the diary again and tried to recollect the arrangements for the day and the nature of the client. What had we talked about and agreed? I studied the details: 6.00 Reception, 8.00 Live Performance, 10.00 DJ.

The client was a jazz musician, and he and his band would be playing a live set at his wedding. Seemed like a strange idea to me but, it was his special day, so he could do what he wanted. I had no intention of working on my wedding day.

Wedding Day? Christ, I don't think I'd ever thought about my own wedding day. Weddings were something other people did and I worked at!

Max and I shut up shop at 3.00 and headed over to the venue. A really lovely space that must have held live music events, but the very high ceiling made me wonder about the acoustics.

Max and I went through the motions and set up the gear. The same way we'd done a million times before. We tested it to make sure it was working and, as suspected, the bass lines disappeared way up into the rafters.

Max looked at me to make sure I was alright. I wasn't but he had his own gig to do, so he left me to the caterers, who kindly fed me some delicious mini patties and some cold Coke.

Eventually, the guests began to arrive from the church. They all looked elated and full of optimism for the new couple. Stylish, modern people. Well-dressed, well-groomed. And there were lots of beautiful little kids running around, children of every shade and hue, all smartly-dressed in scuffed and smudged clothing.

The guests began eating and drinking, and the volume of conversation began to rise. I was used to this. This was part of my job. Background music while friends and relatives laughed and caught-up. I let Traktor and my laptop take the strain. A pre-prepared, background music playlist. Feelgood favourites at low volume.

And, after a few hours of noisy chatter, joyful shrieks, hugging and kissing, the band took to the stage. The groom in his wedding suit. The bride looking up adoringly. A five-piece: upright bass, drums, piano, guitar and the groom on sax.

I turned my volume down and the band began. It was a joy to hear real, high quality musicians on such an auspicious occasion. I thought about the couple's marriage. I didn't know them that well but I thought about a life filled with music. She would always wake in the morning to the sound of her man making music. It seemed idyllic. I had no way of knowing how it would turn out. Maybe a house full of happy kids? Maybe drug addiction and divorce?

So, the band played, and played, and played. On and on and on. The schedule was shot to pieces. The time allotted to me was shrinking and shrinking.

The crowd were watching and appreciating and enjoying but this was not dance music. This was modern jazz for the brain, a million miles from the big band swing of Duke Ellington.

I didn't mind. I was getting paid. I sat and watched pretty waitresses. And the band played on, and on, and on. Naturally, the groom was having a great wedding day. He was in his zone. Playing the music he loved to the people he loved. If he and his bride were having a memorable day, what did it matter?

With 20 minutes to go, the band eventually concluded their final encore and I played 20 minutes of classic, club tunes. People began to dance and looked very confused when I switched off and the janitor began folding-up the tables.

One of my gear ninjas arrived and began dismantling the equipment. Another day, another dollar. Whatever makes them dance ... or not!

It was only midnight. Relatively early. How relieved was I that it had been a low-stress evening? Me and ninja dropped the gear back at the shop and we went our separate ways. I was ready for bed.

I opened my front door. The house still smelt of the flowers Trish had left on my kitchen table. I looked at my phone. There was a selfie from Roz. One of those chaotic group shots full of cheesy smiles and deranged gurning. She and her cohorts were at Heston's sister's birthday party.

I put the kettle on, turned on the telly and sat on my sofa. I was still there when I woke up the next morning.

Chapter Twenty-Five (Sunday)

On Sunday, I'd promised to go and see Marie.

She was less in need of my visits, now that she had the hyperactive Percy tending to her garden. I called ahead to let her know I was coming. I didn't want to find Percy in his underpants again. I sent a text to Roz to let her know where I was, and she said she'd swing by later.

No, I didn't encounter Percy in his underpants but what I did find at Marie's was more disruption than I'd ever seen before. This was a woman who alphabetized her jam flavours and ironed her knickers. Everything in our old house was always in its place. Neat, tidy, ordered and fragrant.

Now, the house looked lived-in. It finally looked as if people lived there! She and Percy had clearly settled into a very 'do it later' lifestyle. The washing-up would be done later. The newspapers on the living room floor would get picked up later. The tidying would get done later but the fun would be had NOW.

Lots of empty wine bottles, lots of half-empty takeaway boxes, lots of Tupperware containers half full of cake. So, this is what love looked like? Mess.

Interesting. It's not that I was the tidiest person it the world. I was definitely not adverse to that lived-in look, but it was interesting to see what love had done to Marie. Virtually changed her personality overnight!

When she greeted me at the door, her hair was still standing on end, and even though she was wearing her apron, she was wearing one of Percy's T-shirts. This I knew because it referred to an Austrian beer festival and almost stretched down to her knees. She didn't mind. It reminded her of the tall and weird one!

I got a warm hug and kiss from her. Definitely a hug of both warmth and gratitude. I looked down at my clothes. My shirt now contained a smudge of flour and a dab of jam.

"Everything okay?" I asked, as Marie went through the motions of making me tea and cake.

She tried to answer. Stumbling and stuttering. Marie just couldn't put it into words. She would start on a theme and then lose her thread. Life with Percy was hard to describe.

She placed a mug of tea in front of me and a plate with a large slab of fruit-filled cake. Her face really was a picture of utter amazement and confusion. She had a zillion words in that vocabulary of hers but seemingly none of them could describe life with her new amour.

She almost looked shocked that someone could have such an effect on her.

"He's not good looking!" she began.

I took a bite from the huge slab of cake. Very fruity. It almost tasted nutritious!

"But he is the most beautiful man I have ever seen!"

This was clearly the 'love is blind' theory at work, a theory that was also working for me! I was no pin-up but, for some strange reason, Roz was knocking back other men in favour of me. Made no sense. Love is blind and also illogical.

"He's not the sharpest tool in the box," she continued. I dreaded to think where this was going! "But he is the wisest man I have ever met."

I detected a theme. And what was this teaching me? The oldest cliché in the book. You should never judge a book by looking at the cover.

And then Marie began to talk about the way he made her feel and, note-for-note, it was almost my same train of thought from Friday morning. As she spoke, I realised we had more in common than previously thought. She was definitely a sibling. The way she talked about the sensations running through her body (although it was traumatising me), there was no getting away from the similarities between us.

"So ... thank you!" she said.

"For what?"

"For bringing him into my life."

When he first lumbered through the door of my shop, I had no idea he'd solve one of the biggest problems in my life. I'd been struggling with my sister's self-esteem for years. Nothing I could say or do made it better. B.P. (Before Percy), there was no way I could convince Marie that she WASN'T a fat, past-it dumpling.

Percy had done what I could never have done: simply treat (and mistreat) her like a lady. Percy had no real idea how much he'd helped me. Marie had been a worry, but now my lovely sister had hope in her heart and dough in her hair. Better and probably friskier times lay ahead?

Around tea time, Roz banged on the door, so that meant another cup of tea and more cake. Not that I was complaining! I spent a lovely afternoon watching my two favourite girls talk about the past and, as Roz talked, she revealed things to my sister that she had never told me.

Roz talked openly about the house. She talked as if it was stuff I knew. Talked as if I wasn't sitting there! It transpired that Raymond and Wendy had been a major (but very secret) item for a while, and Jill had blundered into that relationship for a liaison with Raymond.

Of course, Raymond had got off scott-free (Wendy was besotted with him) but, for Wendy and Jill, from that moment on, things had been very terse and snippy. And it had completely destroyed Jill's impeccable credibility within the house. One minute she was judge and jury, the next she was a home-wrecker!

And, while she was talking about the residents, Roz spilled some beans on Raymond, who had been blighted by anger issues his whole life. Whatever he tried to achieve, whoever he tried to date, his simmering fury always boiled over. The dominant factor in his life had been frustration. Everything frustrated him! He felt a failure, which clouded his decision-making. He was never sure if he was doing the right thing. It had even stopped him from liking his own work which, according to Roz, was actually quite good!

No wonder Roz was anxious to spend less time with these divas and live more of a normal life! I would certainly show her normality, as well as repetitiveness and boredom.

The best thing about Roz's afternoon conversation with Marie was that, every so often, she'd give me a sultry wink or smile. She definitely had plans for me later and I was wriggling in my seat waiting for the sign to go home.

About 5.00, the front door opened and Percy walked in. Marie leapt into his arms and wrapped her legs around him. With ease, Percy held her in his embrace. Very impressive upper body strength! Marie was no Sugar Plum Fairy!

It was the end of his shift and he'd been up since 6.00. Percy looked knackered! He sat at Marie's kitchen table, stretched-out his long legs and closed his eyes. Roz and I looked at him. This was definitely our cue to go.

As we sat in the car ride home, I could see Roz smiling to herself.

"What's tickling you?" I asked.

"I like this," she said. "This. Us. Our life."

"Not too mundane for you?"

Roz laughed and shook her head. "Nooo! You've got some good characters in your soap opera!"

When we got back to my place, no sooner had I closed the front door, then Roz began taking her clothes off! Not in any burlesque kind of way, she was just in a hurry!

With every step, she took something off and, by the time she reached the top of my stairs, she was stark naked. That sweet little bum swished into my bedroom and I said a silent prayer of thanks to whichever gods were listening!

What was there to do? I picked up her clothes and followed her into the bedroom. When I got in there, she was stretched out on my bed, writhing and wriggling, sensually squeezing her boobs and opening her legs, so I could see how cleanly she had been waxed.

"Are you going to kiss me now?" she asked.

Dutifully, I stripped off and joined her on the bed. I began kissing her feet.

She giggled. "Tickles!"

And I continued up and up and up. I kissed her everywhere! And just like the jazz musician on his wedding day, I thought to myself, if he can play solos for two hours, so can I! I was determined to be thorough. Stamina is important!

Just like before, it really felt amazing! Just like before, I got lost in the experience. Totally absorbed in what I was doing and what she was doing. I loved the way she kissed: the softness of her lips, the different kinds of kisses, the way our lips joined. Suddenly, all those R&B slow jamz began to make sense! She made me feel powerful. She made me feel alive.

And, just like before, about two hours later, there reached a point when she was finished and she jumped out of bed. "That was fun!" she said, pulling on my dressing gown and slippers. "I'm famished!"

I lay there, looking at her, exhausted. Spent.

"Come on! The grub ain't gonna make itself!" she said.

"Can I ask you a question?"

She looked at me suspiciously. "A question? You're not going to ask me something daft like how many men have I slept with?"

"No," I replied. No point asking that question! "Do you ever ..." I paused. I really didn't want to screw this up. "Do you ever have that one big orgasm that puts you to sleep?"

No one had ever asked her that. No one had ever cared that much. She'd heard about it, thought about it but never given it THAT much thought, and certainly no one had ever asked her about it.

"Never had one!" she said, timidly. Nervous that I was about to label her as some kind of mutant.

"I guess," she continued, "I must be broken?"

I smiled and got up out of bed. As she had my dressing gown and slippers, I quickly put on some football shorts and an old T-shirt.

"I may have to quote Coldplay!"

She laughed out loud. "Nooo!" she wailed. "Not Coldplay!"

"I'm afraid so."

She smiled. She knew this orgasm business wasn't a serious deal-breaking issue. She now realised I wasn't finding fault, I was just learning about her.

I looked at her solemnly. "I will fix you."

She smiled sweetly. She seemed touched by my outrageous promise. "Will you, darling?"

"Sure," I said. "It will be fun?"

Chapter Twenty Six (Monday)

I hadn't seen the boys since Friday.

I wanted to see them. Damn it, I needed to see them! We hadn't had a mother's meeting since Friday and there was LOTS to catch up on.

There was a decent game of football on the box, so we arranged to meet at The Dog & Duck for beer, a very light (but wholly unhealthy) evening meal and some in-depth gossip about everybody's love lives.

I locked-down one of our favourite tables and made myself at home. This, for me, was the best table in the house: close to the toilets but not close enough to inhale the stench of stale urine, equidistant between two of the biggest screens in the pub, affording a good view to those on both sides of the table, and close to the bar too.

Looking dishevelled and slightly stained, Low was the first to arrive and immediately wanted to know about Roz. There was something voyeuristic about Low's questions. He was ALWAYS happy talking about other people's sex lives, which usually made his line of questioning quite creepy but, on this occasion, he had been very helpful, so I gave him some detail. Not too much, though. Any lurid details would be digested and regurgitated into some five-knuckle shuffle at a later date!

"I'm not going to worry about the knock-out punch," I said to him. "I think it will come in time. We just need the right mood. The right circumstances. She really likes what we're doing! It's good, mate, trust me, it's good!"

Low listened intently. This was his science. Finally, he nodded his approval. "You're right, Wezza. The right circumstances. You need to find out what REALLY turns her on. Just like your motto: whatever makes them dance. You will need to do whatever makes her dance. Find out what she likes and give her exactly what she needs!"

It sounded cold and mechanical but he was right. It was my job not just to be Mr. Right but also Mr. Make It Right. This was a girl who, for some bizarre reason, was into me, so I was halfway to Heaven. If I could set the mood right and put us in the right environment, Roz and I could really hit some heights!

But something was bothering Low. He wasn't looking up and around, scanning the horizon for hotty totty, he was looking down into his beer, reflecting on something.

"This is all changing, Wes. Our vibe. The gang."

This was uncharacteristically sensitive for Low. It almost seemed like he was expressing an emotion (and not just a physical need!)

"You and Roz, Melvin going his own way, Mids losing his mind. What next?"

I could see he was genuinely concerned and, as I had recently been elevated to Group Sage, it was my duty to talk him off the ledge.

"I hear what you're saying," I began, quite an impressive start I thought, "what you're saying is true; things have changed, but there's no real reason for us (the gang) to change. If we want things to stay the same, they can! Honest! Roz is the nuts but I still need you guys."

"It will change!" he maintained. "It can't stay the same forever!"

There was a different look in Low's eyes, as if he was feeling left behind. I'd never seen this expression before. This was the indestructible alpha male.

This was the guy who never got ill and always had the strength to fight not just his corner but yours as well.

"Is there something troubling you?"

Low was really struggling with something but it wouldn't come to the surface. Something he wanted to say but it wasn't even making sense in his head.

"I think," he began, and then he stopped. Whatever he needed to say was clearly out-of-character or embarrassing.

"I think," he began again, "I am jealous of you. Roz is really a top girl and I'm really pissed-off that you found her because, if I'd got to her first, it might've happened."

This was a lot to take in. Low had never said anything like this before. No one had EVER said anything like this to ME. After all, I was the weedy gimp. I was the runt, the after-thought, the also-ran. But things had changed. Now I was the holder of the winning rosette! In previous times, I would've struggled with an answer but now, finally, I had a reply for him.

"You know what, mate? A pretty thing like Roz has done her fair share of beefcakes. I'm sure she's spent time with some pretty spectacular candidates. Why did she choose me? Because I like being in a relationship. I want to be in a relationship. She'd look at someone like you: tall, handsome, dynamic, and she'd think, 'Player. He won't stick around.'"

Low looked profoundly depressed. This was NOT a look I'd seen from our resident sweetboy! "Can't help the way I am, can I?"

I laughed. This seemed funny to me. "My heart bleeds for you, son. You've got some enviable problems!"

Crikey, what was happening to my gang? It was like menstrual cycles synchronising! I'd found an amazing girl and, all of a sudden, my male friends were getting emotional and wanted girlfriends too!

Next through the door was Topper who, by comparison, looked full of the joys of every season. He bounded into the pub and embraced us both! Not our normal greeting but he seemed to want to show his love and appreciation. This was a man who had clearly just been laid!

Topper didn't even speak, he just went to the bar and grabbed beers. He even came back with a large bag of cashew nuts. Replacing protein!

"I gather it went well with you and the brunette?"

"It did!" said Topper, beaming. I'd never noticed he had such white teeth! Had he been on the stain-removing toothpaste?

"Eh? What?" said Low. "Not Topper as well! Have you found a girlfriend too?"

Topper thought about it. I could see his memory banks rounding up random images from the last 48 hours. "Could be?" he said.

Topper sucked on his beer and opened the bag of cashews. "Her name's Zehra. Italian mum, Turkish dad. She's been single all her life. She's 38 now. I don't think she believes she'll ever find a husband!"

"Aww, bless! You're like her knight in dented armour!" Low really sounded jealous now. I'd never seen this side of him before. He'd always been SO happy: ploughing his own furrow, making deposits in whatever orifice was available. He'd always seemed disinterested in the rituals, conventions and obligations of a relationship, and here he was whining about Topper's good fortune.

Topper was too high to be bothered by Low's cynicism. "She is definitely the hairiest woman I have ever been with!"

We both looked at him. It was almost too much information.

"Really nice girl!" Topper rambled, pouring more cashews into his palm and finally remembering to share the bag. "Both her parents passed away a few years ago. She lives on her own. Quite well to do. She runs a cleaning company. You know, those people who arrive when the workers go home?"

Low and I both nodded. It was good to hear Topper talking. He'd been subdued for the last few months.

Low chomped down some cashews and muttered something to himself. "If Baggers comes in and tells us he's getting married, I will eat everyone's bloody hat!"

Topper suddenly looked at Low and noticed a distinct change in mood. "What's up with you?"

"Low thinks the group is changing!" I replied.

"If both of you get girlfriends, it's over!" said Low.

If Low was going to be a drama queen, there was no point getting into it.

"Don't be daft," Topper said, dismissively. "I took her to my workshop! Zehra actually wanted to come downstairs and see where I worked! Her hands are covered in all this ornate jewellery, so I told her what it was: what stones, what value, what style. We talked for hours!"

"And you had sex!" said Low, fishing for some visual images.

"Of course we did! I haven't had any for four months and she hasn't had any for a year!"

"Christ!" said Low, "It must have been a whirlpool of orgasmic juices!"

"I haven't slept as well in ages!" said Topper. "And, in the morning, there was this bloody feast on the kitchen table!"

Sexy and domesticated. It didn't get much better.

Mids still hadn't arrived. I was dreading a phone call from Roz, saying he was there at the house again. Instead I got a text message from the man himself, informing us that he wouldn't be attending our evening, as he was wine-tasting down in the Loire Valley.

Topper shook his head. "He's in a bad way!"

"He'll be alright!" said Low, who now had little sympathy for anyone. "He's got it all: he's bi-lingual, got his own business, got a full head of hair!"

I looked at Mids' text again. He seemed okay. Business as usual. The gang HAD to stay together, if only for Mids! He needed the boys, the banter, the madness, the laughter.

And, finally, Baggers walked through the door carrying just one bag. Just one.

I feared that Low was going to have some kind of mild heart attack! Melvin only carrying one bag was unheard of! This was too much change for Low to handle!

"Where are your bloody bags?"

"Good evening to you too!" he replied, sarcastically. "How are you Melvin? How was your day? Would you like a drink?"

"Bollocks to that!" said Low, assertively. "Where are your bags?"

Melvin looked at him with an amused glare of mock-petulance. It looked quite camp to me but I didn't want to focus on his sexuality too much. He was OCD first and gay second!

"I got given a gift. A very expensive watch. I'm not even into watches but this was a VERY pretty time piece. I put it in one of my bags and I left that bag on an Underground train. There was only dirty clothes in there but it did contain my gift."

"Been to Lost Property?" I asked.

"Not in Lost Property! Gone! It was a very expensive watch!"

"So?" said Low, impatiently. "Where are the bags?"

"No more bags!" said Melvin, simply. "Get my own drink, shall I?"

"I'll go!" Topper got up and went to the bar for him.

"No more bags? Just like that?." I wasn't sure where Low was going but the change in Melvin was unnerving him.

"I don't want to lose any more gifts, do I?" The logic seemed straightforward to Melvin but Low wasn't grasping it. "I need to keep it simple: less bags equals less chance of me losing expensive gifts."

Low nodded. He was finally getting it. Topper returned from the bar with a bottle of beer, which Melvin gratefully began to drink.

"Topper's got a new girlfriend!" I said to Baggers.

"Two legs or four?" he asked.

"Very funny!" said Topper. "You'll like her! She runs a cleaning company; she's neater and more organised than you!"

"I'm impressed!" said Baggers.

I was half-expecting Roz to come through the door but she was out with her mates, I was out with my mates. It was unbelievably mature and civilised. I felt like I was wearing a cravat.

We enjoyed the football match. Quite entertaining for a 0-0 draw. Topper spoke some more about Zehra, and then he suddenly remembered my situation. "So, what happened about Roz?"

Even Baggers looked up!

"I think it's going to be okay."

I looked at Low for approval. He nodded.

"I'm not going to worry about it," I continued. "I think we'll be able to ... get higher! If that makes sense?"

Topper shook his head. "You don't know how lucky you are! With Zehra, nothing!"

This piqued Low's interest. "Nothing? At all?"

"Nothing at all," confirmed Topper. "She absolutely loved what I was doing, and she loved giving me pleasure but ... getting there ... it didn't happen! Early days, though!"

"Early days!" we all repeated in unison, like it was some kind of mantra.

Suddenly, I felt quite lucky. The sparks that flew between Roz and I were a New Year's Eve midnight display compared to Topper's grateful fumbling. It was almost the Kama Sutra at my place and the Enid Blyton books at his!

"But, like I told Wes," said Low, our expert on all matters vaginal, "you just need to adopt his motto: whatever makes them dance. Italian and Turkish? She must be a passionate girl! You just need to set the right mood! She might have erogenous zones you never even thought of!"

We were all silent, as we thought about erogenous zones. This was truly a sign that we were modern, metrosexual men.

Roz had captivated Benjamin. She was a woman he would never forget. Maybe the love of his life? She had that effect on men. To hear Low talk about her in such glowing terms was slightly unnerving but I knew she had his number. He was a much more dynamic package than me but she was done with dynamic packages. Now, she wanted date night, Valentine's Day and shopping trips to IKEA. She wanted to share everything with someone else, no matter how trivial or mundane. She wanted private jokes and someone to rub her abdomen, and a sweetboy like Low would never be able to give her that!

Chapter Twenty Seven (Tuesday)

When I arrived at work, there was a big sign on the window saying 'Tomorrow Is Wesday Wednesday. Come and hear the original breaks!"

All I could do was smile. I wasn't sure how good it was for business but it might while away a few hours?

"I've told all my friends about it!" Max said excitedly, running his fingers through his expensive new hairstyle. "Dudes who make music are coming to hear you! Get some inspiration!"

I wasn't totally sure I was mentor material, but I did have boxes of dusty old 12-inch singles, which looked as if they'd be seeing the light of day tomorrow?

"Two shows a week!" began Max, "And the station want to sponsor my club night! All day all night advertising of my club night! As long as I have a guest DJ from the station every week! Works for me!"

When you're flavour of the month, that trajectory is a beautiful curve! Everything you try ... works! Everything you say ... people listen to! When you're on the rise, everybody wants to be your friend, wants to work with you, wants to hear your opinion.

Max was in a great place right now. People were hanging on his every word. Girls just wanted to hang off his arm! And, because of this trajectory, Max had been able to convince his circle of friends that I was some kind of mystical guru who would lead them along a path of enlightenment to great grooves and full dance floors. After all, I was the holder of the original breaks.

All day I could hear Max on his phones, hyping Wesday Wednesday. Maybe it would bring in a new customer? It was worth a try?

It was quite a busy Tuesday. I looked at the calendar. Was it wedding season? No. For some reason, everybody wanted to hold events. I had a booking for a village fete, a booking for a wedding anniversary, one for a renewing-of-vows party, and another for a retirement party. It was nice to know that music still had the ability to turn an event into a party. Good music still had that magic pixie dust you could sprinkle on a soiree! Did I have a skill or a talent? Trish always used to say to me, "You've got the ability to make people smile." That was one thing I had to thank Trish for: she'd always encouraged me. She'd been a major kick-start in my life.

What kind of future would we have? What kind of friends could we be? If we went for a casual cuppa, would she ever ask, 'How are things with you and Roz?' Why would she? She didn't care. She would never be cheering us from the sidelines, willing us on to happy matrimony.

The shifting sands of a friendship. Moving from lover to friend, or vice versa: tricky! Trish was now the ex. Not a gone-forever ex but a still-in-my-life ex. The former was almost cleaner and simpler! Fortunately, Roz took 'easy-going' to a whole new level, so I knew she would never be threatened by Trish, whatever kind of ex she was!

As we hadn't seen each other on Monday, Roz and I had a hot date for that night. We hadn't really made any firm plans to do anything but any date with Roz was 'hot'! We were in that wonderful 'can't get enough' phase. I definitely couldn't get enough of her and, thankfully, she wanted to see more of me.

I was anxious to appear 'cool', though. Didn't want to be un-cool! I'd observed that in Topper before. He had the tendency to be a bit 'full-on'. A bit too intense too quickly. I made a mental note to talk to him. I didn't want him screwing-up his new relationship with Zehra. And I made a mental note to tell him NOT to tell people she was 'hairy'! Christ, what was happening to me? I was almost developing a new level of sensitivity. First erogenous zones, and now I was able to identify inappropriate banter. It was a breakthrough!

Around lunch time, Trish appeared, carrying coffee and sandwiches. She didn't say a word. She just plonked lunch on the counter, gave Max his grub, and sat on one my stools, eating her sarnie. Looking quite pleased with herself, for some reason.

Would this be the nature of our new friendship: impromptu visits to the shop? I wasn't sure I liked it and I wasn't sure Roz would like it. First, the front door key and now this! Trish was forcing my hand. I didn't want to be an authoritarian but, fairly soon, I would have to give our friendship parameters.

I looked inside the bag. It was one of those flash sandwiches from Pret-A-Manger. Hard to resist! She was softening me up. She had something to tell me. What would it be? Whatever it was, it was giving her great pleasure.

As she continued to sit and chew and smile, I decided to eat my lunch. Whatever her new ploy, nothing would divert me from my course! Roz was my future, Trish was my past.

"You can't trust her, you know! She's too pretty!"

The sandwich tasted amazing, I looked inside to see what was in it. Her new ploy was a 'she's too pretty' manoeuvre. This would be interesting! So, her theory was: all pretty girls are liars and promiscuous.

I looked at her. "Really?"

"Oh, yes! Are you abreast of all her baggage? How much do you know about her past? How many exes are still in her life? How do they feel about her? How does she feel about them? Or have you been too dazzled by those pretty brown eyes to ask?"

And there it was! Trish had this uncanny ability of making me feel two feet tall. Yes, maybe I had been dazzled by Roz? I had assumed that all the men in the house had been 'there', and I already knew that Benjamin would forever be her lovesick puppy but, beyond that, what did I know? Yes, Roz and I had talked for hours on end, but I'd never really drilled down to such subjects. We knew a lot about each other but, no, I didn't have an accurate status report on all her key exes.

I carried on eating and took a sip of this delicious bottle of fruit juice. Damn, Trish was good! I was softening by the moment. What did she want from me? Why wouldn't this woman leave me alone? I'd taken her front door key. I'd told her I was now dating Roz. Hell, I'd kicked her out of bed! Hadn't she got the message yet?

Finally, I lost patience. "What are you going on about?"

Trish reached into her handbag and pulled out her phone. She fiddled with it for a second then handed it to me. I looked at the screen. It was a photo of Roz and Benjamin kissing.

"When was this taken?"

"Yesterday."

My appetite was gone. I put my sandwich down and looked at the screen. It wasn't quite a passionate embrace but their lips looked pretty close together.

"Are you stalking her?"

"I'm protecting you!"

Trish had now entered a brand new arena of weirdness. It was too early to formally call her a bunny-boiler but she was starting to unsettle me. No matter what Roz was thinking or doing, I had moved on and I'd made that very clear. She was one creepy gesture away from, 'Where's your dignity, woman?'

"Why are you stalking her?"

"I'm just trying to show you that she can't be trusted. She's skittish. She likes to flit between the flowers. A pretty thing like that needs a lot of attention from a lot of different men."

This wasn't the Roz I knew. Trish was using a lot of emotive language to de-rail my new relationship. This wasn't the same Roz I'd had so much fun with over the last four weeks. It had really been a month of surprises and thrills. And Trish didn't know the intimacy we'd shared. You can't be half-hearted and be that intimate! She was present. Right there. Making love to me. Giving me pleasure. This was somebody that really liked me and cared about me.

I looked at the photo again. Of course I knew that Benjamin was nuts about her, and would probably stop at nothing to win her back, but this photograph displayed that Roz still had a foot in his camp. Maybe she wasn't sure yet?

"First of all," I began, "you HAVE to stop stalking her! If you damage my relationship, I will NOT be happy. And it will NOT rekindle our relationship!"

"Secondly, I know this guy. He's one of her house mates. He's also one of her exes. And he's grumpy as fuck because she's chosen me! Of course he wants to kiss her!"

Trish continued blithely eating her sandwich. If she could put doubt into my mind, it was a good day's work. She just sat there, masticating, staring at me, confidently holding her position.

"I'm sure there's a good reason for this."

"Is there?" she said. "The body language looked quite clear to me. He's into her and she's into him."

"Stop!" I said. "Just stop!"

"Just trying to protect you, babe. Those kind of girls come and go as they please!"

I really wasn't in the mood for any more of Trish's ham-fisted propaganda. It was embarrassing watching her work. Stooping to stalking was unnecessary. I didn't need help from Trish. If I was making a mistake, I wanted to be left alone to make my mistake.

Having given Trish's key to Roz, when I finally got home, Roz had let herself in and was stretched out on my sofa, looking very comfortable, tall drink in one hand, remote control in the other.

I need answers from Roz and subtlety wasn't my strongest suit. I was evolving as a man but I was still just a few steps up from pond slime.

"I need to ask you some questions," I said.

"Uh oh! That doesn't sound good!"

"Let me get a drink."

When I got back from the kitchen, she was no longer lying on the sofa and had stiffened considerably.

"What's wrong?" she asked.

"Will you answer me honestly?"

"Of course!"

"Is Benjamin an ex?"

"Yes."

"Is he in love with you?"

"Yes."

"Were you ever in love with him?"

"No."

I sat down with my drink and felt marginally better, but now I felt bad about starting our evening with these questions.

"I'm sorry," I said.

"What's wrong?" she asked again.

"I have a slight Trish problem."

Roz looked unbothered, which pleased me greatly. It was truly a blessing to be dating a confident woman. Roz would never have a 'Trish problem'.

"Trish has been stalking you!"

Roz laughed, sipped at her drink and visibly relaxed. "Christ, Wes, I thought we had a real problem!"

Not the reaction I had expected. I'd got Trish to mail the image to my phone, so I pulled out my phone and handed it to Roz. She looked at it.

"It's a photo of me and Benji. So what?"

"You're kissing him!"

"No, he's trying to kiss me! He's always trying to kiss me, as if his kisses are magic and, somehow, I will awake from my nightmare!"

I nodded. Now I felt really stupid! It was not a great way to start the evening. Roz got up, came over and sat next to me. She nuzzled her head beneath my neck. God, she smelt good!

"Listen, Wes, it's just you and me. I've made my decision. I've told them. I'm not a kid anymore! I will come and go as I please. I will date who I want. If I want to bring you home to my place, I will, not that you'd want to!"

"I'm sorry. I had to ask."

"It's cool," she said, softly.

Wow, so this is what it was like! I was finally dating a woman. A strong, independent, confident woman. No baggage, no self-esteem issues, no body issues. Two people on an equal footing, walking together. Who knew such a thing existed?

Chapter Twenty Eight (Wednesday)

When I woke the next morning, I was alone in my bed.

She either didn't need a lot of sleep or didn't like wasting time in bed. Either way, as usual, the jitterbug was up and out, getting on with her day. Jumping out of bed was clearly what she did. Sleep and sex were fun but, once it was done, she wanted to move on to the next fun activity!

Our discussion last night had killed any hope of more sex. The fore-foreplay had not been good. If you want intimacy with someone, do not accuse them of cheating. It's unlikely to arouse anybody! I made a mental note to refine my fore-foreplay. Alcohol and laughter might have worked better?

When I got downstairs, there was a pot of coffee and a note from her. It read, "Last night was amazing!" Sarcasm? Humour? I turned the note over, it said, "We should do nothing more often!"

I looked up the heavens and began talking to the universe, secretly hoping that some kind of god was listening in.

"Thank you for bringing this chick to me!" I said out loud. It sounded ridiculous. Any kind of god listening in would have thought I was a fool!

Today was Wesday Wednesday: Max's mad idea! What had I agreed to?

I opened the door under my stairs and there were my trusty plastic cartons, full to the brim with scuffed and faded sleeves containing my antiques: 12-inch pieces of vinyl.

Back in the eighties and nineties, these had been the tools of my trade. They'd been dropped, sat on, soaked in beer, warped by heat and generally mistreated, but this was how I'd earned my money.

I tried to pull the top carton out and suddenly remembered how heavy these things were. My spine got flashbacks of those early hours when I'd been dog-tired but still had to hump these huge boxes back to my car.

I didn't know what was in the boxes but I knew they were full of tunes 18 and 19-year-olds had never heard before. There were no rarities in there, just big tunes that had always worked for me. My reliable floor-fillers! The grooves and songs that always delivered.

There had even been a couple of occasions where I'd saved the day with these records; revitalised a tired party with my trusted friends.

When I eventually got to the shop, Wesday Wednesday was in full swing! Max had positioned a loud speaker adjacent to the front door so, for the first time in our history, my shop was making noise!

Curious locals were sticking their heads in to see what was going on. It genuinely looked like a private house party! Max was on the turntables, studiously mixing banging new beats, and his mates were hopping and bopping around him, swigging from bottles of Lucozade or Ribena. There were even pretty girls in the shop, which meant there was a lovely smell of perfume. Infinitely preferable to our customary blend of sweat, tobacco and kebab!

Max's friends looked at my record cartons as if I was carrying The Ark Of The Covenant. Holy Scriptures containing words passed down by James Brown and Nile Rodgers!

I hung up my jacket and felt all of these eyes on me. I turned round and there they all stood, Max's friends and followers, hushed in silent reverence, waiting for my sermon.

I casually flicked through the first box and found 'Good Times' by Chic on a grey Atlantic label. It seemed as good a place to start as any. I put the needle on the record and glorious music filled the air.

Most of the boys in the shop were just staring at the vinyl. What was this sorcery? While the girls, as you would expect, were just responding to the music and dancing.

Max held out his hand to shake mine. "Choon!" was all he could say. And then all his friends wanted to shake my hand, as if that would instantly imbibe them with mystical disco wisdom.

Surely they weren't going to shake my hand after every song?

At that point, a policeman came to the front door of our shop and stood in our doorway. He looked around the shop, realised what kind of business we were in and put his thumb up with approval. I reciprocated with my own thumb and the police man moved on.

It was 11.30 on a Wednesday and I had pretty, young girls dancing in my shop. The day was going well!

I continued flicking through my box of tricks and found 'Brick House' by The Commodores on a blue Motown label.

If nothing else, these tracks were acting as an effective advertisement for the gear in my shop. When the 'Brick House' bass line kicked-in, even the boys began to jerk involuntarily! Almost as if the music had taken over their bodies! It was a beautiful sight to see. It gave me great pleasure to introduce art to a young audience. These were tomorrow's music-makers and decision-makers. They needed good influences and healthy DNA.

It was fairly easy to select these records. The fruit juice was flowing, the husky teenage tonsils were in full voice. There was laughter, clapping and singing. Practically every one of these songs was a cherry-popper, entering their ears for the very first time.

Next, I pulled for The Whispers' 'And The Beat Goes On' on a black Solar Records label. It sounded so good! There were now two yummy mummies in my shop, both dancing to the music with their babies strapped to their chest. Where had they come from? My Wednesday was getting more surreal by the minute!

One of the mothers had picked up a brochure from the counter. It was too loud in there for conversation, so she waved the brochure at me in that universal language all DJs understand. I waved my arms in a 'Sure! Take it!' kind of way.

So, not only was Wesday Wednesday a school disco for impressionable teenagers and a coffee morning for new mothers, it was about to become a slapstick pantomime!

For some reason, Marie had decided to bring me cake and, for some reason, Percy was with her. Marie came into the shop, caught my eye and shrugged her shoulders, as if it say, 'What the funk is going on here?'

I shrugged my shoulders and, with a slight nuance, I was able to reply, 'Damned if I know!'

Marie was waving a cake tin frantically at me and I gestured that she should put it on the counter. Mmm ... cake!

Then, I put on Isaac Hayes' 'Theme From Shaft' on a yellow Stax label, and when that high-hat and wah-wah began, all hell broke loose! As in, Percy began to dance! It was the first time the kids had stopped gawping at me.

It was hard to describe Percy's staccato flailing of his limbs but, while the kids all stopped and stared, one of the yummy mummies actually began dancing with him! Maybe she was a social worker?

Wesday Wednesday was going well! I had one potential new customer, a tin of freshly-baked cake, and Max and his friends seemed to be enjoying themselves.

It was now time to go back. Before disco! And only 'Superstition' by Stevie Wonder would do. The kids were so bemused by the sounds, rhythms and textures, they just stood and stared at the speakers. I could see their young minds blowing one by one. The mummies were in Heaven now, gyrating their bemused babies around the shop, and Percy seemed almost ready to erupt! His long arms and legs seemingly disconnected from his torso and his sense of rhythm!

Max wanted to shake my hand again but he had no words. Not even 'choon'! He was in bassline-bumping bliss! He nodded silently and earnestly, as if we had some unspoken selector signals!

Several of his friends had their phones in the air, checking-in with Shazam to see what the hell these tunes were! While others just stood and listened, watching the vinyl go round and round, wondering if it was the music, the vinyl, the gear or some new kind of legal high?

The shop had never been so congested! There was barely room to swing a cat! Not that we endorse cruelty to animals! And just when I thought I had room for no more customers, Mids staggered-in looking sun-tanned and happier than I'd seen him look in a while. He didn't have wine for me but he did have a huge piece of Brie! A very welcome sight! I signalled he should put it on the counter, Marie embraced him and signalled that she was going into the kitchen to make some tea. Percy was moving and grooving like a randy racoon, and she figured she'd be there for a while, so she might as well make a cuppa?

Mids didn't need to ask what was going on. I'd told him about Wesday Wednesday a while ago, and he'd even suggested having it at his warehouse! He sat himself on one of my stools and just enjoyed the spectacle. Marie had promised him tea and cake, so he was staying too!

There seriously was no room for anyone else in the shop! The door was open, so we weren't hot and sweaty, there was just little room for any serious dance moves, certainly not while the hazardous Percy was in full flow!

And yet, Wesday Wednesday had just one final guest. Her ladyship herself!

Roz stood in the shop doorway and smiled. Such a beautiful smile! The Hot Chick Gods had definitely smiled on me! There wasn't much room to move but Roz managed to get past Mids, past the yummy mummies, past Percy, past the pretty young things, and then past Max's nerdy friends. Suddenly, she was beside me! Rubbing her boobs against my arm!

We exchanged a quick kiss, a subtle squeeze and then, deftly, I switched turntables, introducing the dynamic and complex yet simple sound of 'Soul Power' by James Brown on a red Polydor label.

This insane event was spinning out of control! The girls were screaming, the boys were whistling, and all Roz wanted to do was distract me! It wasn't hard. But it was getting there!

She bent over slowly and seductively and reached into her bag. Out came a box of grapes, which she opened and began feeding to me!

Max and his friends were spellbound. They'd heard about the superstar DJ phenomenon and been sorely tempted by the glamour and the lifestyle but, now, watching this glamorous woman feed me grapes as I played the best dance music ever ... well ... they were sold! This was the life for them!

I wasn't sure spinning scratchy vinyl in my grubby shop on a wet Wednesday was the glamorous life, but they all seemed suitably impressed.

Marie emerged from the kitchen with two cups of tea and I could see she and Mids make a start on the cake. As Mids stuffed a huge slice into his mouth, he put his thumb up with approval. It was good to see him happy. He had tea, cake and a sun tan. What more could he need?

It was time for some spiritual awakening, so I decided to play Max and his friends Earth Wind & Fire. Few intros are as dramatic as 'In The Stone' but when the groove kicked-in, it almost seemed like music-makers in the room had seen the light. One guy was deer-in-the-headlights transfixed. He didn't move. Rooted to the spot. Soaking up the joyous sound of the Phoenix Horns!

And even though there was no room for another adult in the shop, there was room for a small person, and suddenly there was an 8 or 9-year-old boy by my side. He was watching the vinyl, watching Max's friends, watching crazy Roz feeding me grapes.

He was saying something but I couldn't hear him above the din. I bent down, so he could whisper in my ear.

"What's this music?" he said.

"Disco!" I said.

"What's disco?" he asked.

All of a sudden, there was a frantic woman standing in the shop doorway. Clearly, this was her son! I waved at her and pointed downwards, so she could see where he was.

"What's that?" he said, pointing at the record.

"It's a record!"

"What's a record?" he said.

These were not questions I could answer. Just like Johnny Nash said, "There are more questions than answers."

The mother fought her way through the crowd and rescued her son. "Thanks!" I saw her mouth at me. I nodded. Wesday Wednesday could be a crèche too!

Roz was smiling at me. I think she was quite proud of me but I definitely detected some lasciviousness! Maybe wishful thinking on my part?

"What?" I asked.

She looked around her and waved her arms. "Look at this? What the hell is going on in here today? Bizarre happenings! I love it! Our life together: it's going to be fun!"

Our life together. I liked the sound of that.

Printed in Poland
by Amazon Fulfillment
Poland Sp. z o.o., Wrocław